LEEDS COLLEGE OF BUILDING LIBRARY
CLASS NO. HIL
BARCODE T38831

Reginald Hill

Reginald Hill is a former
resident of Yorkshire ... ing
crime novels. ... scoe, the best
detective duo ... bar none' *(Daily Telegraph).*

His writing career began with the publication of *A Clubbable Woman* (1970), which introduced Chief Superintendent Andy Dalziel and DS Peter Pascoe. Their subsequent appearances (*Good Morning, Midnight* is the twentieth in the series), together with the adventures of Luton lathe operator turned PI Joe Sixsmith have confirmed Hill's position as 'the best living male crime writer in the English-speaking world' (*Independent*) and won numerous awards, including the Crime Writers' Association Cartier Diamond Dagger for his lifetime contribution to the genre.

The Dalziel and Pascoe novels have now been adapted into a successful BBC television series starring Warren Clarke and Colin Buchanan.

LEEDS COLLEGE OF BUILDING WITHDRAWN FROM STOCK

£2.20

BARTER BOOKS
ALNWICK STATION
NORTHUMBERLAND

Praise for Reginald Hill and *Good Morning, Midnight*

'Reginald Hill is back with the kind of writing and plotting that made his award-winning *On Beulah Height* so riveting. *Good Morning, Midnight* is a real treat. The characters are deftly drawn, the plot constantly delivers surprises and the assured narrative demonstrates again what a terrific comic writer he is' PETER GUTTRIDGE, *Observer*

'Literate without being pedantic, humorous without undercutting suspense, Hill's book will keep you reading far beyond the midnight hour' FRANK WHITTLE, *Sunday Express*

'A new Dalziel and Pascoe can usually be relied on to brighten up the day and Reginald Hill's latest *Good Morning, Midnight* arrives as a literary supernova . . . Mischievous and incredibly good' MARTIN RADCLIFFE, *Time Out*

'The writing is brilliant, witty and erudite . . . as enjoyable as anything Reginald Hill has ever produced' TJ BINYON, *Evening Standard*

'He has the boldest vocabulary of any mainstream British crime writer. You feel Hill delighting in words' MARK LAWSON, *Guardian*

'One of Britain's most consistently excellent crime novelists' MARCEL BERLINS, *The Times*

'Always the master of the complex plot, Reginald Hill has produced another fine mystery with its roots in the past, in which the long relationship between the two detectives continues to develop . . . a reminder of the cunning and often dazzling prose that made him one of the best crime writers ever' SUSANNA YAGER, *Sunday Telegraph*

'Unfolds compellingly and displays all his familiar intelligence and wit. *Good Morning, Midnight* shows Hill on top form' JOHN DUGDALE, *Sunday Times*

'Reginald Hill is as ingenious a concoctor of plot as Ian Rankin, and, like Rankin, he knows how to keep the story moving . . . His narrative is always compelling . . . highly enjoyable' ALLAN MASSIE, *Scotsman*

'The fertility of Hill's imagination, the range of his power, the sheer quality of his literary style never cease to delight' VAL MCDERMID, *Sunday Express*

'Reginald Hill's novels are really dances to the music of time, his heroes and villains interconnecting, their stories entwining' IAN RANKIN, *Scotland on Sunday*

'An increasingly lyrical and always humorous writer, he is first and foremost an instinctive and complete novelist who is blessed with a spontaneous storytelling gift' FRANCES FYFIELD, *Mail On Sunday*

'Probably the best living male crime writer in the English-speaking world' ANDREW TAYLOR, *Independent*

By the same author

Dalziel and Pascoe Novels

A CLUBBABLE WOMAN
AN ADVANCEMENT OF LEARNING
RULING PASSION
AN APRIL SHROUD
A PINCH OF SNUFF
A KILLING KINDNESS
DEADHEADS
EXIT LINES
CHILD'S PLAY
UNDERWORLD
BONES AND SILENCE
ONE SMALL STEP
RECALLED TO LIFE
PICTURES OF PERFECTION
ASKING FOR THE MOON
THE WOOD BEYOND
ON BEULAH HEIGHT
ARMS AND THE WOMEN
DIALOGUES OF THE DEAD
DEATH'S JEST-BOOK

Joe Sixsmith novels

BLOOD SYMPATHY
BORN GUILTY
KILLING THE LAWYERS
SINGING THE SADNESS

FELL OF DARK
THE LONG KILL
DEATH OF A DORMOUSE
DREAM OF DARKNESS
THE ONLY GAME

REGINALD HILL

GOOD MORNING, MIDNIGHT

HarperCollins*Publishers*

This novel is entirely a work of fiction. The names,
characters and incidents portrayed in it are the work of
the author's imagination. Any resemblance to actual persons,
living or dead, events or localities is entirely coincidental.

HarperCollins*Publishers*
77–85 Fulham Palace Road, London W6 8JB

www.harpercollins.co.uk

This paperback edition 2004

3

First published in Great Britain in 2004 by HarperCollins

Copyright © Reginald Hill 2004

Reginald Hill asserts the moral right to
be identified as the author of this work

A catalogue record for this book
is available from the British Library

ISBN 0 00 712343 4

Typeset in Meridien by Palimpsest Book Production
Limited, Polmont, Stirlingshire
Printed in Great Britain by
Clays Ltd, St Ives plc

All rights reserved. No part of this publication may be
reproduced, stored in a retrieval system, or transmitted,
in any form or by any means, electronic, mechanical,
photocopying, recording or otherwise, without the prior
permission of the publishers.

For Max and Mattie
and in memory of Pip
and all those other
companions of creation
right back to Pangur Ban

messe ocus Pangur Ban
cechtar nathar fria saindan:
bith a menmasam fri seilgg,
mu memna cein im saincheirdd.

Good Morning – Midnight –
I'm coming Home –
Day – got tired of Me –
How could I – of Him?

Sunshine was a sweet place –
I liked to stay –
But Morn – didn't want me – now –
So – Goodnight – Day!

EMILY DICKINSON (1830–86)

March 1991

1

by the waters of Babylon

The war had been over for three weeks. Eventually the process of reconstruction would begin, but for the time being the ruins of the plant remained as they had been twenty-four hours after the missiles struck. By then the survivors had been hospitalized and the accessible dead removed. The smell of death rising from the inaccessible soon became intolerable but it didn't last long as the heat of the approaching summer accelerated decay and nature's cleansers, the flies and small rodents, went about their work.

Dust settled, sun and wind airbrushed the exposed rawness of cracked concrete till it was hardly distinguishable from the baked earth surrounding it, and a traveller in this antique land might have been forgiven for thinking that these relicts were as ancient as those of the great city of Babylon only a few miles away.

Finally, with the smells reduced to a bearable level and the dogs picking over the ruins showing no signs of turning even mangier than usual, some bold spirits living in the vicinity began to make their own exploratory forays.

The new scavengers found a degree of devastation so extensive that even the most technically minded of them couldn't work out the possible function of the plant's wrecked machinery. They gathered up whatever might be sellable or tradable or adaptable to some domestic purpose and left.

But not all of them. Khalid Kassem, at thirteen counting himself a man and certainly imbued with a sense of adventure and ambition which was adult in its scope, hung back when his father and brothers departed. He was small for his age and slightly built, factors usually militating against his efforts to be taken seriously. In this case, however, he felt they could work to his advantage. He'd noticed a crack in a collapsed wall which he felt he might be able to squeeze through. Earlier while scavenging in the ruins of an office building he had come across a small torch, its bulb miraculously unbroken and its battery retaining enough juice to produce a faint beam. Instead of flaunting his find, he had concealed it, and when he spotted the crack and shone the light through it to reveal a chamber within, he began to feel divinely encouraged in his enterprise.

It was a tight squeeze even for one of his build, but eventually he got through and found himself in what looked to have been a basement storage area. There was blast damage here as there was everywhere and much of the ceiling had been shattered when the floors above had come crashing down, but no actual explosion seemed to have occurred in this space. Among the debris lay a scatter of metal crates, some intact, one or two broken open to reveal cuboids of some kind of lightweight foam cladding. Where this had split, Khalid's faint beam of light glanced back off dully gleaming machines. He broke some of the cladding away to get a better look and discovered the machine was further wrapped in a close-clinging transparent plastic sheet. Recently on a visit to relatives in Baghdad, he had seen a refrigerator stacked with packets of food wrapped like this. It was explained to him that all the air had been sucked out so that as long as the package remained unopened the food inside would remain fresh. These machines too, he guessed, were being kept fresh. It did not surprise him. Metal he knew was capable of decay, and machinery was, in his limited experience, even harder to keep in good condition than livestock.

There was unfortunately no way to profit from his discovery. Even if it had been possible to recover one of these machines, what would he and his family do with it?

He turned to go, and the faint beam of his torch touched a crate rather smaller than the rest. A long metal cylinder had fallen across it, splitting it completely open, like a knife slicing a melon. It was the shape of its contents that caught his eye. Obscured by the cylinder resting on the broken crate, this lacked the angularity of the vacuum-packed machines. It was more like some kind of cocoon.

He put his torch down and, by using both hands and all his slight body weight, he managed to roll the cylinder to one side. It hit the floor with a crash that raised enough dust to set him coughing.

When he recovered, he picked up his torch and directed the ever fainter beam downward, praying it might reveal some treasure he could bear back proudly to his family.

The light glanced back from a pair of staring eyes.

He screamed in terror and dropped the torch, which went out.

That might have been the end for Khalid, but Allah is merciful and bountiful and permitted two of his miracles together.

The first was that as his scream died away (for want of breath not want of terror) he heard a voice calling his name.

'Khalid, where the hell are you? Come on, or you're in big trouble.'

It was his favourite brother, Ahmed:

The second miracle was that another light came on in the storeroom to replace his broken torch. This light was red and intermittent. In the brightness of its flashes he looked again at the vacuum-packed cocoon.

It was a woman in there. She was young and

black and beautiful. And of course she was dead.

His brother shouted his name again, sounding both anxious and angry.

'I'm all right,' he called back impatiently, his fear fading with Ahmed's proximity and of course the light.

Which came from . . . where?

He checked and his fear came back with advantages.

The light was coming from the end of the metal cylinder he had so casually sent crashing to the floor. There were Western letters on the metal which made no sense to him. But one thing he did recognize: the emblem of the great shaitan who was the nation's bitterest foe.

Now he knew what had come crashing through the roof but had not exploded.

Yet.

He scrambled towards the fissure through which he'd entered. It seemed to have constricted even further, or fear was making him fat, and for a moment he thought he was caught fast. He had one arm through and was desperately trying to get a purchase on the ruined outer wall when his hand was grasped tight and next moment he was being dragged painfully through the gap into Ahmed's arms.

His brother opened his mouth to remonstrate with him, saw the look on his face and needed no further persuasion to obey when Khalid screamed. 'Run!'

They ran together, the two brothers, straining every sinew forward, like two champions contesting the final lap in an Olympic race, except that in this competition whenever one stumbled, the other reached out a steadying hand.

The tape they were running to was the Euphrates whose blessed waters had provided fertility and sustenance to their ancestors for centuries.

Time meant nothing, distance was everything.

The only sound was their laboured breathing and the swish of their limbs through the waist-high rushes.

Their eyes stared ahead, to safety, to their future, so they did not see behind them the ruins begin to rise into the air and be themselves ruined.

But they knew instantly there were now other faster competitors in the race.

The sound overtook them first, rolling by in dull thunder.

And then the blast was at their heels, at their shoulders, picking them up and hurling them forward as it raced triumphantly on.

Down they crashed, down they splashed. They were at the river. They felt its blessed coldness sweep over them. They let the current roll them at its own sweet will. Then they rose together, coughing and spluttering, and looked at each other, brother checking brother for damage at the same time as the impulses signalling the state of his own bone and muscle came pulsing along the nerves.

'You OK, little one?' said Ahmed after a while.

'Fine. You?'

'I'm OK. Hey, you run well for a tadpole.'

'You too, for a frog.'

They pulled themselves on to the bank and sat looking back at the column of dust and fine debris hanging in the air.

'So what did you find in there?' asked Ahmed.

Khalid hardly paused for thought. He had no explanation for what he'd seen, but he was old enough to know he lived in a world where knowledge could be dangerous.

Later he would say a prayer for the dead woman in case she was of the faith.

Or even if she wasn't.

And then a prayer for himself for lying to his brother.

'Nothing,' he said. 'Just the rocket. Otherwise nothing at all.'

March 20th, 2002

1

dropping the loop

It was the last day of winter and the last night of Pal Maciver's life.

With only fifteen minutes to go, he was discovering that death was even stranger than he'd imagined.

Until the woman left, he'd been fine. From the first-floor landing he had watched her come through the open front door, trailing mist. She tried the light switch. Nothing happened. Standing in the dark she called his name. After all these years she still almost had the power to make him answer. Now was a critical moment. Not make-or-break critical. If she simply turned on her heel and walked away, it wasn't disastrous. Getting her there could still be made enough.

But he felt God owed him more.

She turned back to the open door. Winter, determined to show he didn't give a toss for calendars, had rallied his declining forces. There had been flurries of snow on the high moors but here in the city the best he could manage was a denial of light, at first with low cloud, then as the day wore on with mist rolling in from the surrounding countryside. But still enough light seeped in through the narrow window by the door for her to see the stub of candle and book of matches lying on the sill.

His fingers touched the microcassette in his pocket. Without taking it out he pressed the 'play' button. Two or three bars of piano music tinkled out, then he switched off.

Below in the hall it must have sounded so distant she was probably already doubting she'd heard it at all. Perhaps indeed he'd overdone the muffling and she really hadn't heard it.

Then came the sputter of a match and a moment later he saw the amber glow of the candle.

God might not pay all his debts, but he kept up the interest.

Now the candle's glow moved beyond his range of vision but his ears kept track of her.

Ever a practical woman, she went straight down the passage leading to the kitchen where the electricity mains box was situated high on the wall. He pictured her reaching up to it. He heard her exclamation as the door swung open, releasing a shower of dust and debris. She hated being mussed. He heard the mains switch click down, could imagine her growing frustration as nothing happened.

The glow returned to the entrance hall. Lots of choice here. The two big-bayed reception rooms, the dining room, the music room. But her choice had been preordained. She headed for the music room. The door was locked but the key was in the lock. She tried it. It wouldn't turn. She tried to force it but she couldn't make it move.

She called his name once more, nothing uneasy in her voice and certainly nothing of panic, but with the calm clarity of a summons to supper.

She waited for a reply that by now she must have guessed wasn't coming.

He would have bet her next move would be to cut her losses and walk away. Even if she had the balls for it, he doubted she'd find any reason to come up the gloomy staircase with an uncertain light to confront the memories awaiting her there.

Wrong!

That was exactly what she was doing.

He almost admired her.

As she advanced, he retreated to the upper landing, matching his steps to hers. Would she want to visit the master bedroom? He guessed not and he was right. She went straight to the study door and tried to open it. Oh, this was good. When it didn't budge, she stood still for a moment before stooping like a comic-book gumshoe to apply her eye to the keyhole. By the vinegary light of the candle, he saw her steady herself with her left hand against the central oak panel.

This was better still! God was truly in a giving vein today.

Suddenly she straightened up and he took a step back into the protection of the black shadows of the upper landing. Now she was nothing to him but the outermost edge of the candle's faint aureole on the landing below. But the way she'd stood up had been enough. So had she always signalled by some undramatic but nonetheless emphatic movement – a twist of the hand, a turn of the head, a straightening of the shoulders – that a decision had been reached and would be acted on.

He saw the glow float down the stairs, wavering now as she moved with the swiftness of decision. He heard her firm step across the tiled entrance hall, then out on to the gravelled drive. She didn't close the door behind her. She would leave it as she found it. That too was typical of her.

He waited for half a minute then descended to the hallway. She'd blown the candle out and left it where she'd found it. He pulled on a pair of white cotton gloves and relit the stump, slipping the book of matches into his pocket. He went to the music-room door, removed the key and carefully folded it in a fresh white handkerchief. From the top pocket of his jacket he took an almost identical key, unlocked the door and replaced the key in the same pocket before moving into the kitchen. Here he opened the electricity supply box and reset the mains switch to off. Then he levered off the cover of the fuse box. From his pocket he took the household fuses and replaced them and clicked the mains switch on.

Immediately below the electricity box was a narrow glass-fronted key cupboard, each hook neatly labelled. He opened it, removed the key from his top pocket and hung it on the empty hook marked *Music Room*.

Some of the dust and debris she'd disturbed from the supply box had landed on top of the key cupboard, some had drifted down to the tiled floor. He took a dustpan and brush from under the sink and carefully swept the tiles but the cupboard top he ignored. He tipped the sweepings into the sink and turned on the tap, letting it run while he opened a wall unit and took out two cut-glass tumblers. From his hip pocket he took a silver flask and a small prescription bottle. From the former he poured whisky into both tumblers into one of which he broke two capsules removed from the latter. He shook the mixture up before tossing it down his throat. He downed the other whisky too before lightly splashing water inside the tumblers, which he then shook and replaced upside down on the cupboard shelf.

Now he made his way back to the entrance hall and mounted the stairs. He inserted the key he had wrapped in his handkerchief into the study door. It turned with well-oiled ease. He wiped the handle clean with his glove and pushed open the door.

For a moment he stood there looking in, like an archaeologist who has broken into a tomb and hesitates to confront what he has been so energetic to discover.

And indeed there was something tomb-like about the room. The old oak panelling had darkened to a slatey blackness, heavily shuttered windows kept light and fresh air at bay and the atmosphere was dank and musty with the smell of old books emanating from two massive mahogany bookcases towering against the end walls. On the wall facing the door hung a half-length portrait of a man in rock-climbing gear with a triple-peaked mountain in the back-ground. On one side of the portrait a coil of rope was mounted on the wall, on the other an ice axe. The painted face was severe and unsmiling as it glared down at the huge Victorian desk that loomed like an ancient sarcophagus in the centre of the floor.

Pal Maciver looked up at the man in the portrait and saw his own face there. He drew a deep breath and stepped over the threshold.

It was now that the strangeness started. Hitherto he had been the complete man of action, his whole being concentrated on the working out of his well-laid plans. But as he stepped through the doorway, awareness of that other darker threshold which was getting closer by the minute swept over him like the mist outside, leaving him helpless and floundering.

Then his strong will took command. There was still much work to do. He summoned Action Man back into control, and Action Man returned, but only at the price of a weird fragmentation of sensibility. Far from finding his mind wonderfully concentrated by the imminence of death, he discovered he was split in two, man of action and man of feeling, or rather in three, for here was the strangest thing of all, he found that, as well as the cast in this two-parter, he was audience too, an independent and almost disinterested observer, floating somewhere near the portrait, looking down with pity on that part of him drifting wraithlike in a shapeless swirl of fear and loss and bewilderment and despair while at the same time noting with admiration the way that Action Man was going about his preparations with the dextrous precision of a maid laying a supper table.

Action Man moved across the study floor, placed the candle on the desk, checked that the heavy curtains were tightly drawn across the shuttered windows and switched on the bright central light. Across the desk lay a six-foot length of thread. He picked it up, took out a cigarette lighter, gently pressed the thumb switch to release gas without giving a spark, and ran the thread through the jet. Then he fed the thread through the keyhole, put the key into the lock on the inside of the door, twisted the internal end of the thread round the head of the key so that about three feet hung down, went out on to the landing, once more clicked on his lighter and put the flame to the dangling end. The flame ran up the thread, vanished into the keyhole, emerged on the inside, and ran round the loops on the key. He let it get within a couple of feet of the end then snuffed it out.

With his gloved hand he cleaned off all traces of the burnt thread from the outside of the door, then he closed it and with great care turned the key in the lock.

Against the wall about two feet from the door stood a tall Victorian whatnot. On the shelf at the same level as the door lock rested a portable record player. Its retaining screws had been slackened so that he could lift out the turntable. He made a running loop at the unburnt end of the thread, dropped it over the drive spindle and pulled it tight. Then he fed the burnt end out through the power cable aperture, replaced the turntable and tightened the restraining screws. He picked up a record leaning against the table leg and placed it on the turntable. He plugged the power cable into a socket in the skirting board, set the control switch to 'play' and turned on the power. The arm swung out and descended, setting the stylus in the groove. For the second time that evening the opening bars of that gentlest of tunes, the opening piece 'Of Foreign Lands and People' from Schumann's *Childhood Scenes*, sounded in the house.

He stood and watched as the rotations of the spindle wound the thread into the depths of the machine. Just before it vanished he pinched the end between his thumb and finger, held it, pausing the music momentarily, then let it go.

He switched off the light. Darkness surged back, almost tangible, as if it longed to snuff out the candle. But the tiny flame burnt on, filling the hollows of his face with shadow and turning the peaks to parchment as he went behind the desk and sat down in the ornately carved mahogany elbow chair.

He opened a drawer and from it he took a book, which he set on the desk, a legal envelope and a fountain pen. Out of the envelope he took several sheets of heavy bond paper. He held a single sheet over the candle till it began to burn. He let it fall into a metal wastepaper bin by the chair. He lit a second sheet, did the same, then the others one by one. Tongues of fire showed at the bin's mouth, licking the darkness out of the study's gloomy corners before they shrank and died. The record was still playing. He listened and recognized the fourth of the *Childhood Scenes*. With an effort he summoned up its title. 'A Pleading Child'.

He shook the bin to make sure all the paper was consumed and stirred up the ashes with an ebony ruler, reducing them to a fine powder, some of which drifted up on the residual heat and hung in the air.

Now he rose again and went to the left-hand wall where alongside one of the bookcases a glass-fronted, metal-framed gun case was bolted on to the oak panelling. It was empty, covered with a soft pall of dust which he was careful not to disturb as he opened the door. He reached in, took hold of the gun-retaining clip, twisted it anti-clockwise through ninety degrees, then pulled sharply. A section of panelling came away revealing a recess mirroring the cabinet in size and in function too. Here stood a shotgun, which unlike most other things in that room showed no sign of dusty neglect. It gleamed with a menacing beauty. Alongside it, on a leather-bound diary embossed with the year 1992, rested a pack of cartridges.

He took the gun and cartridges and returned to the desk. The music had reached piece number seven: 'Dreaming'. He sat down with the weapon across his lap, broke it and loaded it. From his pocket he took a piece of string about a foot long with a loop at either end. He slipped one of the loops over the trigger, and leaned the weapon against the desk.

He checked his watch. Waited another thirty seconds. Picked up the fountain pen. Wrote in bold capitals on the envelope **FOR SUE-LYNN**. Set the pen down on the desktop. Checked his watch again. Stood up and went back to the gun case.

Up to this point he had done everything with steady purpose. Now he seemed touched by a sense of urgency.

He peeled off the gloves and tossed them into the secret recess, followed by his lighter, the matchbook, the microcassette, the hip flask and the prescription bottle. Next he replaced the panel, twisted the gun clip, shut the cabinet door, and went back to the chair into which he slumped with a finality which suggested he did not purpose rising again. He let the music back into his ears. Piece eleven was finishing. 'Something Frightening'. Then piece twelve began. 'Child Falling Asleep'.

He listened to it all the way through, asking himself, where had they gone, those thirty years?

As the music faded, he drew the book on the desktop towards him.

The final piece began. 'The Poet Speaks'.

He opened the book. He did not need to look for his place. It fell open with an ease that suggested that this was a page frequently visited.

And now the observer saw that other part of himself, that disembodied swirl of feeling, start to drift back into the corporeal chamber from which it had been temporarily expelled. Like Action Man, it had its calmness too, but this was the calm of despair, the acknowledgement that the end was near, a process perfectly captured by the words the eyes stared at but did not need to see.

> *He scanned it – staggered –*
> *Dropped the Loop*
> *To Past or Period –*
> *Caught helpless at a sense as if*
> *His Mind were going blind –*

Feeling Man, the observer saw, was absolute for death, so completely separated from hope and time and sense and feeling and all the threads of experience which tie us lightly to life that he was far ahead of the meticulous preparation of Action Man for that journey from the familiarity of *now* into the mystery of *next* . . .

The music was coming to an end. The observer could hear it but Feeling Man had ears for nothing but the words of the poem as if they were being read aloud by the soft American voice of their creator . . .

> *Groped up, to see if God was there –*
> *Groped backward at Himself*

. . . while Action Man still went quietly about his business, removing his left shoe and sock, bringing the gun between his legs with the stock firmly on the floor, slipping the loop of string over his big toe, grasping the barrel with both hands and holding it steady against the edge of the desk, then leaning forward and pressing the soft underpart of his chin hard against the muzzle.

Now the quiet voice in Feeling Man's mind speaks the final words

Caressed a Trigger absently
and wandered out of Life

while Action Man lowers his left foot, and Observing Man, rather to his surprise, has time to see the ball of shot burn its way up through jaw and palate, squirting blood from mouth and nostrils and punching out the eyes before emerging through the top of his skull in a fountain of bone and brain which spatters floor and desk and open book.

For a millisec reason and sensation and observation are reunited in one consciousness.

Then the empty body slumps to one side, the record dies away, the fine ash from the wastepaper bin slowly settles, the candle gutters.

Pal Maciver exists no longer.

Except in the hearts and minds and lives of those he leaves behind.

2

bedside manner

Sue-Lynn Maciver stretched her naked body languorously against her lover's hand and laughed.

'What?' said Tom Lockridge.

'I was thinking, first time I felt you inside me, it cost me a hundred quid.'

'Wait till you get my bill for this.'

He spoke lightly but she knew he didn't like being reminded he was still her doctor. When Pal had dropped him, his first reaction had been that her husband suspected something. Once reassured, his second reaction had been that this was a good opportunity for her to come off his list too.

'Don't be silly,' she'd said. 'Why give up the perfect cover for me visiting your surgery, you coming to the house?'

'It's just that, if it ever came out, the GMC don't take kindly to doctors screwing their patients.'

'Really? How else do they expect you to become stinking rich?'

When he didn't laugh, she said, 'Relax, Tom. It's not going to come out, not from me, anyway. I've got even more reason to keep it from Pal than you have from your precious Council. Or your precious wife for that matter.'

She'd meant it. But nonetheless it wasn't altogether displeasing to feel she had a hold over her lover that went beyond his desire.

He removed his hand from between her legs and pushed back the duvet.

She glanced at her watch and said, 'What's the hurry? We've got another hour at least.'

'Just going to the loo,' he said, rolling out of bed.

'Why do men always have to pee after sex?' she called after him.

He paused in the doorway and said, 'I'll draw you a diagram when I get back.'

She made a face at the prospect. Sometimes it wasn't altogether comfortable screwing a man who knew so much about the internal workings of the human body. She reached out to the cigarette packet lying by the phone on the bedside table and lit one. He'd probably give her the anti-smoking lecture, but it was better than a conducted tour of his innards.

The phone rang.

She picked it up and said, 'Hi.'

'Sue-Lynn, it's Jason.'

She stiffened then forced herself to relax.

'Jase, shouldn't you be chasing a little ball around a squash court with my husband?'

'That's why I'm ringing. He hasn't turned up. My mobile's on the blink and I thought he might have left a message with you.'

She stubbed her cigarette out, swung her legs off the bed, found her panties on the floor and started tugging them on one-handed as she replied, 'Sorry, Jase. Not a word. But I shouldn't worry. Probably a customer showed up as he was on his way out. You know Pal. He'd miss his own funeral if he thought there was a deal to be done. How's Helen? Must be close now. Give her my best. Look, got to go. 'Bye.'

She put down the phone and was crouching on the floor searching for her bra when she heard the toilet flush. A moment later, Lockridge came through the door. He was smiling and there was evidence he was having serious thoughts about how to spend the next hour. The smile faded as he saw her rise on the far side of the bed with her bra in her hand.

'Pal's loose,' she said before he could speak. 'Get dressed.'

'Shit. You don't think he's on to us? *Jesus wept*!'

He'd started dragging on his trousers with more haste than care and done something she didn't care to think about with the zip.

'Shouldn't think so, but better safe than sorry . . . oh hell. Did you hear that?'

'What?'

'I don't know. A noise. Downstairs. No . . . on the stairs.'

They both froze, mouths agape, eyes staring, she with her bra round her neck, he with his hand on his fly zipper, like a *tableau vivant* of Guilt Surprised, and were both in a state to take the flash of light that came through the open door as the harbinger of one of heaven's avenging angels.

3

Signora Borgia's guest list

The mist was definitely getting thicker. Much more and they'd be calling it fog, which was bad news. There were enough idiots out there who couldn't drive properly in broad daylight without making things even more problematic for them.

Ignoring the obvious impatience of the cars behind her, Kay Kafka drove her Mercedes E-Class down the quiet suburban roads at five mph under the permitted speed limit and signalled a good hundred yards before she turned into the driveway of Linden Bank.

With the mist and encroaching darkness toning down the unfortunate shade of lavender the Dunns had chosen for their outside woodwork, she was able to re-experience her feelings on first seeing the house. Helen had rung full of excitement to tell her that she and Jason had found a place they both liked but she wanted Kay's approval before committing. Kay had gone along

30

prepared to lie, and had instead been delighted. She'd liked the clean modern lines, the harmonious proportions, the use of rosy brick under a shallow-pitched roof of olive tiles. The prepared lies had come in useful later, however, once the newlyweds had moved in.

At the door Kay only had to ring once before it was flung open by a young woman hugely pregnant.

'You're late,' she said accusingly.

'You too by the look of you.'

The young woman grimaced and said, 'Still a couple of days to go – Kay, it's lovely to see you.'

The two women embraced, not without difficulty.

'Jesus, Helen, you sure it's only twins you've got in there?'

'I know – it's terrible – I may have to let out my smocks.'

They went into the house. Outside the evening temperature was dropping fast. In here as usual the central heating was set a couple of degrees above Kay's comfort level. In anticipation she was wearing only a sleeveless silk blouse beneath her chic sheepskin jacket.

As Helen hung it up she brushed her hand over the fleecy collar and said, 'Hey, have you been on a building site? This is a bit dusty.'

'Is it? You know these old houses. I wish Tony had bought somewhere modern like this,' said Kay removing the silk square with which she'd protected her short black hair from the mist and shaking it gently. 'He sends his love.'

'Give him mine. I really love that blouse,' said Helen enviously. 'Wish I dared let people see the tops of my arms.'

In fact pregnancy became her. Big she was, but with the roseate carnality of a Renoir bather. In the glow of that aura many other women would have been reduced to attendant shadows, but Kay Kafka, pale faced and pencil slim, was not diminished.

They went into the lounge. The first time Kay had come into this room and found it full of light from the huge picture window overlooking the long rear lawn, she had known exactly how she would furnish and decorate it. Now, even after many visits, she had to make an effort not to react to the heavy furnishings, the fitted pink carpet, the gilt-framed Canaletto reproductions and the Regency striped curtains which, closed, at least concealed the Yorkstone patio running down to a solar-powered fountain in red-veined marble with which the Dunns had replaced half of the lawn. The only thing that won her approval was the Steinway upright occupying one corner, which, if Jason had had his way, would probably have been replaced by an electronic keyboard in dazzling silver. Strange, she thought, how people could be so beautiful without having any inner sense of beauty.

Tony, when she had told him about this, had

32

asked, 'So if she bought the right kind of house, how come she put the wrong sort of stuff in it with you looking over her shoulder?'

'Because I wasn't looking over her shoulder, not even when she asked me to,' said Kay. 'It's not my place.'

'Come on. The kid worships you and you're the nearest thing to a mother she ever had.'

'But I'm not her mother and I never want to give her occasion to remind me. In fact, looking back, I suspect she chose the house because she knew in advance I'd like the look of it, which I did. Inside's different. They're the ones who've got to live in it.'

'You're all heart, baby,' said Tony, smiling. He was a man of many contradictions and this capacity to be cynical and affectionate at the same time was one of them.

Now she seated herself gingerly at one end of a long sofa. This was great furniture for lounging in. Helen in her pre-pregnancy days would usually curl up in one of the huge chairs with her legs tucked up beneath her and Kay had had to admit that the setting suited her marvellously well. Herself, even in Helen's company, she liked to stay in control, and felt taken over by the soft cushions and yielding upholstery. Tony had called it a great shagging sofa, and thereafter whenever she sat on it she got a mental flash of Jason and Helen intimately intertwined in its depths.

Now Helen was long past the curling up stage

and presumably the intimate intertwining stage too. She'd brought one of the broad high elbow chairs from the dining room to sit upon, though even this was becoming a tight fit.

'Hope you don't mind – got pizzas coming – cooking's getting hard without doing myself or the Aga serious damage – sorry.'

There'd been a time when Kay had tried to amend Helen's rather breathlessly unpunctuated way of speaking but she'd given up when she saw she was merely creating tension. The same with the girl's taste in interior decoration. This was how she was, and you didn't look a gift horse in the mouth especially when God was the giver.

'Pizza's fine,' she said with a smile. 'Though I hope Jase is making sure you get a slightly more varied diet.'

'Don't worry – I'm sticking to the menu I got from the clinic – more or less – tonight's a treat – triple anchovies – damn! Just when I'd got comfortable.'

The phone in the entrance hall was ringing.

'I'll get it,' said Kay.

She rose elegantly, not an easy feat from the absorbent upholstery, and went into the hall.

'Hello,' she said.

'Kay, is that you? It's Jason. Look, Pal hasn't turned up for squash and I wondered if maybe he'd tried to ring me at home. Could you ask Helen?'

'Sure.'

She called, 'It's Jase. Pal's stood him up. He wants to know if he's left a message here.'

'No, nothing – tell Jase to get himself something at the Club like he usually does – don't want him spoiling our evening just because Pal's spoilt his.'

'Jase, did you get that?'

'Yes. Who needs phones when you've got a wife who could yodel for Switzerland? OK, tell her I'll get myself a pasty, then go up on the balcony and see if I can find a couple of sweaty girls to watch. How are you keeping, Kay?'

'Mustn't complain.'

'Why not? Everyone else does. Probably catch you before you leave. Bye.'

Kay put down the receiver and stood looking at her reflection in the gilt mirror on the wall behind the phone table. Her face wore the contemplative almost frowning expression which Tony had once caught in a snap which he labelled *La Signora Borgia checks her guest list*. She relaxed her features into their normal edge-of-a-smile configuration and went back into the lounge.

4

an open door

'There we go,' said PC Jack 'Joker' Jennison, placing the two newspaper-wrapped bundles on the dashboard. 'One haddock, one cod.'

'Which is which?'

'*Mail*'s haddock, *Guardian*'s cod.'

'That figures. What do I owe you?'

'Don't be daft. Chinese chippie two doors up from the National Party offices, they'd pay good money to have us park outside till closing time.'

'Then they'll be getting a refund,' said PC Alan Maycock. 'We're out of here.'

He gunned the engine and set the car accelerating forward.

'What's your hurry?' asked Jennison.

'Just got a tip from CAD that Bonkers is on the prowl. Don't think he'd be too chuffed to find us troughing outside a chippie, so let's find somewhere nice and quiet.'

Bonkers was Sergeant Bonnick, a new broom at Mid-Yorkshire HQ who was hell bent on clearing out its dustiest corners. Also he was big on physical fitness and had already been mildly sarcastic about the embonpoint of the two constables, saying that watching them getting into their car was like seeing a pair of 42s trying to squeeze into a 36 cup.

'Not too far, eh? I hate cold chips,' said Jennison, pressing the warm packets to his cheeks.

'Don't fret. Nearly there.'

They'd turned off the main road with its parade of shops and were speeding into the area of the city known as Greenhill.

Once a hamlet without the city wall, Greenhill had been absorbed into the urban mass during the great industrial expansion of the nineteenth century. The old squires who bred their beasts, raised their crops, and hunted their prey across this land were replaced by the new squires of coal and steel and commerce who wanted houses to live in that had land enough to give the impression of countryside but without any of the attendant inconveniences of remoteness, agricultural smells or peasant society. So the hamlet of Greenhill became the suburb of Greenhill, in which farms and cotts and muddy lanes were replaced by urban mansions and tarmacked roads.

From the naughty nineties to the fighting forties, many of the great and the good of Mid-Yorkshire paraded their pomp in Greenhill. But after the war, the rot set in. Old ways and old fortunes faded, and though for a while the makers of new fortunes still turned their thoughts to what had once been the *arriviste*'s dream, a Greenhill mansion, there rapidly developed an awareness of their inconvenience and a sense that they were at best *démodé*, at worst crassly kitsch, and by the seventies Greenhill was in steep decline. Many of the mansions were converted into flats, or small commercial hotels, or corporate offices, or simply knocked down to make room for speculative development.

Some areas hung on longer than others, or at least by sheer weight of presence managed to preserve the illusion that little had changed from the glory days. Chief among these was The Avenue, which, if it ever had a praenomen, had long ago shed it as superfluous to general recognition. Here on nights like the present one, with mist seeping in from the already shrouded countryside to blur the big houses behind their screening arbours into vague shapes, still and awe-inspiring as sleeping pachyderms, it was possible to drive slowly down the broad street between the ranks of leafy plane trees and imagine that the great days of Empire were with us yet.

In fact, driving slowly down the Avenue was still a popular pursuit among a certain section of Mid-Yorkshire society, but they weren't thinking of Empire, except perhaps metaphorically. The shade against the elements provided by the trees, the privacy afforded by many of the dark and winding driveways, plus the thinness on the ground of complaining residents, made this a favourite parade ground for prostitutes and kerb crawlers. In the misty aureoles of the elegantly curved Greenhill lampposts, the Avenue might look deserted. But set your car crawling sedately along the kerbside and, like dryads materializing from their trees at the summons of the great god Pan, the ladies of the night would appear.

Except if the car had POLICE written all over it, when the effect was quite other.

Jennison hadn't been able to last out and was already unfolding his parcel, releasing the pungent smell of hot battered fish and vinegary chips.

'Can't you bloody wait till I get parked?'

'No, me belly thinks me throat's cut. This'll do. Pull over here.'

'Don't be daft. We'd have the girls throwing bricks at us for frightening off the punters. I know just the spot. Bonkers'll never find us here.'

He swung the wheel over and ran the car under the plane trees into a gravelled driveway between two stone pillars. Stumps of concrete at their tops suggested that they had once been crowned with some ornamental or heraldic device but this had long since vanished, probably at the same time as the ornate metal gate. Its massy hinges were still visible on the right-hand pillar, however, while on the left, graven deep enough in the stonework to be still readable though heavily lichened, was the name MOSCOW HOUSE.

Leaning over the high ivied garden wall was an estate agent's board reading FOR SALE WITH VACANT POSSESSION.

Maycock drove up the length of the drive till he could see the house. Its complete darkness and shuttered windows confirmed the promise of the sign that there was no one here to disturb or be disturbed by.

'That's funny,' he said as he brought the car to a halt.

'What?'

'Isn't that door open?'

'Which door?'

'The house door, what do you fucking think?'

The two men strained their eyes through the swirling mist.

'It is, tha knows,' said Maycock. 'It's definitely open.'

Jennison leaned across, dropped the warm newspaper packet on to his colleague's lap and switched off the headlights.

'Can't see it myself,' he said. 'Now shut up and eat your haddock afore it gets cold.'

They munched in silence for a while. Then the radio crackled out their call sign and a voice they recognized as Bonnick's said, 'Report your position.'

'Shit,' said Maycock.

'No sweat,' said Jennison.

He switched on his transmitter and said, 'We're in the Avenue, Sarge. Checking out an unsecured property.'

'The Avenue? Which Avenue?' demanded Bonnick, sounding irritated. 'Use proper procedure, full details when reporting location.'

Jennison grinned at his partner and replied mildly, 'Just the Avenue, Sarge. In Greenhill. Thought everyone knew that. The property's called Moscow House. It's on the left-hand side as you're heading east, about one hundred and five metres from the junction with Balmoral Terrace. There's a name on the gate pillar. Moscow House. That's M, O, S, C, O, W. Moscow. H, O, U, S, E. House. Bit misty out here but if you get lost, there's one or two helpful young ladies around who'll be glad to show you the way. Over.'

There was silence, though in his mind Maycock could hear police constables pissing themselves laughing all over Mid-Yorkshire.

'Report back to me as soon as your check's finished. Out,' said the sergeant in a quiet controlled voice.

'Think you've made a friend there,' said Maycock.

'He can please his bloody self.'

'Aye, but we'd best do what you've told him we're doing,' said Maycock, getting out of the car. 'Come on. Let's take a look.'

LEEDS COLLEGE OF BUILDING LIBRARY

'I've not finished me cod yet!' protested Jennison.

But to tell the truth his appetite was fading. For Joker Jennison had a secret. He was scared of the dark, and particularly scared of old dark houses. His fear was metaphysical rather than physical. Muscular muggers and crazy crack-heads he took in his stride. But in his infancy he couldn't sleep without a night-light and as a teenager he'd fainted while watching *The Rocky Horror Picture Show*. On reviving and realizing the damage this was likely to do to his street cred, he had faked every symptom of every illness he could think of, causing a meningitis scare in his school and getting him confined to an isolation ward in the infirmary while they did tests. It had worked as far as his mates were concerned, but on joining the police force (which itself had been an act of denial), he had soon realized that if he fainted every time he had to enter a deserted property with only his torch for light, pretence of illness would get him thrown out as quickly as admission of terror. So he had learned to grit his teeth and keep his true feelings hidden behind the screen of pleasantries that got him his nickname.

Now he remained stubbornly in his seat as his partner mounted the steps to the open door. Moscow House seemed to grow in bulk as he watched, towering high into the swirling mist where it wasn't hard for his straining eyes to detect ruined battlements around which flitted squeaking bats.

Then the mist came rolling down the dark façade as if bent on putting a curtain between himself and Alan Maycock.

'Oh shit,' said Jennison again. What was worse, out here alone or in there with his partner?

That part of his mind still in touch with reason told him that if anything happened to Maycock he'd have to go into the house anyway.

With a sigh of desperation, he rolled his bulk out of the car, crushed the remnants of his fish supper into a ball and hurled it into the darkness, then jogged towards the house shouting, 'Hang about, you daft bugger. I'm coming!'

5

a tight cork

'What do they put these things in with? Sledgehammers?' snarled Cressida Maciver, gripping the bottle between her knees and hauling at the corkscrew with both hands.

Ellie Pascoe smiled uneasily and glanced at her watch. Half eight, two empty bottles lying on the floor, and they hadn't even eaten yet. Nor could her sensitive nose detect any evidence of food in preparation wafting from the kitchen, and Cress was one of those cooks who couldn't scramble an egg without sprinkling it with spices.

But it wasn't the thought of going hungry that caused her unease. It was the fact that on a couple of previous occasions, even with food, the opening of a third bottle had been closely followed by an attempt at seduction which came close to sexual assault. After the second time, Ellie had been ready with various stratagems to pre-empt the well-signalled pounce, and though their farewell hug sometimes came close to frottage, she had managed to escape without damage. Sober, next time they met, Cress seemed to have forgotten everything in the same way that, drunk, she clearly had no recollection of Ellie's having confided in her that once, at university, curiosity and a determination not to appear repressed or naive had got her into a female lecturer's bed, but the experience had done nothing for her and wasn't one she had any desire to repeat.

Usually she got a taxi home, but when her husband, Detective Chief Inspector Peter Pascoe had announced they'd need a baby-sitter as piles of neglected paperwork were going to keep him at his desk deep into the evening, she'd declared that what they lost on the sitter they could gain on the taxi and arranged for him to pick her up about ten thirty, which was the usual danger time. Now the schedule was blown to hell, and as well as uneasy, Ellie felt cheated. She was very fond of Cress, and in matters of taste generally, politics sufficiently, and humour absolutely, they shared so much that their evenings together before the hormones took over were a delight which tonight looked like being cut well short.

The assaults always occurred when Cressida was between men, which was pretty frequently. The intensity of her commitment was more than most could abide for long. The journey from feeling adored and cosseted to feeling cribbed, cabined and confined was a short one, in some cases taking only a matter of days. In the aftermath of break-up, Cressida always turned to her female friends for comfort. Men were only good for one thing, and that was overrated. Passion was for pubescents. Female friendship was the thing. Which sensible life-view ruled her mind until the opening of the third bottle, when a meeting of mature female minds was suddenly discarded in favour of a close encounter of mature female flesh.

The last break-up seemed to have been even more than usually traumatic.

'I really liked the guy,' she bewailed. 'He had everything. And I mean everything. Including a Maserati. Have you ever had sex in a Maserati, Ellie?'

Ellie pursed her lips as if running though a check list of top cars, then admitted she'd missed out.

'Never mind,' said her friend consolingly. 'The driving position's fabulous but the shagging position's absolute agony. But you wouldn't believe a guy driving a car like that would turn out to have five kids and a religion that won't let his wife entertain the idea of divorce.'

Her eyes glinted malevolently.

'Maybe if I had a word with his wife that would change her religion,' she added.

'Cress, you wouldn't.'

'Of course I wouldn't. Not unless provoked. And why the hell am I wasting quality time with my dearest friend talking about that sunburnt shit of a witch doctor?'

She gave a mighty heave at the corkscrew and succeeded in hauling it out of the bottle, but only at the expense of leaving half the cork in the neck.

Oh well, that should delay matters a little, thought Ellie, offering up a prayer of thanks to whatever it was that almost certainly wasn't there.

As if to reproach her for this qualification in her devotion, the phone rang.

'Shit,' said Cressida. 'See what you can do with this sodding thing, will you?'

As soon as she left the room, Ellie pulled out her mobile and pressed her husband's speed-dial key. He answered almost immediately.

'Peter,' she whispered. 'It's me.'

'What? It's a lousy line.'

'Just listen. I need you earlier.'

'Ah,' he said. 'Second bottle time already, eh?'

He was quick. That was one of the good things about him. One of many good things.

'Third,' she said. 'No sign of food and she's been dumped again. Some medic. She's started on about the problems of sex in a Maserati.'

'Poor thing. Can't you tell her you've got a headache? Always works with me.'

'Ha ha. Can you get here soon? Say it's some problem with the sitter.'

'I'm on my way. Fifteen minutes tops. Hang in there, girl.'

She'd just got the phone into her bag when Cressida came back into the room.

'Sue-Lynn,' she said. 'My sister-in-law. Wants to know if I've heard from Pal. Seems he didn't turn up for his squash with Jase and nobody knows where he is. Silly bitch.'

In the five years of their friendship, she'd never talked in any detail about her family, not even her brother Pal with whom she was close and who'd been indirectly responsible for bringing Ellie and Cress together. He ran an antique shop called Archimagus in the town's medieval area near the cathedral. Ellie had been in a couple of times without buying anything and without registering more about the proprietor than that he was a good-looking young man who after a token offer of help became a non-hassling background presence. On the third occasion when she expressed interest in a seventeenth-century knife box in walnut with a beautiful mother-of-pearl butterfly inlay on the lid, he'd answered her questions with an eloquent expertise that very subtly implied that only a person of the most sensitive taste would have selected this item above all the rest of his stock. Finally he suggested she took it home to see how it looked *in situ*, no obligation, which had made a young woman who'd just come into the shop roar with laughter.

'I bet he hasn't mentioned the price yet,' she said.

On reflection, Ellie had to admit this was true.

A price was mentioned. Ellie looked at the newcomer and raised an eyebrow enquiringly.

She pursed her lips, shook her head and said, 'That the best you can do for a friend of your sister?'

'You two are friends?' said Pal.

Cressida had looked at Ellie, grinned and said, 'No, but I think we could be.'

To which Pal had replied, 'So let me know how it works out, then we can discuss a possible price cut.'

It had worked out well and the knife box now adorned the Pascoe dining room. But though her friendship with Cressida burgeoned, the brother never became anything more than an antiques dealer with whom she was on first-name terms. As for the rest of the family, Ellie had picked up that there was a younger sister, and also that they'd lost their parents some time in childhood, but she'd made no attempt to pry into the exact nature of the evident tensions and problems Cress's upbringing had left her with. This didn't mean she wasn't curious – hell, they were friends, weren't they? And knowing your friends was even more important than knowing your enemies – but in Ellie's book though mere curiosity might get you nebbing into the life of a stranger, it was never enough to justify sticking your nose into the affairs of a friend.

But if the confidences came unasked, she was not about to discourage them, particularly in a situation where they also served the useful function of postponing the threatened pounce.

'You're not worried?' she said.

'No. He's probably still at work, giving discount.'

'Sorry?'

Cressida grinned.

'Well-heeled ladies love their *objets d'art* but love their money even more. Pal says I'd be amazed how many of them after a bout of haggling will say, "Do you give a discount for cash, Mr Maciver? Or something . . . ?"'

'I presume you didn't say this to your sister-in-law?'

'Thought about it, but in the end I just said if she was really worried she should ring the police and the hospitals.'

'Decided to go for reassurance then.'

'You needn't concern yourself about Sue-Lynn. Self-centred cow. Any worries she's got will be about herself, not Pal.'

'But his squash partner is worried too . . . Jase, you said?'

'Jason Dunn. My brother-in-law,' said Cressida, sounding rather surprised, as if she'd just worked out the relationship.

'So, married to your sister?'

'Yeah, Helen the child bride.'

'Lot younger than you then?' said Ellie.

'She's younger than everyone,' said Cress dismissively. 'Like Snow White. Doesn't get any older no matter how often you see the picture. Only this one still adores the wicked stepmother.'

'Stepmother?' This was completely new. 'I didn't know you had a stepmother.'

'Not something I boast about. You don't want to hear all this crap. Haven't you got that bottle open yet?'

'Sorry. It's this broken cork. This stepmother, is she really wicked?'

'Goes with the job, doesn't it? She's a pain in the arse anyway. You've probably seen her name in the papers. You wouldn't forget it. Kay Kafka, would you believe? Why do Yanks always have these crazy fucking names? Here, let me try.'

She grabbed the bottle from Ellie and began poking at the broken cork.

Ellie, feeling that a gibe about names didn't come well from someone called Cressida who had a brother called Palinurus, was by now sufficiently interested in the family background to have pursued it even without its pounce-postponing potential.

'So you don't care for your stepmother? And Pal?'

'Hates her guts.'

'But Helen took to her?'

'She was only a kid when Dad remarried. It was easy for Kay to sink her talons in. Me and Pal were older, our shells had toughened up.'

'And when your father died . . . when was that?'

'Ten years ago. Pal was of age so out of it. I was seventeen so officially still in need of a responsible adult to care over me. I was determined it wasn't going to be Kay even if it meant signing up with dotty old Vinnie till I made eighteen.'

'Vinnie?'

'My aunt Lavinia. Dad's only sister. Mad as a hatter; you need feathers and a beak before she'll even speak to you. But being a blood relative did the trick and I was able to give Kay the finger.'

'But Helen thought different?'

'Don't think thought entered into it. She was only nine. Pal and I tried to get her out of the clutches, but she went all hysterical at the idea of being separated from Kay. Poor little cow. Not much upstairs, and I'm sure Kay preferred it that way. She's a real control freak. Probably hand-picked Helen's husband with that in mind too.'

'Sorry?'

'Jason. He's a PE teacher at Weavers, so not what you'd call an intellectual giant. But a real hunk. And hung. Known as a bit of a stud before Helen hooked him. They say he fucks like a Rossini overture.'

This was an interesting concept but not one that Ellie, in her present antaphrodisiac mode, felt it wise to pursue.

'So Helen's stayed close to her stepmother? Which means you and Pal aren't all that close to Helen?'

Cressida shrugged.

'She made her choice.'

'But Pal plays squash with Jason?'

'Yes, he does,' said Cressida. 'Can't think why, especially as I'm sure Jase must whup the shit out of him and Pal's not a good loser. Still there's nowt so queer as folks, is there? And most of us are even queerer than we think.'

She gave Ellie what could only be described as a suggestive leer, then said, 'Fuck this,' and drove the broken segment of cork down into the bottle, squirting wine over her hand and forearm.

She raised her fingers to her mouth and licked the red drops off, her eyes fixed on Ellie and a tiny smile twitching her lips.

'More ways of popping a reluctant cork than one, eh?' she said. 'Pass your glass.'

6

a fishy smell

Moscow House was full of light, which the shuttered and curtained windows kept penned within. Only through the open front door did any escape to offer a weak challenge to the besieging fog.

Finding the electricity switched on had been a big bonus, particularly for Jennison, but he still stuck close to his partner as they went methodically through the downstairs rooms, then headed upstairs.

'Hello hello hello,' said Maycock as he pushed open a bedroom door to reveal a double bed, neatly made up, though not with fresh linen. 'This looks like it's still in use.'

'Yeah. Hey, do you think some of the girls might have been using this place to bring their punters?'

'Could be.' Maycock sniffed the air. 'Smell a bit sexy to you?'

Jennison sniffed.

'Nah,' he said. 'Think it's thy haddock.'

There was only one door they couldn't open.

Some of Jennison's uneasiness returned. In haunted houses there was always one door that was locked, and when you opened it . . .

Maycock was kneeling down.

'Key's in the lock on the inside,' he said.

Jennison said hopefully, 'Maybe one of the girls heard us come in and she's locked herself in here.'

'Could be.'

Maycock banged his fist against the solid oak panel and called, 'It's the police. If there's anyone in there, come on out.'

Jennison stepped back in alarm, recalling tales of vampires and such creatures who could only join humankind if invited.

Nothing happened.

Maycock stooped to the keyhole again. Once more he sniffed.

'More sex?' said Jennison.

'Bit of a burnt smell.'

'You think there's a fire in there?'

'No. Not strong enough. Listen.'

He pressed his ear to the door.

'Can you hear something?'

'What?'

'Sort of whirring, scratching noise.'

'Scratching?' said Jennison unhappily, his imagination reviewing a range of possibilities, none of them comforting.

'Yeah. Here, give it a try with your shoulder.'

Obediently, Jennison leaned against the door and heaved.

'Jesus, you couldn't open a paper bag like that.'

'You try then. Didn't I hear you once had a trial for Bradford? Or were that a trial *at* Bradford for masquerading as a rugby player?'

Provoked, Maycock hit the door with all his strength and bounced back nursing his shoulder.

'No go,' he said. 'Bolted as well as locked, I'd say.'

'Better call this in,' said Jennison.

He spoke into his personal radio, gave details of the situation, was told to wait.

They went to the head of the stairs and sat down.

'Not one of my best ideas, this,' admitted Maycock. 'We'd have been better off eating our nosh outside the chippie, and bugger Bonkers.'

Jennison surreptitiously crossed himself and wished he had some garlic. He knew that at times of psychic stress it was a dangerous thing to name evil spirits as that could easily summon them up. So it came as a shock but no surprise when out of the air came a familiar voice, saying, 'So there you are, making yourselves comfortable. OK, what's going off here? And why does your car smell like a chip-shop?'

They peered into the hallway and found themselves gazing down at the slim athletic figure of Sergeant Bonnick who'd just come through the open door.

They scrambled to their feet but were saved from having to answer by the radio.

'Keyholder to Moscow House is a Mr Maciver, first name Palinurus. Just say if you need that spelt, Joker. We've rung the number given and got hold of Mrs Maciver. She got a bit agitated when we told her we wanted to talk to her husband about Moscow House. She says she doesn't know where he is, in fact nobody seems to know where he is, and he's missed some kind of appointment this evening. I've passed this on to Mr Ireland. Hold on. He's here.'

Ireland was the duty inspector.

'Alan, you're sure there's a key on the inside of that locked door?'

'Certain, sir.'

'Then I think from the sound of it you ought to take a look inside. You need assistance to break in?'

Bonnick spoke into his radio.

'Sergeant Bonnick here, sir. No need. I've got a ram in my boot. I'll get back to you soon as we're in.'

He tossed his keys to Jennison, who set off down the stairs.

'Be prepared, eh, Sarge?' said Maycock. 'Good idea carrying everything you might need around with you.'

'Not always, else you'd be towing a mobile chippie,' said Bonnick. 'Show me this locked room.'

He examined the door carefully and stooped to check through the keyhole.

'Key's still there,' he said.

'Well, it would be,' said Maycock. 'Seeing as I just saw it.'

'Not necessarily. Not if there's someone in there to take it out,' said Bonnick.

'We did shout.'

'Oh well then, they were bound to answer,' said the sergeant. 'God, when did you last take some serious exercise?'

Jennison had returned, carrying the ram. He was slightly out of breath. Outside, with the mist turning even the short journey from front door to car into a ghostly gauntlet run, he hadn't been tempted to hang about.

'All right, which of you two still has something resembling muscle under the flab?'

'Al had a trial for the Bulls,' said Jennison.

'That right, Alan? Let's see you in action then.'

The constable hit the woodwork four or five times with the ram with no visible effect except on himself.

'They knew how to make doors in them days,' he gasped.

'They knew how to make policemen too,' growled Bonnick. 'Give it here.'

He swung it twice. There was a loud splintering. He gave Maycock a told-you-so look.

'Yeah, but I weakened it,' protested the constable.

'Let's see what's inside, shall we?' said Bonnick.

He raised his right foot and drove it against the

58

door. It flew open. Light from the landing spilled into the room.

'Oh Jesus,' said Bonnick.

But Jennison, whose fear of the supernatural was compensated for by a very relaxed attitude to real-life horror, exclaimed, 'Ee bah gum, he's made a reet mess of himself, hasn't he, Sarge!'

7

a British Euro

The company of her stepdaughter was always a delight to Kay Kafka. They shared an affection which went all the deeper because it involved neither the constraints of blood nor the coincidence of taste and opinion. Indeed, during these regular Wednesday evening encounters, they rarely strayed nearer the harsh realities of existence than a discussion of films and fashions and local gossip, but what might (in Kay's case at least) have been tedious in the company of another was here rendered delightful by the certainty of love.

In recent months, however, the approach of harsh reality in the form of the soon-to-be-born children had provided another topic, which could have kept them going for the whole visit if they'd let it. Even here, there wasn't much harshness in evidence. It had been so far a comparatively easy pregnancy, and, bulk apart, Helen seemed to be enjoying her role as serenely glowing mother-in-waiting. So they would move easily over the wide range of pleasurable preparations for the great day – baby clothes, pushchairs, nursery decoration and, of course, names. Here Helen was adamant. Superstitiously she'd refused all offers to identify the gender of the twins, but if one were a girl, she was going to be called Kay.

'And I don't care what you say,' she went on, 'they're both going to call you grandma.'

Which had brought Kay as close to tears as she'd been for a long while. She'd told the children to call her Kay when she married their father. The two elder ones did their best to avoid calling her anything polite, but Helen was young enough to want, eventually, to call her mum. Realizing the problem this would give the girl with her brother and sister, Kay had resisted.

'I want to be her friend,' she explained to her husband. 'The lady's not for mummification.'

But she never explained to him just how very hard it was for her to resist.

Grandma was different. She had no resistance to offer here. And even if she had, she doubted if it would have made a difference. Helen had powers of obduracy which could sometimes surprise. In this at least she resembled her dead father.

So she'd smiled and embraced the girl and said, 'If that's what you want, that's what I'll be. Thank you.'

It had been a good moment. One of many on these Wednesday evenings. But tonight seemed unlikely to contribute more. Somehow Jason's phone call had disturbed the even flow, then the fog delayed the pizza delivery and when they finally turned up, they were what Kay called upper-class anglicized – pale, lukewarm and flaccid with not much on top. But the real downer was the fact that, as she entered the finishing straight of her pregnancy, it seemed finally to be dawning on Helen that the birth of the twins wasn't just going to be a triumphal one-off champagne-popping occasion for celebration, it was going to change the whole of her life, for ever.

Kay tried to be light and reassuring but the young woman was not to be jollied.

'Now I know why you would never let me call you mum,' she said. 'Because it would have made you my prisoner.'

'Jesus, Helen,' exclaimed Kay. 'What a weird thing to say.'

'I come from a weird family,' said Helen. 'You must have noticed. Talking of which, I wonder if Pal turned up.'

On cue the answer came with the sound of the front door opening. A moment later Jason looked into the room. In his mid twenties, six foot plus, blond, beautifully muscled and with looks to swoon for, he could have modelled for Praxiteles. Or Leni Riefenstahl. If his genes and Helen's melded right, these twins should be a new wonder of the world, thought Kay, smiling a welcome.

'Hi, Kay,' he said. 'It's all right, sweetie, I'm not going to disturb you. Any word from Pal?'

'No, nothing. He didn't show at the club then?'

'No. What the hell's he playing at? I hope nothing's wrong.'

The phone rang.

He said, 'I'll get it,' and retreated to the hall, closing the door firmly behind him.

'Why's he so worried?' said Helen irritably. 'It's not as if Pal was ever the most reliable of people.'

'Oh, I always found him pretty reliable,' said Kay sardonically.

She regretted it as soon as she said it. Family relationships were a no-go area, again one of her own choosing. Many times in the past it would have been easy to swing along with Helen as she took off in a cadenza of indignation at the attitude and behaviour of her siblings, but, as she'd explained to Tony, 'In the end, they're blood family, I'm not, and nothing's going to change that.' To which he'd replied in his mafiosa voice, 'Yeah, family matters. You may have to kill 'em, but you should always send a big wreath to the funeral. It's the American way. That's one of the things I miss, being so far from home.'

She sometimes thought Tony made a joke of things to hide the fact he really believed them.

Helen gave her a sharp look and said, 'OK, I know he's been an absolute bastard with you –

me too – but things change and lately you've got to admit he's been trying. These games of squash with Jase, a year ago that wouldn't have been possible, but it's a kind of rapprochement, isn't it? You know Pal, he would never just come straight out and say, "Let's forget everything and start over," he'd have to come at you sideways.'

Sideways. From above, beneath, behind. Oh yes, she knew Pal.

She smiled and said, 'Yes, the games obviously mean a lot to Jason. And no one likes being stood up.'

Through the closed door they heard the young man's voice rise. They couldn't make out the words but his intonation had alarm in it.

He came back into the room.

'I've got to go out again,' he said.

He was making an effort to sound casual but his fresh open face gave the game away.

'Why? What's happened?' demanded Helen.

'Nothing,' he said. Then, seeing this wasn't a sufficient answer, he went on, 'It was Sue-Lynn wanting to know if I'd heard anything yet. The police just rang her. They wanted to contact Pal as the keyholder of Moscow House. They wouldn't give any details, but it's probably just a break-in, or vandalism. You know what kids are like. I blame the teachers.'

His attempt at lightness fell flat as an English comic telling a kilt joke at the Glasgow Empire.

'So where are you going?' asked Helen.

'Sue-Lynn said she's going down to Moscow House. I thought maybe I should go too. She sounded upset.'

'Since when did you give a damn how Sue-Lynn sounded?' demanded his wife.

Kay said, 'No, you're quite right, Jase. It's probably nothing, but just in case . . . Hang on, I'll come with you.'

She stood up. Helen rose too, rather more slowly.

'All right, we'll all go,' she said.

'Helen, love, don't be silly,' protested Jason. 'In your condition . . .'

'I'm pregnant,' she snapped, 'not a bloody invalid. And Pal's my brother.'

There we go, thought Kay. Blood.

She said brightly, 'This can hardly have anything to do with Pal if the police are trying to get hold of him as the keyholder, can it?'

It rang as true as a British Euro.

'All right. Come on,' said Jason, who knew when argument was useless.

They got their coats and went out. It took some time to ease Helen into the car, even though it was a big Volvo estate. Jason's beloved MR2 had gone in the fourth month of pregnancy when he'd had to admit its impracticality as a vehicle for his expanding wife and his imminently expanding family.

Finally they were on their way.

Kay looked back at the house as they passed through the gateway. Even at this short distance the mist made it look different, strange, unattainable.

For whatever reason, she found herself thinking that these cosy Wednesday evenings were over for ever.

8

another fine mess

What's keeping the useless bastard? Ellie Pascoe asked herself.

Anything less serious than a terrorist attack necessitating the sealing off of the city centre would be paid for with bitter rue.

She glanced surreptitiously at her watch.

It was a mistake.

The thing about Cressida's pounce was that, though you knew it was coming, it always took you by surprise.

One moment she was sitting opposite, attempting to squeeze a final drop out of the now empty bottle, the next she was on the arm of Ellie's chair, pinning her down with the expertise of a pro wrestler and trying to thrust her tongue down Ellie's throat.

Unable to move and unable to speak, Ellie did the only thing left to her. She bit.

'Christ Almighty!' exclaimed Cress, jerking her head back. 'So you like it rough? Suits me.'

The door bell rang.

And kept on ringing.

One thing about a cop, he might come late, but when he arrived you knew he was there.

'Who the hell is that?' said Cressida angrily.

Her body-lock grip relaxed sufficiently for Ellie to counterattack. She rolled Cressida off the arm of the chair and rose to her feet.

'Don't know,' she said, 'but I don't think he's going to go away.'

She headed for the door and opened it. Her husband stood there, framed in thick mist, like a visitor from another world.

'Hello, darling,' she said, her voice bright, her eyes brighter as they flashed *Where the hell have you been?* 'You're a bit early. We haven't even eaten yet.'

'Sorry, bit of an emergency. I rang home to check things, and the sitter's not feeling too well. Unfortunately something's come up at work and I'm going to be a bit tied up myself, so I thought I'd better get you there.'

He sounded like a second-rate actor in a third rate soap.

'Oh dear. What a pity. Cress, I'm sorry. I've got to go. Perils of domesticity, eh?'

Cressida was standing behind her, looking like she didn't believe a word of it. Don't blame her, thought Ellie. If Peter had sounded stilted, she sounded like a parody of provincial rep. All she lacked was a French window and a tennis racket.

But no time to hang about for the reviews.

She grabbed her coat, gave her friend a quick hug and followed Peter down the steps of the narrow Edwardian terrace house to his car.

The police radio crackled into life as he opened the door.

Ellie, used to the background when she travelled with her husband, didn't pay any attention till he grabbed the mike, identified himself and asked for details.

Shit, thought Ellie. How often did it happen that your lying excuses turned true? He'd said he was tied up with something and now God was making sure he was, which was a shame as, whether in reaction from or reaction to her friend's probing tongue she didn't care to know, she wouldn't have minded getting home full of wine for an early night . . .

She felt herself pushed aside as Cressida came bounding down the steps and thrust her head into the car.

'What was that about Moscow House?' she demanded.

Pascoe looked at her in amazement then tried to ease her backwards.

'Nothing to bother yourself with, just a routine call . . .'

'They're talking about ambulances, aren't they? That's Moscow House in the Avenue, right? Jesus! Ask them what the hell's going on. Ellie, that's our house. Don't you understand – that's our house!'

And as she looked appealingly at her friend, her name Maciver was spoken quite distinctly on the radio.

Pascoe switched it off.

'Your house . . . ?' he said.

'It's the family house, where I grew up . . . It belongs to us now, the three of us, only . . . What's going on there? Has this got anything to do with Pal going missing?'

Pascoe looked at Ellie, who said, 'Pal's Cress's brother. He didn't turn up for a squash match this evening and no one knows where he is . . .'

Pascoe said, 'Probably some simple explanation. Ellie, I'll have to call by there, check what's going off. Maybe it's best if you hang on here till I see how long I'm going to be. You can always get a taxi.'

He sounded very relaxed about things and it all came over much more convincing than before, but Ellie got the real message. He'd heard something that suggested to him it might be a good idea if she stuck with Cressida for a while longer.

But that wasn't an option.

Cressida said, 'I'm coming with you.'

'I'm afraid that's not possible,' said Pascoe firmly. 'Against regulations, you see . . .'

'Sod regulations. OK, if you won't take me, I'll drive myself.'

'Pete,' said Ellie urgently. 'I don't think that would be wise . . . we've drunk quite a bit of wine, and with this mist . . .'

Pascoe shook his head and gave her his another-fine-mess-you've-got-me-into look, then said, 'All right, Cress, get in. But when we get there, you stay inside the car till I check what's happening, OK?'

'Yeah yeah, anything,' said Cressida, tumbling into the back seat.

Fat chance, thought Ellie.

She went back up the steps and closed the door, wondered too late if Cress had her keys with her, thought *That's her problem!* and got into the other rear seat.

Cressida was looking at her suspiciously. She might be tipsy and she might be worried but her brain was still working.

She said, 'So what's happening about your baby-sitter emergency?'

Oh hell, thought Ellie. In her experience lies always got you into trouble.

She said, 'Don't worry, I'll think of something.'

'I'm sure you will,' said Cressida.

9

the battle of Moscow

It was almost a dead heat at Moscow House with Pascoe's ancient Golf just pipping Sue-Lynn's Alfa Romeo Spider, closely followed by Jason Dunn's Volvo estate.

PC Jennison had been stationed as custodian of the gate by Sergeant Bonnick with the uncalled-for comment that here at last was a task suited to his excessive girth.

'No one gets past, right?'

'Not even Mr Dalziel, say?' said Jennison uneasily. *Or the Four Horsemen of the Apocalypse?* his restless imagination added.

'No one unofficial, idiot! Do I have to spell it out? Our lot you wave through. Anyone else, you block their passage, which shouldn't be difficult with your gut, then you contact me in the house. And keep a log of names and times in your note-book. You got that?'

'Yes, Sarge,' said Jennison.

So far all that had turned up had been Inspector

Ireland, an ambulance and the duty Medical Examiner, plus one of the working girls whose curiosity had been strong enough to keep her from joining the general migration to other beats once the flashing blue lights had signalled the end of trade in the Avenue for the night. When first she appeared, Jennison had experienced a pang of bowel-loosening terror. With long black hair and a face as pale as death, she looked as if she'd just stepped out of a Transylvanian tomb. But when she smiled at him without revealing fangs and spoke to him in a friendly and indeed rather flattering way, he quickly relaxed. Any remaining suspicion that she might be one of the Undead faded when his expert gaze took in the substantial and shapely body beneath the short leather dress, a judgment he was able to confirm tactilely when he put his hands on her buttocks and pushed her out of sight behind the gate column when a car approached.

This turned out to be Pascoe. On recognizing the DCI, Jennison stood aside and waved him through, only realizing as the car went by that there were two women in the back.

So what? he thought. Bonkers could hardly blame him if the DCI brought his friends and family along. But even as the disclaimer formed in his mind, the Volvo and the Spider loomed out of the mist and went sweeping by before he could re-interpose his large frame.

He took out his radio, weighed the pros and

cons of contacting the sergeant, decided that a plea of misunderstanding was better than a confession of inefficiency, and put it away again.

In his notebook he noted the time, then added, in his old-fashioned round schoolboy's hand, *Mr Pascoe and party.*

'OK, Dolores,' he said, and watched with a classical appreciation as the young tart slipped like a shy nymph from behind the sheltering column.

Heading up the drive, Pascoe was aware of headlights blooming behind, but thought nothing of it. As some of his civilian acquaintance liked to point out, if you got burgled and wanted a cop while the clues were still hot, it could be twenty-four hours before you saw one; but if you moved beyond the reach of human help by getting yourself killed, then every police vehicle in the county would be rushing to your door.

He saw an ambulance parked before the house alongside an Audi A6 Avant. In the passenger seat of the ambulance a paramedic was carefully puffing cigarette smoke out of his open window. By his side, the driver was talking into his radio mike.

Pascoe read the scene clearly. It wasn't good news. Their disposition meant there was nothing for them here except body recovery. The driver would be talking to his Control, asking for instructions. Which were most likely to be, don't hang around waiting for the cops to tell you they've finished with the corpse, which could take forever. Get back here, plenty of other work to do.

He applied the handbrake, turned to the women in the rear and said, 'Stay in the car, please, until I've checked things out.'

Perhaps he should have applied the rear-door child-locks, but locking Ellie in wasn't something a man did lightly. Anyway he couldn't see how this situation could prove more problematic than many others he'd dealt with over the years.

He soon found out.

Alongside them the ambulance had started up and begun to move away. Cressida flung her door open and ran after it, beating her fist against its rear doors. An Alfa Spider slewed to a halt across the drive, forcing the ambulance to stop, and another woman half fell out and began shouting at the paramedic through his open window. Behind the Spider, a Volvo estate came to rest rather more sedately. Its male driver emerged with athletic grace, a blond young man, lovely to look at, the perfect type of the Handsome Sailor. He looked ready to join the assault on the emergency vehicle but was called to order by a scream from the rear of his car and, with evident reluctance, turned to assist a pregnant woman out of the back seat.

From the opposite door a tall slim woman slipped out and stood assessing the scene with a calm unblinking gaze. The woman from the Spider was demanding to know who was being taken to hospital and insisting if it was her husband that she should be admitted to ride with him. The paramedic was trying without much success to convince her the vehicle was empty and they'd been called away on another emergency. Cressida was wrestling with the rear door handle. The pregnant woman, magnified by a trick of the headlights and mist so that she could have modelled for Gaea, heavy with Titans, was now advancing with majestic instancy. By her side the Handsome Sailor seemed divided between wanting to guide her ponderous steps and wanting to get to the ambulance, presumably to add his vote to the demand for information. The driver out of frustration leaned on his horn. Sergeant Bonnick, attracted by the noise, appeared in the open doorway of Moscow House. The paramedic, realizing that nothing but proof ocular was going to convince the women that the ambulance was empty, climbed out of the cab and went round to the rear doors. Another set of headlights came swimming up the drive.

'Peter,' said Ellie, who was standing alongside her husband viewing the activity, 'I think it's time to exercise your authority.'

'Not to worry,' said Pascoe with the calmness of one in no hurry to confront a belligerent drunk, a hysterical wife (widow?), and a woman who looked as if a good sneeze could send her into epeirogenic contractions. 'When they realize the cupboard's bare, they'll settle down.'

'Wimp,' said Ellie.

The paramedic pushed Cressida to one side and pulled open the doors.

Everyone, including the trio from the Volvo, peered inside.

For a moment it looked as if Pascoe was right.

There was a moment of complete and blessed silence.

Then it was broken by the slamming of a car door, presumably belonging to the newly arrived vehicle invisible behind the Volvo's dazzling headlights.

The noise cracked through the stillness like a starting gun and had much the same effect.

Cressida turned her attention from the ambulance's emptiness to the others around her, seeming to register them for the first time. Her attention focused on the tall slim woman.

'What the fuck are you doing here?' she demanded.

'Hello, Cressida,' said the woman mildly. 'I think we ought to ask someone in authority just what's happened here, don't you?'

'Oh, you do, do you? Well, any interest you might have had in what happens here ended ten fucking years ago. Now all you're doing is trespassing. Get off my property before I throw you off,' snarled Cressida, taking an aggressive step towards the tall woman.

'Your property, Cress? What do you mean, *your* property? It's as much mine as yours, and Kay's here with me, so just shut up!'

This was Gaea, her voice shrill, her pretty face contorted.

'Jesus Christ, can't you two just grow up and stop acting like a pair of sodding schoolgirls! It's Pal, my husband, your brother, we should be worried about here, not who owns what, right?'

This was the Spider Woman. Her reproaches, far from calming things down, merely drew the fire of both the sisters, who seemed united in dislike of their sister-in-law if nothing else.

The Handsome Sailor meanwhile was heading towards the house. He looked in superb shape but Bonnick, who made such a big thing of physical fitness, ought to be able to take care of him, thought Pascoe. On the other hand once the trio of quarrelling women diverted their attention from the ambulance and each other to what lay inside the house, even the redoubtable Bonnick could be in bother.

The blond reached the doorway, the sergeant spoke to him, the young man began to push past, Bonnick tried to apply a basic armlock which the other evaded with practised ease. Realizing he was dealing with someone who'd done the same unarmed-combat courses as himself, the sergeant threw restraint to the winds and the young man to the ground, only to have his legs swept from under him. Next moment, the two were grappling on the doorstep, while the angry voices of the three women rose in volume and intensity.

Definitely time to assert his authority, thought

Pascoe, taking a deep breath. At least things couldn't get any worse.

He was of course wrong.

As he moved unhappily towards the ambulance, he heard a great voice as of a trumpet speak to him from the darkness behind the headlights.

'Evening, Chief Inspector. I'm glad to see you've got everything here under control.'

And out of the mist into the light stepped the bulky figure of Detective Superintendent Andrew Dalziel.

10

a shark in the pool

It would be hard to describe Andy Dalziel as a soothing presence, but like a shark dumped in a swimming pool, he provided a new and unignorable focus of attention.

Reactions to his arrival were various.

Pascoe said, 'What the fuck's he doing here?'

Ellie said, 'God alone knows, but I'm sure if we wait he'll tell us.'

The wrestlers carried on wrestling.

Cressida, Spider Woman and Earth Mother regarded him with wary neutrality.

Only the tall slim woman looked pleased to see him.

'Andy, it's so good to see you again,' she said, smiling as if she meant it.

She stepped forward to meet him, holding out her hand.

'You too, Kay,' said Dalziel, taking the hand. 'Though mebbe not here.'

'On the contrary,' said the woman, who had a

soft unobtrusive American accent. 'Here is perfect. We need to know what's going on, and I'm sure if anyone can tell us, you can.'

'I'd best find out then,' he said, releasing the hand, which he'd been holding in a kissing rather than a shaking grip. 'Ladies, if you'd just be patient a bit longer . . .'

Cressida looked as if she might be about to assert that in her view patience was for monuments but subsided as his gaze locked with hers for a second before passing on to the ambulance crew.

'Detective Superintendent Dalziel,' he said. 'What's going off, lads?'

'Nothing for us here.' The driver glanced towards the women and lowered his voice. 'Just body removal, and your lot don't know when that will be authorized.'

'So you thought you'd shog off home?'

'No! We got an all-units call. Big pile-up in fog on the bypass.'

'Oh aye? Then what are you still skiving round here for?' demanded Dalziel.

Indignation at the injustice of this rose in the ambulance men's eyes, decided it didn't care for the view, and dived back under.

'Right, we'll be off then,' said the driver.

The ambulance pulled away. Kay Kafka put her arm as far round the Earth Mother as it would go. The other two women exchanged a glower then concentrated on the Fat Man's retreating

LEEDS COLLEGE OF BUILDING LIBRARY

figure. On the doorstep the Handsome Sailor had been subdued, but only after Bonnick had been reinforced by the arrival of PC Maycock. For the moment peace was restored.

'Right, sunshine,' said Dalziel. 'What's going off then, apart from bloody chaos?'

'How should I know?' retorted Pascoe. 'I just got here myself. I'm not psychic.'

'Hoity-toity,' said Dalziel. 'See you brought the family. Little Rosie's in the back of the car, is she?'

'No, she isn't. I just happened to be picking up Ellie when I heard the call.'

'So none of that lot's with you?'

'Well actually, Cressida – she's the one with the hair – it was her house I was picking up Ellie from . . .'

'So you said, "Fancy a lift, luv?" Kind of you, Peter. Gets the Force a good name. Did you pick up the others en route?'

'Of course not,' said Pascoe indignantly. 'They all turned up after I got here, which was when the trouble started. How the hell did they get past Jennison on the gate anyway?'

'How owt gets past yon bugger, I don't know. Man can't have any self-respect to let himself get in that shape,' said Dalziel sanctimoniously. Perhaps, thought Pascoe incredulously, he sees himself as slim!

'Any road,' he went on, 'I gather there's a body in here and I'd say this gang have all turned up 'cos they're worried it's Pal Maciver. So let's go in and see if we can put them out of their misery. Or do I mean into it?'

He strode towards the front door. As he passed Ellie he said, 'What fettle, luv? Enjoying your night out?'

'Always a pleasure watching professionals at their work, Andy,' she replied.

Pascoe said to her, 'Look, I'm going to be tied up here for a while. Why don't you take the car and head off home?'

'Before I find out what's happened? You're joking. Besides, Cress might need me.'

'I thought that was why I had to pick you up early,' said Pascoe.

He caught up with Dalziel at the door.

'You all right, Sergeant?' the Fat Man said to Bonnick.

'Fine, sir.'

'Good. And how about you, son?'

Dunn said, 'Look, I'm sorry – I was out of . . . but I was worried – we'd heard that . . . and he didn't show, so I thought that . . . that . . . that . . .'

He stammered to a halt. He really was Billy Budd, thought Pascoe.

'What's your problem, lad?' enquired Dalziel. 'Apart from not being able to finish sentences? Here, don't I know you?'

'I don't think so – please, I didn't realize . . .'

'Yes I do. Rugby club. You sometimes turn out for the seconds, right? Open side? But you can't play regular because of your work, or summat?'

'That's right. I teach PE at Weavers and that means my Saturdays are pretty well spoken for.'

'PE, eh? That explains about the sentences. Pity, but. You looked a lot better prospect than yon neanderthal that plays for the firsts. No finesse. Kicks folk right in front of the ref. Any of them ladies back there belong to you?'

'That's my wife, Helen . . . the pregnant one.'

'That right? Planning to get all your family over at once, are you? So she'd be Helen Maciver as was, right? Now Mrs Dunn as is. I'm getting there. Mrs Kafka I know. And yon Cressida, I remember her. The other is . . . ?'

'Sue-Lynn, Pal's wife.'

'Oh aye. All here then. Some bugger must've sent invitations.'

'Is Pal in there?' said Dunn pleadingly. 'Has something happened to him?'

'I've no idea. Any reason to think it might have done?'

'No. I mean, he didn't turn up . . . we play squash on Wednesday evenings and when he didn't show . . .'

'Stood you up, did he? And that makes you worry something's happened to him? I see. People stand me up, it's when they do appear that something's likely to happen to them. Maycock, you reckon you can keep this mob at bay?'

'No problem, sir.'

'Good lad. Sergeant, lead on. Let's see what all the fuss is about.'

'Please, can't I come with you?' pleaded Dunn.

'Nay lad,' said Dalziel kindly. 'I think most likely you're under arrest. Often happens when you assault a police officer. That right, Sergeant?'

'Yes, sir,' said Bonnick.

'Don't worry too much, but. It probably won't delight the governors at Weavers but it will really impress the kids. Now I'm going to give you a choice. You can either sit in a car handcuffed to the wheel till we're ready to deal with you, which could be hours. Or you can promise to be a good boy and go and take care of that poor wife of thine before she explodes. Which is it?'

'No more trouble, really. I'm very sorry,' said Dunn.

'Good lad. Off you go. Now, Sergeant, fill me in.'

He listened carefully to Bonnick's digest of events as they entered the house and climbed the stairs, only interrupting to ask, 'What made Tweedledum and Tweedledee come up the drive in the first place?'

There was a slight hesitation before Bonnick said, 'Just a random check, I think, sir. Also some of the girls bring their punters up these drive-ways, I believe, and we've been doing a bit of a blitz on kerb crawlers recently.'

'Very conscientious pair of officers, then,' said Dalziel. 'You're lucky to have them.'

The old sod knows that most likely they were skiving, thought Pascoe, but he wouldn't have rated Bonnick if he'd said so.

When they reached the landing, he saw a uniformed inspector standing by a door with a splintered frame. This was Paddy Ireland, a small, rather self-important man, whose trousers always looked as if they'd been re-pressed after he put them on. He turned and acknowledged Dalziel with a parade-ground salute. Behind him through the doorway Pascoe could see a man in a white coverall whom he recognized as Tom Lockridge, one of a small group of local doctors registered as police medical examiners. He was looking down at a man slumped at a desk. At least Pascoe assumed it was a man. Too little of the head remained to make confirmation certain at this distance.

'Poor bastard,' said Dalziel. 'Any ID?'

'Haven't been able to check, sir,' said Ireland. 'Thought it best to disturb things as little as possible till SOCO had got their photos.'

'There's a car parked round the back of the house,' said Bonnick. 'Blue Laguna estate, registered owner Mr Palinurus Maciver, who's also the designated keyholder of the property, so it seems likely . . .'

'Let's not jump the gun, if you'll pardon the expression,' said Dalziel. 'Dr Lockridge, how do? What can you tell us?'

Tom Lockridge had emerged from the room. He didn't look well.

'He's dead,' said Lockridge.

'Don't reckon you're going to get any argument

there,' said Dalziel, peering towards the shattered figure. 'But it's always good to have these things confirmed by an expert. Saves us laymen wasting time with the kiss of life. You wouldn't like to give us just a bit of detail, but, Doc?'

'Not long dead,' intoned Lockridge dully. 'Two to four hours, maybe. Cause of death, probably self-inflicted gunshot wounds to the head . . .'

'Probably?'

'You won't know for certain till the pathologist has taken a look, will you?' said Lockridge, sparking slightly.

'Won't know what? That they killed him or that they were self-inflicted?'

'What? Both. Either. They look to be self-inflicted. He took his shoe and sock off . . .'

'Why do you think that was?'

'I presume so he could pull the shotgun trigger with his toe.'

'You're a bugger for presumptions, Doc. Mebbe he were a freemason. Didn't notice an apron, did you?'

This was a facetious callosity too far, thought Pascoe.

Lockridge evidently thought so too.

'Mr Dalziel,' he said very formally, 'as a doctor, I know the therapeutic value of gallows humour, but I still find your tone offensive. I hope you will take pains to control it before you break the sad news to Mr Maciver's relations.'

'Mr Maciver? That's Mr Maciver, is it? How can you tell?'

They all stared towards the shattered head.

'I don't know . . . I just assumed, with him going missing . . . Yes, I'm sure it's Pal . . . I used to be his doctor, you see.'

'Is that right? So how about distinguishing marks? Something that 'ud spare us having to give his nearest and dearest a close-up of that?'

'He does . . . did . . . does have a distinct naevus at the base of his spine.'

'Naevus? Like in Ben Naevus, you mean?'

'Birthmark,' explained Pascoe, he knew unnecessarily.

'Oh aye. But you've not taken a look?'

'No. I assumed you'd want the body left as undisturbed as possible till your SOCO people had finished in there.'

'SOCO? You think there's been a crime then, Doc?'

'I know there's been a suspicious death. Now, if you'll excuse me, I'll be on my way. You'll have my report as soon as possible.'

He started to peel off the protective overall but Dalziel said, 'Hang about, Doc. Do us a favour. Just pop back in there and check out yon naevus thing, just so's we can be sure.'

For a moment Lockridge looked as though he might refuse, then he turned, went back into the room, pulled the dead man's shirt-tail out of his trousers, peered down for a moment, then returned.

'It's him,' he said shortly. 'Can I go now?'

He didn't wait for an answer but removed his overall and hurried away down the stairs.

'Bit pale round the gills, weren't he?' said Dalziel. 'And he didn't even tuck the poor sod's shirt back in.'

'He knew the guy. Bound to be a bit of a shock, seeing him dead,' said Pascoe.

'Don't be daft. He's a doctor. Spends his life looking at dead folk that were alive on his last visit. Show me a quack who's not used to it and I'll pay hard cash to get on his panel.'

'Perhaps he was a friend as well as a patient.'

'Former patient. Aye, that might do it. Someone you think you know tops himself, it makes you wonder about all the other buggers you think you know.'

'Tops himself? Getting a bit ahead of the game, aren't you, sir?' said Pascoe.

'That's how you win matches, lad. Any road, door locked and bolted on the inside. Windows with the kind of shutters that 'ud keep a tax inspector out. Gun between his legs, shoe and sock off. Lots of little hints there, I'd say.'

'Nevertheless,' said Pascoe obstinately.

'Oh God, you been at the John Dickson Carr again? What more do you want?'

'A note would be nice, for a start.'

'A note, eh? Any sign of a note, Paddy?'

Inspector Ireland let out a long-suffering sigh. The fact that he was a teetotal Baptist born in

Heckmondwyke and able to trace his ancestry back a hundred and fifty years without any sign of Irish blood hadn't saved him from being nicknamed Paddy, and the more he protested, the more he found himself treated as a fount of knowledge on all matters Eireann.

'Name's Cedric,' he said. 'Couldn't say. I followed procedure and kept out to minimize the risk of contamination.'

'But you've been inside, Sergeant, and I've no doubt Tweedledum and Tweedledee went clumping all over the place.'

'Yes, sir,' said Bonnick. 'Didn't see a note though.'

'Pity,' said Dalziel. 'There ought to be something . . .'

'To confirm it's suicide, you mean?' said Pascoe triumphantly.

'No,' said the Fat Man irritably. 'In fact, if you studied your statistics you'd know that seventy per cent of genuine suicides don't leave a note, while ninety-seven per cent of fakes do . . . Hang about. Not a note. A book! Now I recall. There ought to be a book. Isn't that a book on the desk, Sergeant?'

'Yes, sir,' said Bonnick, surprised. 'There is a book.'

'Didn't notice what it was, did you?'

'No, sir. Got a bit splattered with blood and stuff. You'd need to scrape it off first.'

'Not squeamish, are you? Doesn't come well from a sergeant, squeaming.'

'Just following procedure, sir, touching as little as possible till the scene's been examined.'

'Which will be when? You did give SOCO the right address, didn't you, Paddy?'

'Of course I did,' Ireland assured him, looking offended.

Three things were troubling Pascoe. One was the suspicion that the Fat Man had just invented the suicide note statistics. The second was his apparent power of precognition. *There ought to be a book*. And lo! there was a book!

The third was the still unanswered question of why the hell he was here at all. Off duty, what had there been in a shout to a possible suicide to bring him hurrying from the comfort of his fireside? Even the fact that his inamorata, Cap Marvell, was away at present didn't explain that.

His speculations were interrupted by noises below. Fearful that Cressida had led an assault, he peered over the balustrade and saw to his relief that the SOCO team had finally arrived. They paused to pull on their white coveralls and then came up the stairway.

'About bloody time,' said Dalziel. 'Don't be all night at it, will you? And try not to leave a mess.'

He set off down the stairs. Pascoe hurried to catch up with him.

'Sir,' he said. 'Do I take it you're assuming control of this case?'

'Me? Simple suicide? Nay, lad, you got here first, you're the man in charge.'

'In that case, there's a couple of questions I'd like to ask you . . .'

'Not now, lad, not when there's a poor woman out there waiting to be told she's a widow,' reproved the Fat Man.

So saying, he pulled open the front door, bounced Maycock aside with his belly and stepped out into the night.

11

$SD+SS=PS$

Out here, the mist was in total control. It gave bulk while it removed substance. Somewhere in the wooded garden, an owl uttered a long wavering screech that made Pascoe's nape hair prickle.

Helen and Jason had got back into the Volvo, Ellie was talking to Cressida alongside the Spider, and Kay Kafka was standing to one side with a mobile to her ear.

'Where's the wife gone?' said Dalziel.

'I don't know,' said Pascoe. 'But as I'm in charge, I think I ought to be the one who breaks the news.'

Meaning, until he knew different, this was a suspicious death and everyone connected with the dead man was a suspect.

'You reckon? Sometimes these things are better coming from a more sensitive and mature figure,' said Dalziel. 'Where the hell's the daft tart got to anyway?'

Pascoe spotted a movement in the front seat of the Audi that had been parked outside the house when he first arrived. Its headlights came on and the engine started as he peered towards it. The front passenger door opened and Sue-Lynn got out. The car pulled away and he recognized Tom Lockridge's profile as it went past.

'I think the doctor may have saved us the bother,' he said. 'He can't have heard of your sensitive bedside manner.'

'Don't know how. It's famous in three counties . . .'

'. . . the county court, the county jail and the County Hotel,' Pascoe concluded the old joke. He watched as the Fat Man advanced to meet the approaching woman and heard him say in a gently melancholy voice, 'Mrs Maciver, Tom Lockridge has told you the dreadful news, has he? I'm so sorry.'

She looked as if she didn't believe him and said, 'Can I see my husband now?'

'Soon,' said Dalziel. 'Come on inside and let's find you somewhere to sit for a bit . . .'

He started leading her towards the house.

Pascoe said, 'Sir, a quick word.'

'Excuse me, luv,' said Dalziel.

He stepped aside with Pascoe and said in an irritated tone, 'What?'

'You can't take her inside, sir.'

'Why the hell not?'

'Until we can confirm suicide, the whole house

is a crime scene, and you don't escort a principal suspect on to a crime scene.'

'Principal suspect? You crazy or what, lad?'

'Just quoting you, sir. SD+SS=PS, that's what you're always drumming into the DCs, isn't it? Suspicious death + surviving spouse = prime suspect. Sir.'

'Keep your voice down! You'll be getting us all sued. What did you have in mind then? Take her down the nick and shine a bright light into her eyes?'

Over Dalziel's huge shoulder Pascoe saw that Cressida and Kay had advanced to confront Sue-Lynn with Ellie not far behind.

'What's happening?' Cressida demanded. 'What have they told you?'

Sue-Lynn said, 'He's dead.'

'Oh Jesus. What happened? How . . . ?'

'He shot himself. Just like your pa.'

'Shot himself? In there? When?' cried Kay.

'What the hell does it matter when?' exploded Cressida. 'Just now. Ten years ago. That's two down. Are you done now, bitch?'

'Cressida, I'm so sorry, I'm truly deeply sorry . . . this is dreadful, dreadful . . .'

Of the three women, it was Kay Kafka who looked the most genuinely distressed, observed Pascoe. The emotion that twisted Cressida's face was anger, while Sue-Lynn's features were mask-like which might be the result of shock or just the glazing effect of her complex make-up.

Jason Dunn was out of his car now, once more torn between his eagerness to join the group and find out what was going on and his desire to help his wife, who was also trying to re-emerge from the Volvo.

Sue-Lynn said, 'You two want to stay out here and fight, that's your business. I want to see him. Superintendent, I insist you take me to see him. Right now!'

She spoke in the voice that got waiters and shop assistants jumping.

Dalziel scratched his crotch reflectively, then replied in a fawning Heepish tone, 'I'm sorry, Mrs Maciver, I know what you must be feeling, but it's not my decision. Chief Inspector Pascoe's in charge here. It's him who's calling the shots.'

Not the most diplomatic of phrases in the circumstances, thought Pascoe as he sought for the right words to pour oil on these turbulent waters.

But he was saved from proving his diplomatic skills by a long, wavering cry, which for a second he thought was the owl again.

Then it was joined by a male voice raised in alarm and, looking towards the Volvo, he saw that Helen Dunn had sunk back into the car.

'Help me!' cried Jason. 'Please someone, help me! The baby's coming!'

Kay set off at a run with the other women close behind.

'I've seen your bedside manner,' said Pascoe to Dalziel. 'So, how's your obstetrics?'

96

He didn't wait for an answer but went to his car and said tersely into his radio, 'DCI Pascoe at Moscow House in the Avenue, Greenhill. Get an ambulance down here fast as you can. Woman in labour.'

'By God,' said Dalziel behind him. 'This is one up for community policing. Don't worry if your loved one snuffs it. Your modern caring force comes fully equipped with a replacement.'

'Better than that, Andy,' said Ellie who'd come running back from the Volvo. 'Two for the price of one. They say she's having twins.'

'Size of her, I'm surprised it's not a football team,' said Dalziel. 'What's happening?'

'Her waters have broken. You've got an ambulance coming, I take it?'

The radio crackled and a voice said, 'Control to Mr Pascoe. Re that ambulance for Moscow House, could be a delay. There's been a pile-up in fog on the bypass and they're a bit stretched.'

'So's that poor girl,' said Ellie. 'Look, if it's going to take that long, I think we ought to get her into the house.'

Dalziel looked at Pascoe and raised his eyebrows.

Pascoe said, 'Wouldn't it make more sense to drive her direct to hospital?'

'If things happen as quickly as I think they might, she doesn't want to be bouncing around in the back of a car,' retorted Ellie. 'There's light in there, isn't there? And I'm sure it's a damn sight warmer than out here. I'll get it organized.'

She didn't wait for an answer but returned to the Volvo.

'Shit,' said Pascoe.

'Best-laid plans, eh?' said Dalziel. 'Not to worry. Thank your lucky stars it's only a suicide, not a real crime scene.'

Again that certainty. But no time now for deep questioning. Pascoe headed for the house to reorganize his defences.

Maycock he relocated at the foot of the stairs.

No civilian goes up there,' he commanded. 'And I mean no one. Anyone tries, stop 'em. Anyone persists, arrest 'em. Anyone resists arrest, cuff 'em. Is there any other way up there?'

'There's a back stair,' said Sergeant Bonnick, coming down from the landing, followed by Inspector Ireland. 'What's going on, sir?'

Pascoe explained.

'You cover that back stair, Sergeant. Same as here. No one goes up it, OK? Paddy, how are they doing up there?'

'You know SOCO. Slow but sure,' said Ireland, for once not reacting to his sobriquet. 'When they've finished the study, they want to know how much of the rest of the house you want done.'

'Tell them to have a look round upstairs,' said Pascoe. 'Doubt if there'll be much point down here once this mob start milling around, but let's try to keep their movements as confined as possible.'

He went across the hall and flung open a door that led into a large bay-windowed drawing room full of bulky pieces of furniture shrouded in dust sheets.

'You reckon there's something dodgy about this suicide, Pete?' said Ireland, curious why Pascoe should have any concern about the ground floor.

'I hope not,' said Pascoe. 'But if there is, I don't want things muddied by having the whole place turned into a maternity hospital. We'll put Mrs Dunn and the others in here till the ambulance comes, and we'll try to keep them in here.'

'You'll be lucky,' said Ireland with the cynicism of a father of five, four of whom had been born at home. 'Woman in labour, every female within half a mile becomes Queen of the Universe.'

'We'll just have to do our best, but if any of them do have to come out, I want to know the reason why and I want a record kept of exactly where they go. And I mean exactly. Got that, Paddy?'

'Yes, sir,' said Ireland placatingly. 'I've got it.'

He's wondering why I'm being so neurotic, thought Pascoe.

Maybe I should wonder the same.

Does my sensitive nose really scent something untoward about this business, or am I merely reacting to Fat Andy's ready acceptance of suicide and mysterious hints of preknowledge?

He heard voices in the hallway and went out. The birthing party had arrived, with Helen supported by her husband and Dalziel, Ellie and Kay Kafka in close attendance, and Cressida and Sue-Lynn bringing up the rear. The last two both looked pretty subdued. Not surprising. Husband and brother lying dead upstairs, sister and sister-in-law giving birth below. It was a situation to subdue a Tartar.

'In here,' said Pascoe.

'Couldn't we get her to a bedroom?' said Dunn.

'Don't be daft, we'd need a sodding crane,' said Dalziel.

And a cry of pain from Helen persuaded her husband.

Ellie said, 'Is the water supply turned on?'

Pascoe looked at Ireland, who said, 'Yes, ma'am.'

'Heaters too?'

'I'll check.'

'Thank you.'

Pascoe looked at Ellie curiously. Those scenes in old movies where birth was accompanied by the boiling up of untold and unused gallons of water had always amused her greatly.

She said, 'What?'

He said, 'Nothing.'

There was a shriek from the lounge.

'I'd better get in there,' said Ellie.

As she went in, Dalziel came out.

'No place for a sensitive soul,' he said. 'Out in the desert they say Bedouin lasses just drop their kids on the march, hardly break step. Don't need fifty other women all running around like blue-arsed fleas. No word on that ambulance? Mebbe I should talk to the buggers.'

'I don't think that would help,' said Pascoe sharply. 'It will get here as soon as possible, and it will either be in time or it won't, and all the shouting in the world won't make any difference.'

'Don't take it out on me, Pete.'

'Take what out?'

'Come on! Woman so pregnant she can hardly walk, shocked by news that her brother's topped himself. Doctor and ambulance already at scene. And you let 'em both go! Not the best career move you ever made, lad.'

Pascoe reached forward and seized the Fat Man's arm.

'You reckon?' he grated into his superior's smiling face. 'Well, here's what I suggest we do during the few remaining moments of my beautiful career. Let's find somewhere quiet where you can bring me up to speed on exactly what it is you know about this place and these people that I don't, OK?'

'Thought you'd never ask,' said Andy Dalziel.

12

cold, strange world

Dalziel and Pascoe sat side by side at the head of the staircase.

'Can't credit you know nowt,' said Dalziel. 'Where were you ten years back?'

'I don't know. Where were you a week last Tuesday?'

'Not the same thing,' said Dalziel. 'Anyone can lose a day, but I can tell you exactly where I was ten years ago.'

'Bully for you. But hang about . . . Ten years . . . March . . . I remember! I was on my back in bed.'

'Oh aye? Dirty weekend?'

'No. Ellie and I had been away to Marrakesh and I picked up hepatitis.'

'Like I said, dirty weekend.'

'Ha. Anyway, that accounts for me for a month or more. So, where were you that you can be so exact about?'

'Me?' said Dalziel. 'Easy. I were here.'

'Here?'

'Aye, lad. Don't recollect sitting on the stairs, but I was certainly in this house. And for much the same reason. It's ten years ago to this very day that Pal Maciver Senior, that's the dad of this lot, him on the wall in the breeks and woolly hat, locked himself in his study, tied a bit of string round the trigger of a Purdy shotgun, looped the other end round his big toe, and blew his head to pieces.'

'Ah,' said Pascoe.

For a moment there didn't seem anything else to say. Then there seemed to be so much that he took another moment to marshal his words.

'In his study . . . that's the same room . . . and he had an open book on his desk?'

'That's right. But as I've not seen it yet and Bonnick says it were too covered with blood and brain for him to read the title, I can't say if it's the same book.'

'But if it were, by which I presume you'd mean the same title not necessarily the same volume, what would that be?'

'Book of poems. Funny little things. Some Yankee bint. Eleanor Dickson, summat like that.'

'Emily Dickinson?'

'That's the one. Bit weird. Might have guessed you'd know her.'

Ignoring this aspersion on his literary taste, Pascoe was running through what little he knew about the Maciver family history already. He'd met Cressida a couple of times, found her somewhat over intense, and when foolishly he'd wondered aloud how Ellie had come to make a friend out of an aggressive man-basher who, every time she got drunk, attempted to rape her, he'd been lectured on not judging by surfaces. Underneath it all, he was told, Cress was really dreadfully in need of reassurance, and love, probably due to childhood trauma caused by the early death of her parents, which she never talked about.

'I think she was heavily dependent on her brother and they're still very close, but when he got married, that left a gap in her life. She's always looking for a strong man to lean on. Trouble is, the bastards always keel over!'

None of this seemed relevant, so he said to Dalziel, 'This is a copycat suicide then? That's what brought you running?'

'Strolling,' said the Fat Man. 'Aye, you're right. Lightning striking twice and all that. Idle curiosity.'

Liar, thought Pascoe, not knowing why he thought it, but knowing he was right.

'But it can't be exactly copycat, can it?' he said. 'This Pal Maciver, the father, I mean, must have been a good bit older – family established, second wife.'

'Mid forties,' agreed Dalziel. 'His lad must be – must have been – barely thirty. At university when it happened, I recall.'

'And Cressida?'

'Boarding school. Final year. She were head girl.'

'That figures. And the younger daughter, Helen?'

'The mobile incubator? She'd have been about nine. She were away in the States with her stepmother. That's her you saw out there, the classy one.'

Pascoe noted the epithet. In Dalziel's wordhoard, it usually signified approbation.

'She still lives round here?'

'Aye.'

'Kay Kafka, wasn't it? That her own name?'

'No. She got married again.'

'To someone called Kafka? That would be one of the Mid-Yorkshire Kafkas?'

'Don't be racist,' reproved Dalziel. 'I once knew a family of Chekhovs, had a farm near Hebden Bridge. Mind you, owt's possible near Hebden Bridge.'

'This Kafka, was he from Hebden Bridge then?' pressed Pascoe.

'No. A Yank. Her boss,' was the short reply.

There was definitely something here, thought Pascoe. Something not said. He recalled seeing the pair of them meeting beside the ambulance. If she weren't so slim, he'd have guessed that Dalziel fancied her. But it had long since been established that Mid-Yorkshire CID's answer to God liked women in his own image, which was to say, with more meat on them than a Barnsley chop.

He said, 'So what was the verdict?'

'Suicide while the balance of his mind was disturbed.'

'Disturbed by what?'

'Summat at work they reckoned.'

'And work was . . . ?'

'Ash-Mac's, machine-tool factory on the Blesshouse Industrial Estate. Used to be Maciver's. Pal Maciver's dad, that's our corpse's granddad, founded it before the last war.'

'Was he called Palinurus too?'

'Liam. Came across from Ireland to make his fortune and didn't do so badly.'

'Why'd he stick his son with a name like Palinurus?'

'Story is, back home Liam was a blacksmith, no education, but a lot of business sense. Made money some dodgy folk considered was rightly theirs, which was why he left. Came here, used his money to set up in business . . .'

'As a blacksmith?'

'Blacksmith makes things out of metal. Machine-tool business is just the posh end of blacksmithery. Any road, soon he were doing well, married a local lass, and decided he really ought to get himself an education. Got talking to some schoolteacher over a drink one night who told him the greatest literary work of the century had come out of Ireland and it were called *Ulysses*. You heard of it?'

'Of course. Joyce.'

'Aye, her. So Liam went off, determined to read

all he could about this Ulysses, only when he asked at the library they got the wrong end of the stick and provided him with lots of stuff about myths and legends and the Trojan War and such, all of which he downed like a gallon of Guinness, and when his missus dropped a sprog, he looked for a name in this lot, and came up with Palinurus.'

'Strange choice.'

'Why's that?'

'He was Aeneas's helmsman who dozed off at the helm and fell overboard.'

'Oh aye. Drowned, did he?'

'No, actually. He made it to the shore, the first of the Trojans to reach Italy. Only the natives didn't like the look of him so they beat him to death and chucked him back in the sea.'

'Well, there you go,' said Dalziel. 'Could be Liam thought it 'ud be a useful reminder to his lad every time he heard his name that, if he didn't keep his eyes open, he could end up in a foreign land being shit upon by strangers.'

Pascoe said, 'A little career advice with the paternal sex talk would have been more direct.'

'He was Irish, remember. They don't do direct. And back then I don't suppose they did sex talks. But old Liam was right up to date when it came to making money. Lots of demand for machine tools during the war and in the post-war years. Everything seemed to be going his way. You'll recall the other Mac? Mungo Macallum?'

'The armaments man? Before my time, but I met his daughter, the pacifist.'

'Old Serafina. Aye, I remember that. When Ellie got herself into bother with the funny buggers. Well, Mungo and Liam were sort of rivals for a bit, each looking for skilled men and cheap labour. Scotch Mac and Irish Mac they called them. But when Mungo died in the fifties and Serafina set about turning his business into money to finance her causes, Liam filled his boots. Plant, orders, workers, the lot. By the time his boy – let's call him Pal Senior and the headless wonder back there Pal Junior, wouldn't want your brain to overheat – when Pal Senior took over, the business were booming. Pal Senior had an education, nowt special but enough to set him up as an English gent. Did all the things gents are supposed to do, like tearing foxes into shreds and blowing small birds to smithereens.'

'Which is how he had the shotgun to blow himself to pieces?'

'Aye. Could've been one of the birds fought back, of course. No, we'd have noticed the bird-shit. Gave all that up in his thirties when he had his accident.'

'Shooting accident?'

'No. As well as huntin' and shootin', he were a bit of a climber in every sense. Yon painting in there shows him at his peak – that's a joke. You know how those mad buggers like to make life difficult for themselves. Well, he were the first to climb some Scottish cliff, solo, at midnight, on Christmas Day, bollock naked, or summat like that. It were on that mountain in the background. As you can see, him having his picture painted, he were chuffed to buggery. Ironic really.'

'Why so?'

'He went back next year and fell off. Broke this and that. Most of it mended, except his left leg. Couldn't bend it after that. Not many mountains you can hop up, so it were goodbye to all that. Old Liam was failing, so Pal threw himself into the business, heart and soul. It was his pride and joy, and he was coining so much he were able to put a few down payments on a peerage with the Tories. But all that changed, both the coining and the payments, after seventy-nine when old whatsername started running around like a headless chicken, putting folk out of work. Suddenly it were like Maciver's was falling off a mountain too. Order book empty, men laid off. Terrible times.'

'Terrible,' agreed Pascoe. 'And this is when the takeover happened?'

'Aye. It were looking like rags-to-rags in three generations when this Yank outfit, Ashur-Proffitt Inc, came sniffing round. Pal Senior had a choice between accepting their offer or seeing the rest of his workers laid off. So, no choice. Maciver's became Ashur-Proffitt-Maciver's, a.k.a. Ash-Mac's, and Pal Senior got a fistful of dollars and a seat on the Board, executive director or some such thing. More of a face-saver than a real job, from the sound of it.'

'And that got to him?'

'So they reckoned,' said Dalziel, yawning. 'Lots of lolly and nowt to do, sounds like heaven to me, but.'

'So what did you reckon?' asked Pascoe.

'Me? I reckoned he killed himself and that's all I needed to know. He did it by himself, no one helped him. He weren't hypnotized or under a spell or owt like that. Simple suicide.'

'Oxymoron,' said Pascoe. 'Suicide's never simple.'

'Oxymoron yourself,' retorted Dalziel. 'From our point of view, it's always simple. Forget the wherefores. The only question is, was it or wasn't it unassisted suicide? If it was, no crime, so no investigation necessary. End of story.'

'Except that Pal Junior back there's written another chapter.'

'Sequel, more like. Never as good as the original. I mean from the look of it, he couldn't even be bothered to write himself new lines, just used his dad's.'

'What about old Liam? How did he die?'

'Natural causes. Got his three score and ten in, so nowt to concern us there. All you need to do, Pete, is get this wrapped up with minimum pain to the living.'

'One way or another, they seem quite capable of inflicting enough pain on each other,' said

Pascoe. 'This Mrs Kafka, if she married a Yank, how come she's still living round here? He doesn't happen to work at Ash-Mac's, does he?'

It was a shot in the dark, or rather in the twilight when you see things dimly without always being certain what it is you're looking at.

'Aye. Boss man. Here, isn't that the ambulance?' Dalziel said, cupping his ear.

It was, thought Pascoe, one of his more pathetic attempts at diversion.

'I don't think so,' he said.

'No? It's old age. Plays tricks on the senses,' said the Fat Man sadly.

Pascoe smiled. When Dalziel played the ageing card, a wise man hoarded his trumps. Then all at once his own ear caught the wail of a siren drawing closer.

'Thought I heard it,' said Dalziel complacently. 'Nice to know the cavalry sometimes does turn up in time.'

Then came another sound which had both men jumping to their feet.

The piercing yell of a baby, indignant at being launched from its warm safe haven into a strange, cold world.

Now it became a duet.

'So much for the cavalry,' said Pascoe as they hurried down the stairs.

The front door opened to admit two paramedics at the same time as Ellie appeared in the doorway of the lounge. Her hands were bloody, her expression exultant. She could have posed for the Triumph of Motherhood, thought Pascoe. Or Clytemnestra on bath-night.

'Twins,' she declared. 'Boy and a girl.'

'Excuse us, luv,' said one of the paramedics, pushing past.

'Everything OK in there?' said Dalziel.

'Mother and babies doing fine,' said Ellie. 'I think they might want to take a look at poor Jason though.'

'The dad? He ought to be out here flashing the cigars,' said Dalziel. 'Let's have a look in the kitchen, see if there's owt to wet the babies' heads with.'

'Sir,' said Pascoe warningly.

'Oh aye. Crime scene. Not to worry. I always carry emergency rations.'

He went out into the fog.

Ellie said, 'Crime scene?'

'Just a form of speaking. You OK, Mother Teresa?'

'I'm fine. You look tired.'

'It's been a long day,' he said.

Somewhere distantly a church clock began to strike midnight. In the muffling fog it sounded both familiar and threatening, like the bell on a warning buoy tolled by the ocean's rhythmic swell.

'And here's another one starting,' said Ellie.

March 21st, 2002

1

the Crunch Witch

It was the first day of spring and Detective Constable Hat Bowler was lost in a forest.

It wasn't an uncommon experience. He slept as little as possible these days, knowing that as soon as he closed his eyes he would reawaken among trees crowding so close they admitted only enough light to show him there was no way out.

Dr Pottle had nodded, unsurprised, and said, 'Ah yes. The primal forest.'

It was Peter Pascoe who'd taken him to meet the psychiatrist.

Not that there was anything wrong with him.

After the death of . . . after her death . . . after . . .

After the woman he loved more than life itself had died in a car accident . . .

That had been on a Saturday in late January. He had turned up for work on Monday morning, no bother. Pascoe had taken one look at him and insisted he went to see his GP. The idiot recommended complete rest and psychotherapy. Hat passed this on to Pascoe, expecting him to share his exasperation. Instead the DCI had gone all po-faced and said if he didn't follow his GP's advice voluntarily, it would be made official and entered on his record, to be read by every member of every promotion board Hat ever applied to.

This was an empty threat to a man with no future. But he had neither the energy nor the will to resist, so he went to see Dr Pottle and answered questions about his dreams for much the same reasons.

The chain-smoking Pottle listened, his head shrouded like Kilimanjaro, then said, 'If you ever did manage to get out of the forest, what is it you would hope to find?'

He couldn't even bring himself to say her name which was a mark of how delusional he knew all hope to be.

'Yes,' said Pottle as if he had answered. 'It can be a terrible thing, hope.'

'Thought that was what you tried to give people,' said Hat.

'Oh no. Change is my game. But I never guarantee it will be for the better.'

Today – this morning, this evening, whatever time of dream it was – for the first time there was change. The trees stood far apart, a broad track wound between them and eventually he found himself walking through beams of hazy sunlight

116

laced with birdsong which his ornithologist's ear told him signalled morning.

At first he advanced rapidly, but soon began to slow, not because of any obstacle in his path but because he was finding out just how terrible hope could be.

So it was at the same time both huge disappointment and huge relief when he emerged from the trees into a sunlit clearing and found the path had led him to . . .

A gingerbread house!

He knew where he was. And he knew why his poor beleaguered mind had chosen to escape here. This was the land of childhood, a time before love and pain and loss.

Except of course in stories. It was Hansel and Gretel who got lost in the forest and found the gingerbread house. Only it wasn't just a house, it was a trap, set by the dreaded Crunch Witch. You nibbled away at the gingerbread and she caught you and then you too got turned into gingerbread, ready to be nibbled at.

Well, tough tittie, Witch! He wasn't hungry. And he didn't like gingerbread.

With a heart almost as light as his head, he moved forward. Immediately a blackbird skulking under a blackcurrant bush stuttered its alarm call and Hat came to a halt as the Crunch Witch appeared in the house's open doorway.

She was tall and square-faced with vigorous grey hair neatly coiled in a bun beneath some kind of small feathery hat. A pair of round spectacles, one arm of which had been repaired with sticking plaster, perched on the end of her slightly upturned nose. She was dressed in a sky-blue T-shirt and olive-green slacks tucked into black Wellington boots. No broomstick, though she did carry a rough-hewn walking stick which might serve in an emergency. This apart, she looked most unwitch-like. Indeed, there was something slightly familiar about her appearance . . .

Then the blackbird flew up and settled on her shoulder, and the little hat stood up on her hair bun and stretched its wings and he saw it was a great tit.

Dreams are like mad people – in the end they always give themselves away.

Reassured, and curious as to where this might lead, he moved forward again.

'Good morning to you,' said the Crunch Witch.

'And to you,' said Hat. 'Lovely day.'

The closer he got, the more he realized that he was going to have to watch his step with this one. Spotting he wasn't mad about gingerbread but loved birds, she'd changed the house into a simple thatched cottage, constructed of a dark orange brick with gingery tiles and birds flying in and out of the windows.

And there was more. Closer, he could identify the source of his feeling of familiarity. It lay in her sky-blue T-shirt, which bore an image of a small soaring bird and the legend *Save the Skylark*.

She said, 'Snap,' looking smilingly at his chest.

He glanced down to confirm that he was wearing exactly the same T-shirt.

'Oh yes,' he said.

He focused on the blackbird on her shoulder. It returned his gaze assessingly.

'Does he talk?' he asked.

'Talk?' she frowned. 'He's a blackbird not a bloody parrot.'

As if it too had been offended, the bird spread its wings and sprang straight at Hat's head. He ducked, felt its beak tug through his hair and then it was gone.

'Jesus,' he gasped.

'Shouldn't walk around with twigs in your hair,' said the witch. 'Crackpot probably thinks you've been out scavenging nest materials for him.'

Hat put his hand to his head and realized she was right. There was quite a bit of undergrowth adhering to his hair, but at least he didn't have a tit nesting there.

'Crackpot?' he said.

'First time he came into the house he tried to perch on the handle of a cream jug. Over it went and broke. So, Crackpot. Now, how can I help you?'

He said, 'I got a bit lost in the forest . . .'

'Forest!' This seemed to amuse her. 'Well, if you'd kept on the track which goes around my garden, you'd have arrived at the road in a couple of minutes.'

'Your garden?' he said, looking round.

More magic. The clearing was now enclosed by a ragged thorn hedge with a ramshackle osier gate. Most of the ground was covered with rough grass, aglow with tiny daffodils, but alongside a lean-to greenhouse on one side of the cottage were the regular furrows of a small kitchen garden in need of work after the depredations of winter.

The witch said, 'You don't look too well, young man. Not had your breakfast, I bet. I'm just having mine. Step inside and let's see if there's anything to spare.'

Very cool! Disorientate him with the garden then lure him inside with food.

He said, 'That would be nice, long as it's not gingerbread.'

Show her he was on to her game!

She said, 'Fortunately it's not my first choice for breakfast either, but if you want a menu, you'd better find yourself another restaurant.'

She turned and went inside, walking rather stiffly and leaning on her stick.

Hat, feeling himself reproved, followed.

He found himself in a shady old-fashioned kitchen entirely free of anachronistic technology. His nose, sensitized by the chill morning air, caught a whiff of something vaguely familiar from his old life, quickly swamped by the delicious odour of new baked bread traceable to a rough-hewn oak table on which three tits were

120

assaulting the dome of a cob loaf while a robin was doing its best to open a marmalade pot.

'Samson, you little sod, leave that be!' roared the witch. 'Impy, Lopside, Scuttle, what do you think you're playing at?'

The birds fluttered off the table but with little sign of panic. The tits settled on a low beam, the robin perched on the edge of an old pot sink, all casting greedy eyes back at their interrupted feast.

The witch picked up a long thin knife and Hat took a step back. But all she did was trim the pecked dome off the loaf then carve a thick slice from the remainder.

'Help yourself to butter and marmalade while I mash a new pot of tea,' she said.

She turned away to place a big blackened kettle on the hotplate of a wood-burning stove. Hat spread the bread thickly with butter and marmalade and sank his teeth into it. God, it was delicious! The best food he'd tasted in weeks. In fact the only food whose taste he'd noticed in weeks. This was a good dream.

One of the tits fluttered down on to the table and eyed him boldly.

'Sorry, Scuttle,' he said. 'I've waited a long time for this.'

The witch glanced round at him curiously.

'How did you know that one was Scuttle?' she asked.

'Two blue tits and a coal tit, not hard to guess which one's Scuttle,' he said.

'So, apart from your problem with blackbirds and parrots, you do know something about birds. That what you're doing out so early? Bird-watching?'

'Not really,' said Hat, thinking, *You know exactly what I'm doing!*

She turned to face him across the table.

'You're not an egg collector, are you?' she demanded.

'No way!' he replied indignantly. 'I'd lock those sods up and throw away the key.'

'Glad to hear it,' she said. 'So if you're not twitching and you're not thieving, just what are you doing wandering round my garden so early in the morning? You don't have to tell me, but unsatisfied curiosity only gets you one slice of bread and marmalade.'

She smiled at him as she spoke and he found himself returning the smile.

He certainly wanted some more bread, but what answer could he give?

He was saved from decision by the sound of a cracked bell.

'Clearly my morning for dawn raids,' she said.

The bell rang again.

'Coming, coming,' she cried, turning to open a door into a shady corridor that ended at another door, this one with a letter box and an upper panel of frosted glass against which pressed a face.

Hat sliced himself some more bread as she moved away. Even in dreams, a young cop had to take his chances. As he sank his teeth into it, he kept a careful eye on the Crunch Witch to see what reinforcements she may have conjured up.

She opened the front door.

A man stood there. He too carried a walking stick, this one ebony with a silver top in the shape of a hawk's head, and he wore a black trilby which he removed as he said, 'Good morning to you, Miss Mac.'

'And to you, Mr W,' said the witch. 'Why so formal? You should just have come round the back.'

'I'm sorry, it's so early, I thought I'd better be sure . . .'

'That I was decent? How thoughtful. But you know what it's like at Blacklow Cottage: up with the birds, no choice about it. Come on in, do.'

She led the newcomer into the kitchen. He moved easily enough though with a just perceptible drag of the left leg suggesting that, like the woman's, his stick was not simply for ornament. He stopped short when he saw Hat.

'I'm sorry,' he said again. 'I didn't realize you had a guest.'

'Me neither till five minutes back,' said the witch. 'Mr Waverley, meet . . . sorry, I don't think I got your name?'

'Hat,' said Hat. This little rush of names made him uneasy. Not Waverley, that had no resonance. But Blacklow Cottage set up some kind of vibration . . .

'Mr Hat,' said the witch. 'Sit yourself down, Mr W. I'm just making a fresh pot of tea.'

She turned back to the stove. Hat studied Waverley openly and without embarrassment. (Pointless letting yourself be embarrassed in a dream.) Waverley returned the gaze with equal composure. He was in his early sixties, medium height, slim build, with a long narrow face, well-groomed hair, still vigorous though silvery, alert bluey-green eyes, and the sympathetic expression of a worldly priest who has seen everything and knows to the nearest farthing the price of forgiveness. He was wearing a beautifully cut grey mohair topcoat, which reminded Hat that despite the sunshine this was a pretty nippy morning.

He shivered, and this intrusion of meteorology bothered him like the name of the cottage. First the taste of food, now weather . . .

'Do you live locally, Mr Hat?' asked Waverley.

He had a gentle well-modulated voice with perhaps a faint Scots accent.

'No,' said Hat. 'I got lost in the forest.'

'The forest?' echoed the man in a faintly puzzled tone.

'I think Mr Hat means Blacklow Wood,' said the witch with that nice smile.

'Of course. And you're quite right, Mr Hat. As you clearly know, this and one or two other little patches of woodland scattered around the area are all that remain of what used to be the great

Blacklow Forest when the Plantagenets hunted here.'

Blacklow again. This time the vibration was strong enough to break the film of ice through which he viewed dreams and reality alike.

Now he remembered.

A dank autumn day . . . but his MG had been full of brightness as he drove deep into the heart of the Yorkshire countryside with the woman he loved by his side.

One of those small surviving patches of Blacklow Forest had been the copse out of which a deer had leapt, forcing him to bring his car to a skidding halt. Then he and she had pushed through the hedge and sat beneath a beech tree and drunk coffee and talked more freely and intimately than ever before. It had been a milestone in what had turned out to be far too short a journey.

Yesterday he'd driven out to the same spot and sat beneath the same tree, indifferent to the fall of darkness and the thickening mist. Nor when finally he rose and set off back to the car did he much care when he realized he'd missed his way. For an indeterminate period of time he'd wandered aimlessly, over rough grass and boggy fields, till he'd flopped down exhausted beneath another tree and slept.

The fog had cleared, the night had passed, the sun had risen, and he, waking under branches, imagined himself still sleeping and dreaming . . .

The woman placed the teapot on the table and

said, 'So what brings you out so early, Mr W?'

The man glanced at Hat, decided he was out of it for the moment, then said, 'I'm afraid I'm the bearer of ill news, Miss Mac. I take it you've heard nothing?'

'Heard what? You know I don't have any truck with phones or wireless.'

'Yes, I know. But I thought they might have . . . no, perhaps not . . . I'm sure that eventually someone will think . . .'

'What, for heaven's sake? Spit it out, man,' said the woman in exasperation.

'Perhaps you should sit down . . . As you will,' said Waverley as the woman responded with a steely stare that wouldn't have been out of place on a peregrine. 'I heard it on the radio this morning, then rang to check details. It's your nephew, Pal. It's very bad, I'm afraid. The worst. He's dead. Like your brother.'

'Like . . . ? You mean he . . . ?'

'Yes, I'm truly sorry. He killed himself last night. In Moscow House.'

'Oh God,' said the woman. 'Laurence, you are again my bird of ill omen.'

Now she sat down.

It seemed to Hat, who had emerged from the depths of his introspection just in time to take in the final part of this exchange, that the soft chirruping of the birds, a constant burden since he entered the kitchen, now all at once fell still.

The woman too sat in complete silence for almost a minute.

Finally she said, 'This is a shock, Laurence. I'm prepared for the shocks of my world, but not for this. Am I needed? Will anyone need me? Please advise me.'

'I think you should come with me, Lavinia,' said the man. 'When you have spoken to people and found out what there is to find out, then you will know if you're needed.'

The shock of the news had put them on first-name terms, observed Hat. It also underlined his obtrusive presence.

He stood up and said, 'I think I should be on my way.'

'Don't be silly,' said the woman. 'Carry on with your breakfast. I think you need it. Laurence, give me five minutes.'

She stood up and went out. The birds resumed their chirruping.

Hat looked at Waverley and said uncertainly, 'I really think I ought to go.'

'No need to rush,' said Waverley. 'Miss Mac never speaks out of mere politeness. And you do look as if a little nourishment wouldn't come amiss.'

No argument there, thought Hat.

He sat down and resumed eating his second slice of bread on which he'd spread butter and marmalade to a depth that had the robin tic-ticking in admiration and envy.

Waverley took two mugs from a shelf, and poured the tea.

'Is there anywhere I can give you a lift to when we go?' he said.

'Thank you, I don't know . . .'

It occurred to Hat he had no idea where he was in relation to his own vehicle.

To cover his uncertainty, he said, 'Did you come by car? I didn't hear it.'

'I leave it by the roadside. You'll understand why when you see the state of the track up to the cottage. Miss Mac doesn't encourage callers.'

Was he being warned off?

Hat said, 'But she makes them very welcome,' with just enough stress on *she* for it to be a counter-blow if the man wanted to take it that way.

Waverley smiled faintly and said, 'Yes, she has a soft spot for lame ducks, whatever the genus. There you are, my dear.'

Miss Mac had reappeared, having prepared for her outing by pulling a cracked Barbour over her T-shirt and changing her wellies for a pair of stout walking shoes.

'Shall we be off? Mr Hat, you haven't finished your tea. No need to rush. Just close the door when you leave.'

Hat caught Waverley's eye and read nothing there except mild curiosity.

He said, 'No, I'd better be on my way too. But I'd like to come again some time, if you don't mind . . . Sorry, that sounds cheeky, I don't want to be . . .'

'Of course you'll come again,' she interrupted as if surprised. 'Good-looking young man who knows about birds, how should you not be welcome?'

'Thank you,' said Hat. 'Thank you very much.'

He meant it. While he couldn't say he was feeling well, he was certainly feeling better than he had done for weeks.

They went out of the door he'd come in by. She didn't bother to lock it. Waste of time anyway with the window left open for the birds.

They went down the side of the cottage, Miss Mac leaning on the stick in her right hand and hanging on to Waverley's arm with the other as they headed up a rutted track towards a car parked on a narrow country road about fifty yards away.

If Hat had thought of guessing what sort of car Waverley drove, he would probably have opted for something small and reliable, a Peugeot 307 for instance, or maybe a Golf. His enforced absence from work must have dulled his detective powers. Gleaming in the morning sunlight stood a maroon coloured Jaguar S-type.

He said, 'That lift you offered me, my car's on the old Stangdale road, if that's not out of your way.'

'My pleasure, Mr Hat,' said Waverley. 'My pleasure.'

2

the Kafkas at home

Some miles to the south, close to the picturesque
little village of Cothersley, dawn gave the mist
still shrouding Cothersley Hall the kind of fuzzy
golden glow with which unoriginal historical
documentary makers signal their next inaccurate
reconstruction. For a moment an observer viewing the western elevation of the building might
almost believe he was back in the late seventeenth
century just long enough after the construction
of the handsome manor house for the ivy to have
got established. But a short stroll round to the
southern front of the house bringing into view
the long and mainly glass-sided eastern extension
would give him pause. And when further progress
allowed him to look through the glass and see a
table bearing a glowing computer screen standing
alongside an indoor swimming pool, unless
possessed of a politician's capacity to ignore contradictory evidence, he must then admit the sad truth
that he was still in the twenty-first century.

A man in a black silk robe sat by the table staring at the screen. He didn't look up as the door leading into the main house opened and Kay Kafka appeared, clad in a white towelling robe on the back of which was printed IF YOU TAKE ME HOME YOUR ACCOUNT WILL BE CHARGED. She was carrying a tray set with a basket of croissants, a butter dish, two china mugs and an insulated coffee-pot.

Putting the tray on the table she said, 'Good morning, Tony.'

'He's back.'

'Junius?' That was the great thing about Kay. You could talk shorthand with her. 'Same stuff as before?'

'More or less. Calls himself NewJunius now. Broke in again, left messages and a hyperlink.'

'I thought they said that was impossible.'

'They said boil-in-the-bag rice was impossible. His style doesn't improve.'

'You seem pretty laid-back about it.'

'Why not? Some bits I even find myself agreeing with these days.'

'What bits would they be?'

'The bits where he suggests there's more to being a good American than making money.'

'You tried that one out on Joe lately?' she asked casually.

'You know I did, end of last year when the dust had started to settle after 9/11. There were no certainties any more. We talked about everything.'

'Then after that Joe said it was business as usual, right?'

'Not so. You've got Joe wrong. He feels things as strongly as me. I don't see him face to face enough, that's all.'

'He's only a flight away,' she said gently.

It wasn't a discussion she wanted to get into. Joe Proffitt, head of the Ashur-Proffitt Corporation, wasn't a man she liked very much, but she didn't feel able to speak out too strongly against him. Last September she knew that every instinct in Tony Kafka's body had told him to head for home, permanently. But with Helen three months pregnant, he'd known how his wife would feel about that. So Tony was still here and, as far as she could detect, Joe Proffitt's business certainties had hardly been dented at all.

'Yeah, I ought to go more often. It's as quick going to the States as it is getting to London with these goddam trains,' he grumbled. 'Look at me, up with the dawn so I can be sure to be in time for lunch barely a couple of hundred miles away.'

'You'll have time for some breakfast?' she said.

'No thanks. I'll get some on the train. What time you get back last night?'

'Late. Two o'clock maybe, I don't know. You didn't wait up.'

'What for? You may not need sleep but I do, specially with an early start and a long hard day ahead speaking a foreign language.'

'I thought it was just Warlove you were meeting?'

'That's the foreign language I mean.' They smiled at each other. 'Anyway, last night when you rang, you didn't think there was anything there to lose sleep over. Has anything changed? I'll get asked.'

'You think they'll know already?'

'I'd put money on it,' he said.

'It's cool,' she said pouring herself some coffee. 'Domestic drama, that's all. Main thing is Helen's fine and the twins don't seem any the worse for being a tad early.'

'Good. Born in Moscow House, eh? There's a turn-up.'

'Like their mother. Nature likes a pattern. She wants to call the girl Kay.'

'Yeah, you said. And the boy?'

'Last night she was talking about Palinurus. Of course she's very upset over what happened and later she might get to thinking . . .'

'A bit ill-omened? Right. And your fat friend is quite happy, is he?'

'Copycat suicide, no problems.'

'Copycat suicide? He doesn't find that a bit weird?'

'I think in his line of business he takes weird in his stride. I'm having a drink with him later, so I'll get an update.'

'Who was it said an update was having sex the first time you went out?'

'You, I'd guess. No passes from Andy. He is, despite appearances, a kind man.'

'Yeah,' he said, as if unconvinced.

Silence fell between them broken by the distant chime of the old long-case clock standing in the main entrance hall. Though it looked as if it had been there almost as long as the house, in fact it had come later than its owners. Kay had spotted it in an antique shop in York. When she'd pointed out the inscription carved on the brass dial – *Hartford Connecticut 1846* – Tony had laughed and said, 'Real American time at last!' She'd gone back later and bought it for his birthday. He'd been really touched. It turned out to have a rather loud chime which she'd wanted to muffle, but he'd refused, saying, 'We need to make ourselves heard over here!' In return, however, he'd conceded when she resisted his proposal to set it five hours behind Greenwich Mean Time.

Now its brassy note rang out eight times.

'Gotta go,' said Kafka. 'Let me know how you get on with Mr Blobby, if you've a moment.'

'Sure. Tony, you're not worried?'

'No. Just like to show those bastards I'm on top of things.'

'You're sure they're not getting on top of you?'

'Why do you say that?'

'I don't know . . . sometimes you get so restless . . . last night when I got in you were tossing and turning like you were at sea.'

For a moment he seemed about to dismiss her

worries, then he shrugged and said, 'Just the old thing. I dream I hear the fire bells and I know I've got to get home but I can't find the way . . .'

'Then you wake up and you're home and everything's fine, Right, Tony? This is our home.'

'Yeah, sure. Only sometimes I think I feel more foreign here than anywhere. Sorry, no. I don't mean right here with you. That's great. I mean this fucking country. Maybe all I mean is that America's where all good Americans ought to be right now. We are good Americans, aren't we, Kay?'

'As good as we can be, Tony. That's all anyone can ask.'

'I think a time's coming when they can ask a fucking sight more,' he said.

Abruptly he stood up, removed his black robe and stood naked before her except for the thin gold chain he always wore round his neck. On it was his father's World War Two Purple Heart, which he wore as a good-luck charm.

'Pay me no heed,' he said. 'Male menopause. I could pay a shrink five hundred dollars a session to tell me the same. Give my best to Helen.'

He turned away and dived into the swimming pool.

He was in his late forties, but his stocky body, its muscles sculpted into high definition by years of devoted weight training, showed little sign yet of paying its debt to age.

He did a length of crawl, tumble turned, and came back at a powerful butterfly. Back where he started, his final stroke brought his flailing arms down on to the lip of the pool and he hauled himself out in one fluid movement.

When he stops that trick, I'll know he's over the hill physically, thought Kay.

But where he was mentally, even her penetrating gaze couldn't assess.

She watched him walk away, his feet stomping down hard on the tiled floor as if he'd have liked to feel it move. When he vanished through the door, she turned the laptop towards her and began to read.

ASHUR-PROFFITT & THE CLOAK OF INVISIBILITY

A Modern Fairy Tale

Once upon a time some cool dudes in the Greatest Country on Earth decided it would be real neat to sell arms to one bunch of folk they didn't like at all called the Iranians and give the profits from the sale to another bunch of folk they liked a lot called the Contras. At the same time across the Big Water in the Second Greatest Country on Earth some other cool dudes decided it would be real neat to sell arms to another bunch of folk called the Iraqis that nobody liked much except that they were fighting another bunch of folk called the Iranians that no one liked at all. But it didn't bother the cool dudes in either of the two Greatest Countries on Earth to know what the other was doing because in each of the countries there were people doing that too and as Mr Alan Clark of the second G.C.O.E. (who was so cool, if he'd been any cooler he'd have frozen over) remarked later, 'The interests of the West were best served by Iran and Iraq fighting each other, and the longer the better.'

But the really amazing thing about all these dudes on both sides of the Big Water was that they were totally invisible – which meant that, despite the fact that everything they did was directly contrary to their own laws, nobody in charge of the two Greatest Countries on Earth could see what they doing!

She scrolled to the end, which was a long way away. Tony was right about the style. Once this kind of convoluted whimsicality had probably seemed as cool as you could get without taking your clothes off. Now it was just tedious, which was good news from A-P's point of view. Only the final paragraph held her attention.

There was a time when you could argue a patriotic case – *my enemy's enemy is my friend so treat them all the same then sit back and watch them knock hell out of each other* – but no longer. Hawk or dove, republican or democrat, every good American knows there's a line in the sand and anyone who sends weapons across this line had better be sure which way they're going to be pointing. The Ashur-Proffitt motive is no longer enough. It's time we asked these guys just whose side they think they're on.

She sat back and thought of Tony, of his admission that he felt foreign here. Could it be that now that the twins were born, he thought she might be persuadable to up sticks and head west? Funny that it should come to this, that he whose own father had been born God knows where should be the one who spoke of being a good American and going home, while she whose forebears, from what she knew of them, had been good Americans for at least a couple of centuries, could not bring to mind a single place in the States – save for one tiny plot covering a very few square feet – that exerted any kind of emotional pull. OK, so she agreed, home was a holy thing, but to her this was home, all the more holy since last night. Tony would have to understand that.

The script had vanished to be replaced by a screen saver – the Stars and Stripes rippling in a strong breeze.

She switched it off, leaned back in her chair and closed her eyes. Tony was right. She didn't need much sleep and she'd perfected the art of dropping off at will for a pre-programmed period. This time she gave herself forty minutes.

When she woke, the sun was up and the mist was rising. She stood up, undid her robe, let it slide to the floor, and dived into the pool. Her slim naked body entered the water with barely a splash and what trace of her entry there was had almost vanished by the time she broke the surface two-thirds of a length away.

She swam six lengths with a long graceful breast stroke. Her exit from the pool was more conventional than her husband's but in its own way just as athletic.

She slipped into her robe. The legend on the back didn't amuse her but it amused Tony and his bad jokes were a small price to pay for all he'd done for her. But some stuff she needed to deal with herself. Like last night. Something had happened that she didn't understand. If she could work it out and defend herself against it, she would. But if it turned out to be part of that darkness against which there was no defence, so what? She'd dealt with darkness before.

In any case, it was trivial alongside the thing that had happened that she did understand. The birth of Helen's twins. Most dawns were false but you enjoyed the light even if you knew it was illusory.

Whistling 'Of Foreign Lands and People' from Schumann's *Childhood Scenes* she walked back through the door into the house.

3

a nice vase

By ten o clock that morning, with the curtaining mist raised by a triumphant sun and the brisk breeze that cued the wild daffodils to dance at Blacklow Cottage rattling the slats on his office blinds, Pascoe was far less certain about his uncertainties.

Dalziel had no doubts. His last words had been, 'Tidy this up, Pete, then dump the lot on Paddy Ireland's desk. Suicides are Uniformed's business.'

He was right, of course, except that his idea of tidiness wasn't the same as Pascoe's, which was why on his way to work he diverted to the cathedral precinct where Archimagus Antiques was situated.

The closed sign was still displayed in the shop door, but when he peered through the window he saw someone moving within. He banged on the window. A woman appeared, mouthed 'Closed' and pointed at the sign. Pascoe in return pressed his warrant against the glass. She nodded instantly and opened the door.

'I didn't know what to do,' she began even before he stepped inside. 'It was on the news, you see, and I didn't know if I should come in or not, but David said he thought I should, not to do business, but just in case someone from the police wanted to ask questions, which you clearly do, so he was right, and he'd have come with me but he felt he ought to go round to see poor Sue-Lynn, and I would have gone with him only it seemed better for me to come here.'

She paused to draw breath. She was tall, well made and attractive in a Betjeman tennis girl kind of way. As she spoke she ran her fingers through her short unruly auburn hair. Breathlessness suited her. Early twenties, Pascoe guessed, and with the kind of accent which hadn't been picked up at the local comp. She was dressed, perhaps fittingly but not too becomingly, in a white silk blouse and a long black skirt. She looked tailor-made for jodhpurs, a silk headsquare and a Barbour.

'I'm DCI Pascoe,' he said. 'And you are . . . ?'

'Sorry, silly of me, I'm babbling on and half of what I say can't mean a thing. I'm Dolly Upshott. I work here. Partly shop assistant, I suppose, but I help with the accounts, that sort of thing, and I'm in charge when Pal's off on a buying expedition. Please, can you tell me anything about what happened?'

'And this David you mentioned is . . . ?' said Pascoe, who'd learned from his great master that the easiest way to avoid a question was to ask another.

'My brother. He's the vicar at St Cuthbert's, that's Cothersley parish church.'

Which was where the Macivers lived, in a house with the unpromising name of Casa Alba. Cothersley was one of Mid-Yorkshire's more exclusive dormer villages. The Kafkas' address was Cothersley Hall. Family togetherness? Didn't seem likely from what he'd gathered about internal relationships last night. Also it was interesting that the brash American incomers should occupy the Hall while Maciver with his local connections and his antique-dealer background should live in a house that sounded like a rental villa on the Costa del Golf.

'And he's gone to comfort Mrs Maciver? Very pastoral. Were they active churchgoers then?'

'No, not really. But they are . . . were . . . very supportive of church events, fêtes, shows, that sort of thing, and very generous when it came to appeals.'

What Ellie called the Squire Syndrome. Well-heeled townies going to live in the sticks and acting like eighteenth-century lords of the manor.

'Miss Upshott,' said Pascoe, cutting to the chase, 'the reason I called was to see if you or anyone else working in the shop could throw any light on Mr Maciver's state of mind yesterday.'

'There's only me,' said the woman. 'He seemed fine when last I saw him. I left early, middle of the afternoon. It was St Cuthbert's feast day, you see, and David, my brother, has a special service for the kids from the village school, it's not really a service, their teacher brings them over and David shows them our stained-glass windows and tells them some stories about St Cuthbert which are illustrated there. He's very good, actually, the children love it. And I like to help . . . Sorry, you don't want to hear this, do you? I'm rattling on. Sorry.'

'That's OK,' said Pascoe with a smile. She was very easy to smile at. Or with. 'So you don't know when Mr Maciver left the shop?'

'Late on, I should think. Wednesday's his squash night, you see, and he doesn't care to go home and have a meal before he plays so usually he'll stay behind here and get on with some paperwork then go straight to the club . . . but what happened yesterday I don't know, of course, because . . .'

Her voice broke. She looked rather wildly around the shop. Perhaps, thought Pascoe, she was imagining how it might have been if he'd killed himself here and she'd come in this morning and found him.

Comfort, he guessed, would be counter-productive. The English middle classes paid good money to have their daughters trained to be sensible and practical. That was their default mode. Just press the right key.

'So you help with the accounts?' he said. 'How was the business doing?'

'Fine,' she said. 'We've been ticking over nicely through the winter and now with the tourist season coming on, we were looking to do very well indeed.'

'Good. You might like to get your books in order in case we need to take a look. But I shouldn't hang around too long. The press might come sniffing around and you don't want to be bothered with that. Many thanks for your help.'

She said, 'Please, Mr Pascoe. Before you go, can't you tell me anything about . . . you know. Pal was well liked in the village . . . it would be such a help . . .'

Pascoe said carefully, 'All I can say is that it appears Mr Maciver died from gunshot wounds. It's early days, but at the moment we have no reason to believe there was anyone else involved. I'm sorry.'

She said, 'Thank you.'

Unhappiness made her look like a forlorn teenager. Perhaps that's what she was emotionally, a kid who'd had a crush on her charismatic boss.

He turned to the door, letting his eyes run over the stock on display. That was a nice art nouveau vase over there. Would Ellie's discount be still in place now that Pal was dead . . . ?

Come on! he chided himself. This was a step beyond professional objectivity into personal insensitivity.

But it was a nice vase.

4

like father, like son

Tony Kafka sat on the train and watched England roll by, mile after dull mile.

He'd been here . . . how long? Fifteen, sixteen years?

Too long.

He knew plenty of Americans who loved it here. Given the chance, they'd drone on for ever about the easier pace of life, the greater sense of security, the depth of history, the cultural richness, the educational values, the beautiful landscape. If you pointed out that you had as much chance of being mugged in London as New York, that back home there was some sign they were getting through the drug culture that the Brits were just beginning to get into, that you could pick up the fucking Lake District and drop it in the Grand Canyon and not notice the difference, they'd start talking about the human scale of things, small is beautiful, that kind of crap. But if you let yourself be drawn into argument and started cataloguing the strikes against the UK – the lousy transport services, the godawful hotels, the deadly food, the shitty weather – after a while one of them would be sure to say, 'If that's the way you feel, why not get on a plane and head west?'

And that was a killer blow. Nothing to do then but smile weakly and abandon the field. He had no answer to give, or rather no answer he cared to give.

He'd come to do a job. After five years that job had been completed, everything in place and running smooth as silk. Nothing to stop him dropping the lot into the capacious lap of his supremely efficient deputy, Tom Hoblitt.

They'd wanted him back home then. There was a great future there for the taking. And he'd been ready. Then . . .

'More coffee, sir?'

The steward was there, polite and attentive. This morning the service had been excellent and the train was on schedule. Wasn't that always the way of it? Give yourself plenty of time to take account of the usual delays and you got a straight run through. Cut things fine and you could guarantee trouble. Like life.

He drank his coffee, which wasn't bad either, and relapsed once more into his thoughts.

Kay. That's why he'd stayed on. But put simply like that, he'd get nothing but incomprehension. If she'd been a Brit it might have been a reason, he could hear them say. But she was American, so why on earth . . . ?

Then he'd need to explain it wasn't so simple. His relationship with Kay had never been simple.

Look after people, that was the message drummed into him by his father. Look after people, especially if they're kids. How many times had he heard his father tell the tale of how he'd been found wandering lost, not even speaking the language, and this great country had taken him in, and found him a home, and given him a flag and an education? As a kid he'd never tired of hearing the story. Later, growing up and feeling rebellious, he'd dared to question it, not directly but by implication, saying, 'Yeah, you owe them, I see that, but you've paid back, you gave them a couple of years of your life in the war. In fact you almost gave them all of your goddam life.'

And his father had said, 'You know why I didn't? I was lying there, bleeding to death, and this sergeant, he was an Arkansas redneck, never said a good word to me before this, but he never said a good word to anyone so that was no special treatment, he picked me up and slung me over his shoulder and carried me out of there. I was dangling over his shoulder so I saw the bullet that hit him, smelt the burnt cloth where it went through his tunic, saw the blood spurt out and stream down his back. He walked another fifty yards after that, laid me down as gentle as if I'd been a hatful of eggs. Then he sat down and died. A redneck from Arkansas did that. Because I was a soldier. Because I was an American. Because I needed help. So don't talk to me about paying back. I'll never pay back, not if I live for ever.'

Kay had needed help. Once, twice, three, four times. And he'd learned what his father knew, that each time you gave just put you deeper in debt.

But debts personal and debts patriotic were not always the same thing. Last September the world had changed. He'd found himself looking at where he was. In every sense. And wondering if he should be there. In every sense.

An announcement came over the PA. Jesus, they were actually running ahead of time! No wonder the guy sounded smug.

He looked down at his laptop screen, which had gone to sleep. There was stuff he'd planned to bone up on before his meeting, but there was no rush. He was going to have plenty of time to kill. In any case what he wanted to say didn't need facts and figures to back it up.

He stared at the blank screen and with his mind's eye conjured up the Junius article he'd read that morning.

He was pretty certain he knew who Junius was. He'd never hinted his suspicion, to Kay or anyone else. He wouldn't be surprised if Kay had got there before him a long time ago. As to saying anything to anyone else, the likely consequence wasn't something he wanted to have on his already overloaded conscience.

He suddenly found himself thinking of that poor bastard Maciver. Of both poor bastards Maciver. Both ending up sitting at a desk with a shotgun under their chin.

Like father, like son.

Him too. Like his father. If serving your country meant getting wounded, then that was the price you had to pay.

And it still left you in debt.

5

load of bollocks

The first person Pascoe ran into when he entered the station was DC Shirley Novello. He smiled at her. She didn't smile back. She rarely did, and never automatically.

He had long since decided that here was a young officer worth taking notice of. She was sharp, direct, a quick study; could take orders, think for herself, kept in good trim and when put to the test had proved she was physically brave.

All this was on her record. Not on her record, because the modern politically correct police force eschewed such inconsequential trivia, was any comment on her appearance. This erred on the plain side of unremarkable. A strong face untouched by make-up, short mousy brown hair showing no sign of recent acquaintance with coiffeur or coiffeuse, clothes which were usually some variety of loose-fitting combats in colour ranging from drab grey to drab olive.

Pascoe, however, had seen her dressed for

action and knew that the way she looked at work was a deliberate choice. His guess was that here was an officer in a hurry who didn't want to waste time or energy dealing with the Neanderthal dickheads who clutter up every police force. Early in his own career he had let his admiration for the physical attributes of a female colleague show too clearly and he still winced with embarrassment when he recalled how before a raid she had taken him aside and said seriously, 'Peter, your wet dreams are your own affair, but tonight I'd like to be sure you'll be watching my back and not my backside.'

So, though regrettable, there was no escaping the fact that the initial strategies of a young man and a young woman in a hurry must diverge. Perhaps equally regrettable was the fact that there comes a point when they must rejoin. This was the age of the image, of sharp suits as well as sharp minds. For a man just as much as for a woman it was hard to win the hearts and minds of a promotion board if you went around looking like a loosely tied sack of potatoes.

Pascoe hoped that Novello would suss this out. He baulked at the idea of dropping a hint himself, partly because such a comment, however kindly meant, was very much against the spirit of the age, but mainly because he sensed that, despite all his efforts to be approachable, Novello didn't much care for him.

In this he was right, but for the wrong reasons.

What she didn't care for was slim clean-cut men full of boyish charm. What turned her on was a chunky build, good muscular definition and an abundance of body hair. Whenever Pascoe flashed the smile and said something nice to her, he lost all individuality and became a type. But in detective mode, with his mind focused firmly on the task in hand and herself being treated as no more than one of the tools of his job, she admired him greatly. A good-when-she-remembered Catholic girl, she found it easy to think in religious imagery.

There abideth these three, Dalziel, Wield and Pascoe; but the greatest of these (promotion prospects and the present state of the Service being tossed into the pot) had to be Pascoe.

Now the Greatest was asking if the Scariest was in.

'No sign yet, sir,' she said. 'And Sergeant Wield's got the morning off too.'

'So it's only thee and me,' said Pascoe. 'Here's what I'd like you to do.'

Quickly he brought her up to speed on the events of the previous night.

'And, just to be thorough, and in order to see exactly how much of a copycat it is, I'd like you to dive into the evidence store and see what you can find relating to the suicide of Palinurus Maciver Senior. Discreetly. You know how leaky this place is, and I shouldn't like the press making a thing about the copycat element.'

In fact he didn't give a toss about the press, it was Andy Dalziel whose antennae he didn't want to alert.

With only a sigh too light to shake a rose leaf down to indicate she thought this was a more than usually sad waste of her valuable time, Novello strode off.

Pascoe watched her go. *Nice buttocks, shame about the combat trousers*. Then mentally slapped his wrist.

Seated at his desk, he rang Forensic, to be told with some acidity that they too required sleep like normal human beings. So far there was nothing to suggest that Pal Maciver's death had been anything but what it seemed, a suicide bizarrely configured to reproduce an exact imitation of his father's ten years earlier.

Next, witnesses. The circumstances of the previous night hadn't been conducive to getting formal statements from those attending the scene of the death, and the birth. The coroner would certainly want to hear from some of them.

Definitely a job for Uniformed, he could hear Dalziel say. But when Fat Men are away, Thin Men can play, and approaching a newly bereaved wife was surely a task more suited to the diplomatic skills of CID than the *Blitzkrieg* of the plods.

He dialled the Casa Alba number.

A man's voice said, 'Yes?'

He said, 'Could I speak to Mrs Maciver, please?'

'I don't know,' said the voice cautiously. 'Who's calling?'

He identified himself.

'Sorry, thought you might be press,' said the voice. 'I'm David Upshott, the Vicar of Cothersley. I've just been in to see Mrs Maciver, trying to offer what comfort I could at this terrible time, but I'm afraid she's not in a very receptive mood. The doctor's with her now. I'll just let them know who's calling.'

There was a pause of a couple of minutes then a new male voice spoke.

'Tom Lockridge here. That you, Pascoe?'

'Indeed. Any chance of a word with Mrs Maciver, do you think? Either on the phone or, preferably, I could call out there to talk with her . . .'

'Not a good idea,' said Lockridge brusquely. 'I've got her under sedation. I doubt very much she'll be fit to talk to you today.'

'Oh dear. That's a pity.'

'Yes, isn't it? But in the circumstances, Pascoe, I can't imagine what on earth you might want to ask that can't wait. Goodbye.'

Next he rang the hospital where he learned that Mrs Dunn and her twins were doing as well as could be expected and Mr Dunn, after hanging around most of the night, had finally been persuaded to go home and get some rest.

Pascoe started to dial the Dunns' home number, recalled the state he'd been in the day

Rosie was born, and replaced the receiver. Give the poor devil a couple of hours' sleep at least.

Finally he tried Cressida's number and got the answer machine. This was frustrating. If Thin Men were to play, they had to find someone to play with.

On the other hand, perhaps this was the act of some tutelary spirit to save him from his own impetuosity. Disobeying Dalziel was not a path to peace.

He opened a file marked 'Quarterly Crime Statistics' and applied himself to the honing of a report he was preparing thereon.

After half an hour or so of this stimulating activity, he closed his eyes the better to contemplate the rhetorical structure of his peroration.

He was aroused from this creative trance by a cough. Not a Dalzielesque cough, nevertheless a good, firm, I'm-here-and-why-are-you-asleep? kind of cough.

He opened his eyes and saw Novello standing in the doorway, clutching a plastic bin liner. She looked rather dusty.

He yawned and said, 'Shirley, you come bearing gifts but not as a Greek, I hope.'

She had learned to ignore Pascoe's prattery as easily as she did Dalziel's provocations. She advanced to the desk and deposited the bin liner before him.

'I dug up this lot, sir,' she said. 'One file, some bits and bobs. There's a gun down there, but I didn't bring it, seeing as you didn't want to attract attention.'

'A gun? You mean . . . ?'

'The shotgun he used. Yes.'

'Why do we still have that? We said goodbye to deodands a long time ago.'

'Suppose the family could have had it back if they'd wanted, but you wouldn't, would you? I mean, every time you blew a rabbit's head off you'd be thinking . . . well, you'd have to be a bit insensitive.'

'So it wasn't the same gun last night. Bang goes one bit of the copycat.'

'But it still stays close,' said Novello. 'I checked the details of last night's gun. Practically identical. Had to be the other half of a matching pair. And the original permit was for two shotguns. No one seems to have picked up on that at the time.'

'Why should they? It can hardly have been relevant. But hang about – has the permit ever been renewed for the remaining gun?'

'No, sir. Presumably it just stayed in its cabinet in Moscow House.'

'No,' said Pascoe. 'It's a single-gun cabinet and, from the look of it, there hasn't been a gun kept in there since Pal Senior took his out to do the deed. So the other gun must have been kept somewhere else. Interesting, but as I doubt if we can pursue Pal Junior for shooting himself without a permit, not important. Worth mentioning, though. Very conscientious of you. And this stuff you did think worth lugging from the store, anything there you found significant?'

'Significant? Don't know, sir, as I'm not sure what you're trying to signify. But there were a couple of things struck me as a bit odd.'

'Suicides usually are a bit odd, aren't they? I mean, even in our neurotic society, it's a slightly offbeat thing to do.'

'You reckon, sir? Seems to me, a guy gets depressed, waits till his family are out of the way, locks himself in his room, blows his head off, that's pretty conventional stuff.'

'Really? Didn't realize that Vatican thinking was so laid back these days.'

Novello was surprised. Heavy-footed religious trampling from the Fat Man, who numbered Joe Kerrigan, her parish priest, among his drinking mates, she'd come to expect, but Pascoe generally tiptoed through the tulips of personal belief.

She said dismissively, 'I'm talking as a cop, sir, not a Catholic.'

'Which are, I trust, both permanent conditions, having in common the ability to believe several impossible things at the same time and before breakfast. So, on the one hand, a straightforward act of self-slaughter. On the other, an instance of that denial of God which is the unforgivable sin for which Judas stood condemned in the eyes of some theologians far more than for his act of betrayal. The black midnight of the soul which holds no hope of dawn. Strong stuff. Can you really keep it out of your cop-think in a case like this?'

'As easy as calling a doctor and saying a prayer if someone falls ill,' she said with spirit. 'You're mixing up depression and despair, sir. One's a condition of the mind, the other of the soul.'

'And nowadays the Church can tell the difference?' he said smiling.

'Sometimes,' she said. 'But it doesn't matter. God always can.'

There's a conversation killer, he thought.

'OK,' he said. 'So let's get back to the oddities.'

'Maybe I'm overstating it,' she said, starting to empty the bag. 'As you can see, it's a very full file, chaotic, but with all kinds of stuff bundled in that you'd not expect to find when it's not a criminal case. Looks like Mr Dalziel caught the call and stayed in charge.'

Pascoe looked at the confusion of papers on the desk. Definitely a Dalziel file. No pushing it off on to Uniformed here soon as suicide was confirmed.

Odd. Even odder than his appearance last night. Copycat suicide ten years on might just about explain a Head of CID's interest. But why had the Fat Man involved himself so deeply the first time round? Curiouser and curiouser.

Novello said, as if he'd articulated his thought, 'What's really odd is . . . well, judge for yourself, sir. I made a sort of digest.'

She produced a sheet of paper and looked at him enquiringly.

He said, 'I'll stop you if I get bored.'

'OK,' she said. 'On March 18th Mrs Maciver flew to New York with her younger stepdaughter, Helen. On March 20th Mr Maciver killed himself in Moscow House, the family home. His body was found by his son on his return from Cambridge on March 23rd. The news was passed on to the daughter, Cressida, at Brigstone School, Lincoln, and she came home the next day. Mrs Maciver, travelling in America with her stepdaughter, was harder to reach, so she didn't arrive until three days later. Now it gets odd. Turning up at Moscow House, she found she couldn't get in. She contacted the police. We assured her it was nothing to do with us, but we were able to ascertain the locks had been changed on the instructions of Mr Palinurus Maciver Junior. We needed a contact address for Mrs Maciver and the one she gave eventually was c/o Mr Tony Kafka, Cothersley Hall, Cothersley. I expect you know she later married Kafka, who's CEO of Ash-Mac's – that's Ashur-Proffitt-Maciver's, which used to be the Maciver family firm till the Americans took it over in the eighties. Pal Senior kept a seat on the Board but seems it was just for show. There was speculation at the inquest about how much losing the top job could have contributed to his depression.'

'Othello's occupation's gone,' said Pascoe. 'And

eventually the Widow Maciver becomes Mrs Kafka. Wonder how long it took?'

'Nothing in this file about it, sir, but I checked. Eighteen months.'

Pascoe looked at her speculatively and asked, 'Now why should you have checked that, Shirley?'

'Just being thorough, sir,' she said.

Long years of listening to spinners, trimmers, quibblers, equivocators and every other kind of truth-mangler had fine-tuned Pascoe's ear, and he thought he detected something here. A hesitation? A reservation? Something.

He left it for now and asked, 'And the inquest – anything interesting there?'

'Interesting?'

'Emotional outbursts. Wild accusations, that sort of thing. They didn't come across as a very together family last night and this odd business of the young Maciver changing the locks suggests some antagonism.'

'No, sir,' said Novello. 'Seems to have gone off very smoothly. Verdict of suicide. End of story. I checked out the evidence exhibits while I was at it. As well as the shotgun, there was the book they found on the desk. Family can't have wanted that back either. Don't blame 'em. Even cleaned up and dried off for ten years, it's not something you want lying around your coffee table.'

From the bin liner she took a plastic evidence

bag. Pascoe could see what she meant. The book it contained was open, presumably as it had been found on the desktop all those years ago. He'd looked at the volume on the desk last night before it went down to the lab for close examination. The words on the page had been hard to read under the mullock of blood and brain, but he'd made out the page numbers and the numbers of some of the small poems printed on them.

He checked these now against the older book from which the solider matter had been removed, leaving the page severely stained but legible. The page and poem numbers corresponded. Pal Junior's imitation had been exact.

The poem numbers ranged from 1062 to 1068. How many had Dickinson written? He knew little about her except that she was American and responsible for the lines *Parting is all we know of Heaven And all we need of Hell*. Or was that Ella Wheeler Wilcox, someone else he knew absolutely nothing about?

Ellie would know, though he would suffer for admitting his ignorance. She was big on the neglect of female writers. Pascoe smiled as he recalled Fat Andy's riposte after listening to a harangue which he'd deliberately provoked: 'I think I've got it now, lass. If it's got tits and can put two words down on paper, it's a lost genius.'

He ran his eyes over the tiny poems.

The first, 1062, seemed the relevant one.

He scanned it – staggered –
Dropped the Loop
To Past or Period –
Caught helpless at a sense as if
His Mind were going blind –

Groped up to see if God was there –
Groped backward at Himself
Caressed a Trigger absently
And wandered out of Life.

It was, he thought, surprisingly good.
Whoops!
There he went. Patronizing or what? Because
she was female, American, and he knew sod all
about her, he was surprised to be impressed.

The only thing surprising here, he could hear
Ellie say, is your prejudicial ignorance, and I'm
not surprised at that.

He returned his attention to the poems.

1063 had stuff about ashes in it and there had
been a fire in the wastepaper bin. And 1065 began
Let down the Bars, Oh Death – but then got into
sheep imagery. The others had nothing suggestive
in them. At least he couldn't see anything. Maybe
they needed a female eye.

He said, 'You read these poems, Shirley?'
She nodded.
'What did you make of them?'
She shrugged.
'For the tape,' he said smiling.

'Load of bollocks,' she said. 'But I'm not really into poetry and stuff.'

'It's not everyone's cup of tea,' he said.

He'd taken the volume out of the evidence bag now. After all these years, the risk of contamination hardly applied. Set in one place all these years, the spine creaked and cracked as he turned to the title page.

It bore an inscription in an elegant flowing hand.

The World – stands – solemner – to me –
Since I was wed – to You!'
For my darling Pal
from your solemnly loving Kay

'Nice,' said Novello over his shoulder.

'In what way?'

'All ways. If she meant it, brings-a-tear nice. If she didn't, nice one, Kay! Sir, if you don't mind me asking, is there something going on here? Do you reckon there's something dodgy about last night's suicide?'

He said with a smile, 'Just being a good house-wife, Shirley.'

Despite trying to keep it light, he could see she took it as a shut-out. But explaining that he probably wouldn't still be messing with this if his boss hadn't told him to leave it alone wasn't the best example to lay before a subordinate!

Was there anything here to justify further delay

in passing this over to Paddy Ireland? The answer was no . . . except maybe for that suspicion of a hesitation . . .

'Right,' he said negligently. 'That's it, dear. Over to Uniformed. Could you dump this stuff back in the store, then we can both get back to some real work?'

The *dear* worked. He saw her jaw set and guessed he was at last going to get what was bugging her in the form of a Parthian shot.

'Oh, by the way,' she said as she started gathering the tumble of papers together, 'there was *that* –'

That was a tape cassette.

She pushed it across the desk towards him. He looked at it without touching. It was the kind of cassette they used in the interview room but without a label.

He said, 'This was where?'

'Tucked away in one of the box files,' she said. 'Could just have ended up there by accident.'

'You haven't played it then?'

'No, sir.'

Positive without being over emphatic. She was good. But Pascoe had been where she was now.

She'd listened to the tape. It contained something she didn't care to admit she'd heard. She'd been uncertain what to do about it till he'd got up her nose with his *dear*, which had made her decide it would be amusing to leave him to listen

164

to it alone, and later observe surreptitiously how he reacted.

It was time for her to learn that DCs had no secrets from DCIs.

'OK. Probably nothing, but I'll have a listen,' he said.

He took the tape, swivelled in his chair to face the table that bore his computer and other electronic equipment, and loaded it into the cassette player.

Novello, laden with the file material, was trying to negotiate the door.

Pascoe said, 'Tell you what, Shirley. You might as well sit down and listen to this too. Then if it's got to go back with the rest of that stuff, you won't need to make an extra trip.'

She halted, turned, looked at him over the files.

Their gazes locked for a moment. Then she nodded as if getting a message.

'As you wish, sir,' she said, returning to her seat.

He waited till she was settled and pressed the 'start' button.

A familiar voice boomed out. 'Voluntary statement made by Mr Palinurus Maciver Junior in the presence of Detective Superintendent Andrew Dalziel. Date March 27th, 1992. Time one thirty-seven. God, I should be out enjoying me lunch! All the meat pies 'ull be gone. Never mind, duty calls, eh? Off you go, Mr Maciver. The floor's yours. Tell us thy story. But try and keep it short!'

Pascoe looked at Novello and tried to keep his face as blank as hers.

An unlabelled cassette. The super's voice casually breaking several clearly spelled out rules of procedure. Already, without hearing a word of what Maciver might say, he understood Novello's concern – and her well-hidden glee.

He settled back to hear the dead man talking.

6

Pal

I hope you'll be taking this a little more seriously by the time I'm done, Superintendent.

My name is Palinurus Maciver Junior. I am making this statement of my own free will.

This is in relation to the alleged suicide of my late father, Palinurus Maciver Senior. I've already tried to indicate to you what I think really happened. I haven't yet seen any indication that you're acting on my suspicions, which is why I want to make this statement formally.

I think my father was deliberately driven to the point where he took his own life and I think that my step-mother Kay Maciver was involved. I'm not saying directly involved. The bitch made sure she was well out of the way in the States when it happened. That strikes me as being pretty indicative in itself. I don't know the details of what took place. That's up to you lot to find out, isn't it? That's your job – though, God help us, you don't exactly seem desperate to get on with it. Probably there's no physical evidence to find. But deliberately driving a man to the point where some-thing snaps and he blows his head off, that's cold premeditated murder in my book. But it wouldn't surprise me if it turned out that somehow my stepmother was actually in the study with him, pulling the trigger. How could she have managed it when she's got an alibi putting her six thousand miles away? I don't know. Perhaps she's a witch as well as a bitch. Nothing would surprise me about Kay. Yes, she could be a witch. There's certainly something dark about her, and it's pretty plain to see she's got you magicked, Superintendent.

No. Scrub all that out. I don't want her getting away with anything because they say I'm making absurd accusations.

Here's the physical facts as I know them. I hope some of them aren't too physical for you, Superintendent.

To start with, it has to be clear to anyone who knew my father and knows my stepmother that she's an unscrupulous grasping cow who married him partly for his money but mainly so she could lead him on to sell the business to those Yankee pirates she works for. That oily bastard Kafka will be up to his neck in this. Ask yourself where she headed as soon as she realized I was on to her and wasn't letting her back into Moscow House. Straight round to shack up with Kafka, that's where.

But I'm getting ahead of myself.

Let's go right back.

I was fourteen when my mother died, Cress – that's my sister Cressida – was eleven and Helen, that's my other sister, was only three. Mother had Helen late and she was never the same after the birth, physically or mentally. It was a hard time for Dad in so many ways. Problems at home, plus he was fighting to keep the firm afloat while all around him other businesses were sinking like stones under the recession. When mother died, it must have seemed like he'd hit the bottom. His sister, Lavinia – that's my Aunt Vinnie – moved in to look after us. She did her best but she wasn't really up to it. Birds are her thing. She treated us like fledglings, saw we were kept warm and fed on a regular basis, but that was it. She spent more time in the garden than in the house. Which wouldn't have been so bad, being treated like young birds I mean, if she'd followed it through and kept off the predators. But when the witch-bitch turned up on the scene just over a year later, all that Vinnie saw was her best chance of getting out of Moscow and back to her country cottage, which is like an open aviary.

You're looking impatient, Superintendent. Let's cut to the chase. Manufacturing business was in a bad way generally, but in the jungle of international commerce, one firm's disaster is another firm's opportunity. Show signs of weakness and you can guarantee there'll soon be buzzards floating overhead waiting to snack on your juiciest morsels. Ashur-Proffitt in the States was the main buzzard with its eyes on Maciver's. God knows why they fancied us, but fancy us they did and nothing was going to stop them. OK, we were in a bad way, but there was still hope. I mean, look what's happened since. The place is booming, isn't it? If Dad had hung on, found a bit of extra finance somewhere, he'd have been round the corner and Maciver's could have been one of Maggie Thatcher's big success stories.

But Dad was vulnerable, his mind wasn't really on the job, and those Yankee bastards soon sussed out the best way of making sure that's the way it stayed. I'm not saying they planned it from the start, but I don't doubt they did their homework on Dad's personal life pretty thoroughly and soon as someone noticed he was paying as much attention to their top man's PA as he was to their balance sheets, they hit the button.

Did she play hard to get or was it a tit-flash job from the start? I don't know. I've only seen her in the latter mode. That surprises you, Mr Dalziel? It surprised me. All I saw at first was this skinny foreigner with a funny accent that my crazy father wanted us to accept as a substitute for our lovely mother who was hardly cold in her grave. That was bad enough. I didn't believe it could get worse. I had no way of knowing from those first meetings when she was so unremittingly nice to me and Cress and so droolingly gooey over little Helen that here was a sexual predator, completely out of control, thinking of nothing but satisfying her own depraved needs.

No point shaking your head at me like that, Superintendent. I've got a witness. Me!

Almost from the first moment she came to Moscow, she started flaunting herself at me. She never missed a chance to give me a show. I'd go past her bedroom and the door would happen to be wide open and she'd be lying naked on the bed, smiling at me. Or she'd come out of the bathroom in her robe and it wouldn't be *fastened properly. I didn't know what the hell was going on. I was completely confused. I was only fifteen when they got married, for God's sake. Still a minor. Doesn't that make it sexual abuse? That's a crime, isn't it? You can go to jail for that, can't you? You'll have to investigate that, won't you?*

Saying anything when Dad was alive was always going to be hard. In the end I did it, but maybe I left it too late, maybe I did it the wrong way. Some things you've got to stand up and shout out loud to the world, no matter who it hurts. Well, he's gone now, he's beyond hurt, and it's all that bitch's fault and now I'm ready to stand up in any court in the country and tell them the truth about her.

Let's try it out on you for a start, Mr Dalziel, and see how you like it.

The first time, I was having a shower when suddenly the door slid back and it was her. She was naked. I started to ask her what she wanted but she stepped in beside me and put her arms round me and kissed me. It was disgusting, she was like an animal. I thought she was going to eat me alive. I felt like a mouse when a cat's got its teeth into it! The more I resisted, the closer she seemed to wrap herself around me till it seemed I could feel every bit of her. The trouble was that, though I knew it was terribly wrong, I was a healthy adolescent and I spent a lot of time dreaming about girls like most boys do at that age. I'd had no experience beyond a bit of heavy snogging at parties. This was the first time I'd been up close against a naked female, and while my mind was saying No! my body was reacting the way you'd expect. I got hugely excited. She put her hand down to get hold of my prick and as soon as she touched it, I came. She held on for a bit, then said, 'That was a waste, wasn't it? Still, there's always next time.' And she left.

I've never felt so guilty about anything in my life. It felt like it was all my fault. Or if not all, at least fifty per cent. Maybe it was because of the pleasure I'd felt. I was convinced that God was going to punish me. I didn't know what to do except keep out of her way as much as I possibly could. And from then on I always made sure the bathroom door was firmly locked, and my bedroom door too. I was too ashamed to try and talk to anyone. Except Cress. She never liked Kay from the start, you see, and I needed her to help me in keeping guard against her in case she tried anything again.

But she didn't, not at first anyway. What she did was worse. She acted like we had some private understanding, giving me secret smiles, brushing up against me, that sort of thing. But she never actually came on to me in the same blatant fashion, mainly of course because I never gave her the opportunity.

So time went by, years, till I might have begun to think I'd imagined it all if it hadn't been for the way she kept up this we've-got-a-secret thing. Plus I could see that Dad wasn't happy. That bothered me as much as anything. He'd married her to be happy again, and he wasn't. But I was young and I was selfish and all I felt when it came time for me to go to university was relief to be away from her sphere of influence. I went off happy as a sandboy with no thought for poor old Dad.

Then a couple of weeks ago, just before she took off to America, things must have reached some sort of climax. Cress had been home for half-term and when she got back to school she rang me to say Dad was looking like hell. She sounded so worried I took the first chance to duck out of college and head home. I should have checked first. When I got back, I discovered that Dad was away for a couple of nights. I almost went straight back to Cambridge, then I thought, Why the hell should I let this cow keep me out of my own home? We were very polite to each other and of course Helen was there too. She was nine now, old enough to take notice, and she made a good chaperone. One thing Kay didn't want was to risk losing the halo Helen had put round her scheming head.

That night I went out to a pub to eat with some old chums and when I got back, Kay had gone to bed. I went to my room and made sure I locked the door. After a couple of hours I had to get up for a pee. As I came out of the bathroom, I heard a noise downstairs. Someone was playing the piano in the music room. We'd all had lessons, but with Cress and me it never took. Dad, who loved music, was disappointed, but Mother didn't really care so we soon gave it up. Helen was different. She had some talent and Kay, who played a bit herself, kept her at it, which really pleased Dad. One of the first pieces she'd learned, a tune from Schumann's Childhood Scenes, became a sort of signature tune with her. This was what I heard now so I thought she must have sneaked out of bed. Naturally I did the big brother thing and went downstairs to sort her out.

I pushed open the music-room door. It was pitch-black inside, curtains drawn, no light on. I stepped inside saying, 'OK, Sis, time for little girls to be in bed.'

A voice said, 'Suits me fine', and I switched on the light and saw it was Kay on the piano stool. She was stark naked.

I should have just turned and got out of there but I was so angry I advanced instead and began to yell at her. She span round on the stool and faced me, legs splayed, that smile on her face, the one that says, I know more about you than you know about yourself, and she said, 'Got any requests, Pal?'

I grabbed her by the shoulders. I think I meant to drag her out of there by main force, but she just let herself come forward without resistance and next thing I was on my back with her on top of me. I was only wearing shorts so it was bare flesh to bare flesh just like last time, and like last time I could feel myself being aroused. But I wasn't an inexperienced adolescent any more. I tried to push her away but she clung on, wrapping her legs and arms round me, nails digging into my back, laughing like it was a game, and all I managed to do was roll her over so I was on top. By now I admit I wanted to fuck her, I wanted to fuck her so hard it really hurt her. Like rape, I suppose I mean. Not for pleasure but for power.

But I knew that was what she wanted too. For every reason. To satisfy her own depraved needs. For pleasure, and for power too. Once get me inside her and she knew she'd be inside me for evermore.

What would have happened, I don't know. But at

that moment I heard a voice calling her name. It was Helen on the stairs. She must have woken and gone to Kay's room and when she found she wasn't there, she came looking for her.

I don't think any other voice could have put the brake on Kay's lust. Dad, the Archbishop of Canterbury, anybody else and she'd have just clung the tighter and revelled in being caught in flagrante with her stepson.

But not Helen. If in that whole mass of self-centred, self-indulgent, self-advancing, self-pleasuring impulse which makes up her being there is a single spark of unselfish feeling, it's struck by Helen.

She pushed me off, stood up and slipped into her robe, which had been draped across the piano. Then she smiled that smile at me again and said, 'Maybe it will be third time lucky, eh, Pal?'

She went out. I heard her greeting Helen in the hall, her voice perfectly normal, for all the world as if nothing had happened. Jesus, what an actress she would have made! But she's more than an actress, she's Lamia. She uses enchantment to hide the fact that she is really a serpent. I told her that once and she smiled as if I'd complimented her and said she could see from the start that a love of poetry was another thing we had in common. God, she knows how to get under your skin.

Next morning I got up early and packed my bag. I didn't want to be there when my father returned. I needed time to work out how to deal with this situation. She greeted me in the hall nice and easy, as if nothing had happened. She was so convincing that for a moment I began to doubt my own memory! Then I remembered the scratches I'd got on my back where she'd dug her claws into me.

I told her I was seriously thinking of telling my father everything. She just laughed and said, 'In that case, perhaps I shall tell him how you've been lusting after me all these years, which I could just about put up with when you were a spotty little adolescent. But trying to force me to have sex with you now that, on paper at least, you're a grown man is something different. That's attempted rape.'

I got out then. No point in doing anything else. All the way back to Cambridge, I debated how I should tell Dad. This time I knew I had to say something. The bitch was taking Helen on a trip to the States in a couple of days and I suspected that, fearful of what Cress and I might reveal to Dad when we had him to ourselves during the Easter vac, she might try to get in first. I couldn't bear the thought of telling him such stuff face to face, so first of all I rang him in London. But I felt such a coward, and he was so distant and distracted, that I got to the end of our conversation without saying a word. It wasn't till later that I got to thinking maybe the reason he sounded so distracted was that the bitch had already started poisoning his mind against me. I had to do something. I should have been there to meet him when he got back – oh, how I wish I'd gone to meet him – but I chickened out again and wrote a letter. He should have got it the day before Kay and Helen were due to fly to America.

I thought he would ring me straightaway. He didn't. I gave him a day then rang him. There was no answer.

So I left it. It was end of term, I'd be home in a few days anyway. We could talk then.

Instead I found him. Well, you know that. God help me, I found him.

Did he get my letter? I believe so. I think that was what he'd been burning in his wastepaper bin.

Did he have time to say anything to Kay before she left? My bet is he did. But that bitch would have been ready for it. Perhaps she'd already pre-empted my accusation with her own version. So there he was, faced with having to accept either that his wife was a dissolute bitch who'd tried to force herself on his son, or that his son was a depraved monster who'd tried to rape his wife.

Either option was hell. His mind snapped and he took what must have seemed the only other option. And it's all down to that bitch!

She may not have been in the study with him and she may not have pulled the trigger, but she drove him to it and I don't doubt that she did it deliberately. I think she could see he was on the edge and she pushed him as close as she could get, then left. I think she probably told him that if he didn't get things sorted, she was going to go public with her version, accuse me of attempted rape, call in the police. She wanted him to see that, whatever he did, his family was going to be blown apart. Except if he blew himself apart first.

Then she headed for the States. She wanted to be long gone if and when it happened. She must have jumped for joy when she heard the news. Now she'd got it all. My sister, Helen. A huge chunk of Dad's estate.

And now she could spend all the time she wanted with her fancy man, that greasy Yank, Kafka.

You've got to admit she's been quite blatant about it. Soon as she realized she wasn't going to get back inside Moscow House, where does she head? Out to his pleasure palace at Cothersley Hall!

But she's miscalculated badly if she thinks I'm going to take this lying down.

No need to keep glancing at your watch, Super-intendent. I won't keep you from your lunch any longer. This is my statement. You get it typed up and whatever else you do to make it official and I'll sign it. But I wanted you to hear it first, just so that you'll know what you're dealing with next time you go smarming round that bitch. And just in case she's got you so magicked you think you might do her a favour by forgetting about this tape, I shouldn't put your career at risk. I'm going to say it all again at the inquest, and the coroner might be very curious indeed to know why nothing in the police records has prepared him for this evidence.

End of statement. This is Palinurus Maciver Junior speaking. The time is one fifty-three p.m. on March 27th, 1992.

7

amnesia

'Well,' said Pascoe. 'And what do you make of that, Shirley?'

'Sir?'

'Of the tape. You were listening?'

'Sorry, sir. My mind went wool-gathering. I didn't really take it in.'

Meaning – *if you want to say negligently, 'No matter, it was pretty dull anyway,' and toss the cassette into your wastepaper basket, you'll get no quarrel from me.*

'I see. Shall I play it through again then?'

Meaning – *thank you but that's not the way I want to play this, not yet anyway.*

'No need, sir. I reckon I got the gist. Pal Maciver Junior blamed his stepmother for his father's suicide.'

'That's putting it mildly,' said Pascoe. 'Anything more?'

She shrugged as if to say, OK, you keep asking for it, you're going to get it.

'And he also seemed to be suggesting that Mr

Dalziel was far from objective in his attitude to said stepmother and might be disinclined to take these accusations seriously.'

'Which would, if true, be a serious matter,' said Pascoe, curious to see how the young DC was going to deal with this.

'Yes, sir. Though there did seem to be mitigating circumstances.'

'Did there? Such as?'

'Well, it was getting on to closing time,' said Novello very seriously. 'And he was worried about his meat pie.'

Pascoe stared at her. She stared back. Then his face cracked in a grin and after a moment she grinned back.

'However,' he resumed, 'it would seem that mitigation is unnecessary as, if your digest of the investigation is accurate, nothing of Pal Junior's accusations against his stepmother or insinuations against Mr Dalziel ever troubled the official record.'

'No, sir. There's certainly nothing in the file, no signed transcript of the tape and no reference to it, and there was no mention of any of this at the inquest either.'

'No problem then,' said Pascoe briskly. 'So here's what we're going to do. If you're agreeable, that is. You're going to forget you heard this tape. Both times.'

Just a little reminder that the Fat Man didn't have a monopoly of divine omniscience.

'Which tape?' she asked.

'Don't jump the gun,' he said. 'Before amnesia sets in, I'd be interested to hear your reactions to it. Anything at all.'

She shrugged.

'I've met none of these people. I can't even make an educated guess as to whether there's anything in what Maciver said. As to why he changed his mind about hurling all these accusations around, well, in a straight fight, Cambridge undergrad versus the Super, I know where my money would be. But how about you, sir? Weren't you around at the time?'

Pascoe shook his head.

'Sick leave. We established that last night when it became apparent that this latest suicide was a carbon copy of the old one.'

'That's you off the hook then, sir.'

Pascoe opened a drawer and slid the cassette into it.

'What hook would that be, Detective?' he said briskly.

'Hook, sir?' said Novello, interpreting the signal. 'Who said anything about a hook? Shall I take this stuff back down to the store now?'

'No,' said Pascoe. 'Stick it in that cupboard there. I'll pass it on to Mr Ireland later.'

'Mr Ireland?'

'Yes. Once we're completely satisfied no crime's been committed, a suicide, copycat or not, becomes Uniformed's baby.'

'And are we completely satisfied, sir?'

Pascoe hesitated his answer. The trouble was he still didn't know if his reluctance to say yes was caused by anything more than an objection to the Fat Man steamrollering him off the case.

But he didn't doubt that in the apophthegms of the wise from Confucius to Rochefoucauld he could find many variations on the theme that men who try to stop steamrollers end up flat. Presumably Pal Maciver Junior too had tasted the sadness of Dalziel's might. All that passion and hate in his recorded statement, yet none of it had ever got on to the public record.

So what did he do now? He suspected – no, he was certain – that he'd already stepped over the line drawn by Dalziel's instruction to tidy this up and dump it on Paddy Ireland. There was danger in probing further, but was there any point?

Novello was watching him closely. He got the feeling she was following his thought processes even more closely. He remembered as a teenager climbing up on to the high board at the municipal swimming pool and changing his mind when he realized just how high it was. Then his nervous eye had spotted a couple of girls he knew who'd just come in and were looking up at him. So he'd dived.

Happily he was long past such adolescent needs to prove himself.

He said, 'You know what? I think it might be useful to have a look at the scene by daylight.'

She smiled secretly but he saw it. And he recalled that when, after a descent which seemed to go on forever, he'd hit the water in a belly flop that almost stunned him, one of the girls had dived in and helped him to the side.

No use showing off unless you could carry it off.

He said, 'It would be useful to have a fresh pair of eyes along . . .' paused, then went on, 'I'll just see if Sergeant Wield is in,' and reached for his phone.

'Not till later, sir,' said Novello. 'I told you he'd got the morning off.'

'So you did,' said Pascoe. 'In that case, I suppose you'd better come along, Shirley.'

Already he was feeling ashamed of his pettiness.

'OK,' said Novello. 'Shall I drive?'

This was a telling riposte, thought Pascoe as he blew his nose to conceal his alarm. He recalled the one previous time he'd travelled, folded like a foetus, in the front seat of Novello's Fiat Uno. She'd driven like Jehu on a bad prophet day and his abiding memory was of being far too close both to the road and to God.

Self-preservation overcame political correctness. He said firmly, 'No, we'll go in my car.'

And got that secret thought-reading smile again.

8

assignation

The fog had lain thick on Enscombe village all night but it hadn't inhibited the dawn chorus, and Detective Sergeant Edgar Wield had been further cheered by the returning memory that he wasn't due in at work till after lunch. It would have been nice to share a lie-in with his partner, Edwin Digweed, but that was not to be. The Yorkshire Antiquarian Bookdealers Association's annual symposium was starting at the Golden Fleece Hotel that evening and, as the member closest to the action, Digweed had taken on the job of making sure that everything was ready for the delegates' arrival.

Observing that Wield's good cheer seemed to have declined a little over breakfast and putting it down to his own unavoidable absence on his friend's morning off, he apologized again before he left, adding, 'Look, you pass the road end. Why don't you call in and we'll have lunch together? My treat.'

184

'And my pleasure,' said Wield.

In fact his apparent depression of spirits had had nothing to do with Edwin's absence, but was merely a retrospectively pensive mood provoked by the news on local radio of Palinurus Maciver's death in Moscow House the previous night.

By midday, with the sun soaring high in an almost cloudless sky, and the fog and the chill of the previous night vanished like a dream, he was in no mood for retrospection, and as he rode his Thunderbird along the narrow road that led out of Eendale, he sang in a voice to make a rook wince, *'The flowers that bloom in the spring, Tra la, Breathe promise of merry sunshine.'*

Normally his speed of choice would have blown the words back down his throat, but today he was moving at a pace sedate enough, if not to let him enjoy the scent of the flowers as he passed, at least to take in the full beauty of the landscape which in a single night seemed to have shrugged off the debilitations of winter and risen refreshed to garb itself in the clean bright fabrics of spring.

Eventually the road emerged from the steep-sided valley into a flatter, more conventionally pastoral landscape still very attractive in its variety of vernal greens. A couple of miles ahead lay the junction with the main east–west arterial, the fastest way into town for a man in a hurry, which was what Wield usually was as he found himself increasingly reluctant to leave Enscombe village of a morning. Today however he turned off to the left about a mile before the arterial junction, entering what to the casual tourist looked like a pleasant minor country road. But this too had once enjoyed the hustle and bustle and self-importance of a major thoroughfare before the road improvers of the sixties discovered a better, more Roman line for the main east–west route.

Those with farms or houses along the old main road had been mightily relieved to learn that the new highway wasn't going to affect them except by rendering their everyday lives a lot more peaceful. Only the owner of the Golden Fleece, the old coaching inn at Gallow's Cross, had been dismayed, and rightly so. With the passing trade which had been the Fleece's life blood for a century and a half now coursing with ever-increasing force two miles to the south, the Fleece had rapidly declined to a run-down country pub with only its incongruous dimensions to remind anyone of the glory days.

Then, just as rumours gathered strength that it was to be demolished completely to make way for an intensive pig farm, it was bought in the eighties by a national hotel chain specializing in establishments that could combine the snobbish attractions of the country house hotel and the corporate attractions of the conference centre plus health and leisure club.

The old coaching inn was completely refurbished and extended to provide all the necessary concomitants of hospitality in the late twentieth century, and though the result might not have satisfied Prince Charles, with its ease of access to the fleshpots of urban Mid-Yorkshire in one direction and the beauties of rural Mid-Yorkshire in the other, it succeeded in satisfying the demands both of those in search of peace and quiet and those intent on expense-account conviviality.

As a coaching inn, the Golden Fleece had naturally had an entrance straight off the road under an archway into its courtyard, but that was impracticable in days when they might be expecting several dozen cars and now you approached along a sweeping driveway through pleasant parkland under whose scattered trees sheep paused in their grazing and lambs in their gambolling as a leather-clad figure rode by, carolling, '*We welcome the hope that they bring, Tra-la, Of a summer of roses and wine . . .*'

There were plenty of spaces in the car park but Wield's eye was caught by a station wagon so long unwashed that its colour was hard to determine. He parked the Thunderbird next to it, dismounted and peered through the grubby window.

The rear seats were covered with a familiar strew of clothing, maps, empty takeaway cartons plus a Spanish onion and a half-full bottle of Highland Park – the famous emergency rations.

Wield was not much given to flights of fancy but for a moment his mind scrabbled for a parallel among the nasty shocks of fact and fiction – Friday's footprint, Amundsen's flag fluttering over the Pole, Pearce's missed penalty in the '90 World Cup – and found none.

This was Andy Dalziel's car.

On the other hand, even devils must dine, and there was no rational explanation for the deep sense of foreboding the discovery roused in him.

He set off for the hotel entrance. The car park was discreetly screened from the building complex by a box hedge. As he passed through this he came to a sudden stop. A mock Victorian conservatory had been built on the end of the hotel. Through the glass under a potted palm he saw two heads – one fine-boned, short black hair elegantly coiffured; the other solid as an ancient weathered boulder – leaning close together over a wrought-iron table, like a tableau set up by a nineteenth-century narrative painter working on a canvas entitled *The Assignation*.

The woman looked in his direction and said something; the big grey head opposite her began to turn, and Wield took a hasty step backwards with the roar of Teutonic cheers and Antarctic winds echoing in his ears.

Back in the car park, he got on his bike and went looking for a space as far from Dalziel's car as he could get and closer to the path round to the front of the hotel which would keep him out of view of the conservatory.

The cheers and the winds had been replaced

by the song he'd been singing all the way from Enscombe, but now he'd moved on to the second verse.

'*The flowers that bloom in the spring, Tra la, Have nothing to do with the case . . .*'

9

special filling

Kay Kafka said, 'That guy in the biker gear, wasn't it . . . ?'

'Unless he's got a twin, which I doubt,' said Dalziel.

'I thought this was a private unofficial meeting, Andy,' said Kay Kafka.

'Me too. Don't fret, I'll be having a word. So, things all right with you generally, are they, Kay?'

'They're fine. No worries. Not till this thing last night.'

'I've told you, put that out of your mind. Terrible business, but no reason you should be involved.'

'It looks to me as if Pal wanted to involve me,' she said.

'Aye, you're right from what you said. But it hasn't worked. So no problem.'

'I don't need to make it official then?'

'No point,' he said confidently. 'Why complicate what's simple? As things stand, I doubt Paddy Ireland, that's the man in charge, will even want to talk to you. No, forget it.'

'I'll try. But it won't be easy. He was his father's son. My stepson. Helen's brother.'

'He was a nasty twisted scrote.'

'He must have been in great distress to kill himself.'

'Aye, and he wanted to spread it around as much as he could. Like hearing you've got leprosy and drowning yourself in the town reservoir. So you forget it and concentrate on them new grandchildren.'

'Stepgrandchildren,' she corrected.

'I doubt they'll ever see it like that,' he said, emptying his glass. 'They don't know how lucky they are, not yet. Give 'em a couple of years, but, and they'll know.'

She smiled at him fondly and said, 'All this talk of me. How are *you*, Andy? You still with your friend?'

'Cap? Aye, so to speak.'

'So to speak? That doesn't sound too positive,' she said, concerned.

'Nay, all I meant was we don't live together. Not permanent. Like our own space, isn't that what they say? Any road, she's away just now.'

'In her own space?'

'Summat like that. She protests.'

'Not too much, I hope?'

'Feels like it sometimes. I used to take the piss

out of my lad, Pascoe, 'cos his missus were one of these agitating women. God likes a joke.'

'Because now you've got one?'

'Because I've got *the* one. Animal rights, the environment, that stuff. When she says she'll be away a couple of days but don't say where, I stop reading the paper in case I see that Sellafield's been blown up.'

'Your womenfolk are a trouble to you, Andy.'

'Nay, them I think of as mine are worth ten times the trouble,' he said, smiling at her. 'How's that man of thine?'

'He's away too. Just for the day. London, on business.'

'London. Poor sod,' said Dalziel with feeling. 'Still, he'll be back in God's own country tonight.'

'I think he'd need to travel a little further to get there in his case,' said Kay.

Dalziel regarded her shrewdly and said, 'Feeling homesick, is he? Never had him down as the type.'

'I think he feels that after what happened last September it's the place to be. Get the wagons into a protective circle, that sort of thing.'

'How about you?'

'You know me, Andy. This is where I want to be, lots of reasons.'

'And two more since last night, eh?'

'Right. And one big one sitting with me now.'

Something which on a less massively sculpted

face might have passed for a blush glowed momentarily on the Fat Man's cheeks.

He pushed his chair back and said, 'Now I'd best be on my way.'

'Sure you won't have another drink?'

'No. One's enough when I'm driving,' he said virtuously.

'You mean there's a cop in Mid-Yorkshire who'd dare breathalyse you?'

'There's some as 'ud pay for the chance,' he said. 'You coming?'

'I may get a snack here. Sure you won't join me?'

'No fear. They cut the crusts off your sandwiches.'

He stood up. Kay rose too, leaned over the table and kissed him lightly on the lips.

'Thanks, Andy,' she said.

'For what?'

'For being my friend.'

'Oh aye. Is that all?'

'It's a lot. Gets me served quick in pubs,' she said, smiling.

'Not all bad then. Take care, luv. And ring if there's owt worrying you.'

He left and made for the car park. In his car he didn't make for the exit straightaway but drove slowly round till he spotted the Thunder-bird.

'Enjoy your lunch, Sergeant,' he said. And drove away.

* * *

Back in the conservatory Kay Kafka pressed a key on her mobile. She had to wait a few moments before she got a reply. She said, 'Hi, Tony. It's me. Have I disturbed your lunch?'

'Not as much as it's disturbing me,' said Kafka. 'You should see this place, except you can't because they don't let women in. I sometimes think it's a movie set, or something they hire from the National Trust to keep foreign riff-raff in their place. So what's new with Mr Blobby?'

'Everything's fine. Any mention your end?'

'Not yet, but they don't get on to matters of substance till the soup's been served. Soup! If you're looking for a weapon of mass destruction, look no further!'

'Tony, you are being careful what you say?'

'You know me. Soul of discretion. Anyway, I'm outnumbered.'

'I thought it was just Warlove.'

'He's brought that guy Gedye along. The one who looks like a high-class mortician, always measuring you up with his eyes.'

'Tony, don't go neurotic on me.'

'Just because I'm neurotic doesn't mean the bastards aren't creepy. Joke. Now tell me about your chat with Mr Blobby. And the twins, have you been to see them this morning? How do they look in the bright light of day?'

They talked for several minutes more. When the conversation was done, Kay stood up and went through an inner door leading to the spacious hotel lobby, one wall of which was almost filled by a seventeenth-century fireplace in which a twenty-first-century fire looked sadly inadequate. In a deep armchair by the fire, either reading or sleeping behind the *Daily Mirror*, sat a man. Kay approached the reception desk where two young women, one blonde, one brunette, otherwise so alike they could have been clones, were working. The blonde greeted her brightly.

'Hello, Mrs Kafka. And how are you today?'

'I'm fine,' said Kay. 'I'm just going up to the suite. I'll be doing some work on my laptop, so would you like to send some sandwiches up?'

'Of course, Mrs Kafka,' said the young woman, reaching for a key. 'Any special filling you'd like today?'

'A selection will be fine. Thank you.'

As Kay walked away the blonde raised her eyebrows at her fellow worker who mouthed, 'Any special filling. You cheeky cow!' They both giggled.

Edgar Wield lowered his newspaper and watched Kay get into the lift. As it ascended, alongside it the door to the bar swung open, giving him a glimpse of Edwin Digweed sitting with a group of rather dusty, slightly foxed men. Then the door closed again behind a young waiter with golden skin, jet-black hair, sultry brown eyes and a face to turn Jove languid.

The blonde receptionist called, 'Hey, Manuel. Job for you.'

LEEDS COLLEGE OF BUILDING
LIBRARY

'What job? I'm very busy,' he replied without slowing his graceful step.

'Too busy for Mrs Kafka?'

Now he slowed and went to the desk.

The girls spoke to him in voices too low for Wield to catch. After a moment he laughed and moved away, calling over his shoulder, 'Never mind. Your turn will come.'

'Loves himself, doesn't he?' said the brunette.

'And why not? Wouldn't mind giving him a helping hand, how about you?' said the blonde.

She glanced towards the fireplace and saw Wield watching her. A smile lit up her face and she gave a little wave. He gave a wave and a smile back.

'Not thinking of going les, are we?' said Digweed who'd emerged from the bar unnoticed.

'It's Doreen, Tom Uglow's lass from the village,' said Wield.

'Yes, I do know that,' said Digweed a little tetchily. 'Let's see if we can get her to rustle up some sandwiches.'

He went to the desk and spoke to the girls.

When he returned he said, 'They'll be along shortly. The waiter's rather busy at the moment.'

'I bet he is,' said Wield.

Twenty minutes later Wield had finished his beer and, with an afternoon's work ahead of him, had moved on to cranberry juice, which if his partner was to be believed would help him grow up into a big healthy boy. He was thinking if the food didn't arrive soon he would have to leave without it.

'What on earth are they doing with these sandwiches?' grumbled Digweed. 'Churning the cheese? There's the manager. I think I'll have a word.'

A portly man in a pinstripe suit had appeared behind the desk and was talking to the receptionists. Digweed began to rise but before he was out of his chair, the lift door slid open and the handsome young waiter erupted looking like an advertisement for the Wrath of Achilles. The manager glanced towards him, pursed his lips and called, 'Manuel, I've told you before. Use the service lift.'

The waiter didn't even look his way but as he strode towards the main exit made a gesture whose meaning was as unmistakeable in rural Mid-Yorkshire as it was in urban Spain or even Homeric Greece.

Digweed subsided into his chair.

'Not from Barcelona, is he?' said Wield.

'Valencia, I believe,' said Digweed, pronouncing it correctly. 'I think our sandwiches may be some little time.'

'Probably just as well if there's something wrong with your teeth,' said Wield.

10

green peckers

Moscow House in the clear light of day no longer looked like it had strayed out of a Poe short story. True, it was a bit run down, but nothing that a pressure gun and a paint brush couldn't put right in a couple of days. And though the garden could certainly have done with a short-back-and-sides, Pascoe rather liked the wild-meadow look, with brassy daffs trumpeting their triumph over a wilderness of grasses.

He was surprised to find Constable Jennison on guard duty at the front door.

'You still here?' he said.

Jennison, happy to be here in broad daylight, did a comic take to left and right, then said, 'Oh me, sir? Yes, I'm still here. Leastways I was last time I looked.'

Novello, who'd not been a member of Joker Jennison's fan club ever since he'd affected to mistake her for part of a drag act booked to do a turn at the Welfare Club, grimaced at this weak attempt at humour. When I'm DCI, any plod taking the piss will wish he'd stayed in bed with a broken leg that day, she promised herself.

Pascoe grinned broadly and said, 'I mean, you haven't been here since last night, I take it?'

'No, sir. Got relieved about one. Came back on an hour ago and Bonk— Sergeant Bonnick told me I was off the cars today and back down here. I think he blames me for letting that lot up the drive last night.'

Pascoe said, 'Even if you'd checked them, I think we'd have had to let them up to the house. They were family, after all. Anyone been around today?'

'Not since I came on, sir. And the guy I took over from said it had been dead quiet too.'

'A master of the apt phrase. Come on, Shirley. Let's take a look inside.'

As they stepped into the house, Jennison said, 'Sir, can I have a word?'

'Of course,' said Pascoe, turning back to him.

'It's probably nowt, but last night when I were on the gate, I got talking to one of the working girls. Dolores, she said her name was. Sounded foreign. Long black hair, dead white face, but I think she were just a kid really. It's a crying shame. Lovely figure, but. Bum to die for, and legs you could wrap twice round your neck and still leave enough to tie a bow with.'

Behind Pascoe, Novello shook her head, baffled as always by this not uncommon male mix of compassion and salacity. How could these guys feel so sorry for a girl and want to fuck her at the same time?

Pascoe said, 'I hope she didn't distract you from your duties.'

'No, sir. We just talked a bit. I thought she were just naturally nosey like women can be. Once word got round we were on the plot mob-handed, most of the Avenue girls must've realized that was the end of trade last night and took off elsewhere. But not Dolores.'

'I'm beginning to feel a bit like an ancient mariner here, Joker,' said Pascoe.

'No accounting for tastes, sir,' said Jennison. 'Sorry. No, all I wanted to say was, I reckon it was more than just female nebbiness that kept her talking to me.'

'Certainly wasn't your magnetic personality,' muttered Novello.

Pascoe frowned at her and said, 'You're getting within lunar orbit distance of interesting, Joker. Try for a landing, eh?'

'Well, it were nowt really. She just kept on asking for details, like wanting a description of the fellow who'd topped himself, and she were dead keen to know if any of the girls were involved.'

'You got this woman's details, I take it?'

Jennison looked uncomfortable.

'No, sir. Sorry.'

'Jesus. Why not?'

'It weren't till I got to thinking about it later

that it struck me as odd enough to mention. And in any case Mr Dalziel's car turned up while we were talking and I pushed her out of sight behind a tree and when the Super had gone up the drive, she'd disappeared.'

'She shouldn't be hard to find,' said Pascoe. 'I'm sure the girls will be back tonight once the dust has settled. Pick her up and bring her in, will you? And thanks for bringing it to my notice, Joker.'

He went into the house. Jennison gave a modestly self-deprecating shrug and a big wink to Novello, who said, 'Yes, thank you, Jerker,' and followed.

'Think it means anything, sir?' she asked.

'You never know.'

'Pity the plonker didn't mention it last night then.'

Pascoe said gently, 'The plonker needn't have mentioned it at all, Shirley. And you won't get far in CID unless you've got an efficient working relationship with your uniformed colleagues.'

The only efficient working relationship most of that lot want involves their only efficiently working part, thought Novello.

'Yes, sir,' she said, looking around the entrance hall, taking in the high ceilings and counting the doors. 'Big place.'

'Yes,' said Pascoe. 'They knew the meaning of spacious living in those days.'

Living! thought Novello. Spacious, maybe. Like a pyramid.

'How long's it been up for sale?' she asked.

'A few months, I gather,' he said.

'So the estate agent will have a key and there could have been any number of people wandering round at one time or other?'

'I suppose. Why do you say that?'

'Never hesitate to point out the obvious,' she said in a tone of voice at once precise and diffident which it took him a second to recognize as a parody of his own. The words too he recognized as one of his maxims for trainee tecs.

'Someone's certainly been using one of the bedrooms from time to time,' he said.

'Yeah? Maybe one of Jennison's lady friends decided it would be a lot more comfortable than getting shagged up against a tree or in the back of a Fiesta,' said Novello. 'Easy enough to get hold of a key.'

'You think so? How?'

'Make an appointment with the agent and find a chance to make an impression of the key in a bit of putty. Or give the sod a freebie and get one that way. Shall I talk to the agent, sir?'

Pascoe smiled at her indulgently and said, 'Not until we have reason enough to satisfy Mr Dalziel that would be a proper use of police time. The use of the bedroom is interesting but so far not of any apparent relevance. Let's take a look at the *locus in quo*, shall we?'

She smiled back at him. Mention of something basic like shagging to Pascoe often sent him running to his fancy phrases, but it took more than a bit of Latin to impress a good Roman Catholic girl.

She followed Pascoe up the stairs.

On the landing he paused before an oaken door that showed signs of having been assaulted with a battering ram.

SOCO had clearly done a thorough job up here, leaving their print-indicating marks all over the place, including some on the door's lower panel about thirty inches from the ground.

'Now why would anyone need to touch that part of a door?' wondered Pascoe.

'A child?' suggested Novello. 'Or, more likely, whoever it was got here first knelt to look through the keyhole and rested his hand on the panel.'

'Good thinking,' said Pascoe, checking the finger-print report. 'Constable Maycock and Sergeant Bonnick, who had their prints taken for elimi-nation. But also there's a full palm-print from someone else not known. Meaning?'

'I don't know, sir.'

'Me neither. Here's something else. On the doorknob they found prints from Sergeant Bonnick and Constables Maycock and Jennison. No one else.'

He looked at Novello expectantly.

'What about Maciver?' she said. 'He must have turned the knob to get in.'

'You'd think so,' said Pascoe. 'Though I suppose with three other people touching the knob, his prints could have got covered over. But how to explain that on the key there's only one partial, not Maciver's?'

'Keys are crap to dust,' said Novello. 'Partial could have been there for years. And maybe Jennison wiped it clean for a laugh.'

Shaking his head reprovingly, Pascoe pushed the door open.

The study was full of light. The previous night on his command the shutters had been fully opened to check that they were as secure as they looked. They were. In fact the shutter catches were almost melded together by corrosion, and the sash windows were stiff from long disuse, making Pascoe wonder if they'd remained shut ever since the death of Pal Maciver Senior ten years earlier. He'd instructed that they be left open to let some air into the room to waft away the smell of smoke, cordite and death.

Novello found herself staring fixedly at the bespattered desk, trying to imagine what it was that could bring a man to this level of despair or self-hate. She forced her gaze away and tried to get a feel for the rest of the room. Two tall cabinets packed with books, most of them backed with that posh leather that tells the world, *We're so awfully dull, no one ever reads us*; picture of some guy on the wall dressed like a tramp, not bad looking if he lightened up a bit; on one side a coil of rope and on the other an ice axe whose function she recognized from a short but entertaining relationship she'd had with a rock climber who'd almost got her interested in the sport by doing something very ingenious with her on the sports centre climbing wall one night after everyone else had gone. But not even the prospect of a reprise had persuaded her it was worth submitting herself to the violence of wind, weather, vegetation and insect life by joining him on expeditions to godforsaken places like Wales or the Lake District.

'Shirley,' said Pascoe in a tone which suggested that this wasn't the first time he'd said it. 'Still with me? Good. You've just read the file on the previous case. Take me through the sequence of events then.'

Novello refocused.

'They worked out he put a record on the turntable, set it playing, sat down, started to write a note to his wife . . .'

'How do we know it was to his wife?' interrupted Pascoe.

'Because he'd addressed an envelope to her. But he must have changed his mind about the note. Perhaps he decided the poetry book would do just as well. So he set fire to the note, dropped it in the bin, took his shoe and sock off, put his big toe through a loop of twine, the other end of which was tied round the trigger of a shotgun, placed the trigger under his jaw, and blew his head off.'

'Interesting. Why did he set fire to the note? Any speculation there?'

'Nothing in the file, but I presume because he wrote something which didn't sound right when he read it back to himself. Maybe it was something nasty, like he was blaming her. Sir, why are you bothering yourself about what the father did ten years ago? Surely we should be concentrating on what the son did last night?'

'But we know why the son did things the way he did,' said Pascoe. 'Because he was imitating his dad. The question is, why did he want to imitate his dad? And what precisely was it about his dad's death he thought he was imitating? Was it more than just the method and sequence? Was he perhaps trying to tell us he had the same motives? And if that's the case, we've got to be sure we understand why he thought his father killed himself.'

Novello considered this then said, 'According to the tape . . .'

'What tape?' said Pascoe, raising his eyebrows at her.

'Sorry. According to rumour, he thought his father was driven to suicide by a combination of things, but mainly by the behaviour and attitudes of his wife. So perhaps it was the same for Pal Junior.'

'You mean his own wife, Sue-Lynn, not Kay Kafka?'

'The envelope was addressed to Sue-Lynn.'

'But was the poem addressed to her as well, or was that just straightforward imitation of his dad's bad example? And why did he want to imitate his father anyway? What did he hope to achieve by doing that? Better still, perhaps we should ask ourselves, what has he achieved by doing that?'

Novello half hid a yawn and said, 'Not a lot, I'd say, except make us . . . spend a lot of time trawling through the old case.'

She'd been going to say *waste*, but thought that on top of the yawn this might be an implied criticism too far.

But Pascoe was looking at her as if she'd come close to saying something profound.

'You may have something there, Shirley. Would you care to expand?'

She was spared this trial (why did she always feel so *tested* in Pascoe's company?) by Jennison's voice calling, 'Sir? Sir?' from the hall below.

Pascoe went out on to the landing and looked down. Jennison was leaning his bulk against the closed front door as if anticipating an attempt to force it open.

'Yes?'

'Got some people outside would like to speak with you, sir. Two ladies. The sisters, I think they said.'

Cressida. Now sober, he hoped.

'So, one lady's the sister. And the other?'

'No, sir. I think both ladies said they was the sister.'

Helen? Risen so soon from her maternity ward bed? Not likely.

Someone started thumping very hard on the door.

Pascoe said, 'Better let them in,' and started descending the stairs.

Jennison opened the door and Cressida Maciver almost fell in, her face flushed with, he hoped, anger rather than booze. She was followed less precipitately by a woman in her late fifties, leaning, though not too heavily, on a knobbly oak walking stick.

'There you are!' Cressida cried accusingly. 'Was it on your instructions that this fat oaf shut me out of my own house?'

'Miss Maciver,' said Pascoe, deciding to keep it formal for the time being. 'I understand what a trying time this must be for you, but being personally offensive to my officer isn't going to make things easier for anyone. Let's go through here.'

He led them into the kitchen where he knew they could sit without making themselves comfortable. Jennison had followed and was looking round hopefully for any sign of tea-making equipment.

Pascoe said, 'Thank you, Joker. Back on the door if you please,' then turned his attention to the newcomers.

Jennison's confusion was soon explained.

The other woman was Pal Senior's sister, Lavinia Maciver.

Cressida seemed somewhat abashed by Pascoe's

reproof and it was left to the older woman to explain their presence.

'I do not care to be troubled by either telephonic or broadcasting equipment, Mr Pascoe, so I knew nothing of this dreadful business till Mr Waverley, who likes to keep abreast of events, came round to tell me this morning, an act of true friendship, I think you'll agree.'

'Indeed. Er, Mr Waverley . . . ?'

'An old friend. I was naturally shocked. Mr Waverley, thinking I would probably want more information than was available from the media, offered to drive me into town. Our first call was at my niece's house . . .'

She paused and glanced at Cressida as if inviting her input.

The younger woman seized the chance and, to Pascoe's relief, injected a bit of pace into the narrative.

'I was still in bed, still in shock from last night, I reckon. Anyway I got up and Aunt Vinnie and I had a heart to heart and we decided we needed to come and see you people and get the latest news from the horse's mouth. But first we drove out to Cothersley to see Sue-Lynn. Waste of time. No sign of her. Probably it was her day at the beautician's to have her bikini line done. For some reason Aunt Vinnie suggested we called at the Hall to see Kay, but she wasn't in either, for which relief much thanks. Then we went to the hospital to see how Helen was. Stopped to buy some flowers but needn't have bothered. That Yankee bitch had been there already and the place was like Kew Gardens. Spent some time with Helen – Jase turned up as we were going so we had to rap with him too, naturally – then we headed for the cop-shop only to find no one over the rank of tea boy available, so we came on here and struck lucky. Bring us up to date, Chief Inspector.'

'I'm afraid there's little more for me to tell you,' said Pascoe. 'The investigation is proceeding with all possible speed. All violent deaths are treated as suspicious, but in this case I can say that nothing in the preliminary forensic reports contradicts our first impression that your brother died at his own hand.'

'And that's it?' said Cressida incredulously.

What, wondered Pascoe, would she like me to say that wasn't *it?*

But he was familiar enough with the irrationalities of grief not to let the thought show.

'For the time being, I fear it is,' he said gently.

'So what the hell's a big gun like you doing out here?' demanded Cressida.

This was a good question and not one to which he could offer an easy answer.

Novello said, 'Sir . . .'

'What?'

'I thought I heard a noise . . .'

Was she being merely diplomatic to get him off Cress's hook?

He said, 'Where?'

She raised her eyes to the ceiling.

'I'd better check, then. Excuse me, ladies.'

He went out into the corridor and back to the main stair. The front door was ajar and he could see Jennison's substantial frame on the step. Not much chance of anyone having got past him. Unless they had a bum to die for.

He ran lightly up the stairs, and halted when he came to the landing.

The study door was wide open. He remembered pulling it to behind him.

He advanced quietly and looked inside.

A man he'd never seen before was down on one knee by the old record player on which Pal Maciver's farewell music had been played. He supported himself by leaning on a silver-topped ebony walking stick. He looked to be in his sixties and was smartly dressed in an expensive-looking mohair overcoat in charcoal grey and a black trilby.

'What the hell are you doing here?' demanded Pascoe.

The man rose, removed his trilby to reveal vigorous near-white hair, smiled and said, 'DCI Pascoe, is it? Good to meet you. Laurence Waverley. I brought Miss Maciver, both Misses Maciver, here.'

'Did you? Then you'll know that this is a crime scene, Mr Waverley. Would you care to tell me what you are doing here without authority?'

The change of tone was partly a matter of

personal style but also down to the fact that, upright and face on, authority wasn't something you could accuse Mr Waverley of not having.

'Reluctant though I am to shelter behind encroaching age, I have to admit to a slight prostate problem. I came upstairs in search of a loo. Idle curiosity, I fear, made me open the study door. Idle but not altogether morbid. I recall the sorrow occasioned by Mr Maciver Senior's death, and I am distressed that my dear friend, Miss Lavinia, is having to go through this dreadful experience yet again.'

'You knew the father then?'

Waverley's gaze went to the portrait on the wall.

'Only in a professional sense. We were not friends. Few people make friends of a VAT investigator.'

'Ah,' said Pascoe, ushering him through the door on to the landing. 'You're a VAT-man.'

'Was. Safely retired. Please accept my apologies for trespassing in this way, Chief Inspector. I should have realized the study would be treated as a crime scene until the authorities have established beyond all doubt it was suicide. That process, I presume, is not yet complete?'

'Why do you say that?'

'A DCI on site? My slight experience of the police suggests that CID likes to wash its hands of suicides as quickly as possible and get on with the investigation of real crime.'

'Just routine, Mr Waverley. Let's join the others.'

They went down the stairs. Jennison's form was still visible through the front door. Waverley must have entered in the few moments when the constable had been in the kitchen.

Novello looked at the newcomer curiously, then raised an enquiring eyebrow at Pascoe.

'Mr Laurence Waverley,' he said. 'In search of a loo.'

Cressida, who was sitting at the table looking pale and angry, didn't even glance up. Lavinia, standing at the window which gave a view of the extensive and heavily wooded rear garden, turned and smiled.

'There you are, Mr W,' she said. 'Would you believe it, the green peckers are still here. Do you recall the first time we met? We heard one hammering away and I was able to take you right to its nest? I wonder if they're still using that old beech. Of course it may have blown down by now. It was quite rotten ten years ago. Shall we go out and look?'

Waverley glanced at Pascoe, smiled wryly as if to say, *We each deal with death in our own way,* and said, 'Of course, my dear.'

He tried the back door. It was locked. He turned to the glass-fronted key cupboard on the wall under the electricity supply box, but before he could touch it, Pascoe said, 'I wonder, would you mind going out of the front door?'

Once let them start opening other entrances to the house, it would become a public thoroughfare. He glanced at Novello. This was a good chance for her to have a chat with Lavinia out of Cressida's presence.

She gave a little nod as if he'd spoken the instruction out loud and set off after them. He returned his attention to the key cupboard. On its top there was a scatter of fine debris, plaster, mortar, the kind of stuff you'd expect to accrue in an old neglected house, but thicker here than on any other surface. By contrast the tiled floor beneath looked like it had been well brushed.

Behind him there was a sound midway between a sigh and a groan from Cressida. He turned, anticipating a renewed verbal assault now they were alone, but instead found her slumped forward with her head in her hands. For a second he thought she was crying but when she raised her face to him, though pale and drawn, her cheeks were dry.

'Christ, Pete, I could do with a drink,' she said.

He noted that he'd ceased to be a rank and become a name. Fair enough. She was Ellie's friend, and if there were anything to be got out of her, he guessed it was more likely to be offered to Pete than to Chief Inspector.

She rose suddenly and started pulling open cupboard doors. Lots of crockery, but the nearest thing to booze was a row of crystal tumblers. She seemed to lose interest and flopped back down again. Pascoe stared at the tumblers. Glasses left unused for any length of time soon lose their fresh-washed shine and eventually they start collecting dust. These looked like they hadn't been touched for weeks. Or months. Maybe years. Except for two.

Carefully he picked one of them up. It left a damp circle on the shelf as if it had been recently washed and put back not quite dry.

Last night, thought Pascoe. Probably last night someone in the maternity party had wanted a glass of water. Then washed the glass – two glasses – and put them neatly back in place? Not likely, not with them all running around, in Dalziel's elegant phrase, like blue-arsed fleas.

'Pete,' said Cressida helplessly, 'is there something wrong here or am I just being a pain in the arse for nothing?'

He replaced the glass and closed the cupboard, taking his time. Resisting the urge to get irritable because grief had provoked someone into being a pain in the arse was easy. Resisting the equally dangerous urge to be open in response to a simple emotional appeal was much more difficult.

He sat down opposite her and said, 'I honestly don't know, Cress. All I know is that it's my job to look for something wrong so I can be absolutely sure that nothing is. When I'm sure of that, my job's done, but it still leaves you with a brother who was depressed enough to take his own life, and you didn't see it coming. But it's no use blaming yourself. Not seeing something coming doesn't make it your fault.'

'Well, that's a real comfort,' she said with a flash of her previous aggression. 'Whoops. Sorry. There I go again. No, the real trouble is, being a Maciver's like eating out with a bunch of people so drunk no one can remember what they had so in the end it's easiest just to divide the bill so you all pay the same. In other words, we're such a fucked-up family, collective guilt is the order of the day. Not that that stops us pointing the finger at each other, of course.'

She broke off and fixed him with her huge almost violet eyes.

He said, 'Anything you can say that might help us understand Pal could be very useful.'

'Like what?'

'Well, for instance, this mimicking of your father's mode of death. What do you imagine that was all about?'

She looked doubtful for a moment then shrugged.

'Why not?' she said. 'Sitting here in the house I was born in, the house where my mother died and my father and brother topped themselves, maybe I can raise a few ghosts if I tell it like it was.'

11

Cressida

I don't recollect having an unhappy childhood so I suppose I must have had a happy one.

What I am sure of is I was happy when I was around Pal and not so happy when Pal wasn't there.

The thing was Pal and I were really close, a unit, almost twin-like, I'd say, though there were three years between us. There was nothing sexual in it, let me get that out of the way in case you're getting horny thinking this is building up to some big incestuous passion scene. OK, we used each other like biological diagrams when we were trying to get to grips with all the where-do-babies-come-from stuff, but when we moved from theory to practice, we both looked elsewhere. Easy in Pal's case. He was always drop-dead gorgeous. I reckon at least half of my friends wouldn't have been if I hadn't been his sister.

My mother. I was eleven when she died. Periods just started, teens ahead, the age when a girl starts needing her mother most though she imagines she needs her least. Mum was one of those quiet little women you don't notice is there until she isn't. Then you start thinking of all the things you could have done or said to let her know you loved her. That's after you've stopped blaming her for dying, of course.

She'd not been well since she'd had Helen three years earlier. I know girls are expected to go all gooey and maternal when they get a little sister, but maybe there was too big a gap between us. Or maybe it was because Mum had such a bad time, ill through much of the pregnancy and a long hard labour. She was never the same afterwards. She seemed washed out, exhausted, and Helen was a mewling, puking baby who caught everything a baby can catch. Finally though she came through it all. It was like she'd got everything over early and all at once. I don't think she's had anything worse than a cold since she was two and a half. I half believe Mum looked at her, thought, that's you safely out of the woods, relaxed her hold on life, and just slipped away.

Heart failure, the doctors called it. You can't get much vaguer than that. After I stopped blaming her for dying, I blamed Helen. And of course my father.

Daddy never seemed to be around much, which could be why I was so close to Pal. I've got photos of Mum and Daddy together, of course, but it's a funny thing, I don't have any picture of them together in my memory. Not one.

After Mum died, Aunt Vinnie moved in with us for a while. She wasn't quite as eccentric then as she is now, but well on the way. An eleven-year-old girl's capacity for being embarrassed is pretty high and I found Aunt Vinnie acutely embarrassing. I'd have a couple of friends round to the house to play records and suddenly she'd burst in and insist we all went out into the garden to see a lesser twitted willie-warbler, and when we got there it would have gone and we'd hang around for ages waiting for it to come back despite the fact that it was minus two and raining. Girls at school started flapping their arms and whistling whenever they saw me in the playground. I hated it.

But I was talking about Daddy. He needed someone to look after Helen, I can see that. And Vinnie wasn't the answer, not in the long term. Also he needed someone to look after the house. And above all, I realize this now, he needed someone to look after him. Sexually, I mean. He was a big vigorous man and to be honest I don't think he'd been getting much if anything since Mum gave birth to Helen. I was only a kid but growing up fast and girls have an instinct for that sort of thing.

The perfect answer would have been a housekeeper-cum-nanny who fucked, just a matter of advertisement, careful selection, and the promise of a specially big Christmas bonus.

But Daddy was the great businessman. He saw a way to get all three without having to pay out a penny in advertising or wages.

He got Kay.

What were her motives? Not love, I don't believe love. She was younger than I am now, with a good job and great prospects. What the hell was there about a middle-aged Yorkshire businessman with a gammy leg and three kids to attract her? Remember Jane Eyre and Mr

Rochester, you say. Listen, there was nothing romantically mysterious about Daddy, believe me. OK, his father – my granda – was all Irish, but in Daddy the little green genes had long since lost the battle with Yorkshire pudding. Pal was convinced it was some kind of set-up. Ashur-Proffitt were dead keen to get their hands on Maciver's and when Daddy played hard to get, instead of upping the ante, they told Kay to up her skirts. Why did she have to go the whole hog and marry him? Maybe they wanted someone close in there to keep an eye on him in case he still tried to meddle with the way they were reorganizing the company. Maybe she saw the chance of setting herself up after a couple of years with a nice nest egg as a rich divorcée. Maybe she was prescient and foresaw a future as a merry widow.

I don't know. I just know that Pal and I could see from the start that she was doing this purely for herself. The thought of her in my mother's house, in my mother's bed, using my mother's things, made me ill.

She soon caught on that she hadn't got Pal and me fooled, so she concentrated on Daddy and Helen. Four years old, what do you know? She'd lost one woman who devoted the whole of her attention to her. Now here comes another apparently willing and eager to do the same. Helen took to her like a fly to jam. As for Daddy, I don't know what she was doing to him in bed, but he was besotted. Pal and I did what we could by way of resistance, but we both knew we were on a loser.

It was worse for me, I think. Pal was fifteen, his life was full of things that took him out of the house. You know what boys are like at that age. It was all girls and football. We were still close but maybe not the way we'd been a couple of years earlier. Kay's arrival threw us back together, which was the only good thing you could say about it. But it also separated us because I decided I couldn't put up with having to share a house with her all the year round and I spoke to Daddy and told him I'd changed my mind about going away to school.

He'd been keen for both of us to go to boarding school when we moved into secondary education. Pal had refused point-blank. He said all his mates were going to Weavers and that's what he wanted too. When it came to my turn, I followed suit. I'd just started there when Kay came on the scene. Suddenly, boarding school didn't seem such a bad option. I talked it over with Pal and he said he'd miss me but he understood why I wanted to go and there'd be the hols to look forward to. So I went.

From my point of view it turned out great. I was a bit homesick at first, then I thought of Kay and got over it. I soon made friends and pretty soon I started to enjoy myself. I wrote to Pal, of course, describing all my adventures and he wrote back, telling me what was happening back here. But he never mentioned Kay. It wasn't till a lot later that I found out what had been going on almost from the moment I left.

I don't know if she really fancied him. It wouldn't have been surprising. Like I say, he was a hunk in the making by the time he was twelve; in his case the gangly spotty stage hardly lasted a year, and suddenly, in his teens, there he was, a dish fit for a queen. And there was always something a bit royal family about Kay. You know, quiet, controlled, never a hair or a word out of place. The royal family like it used to be. And maybe the idea of having father and son turned her on. I felt from the start she was a bit of a sexual athlete. It doesn't matter how prim and proper the exterior, a woman can usually tell.

Or maybe it was just that it got up her nose when he and I made it so plain she didn't take us in and we didn't like her. She tried the all-girls-together-let's-be-friends approach on me but gave up when she saw it was getting her nowhere. With a boy it's different. You men, all of you in your teens, and some for a long time after, once a woman gets hold of your dick, no matter what your personal circumstances or feelings, you're lost. I know. I've tried it and it works. God didn't give us much in the battle of the sexes but He gave us that.

So she went after him.

She'd bump into him accidentally on purpose. Or he'd be passing the bathroom and she'd come out with a towel over her shoulders, everything on show, and wink at him as they passed. Or she'd be sunbathing topless on the lawn and ask him to rub some sun oil on her back.

Pal didn't know what to do. How do you tell your father something like that? And things weren't so good between them anyway. I think Daddy had some crazy notion of his boy making good in the business world and wresting back control of the old family firm, but from an early age Pal made it clear he wasn't interested in that kind of work. He never took to rock climbing

either or game shooting, and sometimes he'd deliberately put on a real Irish brogue and say he supported
the IRA just to get up Daddy's nose. So now when he'd
have really liked to be able to talk to Daddy, it was
pretty well impossible, especially on this subject. So he
had to suffer in silence and when he did let his antagonism towards Kay show, Daddy would tear a strip off
him for his bad manners!

And there was another complication.

Pal genuinely found Kay's behaviour repellent, I'm
sure of that. But he was a young man, full of rising sap,
and though he'd never admit it, I could see that despite
himself he found it exciting too. It all came to climax,
literally, one day when she followed him into the shower.
From the sound of it she intended to go the whole way,
but for once she underestimated her powers of provoca-
tion and he climaxed before she could get him into her.

This time I was hot for him to tell Daddy but still
he wouldn't. He was too deeply shamed. That's something you have to understand about Pal. He could come
across as pretty laid-back, even cynically amoral, but
underneath it all he was a good caring human being.
I know that sounds like sentimental hokum, but I can't
think of any other way of putting it. Anyway, he made
me promise I'd keep my mouth shut too, and I did. But
only as far as Daddy was concerned. I'd made no
promise about not talking to Kay and I confronted her
one day and told her loud and clear what I thought of
her and I made it plain that if I ever got the slightest
hint she was sniffing around Pal again, I'd tell the
world, damn the consequences.

And that was it. After that it was Cold War between us. I did my best to be polite when Daddy was around but he must have noticed the chilly atmosphere. Fortunately Pal went up to Cambridge soon afterwards (to read Art History, which Daddy made clear he thought was a waste of time) and with me away at school, it was easy to keep contact down to a minimum. But I guess she knew the game was up as far as we were concerned and decided her best bet was to get out of the marriage with maximum profit to herself before one of us let the world know the kind of depraved bitch she was. I think the first thing she did was turn off the sex with Daddy, to put him in the right frame of mind for a generous divorce settlement. I can't say this definitely of course. It's not the kind of thing a man like my father would discuss with his teenage daughter. But I could see they were all over each other in the first two or three years. I remember being horrified at the thought that she might get pregnant. Her baby around the house! God, what a prospect! And I'm sure Daddy was dead keen to start a new family with her. But it never happened. I suspect that Kay made damn sure it never would happen!

Anyway, eventually I could see things had really cooled between them. I was at home for the spring half-term and Daddy definitely wasn't himself. He was distracted, worried, angry, frustrated, all kinds of things. God knows what she was putting him through, but it was something he was finding it hard to deal with.

I went back to school. I talked with Pal on the phone. He said he'd try to get home and have a chat with

Daddy, though he didn't hold out much hope. Daddy wasn't a man for heart-to-hearts. He rang me back a week or so later. He said he'd been home but it turned out Daddy was away for a couple of days. I think Kay might have come on to him again but he didn't want to talk about it on the phone. But he said he was writing to Daddy, putting him straight about the bitch, and he wanted me to be ready to back him up in case Daddy looked to me for confirmation. Like I say, I was ready and willing. Then only a couple of days later I was called to the head's study and given the news.

Kay had taken off to America with Helen and Daddy had blown his brains out.

Oh, I know that she claimed it was just a trip arranged with Daddy's full co-operation and she'd have been back by Easter, but it fell very convenient. When I saw Pal, he confirmed what I'd guessed, that something had happened when he went home earlier in the month. She'd made another big play for him. Once again he'd threatened to tell Daddy, and this time he'd gone through with it. But he suspected that Kay for once had taken his threat seriously and got in first with some story that made him out a sex-crazed monster.

Well, it must have all blown Daddy's mind. Generally he was a tightly controlled man, screwing down the hatches to keep everything inside. But sometimes you knew that all this containment meant was that the explosion was going to be nuclear when it came. I don't know what was going on in his mind. Who can ever tell about anyone? But I do know he ended up alone in this house. Kay was gone. Perhaps he doubted if she'd ever come back. And with her she'd taken our kid sister.

Daddy loved Helen. More than he loved me and Pal, I'd say. That had always been Kay's big hold over him, more even than the sex, I think. She'd made sure Helen worshipped her. The worst thing was when the dust settled, we found there was nothing we could do to get Helen out from under the cow. Daddy's will appointed Kay as our guardian. That didn't affect Pal – he was already in his majority, and I was in hailing distance of my eighteenth too. I even went and stayed with dotty old Vinnie just to make sure I kept myself completely out of the bitch-queen's clutches. But Helen was only nine. Kay was legally entitled to hang on to her, and that's where Helen wanted to be.

Pal wanted to bring everything out into the open in an effort to prove Kay wasn't a fit person, but in the end he took advice which was that to make accusations without firm evidence could just be counterproductive. Better to go down the alternative route and argue the other undeniable strikes against her bringing up Helen, which were that, not being a British citizen, she might decide to go back to the States and live, and Daddy certainly wouldn't have wanted Helen brought up over there. Also if Kay got re-married, and her new husband took against Helen, the fact that there was no blood relationship would make it a lot easier for Kay just to dump her. I'm not sure what the outcome might have been, but suddenly she got married to her boss, Tony Kafka, who turned out to be willing to legally adopt Helen. Also he said that he didn't anticipate moving out of England in the foreseeable future and in addition they gave a firm undertaking that Helen's education would be entirely in the UK.

This cut the ground from under Pal's case. Pal always suspected her and Kafka had something going before she met Daddy, and that it didn't stop after the marriage. But no proof, and anyway it was water under the bridge. Naturally, Helen grew up thinking we were the villains of the piece, but, give Kay her due, she didn't overdo it. She had nothing to gain by an open row with us. The closest we came to that was when she proposed that Moscow House be put on the market. She had no personal interest – Daddy's will left it to the three of us – but as guardian she had Power of Attorney for Helen. Me, I'd have probably gone along with this – I found the place really creepy after Daddy's death – but Pal was adamant. No sale. He reckoned he'd lost every other battle with her, but this one he wasn't going to lose. It was the family house, he said, and should remain in the family till all three of us were in a position to make an adult decision with no outside interference, meaning of course Kay.

Once Helen got to eighteen and got herself married, she soon made it clear she still wanted to sell and Pal dropped his objections, so now it's on the market. Not much interest so far, but eventually it will sell, and when you look at how property prices have shot up in recent years, maybe it wasn't so silly from an investment point of view leaving it be all this time.

As for Kay, she's still very thick with Helen, of course. Don't know how she felt about the improved relations between us and Helen – the house sale going ahead, Pal and Jason playing squash – but she kept out of our hair. Mine anyway. I got the impression Pal might have run across her somewhere, he was still so full of anger whenever she was mentioned. And I knew how he felt when I saw her last night, which was the first time in ages we'd met. It all came flooding back. OK, I was full of booze and terrified of what we were going to find out about Pal. But that didn't explain my reaction. I saw her and I knew what I've always known, that there's a darkness in her that she can't control or hide. She goes out in the daylight, but she belongs to the night.

You said you wanted to understand Pal's frame of mind, why he imitated Daddy's death. I can't help you there, not with anything definite anyway. But one thing I will say. I've no idea how and I can't really explain why, but I'm absolutely certain if you look deep enough you'll find that that cunning manipulative American bitch is somewhere behind my darling brother's death.

12

lunch at the Mastaba (1)

Two hundred miles to the south, Tony Kafka had fled from the dining room of the Mastaba Club as soon as his phone rang, knowing from previous experience how much the members (referred to disrespectfully in St James's circles as Mastabators) disliked being reminded that the Old Queen was dead.

His host watched him go. His name, not unfittingly, was Victor Warlove. His job (how fittingly was a matter of debate) was Under-Secretary in the Department of Overseas Aid. He was a short man, very stout, even his head was stout, and also completely bald, a deficiency he balanced by wearing a Harris tweed suit so hairy, you could have sheared it and got yourself a matching rug.

As if chosen deliberately for contrast, the other man remaining at the table was very thin, very tall, and so smooth of person and suit that a housefly would have found it hard to land on him. This was Timothy Gedye, one of whose passports described him as a civil servant but whose actual job was as hard to get a purchase on as his person.

Warlove picked up a carafe and filled his companion's glass with a wine bright as arterial blood, saying as he poured, 'I often wonder what the Vintners buy one half so precious as the goods they sell.'

Gedye said, 'Perhaps you should change your trade, Victor.'

He had the kind of English face whose mouth only moves under the thin lower lip, spilling each perfectly enounced syllable to drift floorwards like a dried leaf and rustle into a corner.

'And deprive my country of my services? Wouldn't dream of it, dear lad. So, what do you think of him so far?'

'Without prejudice, I'm getting the faintest butterfly-in-the-neighbouring-meadow feeling that our friend's heart may no longer be in it.'

'Oh dear,' said Warlove. 'I do hope you're wrong. He has been a valuable colleague for many years. But I've noticed radical changes in so many of our transatlantic cousins since that sad business, what do they call it? Ten eleven?'

'Nine eleven,' said Gedye.

'That's the one. Was a time when profit and patriotism went hand in hand, you couldn't have one without the other. All changed, all changed. Back in the sixties it used to be commies in the cupboard, now it's terrorists under the bed.'

'I think our friend has particular reason for wanting to swim in the mainstream,' said Gedye. 'What do you know about his background?'

'Not a lot. No idea where he went to school. Not Eton, else I would have known. Winchester perhaps? They have a thing about foreigners.'

Sometimes even Tim Gedye did not know when Warlove was joking.

'I meant his racial background,' he said.

'What's that then? Czech family, first or second generation American, I'd have guessed.'

'We don't guess. Not Czech. Those cheekbones and that nose are not, as you might imagine, Slavic. The family name is, or was, Kafala. Or perhaps it wasn't.'

'You chaps may not guess but you don't mind speaking in riddles,' said Warlove.

'Sorry. His background is Arab, not European. In Islam *kafala* means something like sponsorship or providing support and sustenance, the latter quite literally as it comes from a root word meaning to feed. *Kafala* is their form of looking after homeless, abandoned or orphaned kids. It bears some superficial resemblances to Western adoption, but there are significant differences. In *kafala* the child acquires no automatic inheritance rights, and it has to retain its own family name. You may treat the child as a member of your family and you may even love it like a member of your family, but it is strictly forbidden that you should ever try to fool people into thinking that he or she is in fact a member of your family.'

'Fascinating,' yawned Warlove. 'And no doubt, ultimately, relevant.'

'Indeed. It seems that sometime in the twenties, Kafka's grandfather was discovered wandering around the shed on Ellis Island, age five or six, unaccompanied and unaccounted for. Whether his name was Kafala or something like it, or whether he got called Kafala because he was taken care of under the system, is impossible to say at this remove.'

'And the change to Kafka?'

'That came after the war. Tony's father was drafted in 1943. Good record, got wounded, mentioned in despatches, fitted in well. But when he came out, he quickly realized that not even a Purple Heart stopped a dark-skinned fellow called Kafala from being relegated to the bottom of the social pile. In the army a bit of bad handwriting on his records often resulted in his being called Kafka by mistake. It hadn't seemed to matter all that much in the camaraderie that develops among fighting men, but back in civvy street a bit of experimentation probably quickly revealed that a suntanned Central European called Mal Kafka stood a lot higher up the heap than a brown Middle Eastern called Amal Kafala.'

'Our Tony's basically Arab then? No wonder he's been such a star out there.'

'Indeed. But like his father before him he has

been totally converted to the American dream and, like most converts, he perhaps feels the need to make up in devotion what he lacks in background.'

'Needs to wave a bigger flag, eh? How about religion? Not Muslim, is he?'

'Not so we've noticed. But one thing seems clear from his history, especially with regard to his wife. He may have lost the name, and probably never had the religion, but the concept of *kafala* still plays a large part in his philosophy. Looking after homeless and parentless children. Excuse me.'

A slight agitation was visible to the left of Gedye's breastbone.

'Not having a coronary, are you, old boy?' enquired Warlove.

Ignoring him, Gedye spoke into the air.

'Yes?'

He listened, frowning, and said, 'How certain are you, Larry? . . . I see . . . That puts a different complexion on things . . . Question is, how did he know? Wasn't there some detective . . . ? Yes, check it out. But no action, not while there's still a good chance Mrs Kafka's friend can sit on things.'

Warlove looked round at the other diners. No one was paying any attention.

Marvellous thing, hands-free technology, he thought. While the Mastabators objected vehemently to phones ringing in the club rooms, the sight of a fellow diner apparently talking to himself was too commonplace to cause concern.

'More wine, Tim?' he said. 'Not bother, I hope? Too old for bother.'

'A slight tremor along a thread. Coincidentally on our friend's patch.'

'Oh dear. Do tell.'

Gedye told, concluding, 'Fortunately I have one of my spiders handily placed to keep the vibrations under control. I'm more concerned about the degree to which our American friend could agitate the web by trying to abandon it.'

'Tony's sound, I'm sure of it,' said Warlove, with the slight irritation of a man who doesn't like bother. 'And even if he wobbled, old Joe Proffitt would soon steady him up. He's rock solid.'

'Perhaps. But he may soon have other things to occupy him. Post Enron, the Securities and Exchange Commission have issued their people with fine-tooth combs. A rumour has reached me that they have A-P in their sights.'

'They'll need very sharp eyes to find any nits on Joe,' laughed Warlove.

'I wish I shared your confidence. They could move very soon. And I understand Proffitt has just ordered himself a luxury yacht with space on it for a golf driving range.'

'There we are then. Must feel safe as houses.'

'Hubristic, I think, is the term you're looking for. Ah, here comes our nomad friend at last.'

'And so does the soup. Perfect timing as always, Tony. Everything all right?'

'Fine. My wife. Sorry.'

'The lovely Kay. You're a lucky man. Do tuck in.'

Kafka dipped his spoon unenthusiastically into the gently steaming grey-green pond which had been set before him. True, the wine at the Mastaba was always excellent, but it needed to be. How anyone could call the food here good – or indeed call it food! – baffled him. But if you ate in a tomb, maybe you should expect your soup to be Stygian.

He glanced around the gloomy dining room. It was the size of a small cemetery. Most West End restaurateurs would have crowded a couple of hundred diners in such a space, but here there were no more than twenty discreetly spaced tables, only half of them occupied and most of those by solitary men. Probably resting actors, if his theory about the real nature of the place was right.

As always, soup was the signal for serious business to begin.

'By the way,' said Warlove. 'Hear there was a little bit of bother up your way last night. Anything we should worry about?'

'Under control,' said Kafka indifferently. He'd been right when he guessed they'd know about it. They thought they knew everything. But if they thought they knew what he was thinking, they were wrong.

'Pleased to hear it. Now let's talk turkey, as you chaps say. It's the first day of spring, isn't it? Time of the big clearance sales!'

'You reckon?' Kafka put his spoon down. 'I've been thinking. Maybe it might be a good idea to cool things for a while, in view of the current state of things.'

'The current state . . . ?' said Warlove, faintly puzzled.

'The great war against terrorism, all that stuff – haven't you noticed?'

'Indeed yes. And a splendid marketing opportunity it is, too. Do you have a problem you're not sharing with us, Tony?'

'I'm just wondering in the circumstances whether it's wise . . .' He took his spoon, raised a gill of soup to his lips, then spilled it back into his bowl untasted. Gedye was regarding him with that English look which, without being a sneer, somehow suggested a sneer was on the assembly line.

'Whether it's right,' he concluded defiantly.

'Right?' said Warlove, enouncing the word with great care as though it were foreign. 'In what context would that be?'

'In the context of right and wrong,' said Kafka. 'Is there some other fucking context I don't know about?'

Warlove and Gedye exchanged glances.

'My dear boy,' said the stout man. 'Normally I don't do ethical debate over lunch, even though

I did carry off the prize for Religious Knowledge three years in a row at school. But what I will say is we know *we* are right because we know *they* are wrong. Right? And because they are wrong, every last damn one of them, we either have to trade with none of them or with all of them. We choose all of them because our masters tip us the wink that, if they didn't move in polite circles like the UN, they'd choose all of them too. No harm done because everybody's treated the same. What could be fairer? Now, let's talk plans. Know what I was thinking the other day? Uzbekistan. No idea where it is. Been there once, I think, some fact-finding tour – they do like a jaunt, these ministers – didn't take much notice, but there's a chap in my office always going on about it. In the end I had to listen or send him to Easter Island, and you know, it rather sounds our sort of place. What do you think, Tony? Uzbekistan. Got a real Harry Potter ring to it, hasn't it?'

He smiled like a benevolent uncle at a favourite nephew's birthday party and refilled Kafka's glass.

I mustn't let him do this to me, thought Kafka. He's trying to get me thinking he's Bertie Wooster and I can run rings round him! Remember, over the past fifteen years, this asshole has made A-P huge profits and almost certainly made himself a millionaire into the bargain.

But what made the fat bastard tick? Could it actually be some form of patriotism? There were guys back home who did stuff ten times more outrageous and still claimed they were flying the flag.

More importantly perhaps, what was Gedye doing here with his undertaker's eyes?

'Uzbekistan,' he said cautiously. 'Sounds interesting for the future. But right now it seems to me we need to look at our Gulf shipments. There's one due out of the plant this weekend and I've been wondering whether maybe we should put it on hold.'

'Now why on earth should we do that?' asked Warlove, apparently amazed.

'Because sooner or later there's going to be another goddamn war out there,' said Kafka. 'And it's not going to look good if the place is littered with Ash-Mac gear.'

'Hardly likely. Lessons have been learnt, old boy. They could follow the paper chase we lay nowadays twice round the globe without coming close to Ash-Mac's.'

'That's not my point. It's whether we should be doing this at all with a war on the cards. In a lot of people's eyes, it's a war that's started already.'

'My dear chap, don't get so upset. You take these things far too seriously. What was it Aristotle said? War is just a marketing campaign pursued by other means.'

'Aristotle said that?'

'Onassis,' laughed Warlove. 'Let's have a toast!'

He raised his glass so that the blood-red wine caught a dim ray of sunshine which had somehow sneaked in through the high dusty casement.

'The toast is war,' he declared. 'Gentlemen, I give you war!'

13

hairy chests

As they drove away from Moscow House, Pascoe and Novello exchanged notes.

'The aunt is a few twigs short of a tree, but she's not a nut,' said Novello.

'Nutty enough to go hunting green wood-peckers in the garden of the house where her nephew has just topped himself,' said Pascoe.

'Yeah, that was a bit tedious,' said Novello with the distaste of an unreconstructed townie for rural pursuits that didn't involve taking your clothes off. 'Would have suited Hat Bowler down to the ground. Any word when he'll be giving us the benefit of his expertise again, by the way?'

'When he's ready,' said Pascoe shortly, detecting a certain lack of sympathy for her absent colleague. 'But given that your ornithological small-talk is indeed small, what did you find to chat about?'

Novello noted the shortness and was tempted to be short in reply. Doing extra work because a colleague was injured in the course of duty was one thing. She'd been there herself. But finding your recreational time eaten into because same colleague's girlfriend had died in a motor accident two months ago was a pain. Whoever started these New Men getting in touch with their feelings had a lot to answer for. The only feelings she wanted her men to get in touch with were . . .

She shoved the thought to the back of her mind for later delectation and said, 'Well, that's what I was going to say. OK, we crawled through the undergrowth, looking for birdshit and such, but in between all the twitter, I got the feeling I was getting a good quizzing. Like they felt having little junior me away from big important you was a good chance to find out what was really going on.'

'They?' said Pascoe.

'Yes. If anything, the old geezer was worse. She asked questions direct. He was much more oblique. Wouldn't surprise me if he'd done a bit of this before.'

'He was a VAT investigator,' said Pascoe. 'Did he go for a pee at any time?'

She hid her surprise and said, 'No. I think I'd have noticed.'

Pascoe drove in silence for a while. He'd been pleased to get Cressida separated from the others, but it had never occurred to him that they too might be pleased to get Novello to themselves. He recalled an early warning the Fat Man had given him. 'I can see you're a clever bugger, lad. But are you clever enough to see there's other buggers cleverer? Present company not excepted.'

He said, 'So what did they want to know?'

'The bird lady just wanted details. How exactly had her nephew died? Just how similar was it to her brother's death? The old boy seemed more interested in checking if we thought there was anything dodgy about the business.'

'To which you were suitably noncommittal, I trust.'

'Couldn't tell him what I don't know, sir,' she said spiritedly. 'But he struck me as bright enough to wonder without encouragement why a DCI and DC are sniffing around the *locus in quo*.'

Give him his poncy Latin back.

'Could be,' said Pascoe. 'Check him out, but don't waste time on it.'

'What about the sister – Cressida, is it? Anything there, sir?'

'A trip down memory lane. Thinks her brother was some sort of closet saint. Confirms most of what he said on tape after their father's death. If there were a tape, of course.'

'Seems like every time there's a death in Moscow House, someone points a finger at the stepmother.'

'Yes. Though I suppose to make the copycat exact, it ought to be Sue-Lynn Maciver the finger's pointed at this time.'

'We going to see her too, sir?'

He noted the *we*. Despite herself Novello was getting interested.

'Oh yes. When she rises from her bed of grief. And little sister when she gets over giving birth. More visits to look forward to than a Jane Austen heroine newly arrived in Bath! But our first call is on Jason Dunn who got stood up.'

Novello yawned, a Pavlovian reaction to mention of Austen, who'd been a favourite of her convent-school teachers, the lack of Roman doctrine being more than compensated by the equal lack of sex, violence, bodily functions and male interiorization. To the young Novello, all these dull women seemed to do was visit other dull women and have dull conversations with them. By contrast, discovering the Brontës had been like a pubescent lad chancing on his father's copy of *Playboy*. OK, the books were a bit long-winded in places, but if you persevered, you soon realized that, even though hairy chests were never actually mentioned, Heathcliff and Rochester certainly had them, while it was hard to believe Mr Darcy had any body hair at all.

Her flagging interest in the case was hugely revitalized when they arrived at the Dunn's house and she saw the hunk who opened the door. This was serious sex on the hoof, about six feet four of it, gorgeous to look at with the kind of body that tapers down from broad shoulders to a dinky waist then broadens out just enough to give promise of a deliciously compact ass. Though her own preferences generally ran more to the solid weight-lifting type, she didn't mind making an exception in the event a Greek discus thrower came along, especially unshaven and looking like he'd slept in the clothes he wore.

His eyes ran over her as she guessed they did over any new woman. Nor, she assessed, was he put off by her bromidic clothing. To see the choc bar not the wrapping was one of her own talents. But what conclusion he came to wasn't on offer today. His main focus of interest was the DCI.

'Mr Dunn!' said Pascoe. 'DCI Pascoe. We met at Moscow House. Hello again. And many congratulations.'

'Thank you,' said Dunn, returning his smile.

'I wonder if I can have a quick word.'

The smile faded.

'I was just going to tidy up and then head back down to the hospital,' he said.

'Won't take a minute,' said Pascoe, stepping lightly but inexorably into the house. 'How're they all doing?'

'Fine, they're fine.'

'Good. And you're enjoying the lull before the storm.'

'The storm?'

'When you bring them home. I remember what it was like with one, and you've got two. It's great, of course, but there's no getting away from it, things feel a bit hectic to start with. You got some help? Your family? Helen's?'

They were in a big lounge now. Novello liked the colour scheme. Lovely deep soft furniture and a shag-pile carpet your feet sank into. Shag pile. Oh yes.

'My mother's dead,' he said shortly. 'And Helen's family haven't exactly been close over the years. Except for Kay. Mrs Kafka, Helen's step-mother. She's said she'll come round and help out all she can.'

'Oh good. Not the wicked stepmother then?'

'No, she's great. What did you want to talk to me about, Mr Pascoe?'

'Just to get the sequence of events right about the other night. The coroner likes his tees dotted and his eyes crossed. So if you don't mind. Better now before the family comes home and you don't have a minute!'

Pascoe was glad Ellie wasn't around to hear this breezy old-hand dad act, but it seemed to relax Dunn.

'OK. Shoot.'

'Your squash game was arranged for seven, is that right?'

'Yes.'

'And you usually met at what time?'

'Twenty to, quarter to seven.'

'In the changing room?'

'Yes.'

'And what time did you start getting worried at?'

'When it got to seven, I suppose.'

'He was usually pretty punctual, was he, Mr Maciver?'

'Not bad.'

'So what did you do?'

'I tried to ring him on his mobile. But it was switched off. Then I tried his shop phone. No reply. Finally I rang Sue-Lynn, that's Mrs Maciver, to see if she'd heard anything.'

'That would be about five past seven?'

'Five past, ten past.'

'And then, a bit later, I rang home in case he'd left a message there.'

'A bit later?'

'Towards half past.'

'Not straight after you rang Sue-Lynn?'

'No. I wandered round a bit, thinking he might still turn up.'

'Then you went home?'

'Not straightaway. Wednesday nights Kay comes round, it's a sort of girls' night in and I know how much Helen looks forward to it, so I didn't go home till after nine.'

'Find anyone else to have a bang around with?' said Novello.

'Sorry.'

'I thought you might have looked for another partner. You did have a court booked, didn't you? Evenings, a free slot's worth its weight in balls.'

'You play, do you?' said Dunn, giving her the look again.

'Oh yes. Nothing like it to keep a girl fit.'

'You're right,' he said, giving her a smile. 'I'll watch out for you, maybe we can have a knock around some time.'

'Did you find another partner?' interrupted Pascoe, who'd noted with distaste but also with envy the easy way Dunn had slipped into chat-up mode.

'No, I didn't,' said Dunn. 'I mean, I didn't try. I just had a cup of coffee and mooched around till nine, then headed off home. I hadn't been in long when Sue-Lynn rang. When she said you lot had been asking after Pal too as the keyholder to Moscow House, I thought I should get round there to see what was going on.'

'Why?' said Pascoe.

'Sorry?'

'Why did you think that?'

'Because Pal was missing, obviously.'

'But there can't have been any reason to make you think the two things were necessarily connected. I mean usually when the police ask for a keyholder it's because they believe someone has attempted to break in to a property.'

'Yes, but . . . look, I don't really see the point to your question.'

'I'm just wondering if you had any particular reason to be concerned about Mr Maciver. More than simply that he'd stood you up for a game of squash. The coroner will be very interested in his state of mind, you see, and if you can tell us anything that might throw light upon it . . .'

'No, not really. Last time I spoke to him he seemed perfectly normal.'

'When was that?'

'Tuesday, I think. I rang to check that our game was on. He said, yes, usual time. And that was that. Look, Mr Pascoe, he did kill himself, right? There's not anything else you're trying to get at here.'

'Like what, Mr Dunn?'

'You tell me, you're the cop,' said Dunn, suddenly aggressive.

'Just routine enquiries,' said Pascoe placatingly. 'Thank you, Mr Dunn. You've been very patient. We won't hold you back any more. And congratulations again.'

'Yeah, congratulations,' said Novello.

In the car she said, 'Nice house. Nice furniture. You say he's a teacher?'

'That's right. PE at Weavers.'

'Pay must have improved since I last checked.'

'I think his wife must have inherited quite a bit. You were interested in becoming a teacher, were you, Shirley?'

'No. My parents and my teachers and my parish priest were interested in me becoming a teacher,' she said. 'Wouldn't have minded if it hadn't been for the money. And the kids, of course.'

'Not to mention the dinners.'

'Yes, I'd rather you didn't mention the dinners.'

They laughed. It was a good moment. Good moments were possible, she admitted with slight surprise, even with the Mr Darcys of this world.

14

see me!

Back at the station, Novello was amused to see the DCI move past the Super's door if not exactly on tiptoe, certainly with a stealth that confirmed her judgment that their morning activities did not have the seal of divine approval.

But flee him as you will down the nights and down the days, the Hound of Heaven will get you in the end, or a bit earlier if he answers to the name of Dalziel.

Pascoe's sense of relief at reaching his office unintercepted drained away as he saw protruding from the centre of his desk a paper knife, impaling a sheet of paper across which was scrawled **SEE ME!**

A natural indignation at being summoned like some errant schoolboy rose in his craw. His pride demanded that he didn't rush to present himself instantly so he busied himself examining his in-tray. An evidence bag had been deposited there containing a snakeskin wallet and labelled *Wallet found in jacket of deceased male, Moscow House. Examined and recorded. Nil.* Meaning that, as far as Forensics were concerned, it could be handed over to the grieving widow.

He opened it and shook its contents on to the desk. Not much. Eighty pounds in notes. Three credit cards. A couple of business cards inscribed *Archimagus Antiques*, plus phone, fax and e-mail numbers. And another card, this one an eye-catching gold, embossed in red with the name *JAKE GALLIPOT* and a Harrogate phone number. He thought of ringing it but what the hell for? It would just be procrastination. His risen indignation had declined to a queasy heaviness in the pit of his stomach. Time to face the music. He looked around for some talisman to wear against the impending discord. Finally he opened his desk drawer and took out the tape cassette which Novello had brought to him that morning.

Slipping it into his pocket, he headed for the headmaster's study.

Edgar Wield was standing by the door, his fist raised to knock. He froze as Pascoe approached and mouthed the words, *See me?*

Pascoe nodded and motioned to indicate, you first.

But before they could sort out precedence, the door was flung open to reveal the Arch-fear in a visible form.

'Here they are then, Beauty and the Beast! Don't hang around blocking my light. Step inside, do!'

They advanced and the door crashed shut behind them. The Fat Man then moved to his desk and sat down heavily.

Pascoe contemplated taking a seat also, just to show that senior officers were not to be treated like naughty children, but that would have left Wield standing.

It's always nice to have a good reason for not doing what you're afraid of.

'Right,' said the Fat Man, fixing his Medusa stare on Wield, 'let's start with thee. What were you doing skulking around the Golden Fleece this lunchtime?'

'I weren't skulking. I went there for lunch,' said Wield.

'Not skulking? Coming out of the car park, clocking me in the conservatory, then going into retreat so's you could spy on me through the hedge, and that's not skulking? Nay but, I'd like to see you when you do skulk! Who sent you there?'

His gaze flickered to Pascoe as he spoke.

The neurotic old sod thinks I'm having him tailed! thought Pascoe in amazement.

'No one. There's a booksellers' convention at the Fleece. Edwin's doing the arrangements and I went there to meet him for lunch,' said Wield. For the first time Pascoe found himself envying the sergeant's face. Like a cobbled farmyard, it stayed the same no matter what kind of crap got dropped on it.

'Oh aye?' said Dalziel. 'So not skulking, just dropping in to enjoy a literary fucking lunch. Very reasonable.'

He said this like a Scottish judge pronouncing a Not Proven verdict.

His gaze shifted to Pascoe.

'Chief Inspector, I ran into Paddy Ireland just now. Asked him how he were doing with the Maciver suicide. He said as far as he knew you were still dealing with it. When I went to check, I found out that you'd got Novello to dig up all the files on old Pal's suicide ten years ago, then you'd gone walkabout with her. So spit it out, lad. What the fuck's happened that I don't know about?'

What would dare to happen that you didn't know about? wondered Pascoe.

He said, 'Nothing as far as I'm aware, sir.'

'Nothing? Nay, lad, surely summat must have happened to make you decide to ignore my instructions to offload this business on to Uniformed where it belongs. Or did you just forget mebbe? Early onset of Alzheimer's?'

'No, sir. Just some small loose ends to tie up before I pass it on to Ireland.'

'Small loose ends? So the department grinds to a halt just so's you can play with your small loose ends? Come on then. Give us a flash of one of them.'

Pascoe played the list mentally. It didn't take long and nothing in it was going to be a hit.

'Motive,' he said. 'No note, just the Dickinson poem, which only shows how religiously he was following his father's example. And I think the coroner will want some elucidation of motive a little more persuasive than filial piety.'

'Elucidation of motive? Filial piety? Oh, Pete, Pete, why do I always think you must be scraping the bottom of the barrel when you start coming up with the fancy phrases? *Balance of the mind disturbed*. By what's not our concern. Could be his hamster died or he met the Virgin Mary in Tesco's and she said, "You've been a naughty boy." Doesn't matter. We're cops, not trick cyclists. So that's one loose end the less for you to fiddle with. Any more you want to waggle at me?'

Pascoe, who knew when to stop digging, shook his head.

'Good,' said the Fat Man. 'I'm glad that's sorted. So you'll be handing over everything you've got to Paddy Ireland, right? Straight off. Then mebbe you can get down to the job you're paid for. Now bugger off, the pair of you.'

Wield turned instantly and opened the door.

Pascoe, though he knew like Wellington that sometimes the only choice is between retreating in good order and running like hell, hesitated, feeling deeply resentful.

'Got another fancy phrase for me, Pete?' said Dalziel, not looking up from the file he'd opened.

'No, sir. Just thought you might have been wondering where this had got to.'

He took the Maciver interview tape out of his pocket and tossed it on to the open file. Then he followed Wield out, closing the door very quietly behind him.

They made for Pascoe's office in silence and sat down, looking at each other po-faced for a few moments. Then they began to grin, and finally laughed out loud, but not too loud.

'Beauty and the Beast!' said Pascoe.

'Aye. Wonder which of us he thinks is which,' said Wield.

'No competition. You got off light. I'm the Beast. But it doesn't make any difference. Jemmy Legs is definitely down on both of us. You weren't really trailing him, were you?'

'Do I look mad?' said Wield. 'Pure accident. I went to the Fleece like I said and there he was, having a drink.'

'So why's he reacting like a bishop caught in a brothel?'

The sergeant's face, which was to rough diamonds what rough diamonds are to the Kohinoor, gave next to nothing away as he replied, 'Mebbe the bishop were embarrassed to be caught doing good by stealth. Pete, I know nowt about this Maciver business except what I heard on the news. So what's gone off?'

Pascoe gave a succinct account of the previous night's events. When he'd finished he sat back and said, 'So there it is. Your turn now.'

'For what?' said Wield.

'To fill me in on what you know and I don't. And don't play hard to get. Just spit it out, eh? If I don't like it, I can always wipe it up with thy tie.'

The line was Dalziel's. He tried the voice too, not very successfully, but at least it made Wield relax and smile.

'I'm not playing hard to get,' he said. 'I'm just not sure I've really got owt to tell you. You weren't around when old Pal Maciver topped himself, were you?'

'No. But Andy filled me in last night.'

'Did he now? Then you'll know it all.'

'Wieldy, get on with it or I'll get you crossed off Ellie's Sticky Toffee Pudding list.'

'Threats, is it? All right, here it is for what it's worth. The Super knew Maciver, the father I mean. Didn't like him much. And he knew his wife too, the Yank I mean. Her he liked a lot.'

'Liked? In what sense?'

'Every sense. He once said to me, "Never thought I could fancy a skinny lass, Wieldy. Like mackerel. Don't matter how tasty the flesh is if you've got a mouthful of bones. But yon Kay's a grilse. Full of jilp. Fit for any man's plate."'

Wield's mimicry was spot on, but of course these were his native wood-notes wild, whereas Pascoe was an off-comer, and educated at that.

'You're not saying he put her on his menu, are you?'

'Doubt it. I reckon you'd need a finely tied fly

to get a rise out of our Kay, and Andy tends to fish with sticks of dynamite. But there's definitely something. He knew her before her man topped himself, that was clear.'

'Did he now? And this showed, did it?'

'Oh yes. There was a proper investigation, don't misunderstand me. It was a bad situation, you could feel it from the start. There was bad feeling in that family, lot of crap flying around. Usually is when a rich widower marries a young bride and then snuffs it a few years on, but this felt worse than usual. Andy sat on it. Hard. He appointed himself Kay's guardian angel. It was the son, last night's copycat, who was chucking most of the dirt. Andy choked him off somehow. I expected sparks to fly at the inquest, but I've seen livelier games of carpet bowls. Don't know how the old sod did it, but he did.'

'I thought something like that must have happened,' said Pascoe.

He told Wield about the tape.

'And that was the one you tossed on to his desk just now?' asked Wield.

'That's right.'

'You made a couple of copies, but?'

'Actually, no.'

'Probably wise,' said Wield after a little reflection. 'No point trying to blackmail a man who's got pictures of the Chief Constable in a backless ball gown dancing the tango with the Mayor.'

'You're joking,' said Pascoe alarmed.

'Yeah, I'm joking,' said Wield. 'It were the veleta. Pete, I think the reason Andy got his knickers in a twist about me clocking him at the Golden Fleece was he was having a drink with Kay Maciver. Kay Kafka as she is now.'

'Ah,' said Pascoe.

They sat in silence for a moment, then he asked, 'Anything bother you about what happened ten years ago, Wieldy?'

'I didn't think so,' said Wield slowly. 'You know me, I'm a details man and all the details added up. Man used to being top of the heap finds himself not even on the heap any more. And the heap's changed out of recognition.'

'How so?' asked Pascoe.

'Maciver's, even at its biggest and most successful, were always a family firm. They employed a lot of men but no one ever said good day to Mr Pal without getting good day back with his name attached. No clocking on or clocking off. If you were late, it were noticed. If it happened again you were spoken to and if you didn't have a good excuse, you were warned, but if you did have an excuse, like a new babby disturbing your night so that you overslept, you got offered help. Knocking you up or a change of shift, mebbe.'

'Very patriarchal. And the new regime?'

'Modern streamlined, highly efficient, one warning and you were out on your neck. There wasn't a strong union presence because, under Maciver, there had never been the need for one.

Now the Yankee management was showing Thatcher the way to bash any sign of union life on the head. I checked out the parent firm, Ashur-Proffitt, on the net.'

'You were thorough,' said Pascoe. 'That mean you were worried?'

'If a job's worth doing . . .' said Wield. 'Big corporation, getting bigger, lots of international subsidiaries, financially very buoyant. Made lots of dosh, made enemies too. There were this website, Junius it called itself . . .'

'Junius?'

'Aye. Mean something to you?'

'Vaguely. Junius was the pseudonym of some eighteenth-century guy who used to write letters and articles saying the government was a load of crap. Had a go at the judiciary and George the Third too, if I remember right. They never found out who he was, not for certain, anyway.'

'Sounds like that's where this Junius got his name. According to him at least one of the Ashur-Proffitt subsidiaries was mixed up in that Arms for Iran scandal, remember, when that guy North got done for sanction-breaking, arranging for arms to be sold to the Iranians then subsidizing the Contra guerrillas in Nicaragua with the profits. Lot of stuff about Iraq too.'

'You must have dug deep to get on to this Junius site,' observed Pascoe.

'Not really. Whoever set it up had managed to get a hyperlink in the A-P website, so when you

259

clicked on *More Information about our overseas operations*, suddenly you were transferred to Junius with all this stuff pouring out at you.'

He sounded admiring. To Pascoe, computers were like cars, a tool. In his youth he'd felt fairly competent to deal with minor car troubles, but that had been in a gentler age when lifting up a bonnet revealed as much space as engine. Now every inch was so crammed he had to get his manual out to locate the oil dipstick. With computers he didn't even have that distant memory to console him. Only Andy Dalziel made him feel expert. In face of real experts, like Wield and his daughter, Rosie, he felt only resentful awe.

'All that this stuff did,' continued the sergeant, 'was show me how fast and how far Ash-Mac's had moved from the old Maciver's. It must have been a real shock to Pal senior's system when he realized this. OK, they gave him a token job, but I guess it took a bit of time for it to sink in just how token it was. Mebbe he reacted by trying to throw his weight around till someone took him aside and spelt it out that he was yesterday's man. He must have felt betrayed, Worse, he must have felt he'd betrayed all his employees. I could see how he might have cracked.'

'So, no loose end?' said Pascoe.

'None that I could see. Mebbe none that I wanted to see,' said Wield. 'I put it out of my mind and never gave it another thought. Not till

I caught the news this morning. And I found myself coming over all bothered by it, just like I had before. I thought hard about it, couldn't see any reason why I should be bothered, so I put it out of my mind again. Next thing, I clock Andy head to head with Kay. And suddenly I'm bothered again. And now he's throwing his toys out of the cot.'

'And his teddy's weighted with lead shot,' said Pascoe. 'Wieldy, sorry to go on about it, but you're quite sure this doesn't just come down to sex?'

'You think, mebbe 'cos I'm gay, I can't crack all the hetero codes?'

Pascoe opened his mouth for an indignant denial, changed his mind and said, 'Could be. Took me a long time to suss you out, remember?'

'I remember. But it's not relevant. I don't think the super plays the sex-for-favours game. And anyway, from what I've seen, Andy's not Mrs Kafka's type.'

'Her type being . . . ?'

Wield described the scene with Manuel.

'He went up there looking like he was hot favourite for a gold, came down like he hadn't even got a bronze,' he concluded. 'And seems he's not the first.'

'What?'

'There've been others. Not a lot, three or four, well spread out.'

'How the hell do you know this?'

'Doreen, one of the reception girls, comes from

Enscombe. I got into conversation with her afore I left.'

'God, Wieldy, you live dangerously. If Himself ever found out you were asking questions . . .'

'No chance,' said Wield. 'In Enscombe we know how to keep things close.'

'Except to other members of the coven, eh? What precisely did Doreen say?'

'Not much. Same types: young fellows who really fancied themselves was how she put it. One was a trainee manager – didn't know the others, but they all had two things in common: they started by acting like they were God's gift and they ended chewed up and spat out – her words.'

'Fascinating,' said Pascoe. 'Makes you wonder about that stuff on the tape.'

'Does it?' said the sergeant. 'Well, I'm glad it's nowt to do with me. So what are you going to do with your loose ends, Pete? Try and tie 'em up?'

'Do I look crazy?' said Pascoe. 'Over to Ireland this goes, and good riddance.'

To show he meant it, he started reassembling the contents of Maciver's wallet, which he'd left strewn across his desk.

Wield said, 'What's that?'

'Deceased's wallet and watch for Paddy to return to the widow,' said Pascoe.

'No. That –'

The sergeant's finger touched the golden business card.

'Just a card in his wallet. Why?'

Wield turned the card round and read out the name.

'Jake Gallipot. I thought that's what it said. Hard to miss, even upside down.'

'Mean something to you?'

'There was a Jake Gallipot used to be a DS in South Yorkshire twelve, thirteen years ago. I knew him quite well. Was on a sergeants' course with him and our paths crossed a few times after. Invalided out, in inverted commas. I heard he'd set up some kind of PI agency in Harrogate.'

'It's a Harrogate number,' said Pascoe. 'And there can't be many Jake Gallipots around.'

Wield looked at him and said, 'So?'

Pascoe took the card and replaced it in the wallet.

'So I'll mention it to Paddy Ireland,' said Pascoe firmly. 'I've had it with Maciver. RIP, Palinurus! And with a bit of luck maybe I can too!'

LEEDS COLLEGE OF BUILDING LIBRARY

15

two-mile jigsaw

Kay Kafka sat at her computer looking at the Ashur-Proffitt website.

The site designers, alerted to the Junius invasion, had acted quickly and all traces had been removed. But Kay didn't doubt he'd be back.

When the encroachments first started to occur, she'd looked up Junius in an encyclopaedia. Her motive had been idle curiosity. There she read that the true identity of the writer of the Junius letters had never been established but the most likely suspect was a man called Sir Philip Francis.

'Snap,' she said.

She believed in fate, she believed in various kinds of divination, but she didn't believe in coincidence.

It had to be him. Not Philip Francis, but Francis Phillips. The coincidence was too great. And Frank certainly had cause to hate Ashur-Proffitt, just as she had cause to hate Frank.

She'd debated whether to share her suspicion

with Tony but decided against it. OK, Frank had done her wrong. But that was in another country. And besides, he'd given her the greatest joy in her life and could hardly be held responsible for its greatest pain.

Not that she hadn't taken revenge from time to time, but its nature was generic rather than particular. From the way Tony had talked this morning, he was no longer all that concerned to discover Junius's identity but the reaction of some of his associates could be extreme . . . She pushed the thought from her mind.

Tony had rung a couple of hours earlier, saying the train had been held up, some trouble on the line, God knows how long it was going to take. He had sounded tired and irritable. She had asked him how the meeting had gone. He had snarled something indecipherable except for the words *slug* and *Warlove*. Then they'd been cut off, or he'd disconnected.

It sounded bad. She knew how little he'd been looking forward to this trip and if he'd let the slug see the doubts that had been troubling his mind with increasing frequency, it couldn't have been a comfortable meeting. But her sympathy for her husband was tempered by more personal considerations. His talk of 'going home' troubled her. This was home now, all the more so since last night. He must see that. So in a way she and Warlove could find themselves allies in this, neither wanting Kafka to chuck in the towel and head for retirement. And what would he do back in the States anyway?

Write his memoirs, he'd once replied when she'd questioned him.

She prayed he hadn't hinted that, not even in jest, to Warlove. She had no illusions about the likely consequences of such a threat.

No, she reassured herself. Tony wasn't stupid. But he was brave and that was sometimes almost as bad.

She switched off the computer, stood up and went into the lounge. Here she sat down, hesitating between the television and the scatter of newspapers on the table by her chair. Finally ignoring both she picked up the chunky volume which lay beside the papers. On its cover was a sketch of an oval-faced woman, lips pursed, mouth slightly askew, hair severe, expression unsmiling. If the artist had caught her well, here was a woman contained, giving nothing away.

Except wisdom to the devotee.

Kay closed her eyes, opened the book, put her forefinger on the page, opened her eyes and read where her finger had rested.

1742
The distance that the dead have gone
Does not at first appear –
Their coming back seems possible
For many an ardent year.

And then, that we have followed them,
We more than half suspect,
So intimate have we become
With their dear retrospect.

Twice she read the poem, her face as unrevealing as the sketch on the cover.

Distantly she heard a door open and close.

She closed the volume, stood up, went to a sideboard on which stood decanters and tumblers and poured two fingers of scotch into one of them.

A moment later the lounge door opened and Tony Kafka came in.

She handed him the drink, which he downed in a single gulp.

'Hi,' he said, handing the glass back for a refill.

'Hi. Hard day?'

'You could say that.'

'You shouldn't let Warlove get to you.'

'Not just Warlove. I told you, Gedye was there too.'

'So? He's on our side, isn't he?'

He finished the second scotch.

'Is he? I'm not sure which side is which any longer. Things have changed back home, but not here, not with guys like Warlove. Business as before. The Brits call nearly all the shots now but you can bet your sweet ass when the shit hits the fan it will be all "Tut-tut, old boy, what can you expect from a Yankee business?"'

'You didn't say this?' she asked, alarmed.

'Not in so many words. Hey, don't look so worried, they probably got the message, but they don't kill the messenger any more, not when he's got scary friends back home. I spoke to Joe on the train, put him in the picture far as I could on an open line. I said I'd ring him again when I got back here, but we agreed we ought to bring forward next month's strategy meeting, so I'll be heading home in the next day or so.'

Home, she thought.

She said, 'You will be careful, won't you, Tony? Don't go too far out on a limb till you're sure Joe and the others are with you, not sitting on the ground watching Warlove and his friend get to work with a chainsaw.'

'Don't you worry about me. I'm always the one sitting with my back to the wall so I can watch the saloon door.'

He had filled his glass for the third time and was looking at it doubtfully. Gently she took it from him.

'You'll need a clear head if you're going to ring Joe again.'

'Yeah, you're probably right. I had a few on the train. Fuck all else to do. These fucking trains! The Brits have invented the time machine – you get in and when you get out again centuries have passed!'

'What caused the delay this time? Leaves on the line?'

'Not leaves,' he said. 'Flesh. Some sad bastard decided to step in front of us.'

'Jesus. Man? Woman?'

'Who knows? For a change, we were really moving when it happened. I guess they'll be doing a two-mile jigsaw to put the poor devil together again. Time of the year for suicides, it seems. First Pal, now this. Don't they say such things go in threes? Who's next, I wonder?'

She went to him and put her arms around him. He stood quite still in the embrace, neither responding to it nor attempting to move from it.

In the entrance hall the old American long-case clock began to strike midnight. Tonight its brassy chime sounded particularly triumphant, as if to say, *At last I've got someone to hear.*

March 22nd, 2002

1

870

It was the kind of spring morning to make a young man's fancy turn to thoughts of new baked bread and home-made marmalade, while Ellie Pascoe's matutinal kiss was more than usually passionate, resulting in Peter Pascoe arriving late at work, but lighter of step and lighter of heart than usual.

The lightness of step was not enough to get him past Paddy Ireland's ground-floor office undetected, and the lightness of heart didn't last long either.

'Morning, Pete,' said the inspector. 'Got a letter here. Think it must be yours.'

'Got my name on it, you mean?' asked Pascoe.

'Not exactly.'

He turned toward his desk and stood pointing at an envelope like the Spirit of Christmas Yet to Come inviting Scrooge to look at his own headstone.

The envelope bore a local postmark with yesterday's date and was addressed in crude block capitals to

'It says Maciver,' Pascoe objected. 'We've agreed that's your business.'

'It says murder,' retorted Ireland. 'That's CID business.'

'I see you opened it all the same. What's the message?'

Ireland picked up a clear plastic evidence bag containing a sheet of A4 paper.

Printed on it in the same hand that had written the address was the number **870**.

'What's this?' said Pascoe. 'A date? A hymn number? An alternative solution to the mystery of Life, the Universe and All That?'

'Don't ask me,' said Ireland. 'I don't do riddles. Pete, correct me if I'm wrong, but it seemed to me out at Moscow you had some real doubts about this business.'

'All of which have faded away, like the youth of the heart and the dew in the morning. I am a doubt-free zone. By Order. Even if I were burning up with doubt, I hardly think this would have poured oil upon it. Dotty anonymous letters full of specific accusation with lurid detail are par for the course after a suicide, so there's certainly no need to get our knickers in a twist about a number.'

He offered the bag to Ireland, who ignored it as he opened a file on his desk.

'Got the post mortem report,' he said. 'Confirms death by gunshot.'

'Self-inflicted?'

'They found nothing to suggest different. Except maybe traces of diazepam in Maciver's system.'

'Diazepam?' The second half of the twentieth century had put drugs in all their forms firmly on the detective curriculum and Pascoe did not need to reach for his pharmacopoeia to know that diazepam was used in the treatment of nervous disorders, its best known commercial manifestation being valium. 'How much?'

'You can read it yourself,' said Ireland, turning the file towards Pascoe, who didn't even glance at it as he said, 'Paddy, this is for the coroner, not me. Most likely explanation is Maciver took a valium tablet to steady his nerves before he blew his head off. Fairly commonplace. Probably had a stiff drink too. Were there traces of alcohol?'

Ireland nodded.

'There we go then.'

'They found alcohol in his blood. We didn't find a glass in that room. I've double-checked the SOCO report and photos. No glass.'

'So he washed the drug down with a drink straight from the bottle.'

'No bottle either.'

'So he did it in his car on the way to Moscow. And if there's no bottle in his car, he tossed it out of the window. Or maybe he had a drink in the

275

kitchen. Come to think of it, when I was there yesterday, I noticed a couple of glasses looked like they'd been used recently.'

'He used two glasses for his drink then? And the bottle?'

'That's for you to work out, Paddy.'

'Sounds more like your line of country,' said Ireland stubbornly. 'Look, at least read the post mortem report, then you can initial the file, just to keep the record straight. And you might as well initial that you've seen the letter too. Then I'll be covered if things go pear-shaped.'

He smiled as he spoke to take the edge off the implicit threat. Irritated, Pascoe picked up the file and the evidence bag and bore them upstairs to his own office where he tossed them into his in-tray and tried to concentrate on other matters.

But the tragedy at Moscow House kept rattling around his head.

Last night, Ellie had asked him about the case and he'd told her it was out of his hands, making a comic story of himself and Wield being summoned to the head's study. He'd been rather taken aback when she'd said, 'Maybe the trouble is you'd much rather it were murder than suicide, Peter.'

'Why do you say that?' he asked.

'Perhaps because you find murder much easier to deal with.'

He'd lain in bed thinking about this. And she was right of course, damn her.

OK, most murder involved huge human tragedy, but you could usually sideline this in the wholehearted pursuit of the perpetrator. It was the murderer's state of mind you tried to reconstruct in your efforts to get close to him or her. This was cerebral work. No matter how deeply the effort to get inside the killer's psyche engaged your emotions, it was still your intellect calling the shots.

But when you got to thinking about the mental condition of someone who was so deep in darkness that death was the only escape route, then you were chasing your own soul's tail round and round. He had woken this morning with the image of Pal Maciver slipping his toe through the noose of string still in his mind till Ellie had banished it in most delightful fashion.

Now it was back.

Stop it! he admonished himself. Put it out of your mind. Diazepam . . . it meant nothing . . . he'd offered a perfectly good explanation to Ireland. As for the letter, clearly the work of some malicious trouble maker who couldn't even be bothered to invent some good juicy accusations!

870 . . . it was meaningless . . . 870 . . .

He closed his eyes and tried to relax into free association. After a while he found that 870 was being partnered by another number, equally obscure.

1062.

Where the hell had that come from?

Then he remembered.

He stood up and stooped to unlock his cupboard and from it took the bin liner containing the relicts of Pal Senior's suicide. From it he plucked the volume of Emily Dickinson's poetry. It was still open at the blood-spattered page containing poem 1062.

He turned the protesting pages back till he came to poem 870:

> *Finding is the first Act*
> *The second, loss,*
> *Third, Expedition for*
> *The 'Golden Fleece'*
> *Fourth, no Discovery –*
> *Fifth, no Crew –*
> *Finally, no Golden Fleece –*
> *Jason – sham – too.*

He read it through three times and was still no closer to a meaning – either the poet's or the sender's.

No matter. It was an extra feather of doubt fluttering down on to the scales. At the very least he wanted another set of initials on the file.

Carefully he copied out the poem on a sheet of paper. Then, carrying it in his hand like a talisman, he headed for Andy Dalziel's room.

2

flying with the cormorants

Hat Bowler had woken up later and feeling better than he had for many weeks. And his dream memory hadn't been of dark forests but of budding fruit trees enchanted with nesting birds. He'd also been very hungry, and when an examination of his fridge had revealed nothing to tempt a starving hyena, it had seemed not so much reasonable as inevitable that ten minutes later he should find himself in his car, driving towards Blacklow Cottage.

It was only as he got within a couple of miles of his destination that he took that further step towards normality which involves acknowledgment of the feelings, needs and rights of other people.

What the hell did he think he was doing?

OK, the Crunch Witch had invited him to drop by any time. But she wasn't the Crunch Witch, she was Miss Lavinia Maciver, a slightly eccentric lady of a certain age and a certain class, probably conditioned in infancy to atone for the relief at seeing the back of an unwelcome visitor by pronouncing some token platitude about hoping they'd return soon. Even in her worst-case scenario, she could hardly have envisaged that her invitation would be taken up the following day!

Plus there was the fact that she was in the midst of a family tragedy. What was it that guy Waverley had said? He tried to separate the words from the powerful memory of marmalade. Something about some relative topping himself?

No way could he just turn up on the doorstep again today.

Yet the MG was whipping along the narrow country roads at undiminished speed, and instead of looking for somewhere to stop and turn, his mind was busy devising a succession of reasons for his visit, each less plausible than the last.

That small advance party of his personality which had its beachhead on the shores of normalcy was able to observe wryly that the main body still had a long way to travel, further proven by the fact that he didn't just keep on driving when he saw that the spot by the roadside where Mr Waverley had left his car the previous morning was already occupied.

And not by Mr Waverley either (with whom he could at least claim a brief acquaintance), not unless he owned an Alfa Spider as well as a Jag. This didn't seem likely, but then the S-type had come as a surprise, so why not?

He parked the MG behind it, got out and touched the Spider's bonnet. Still hot, so not long arrived. Nice to find himself acting like a detective again. Time perhaps to act like a social being and not inflict his personal troubles on a near stranger and her newly arrived friend.

He heard voices from the house, one raised and shrill, the other just a murmur. Then two figures emerged from the door.

One was Miss Maciver, the other presumably her guest.

She was a woman aspicked in her mid twenties, good looking in a glossy magazine kind of way, blonde hair carefully natural, face as perfectly painted as a Victorian portrait, olive silk blouse over firm free-standing breasts and matching jeans hugging slim hips and long legs.

She was the one doing the shrill shouting.

'I don't believe you. You're all the same, you Macivers. Twistier than a hangman's rope!'

She tottered towards the car, her high narrow heels completely unsuited to the rutted track. As she got nearer, Hat could see that beneath the cosmetic mask her face looked wrecked.

Miss Mac followed her, leaning rather more heavily on her stick than she had done the previous day and saying, 'Do come back inside, my dear. Honestly, I know nothing about it. I'm sure if we talk quietly . . .'

'Talk? I'll be letting my solicitor do the talking, soon as I find one to replace that cheating bastard Pal hired. Takes a one to hire a one, doesn't it?'

'Please, dear, don't talk like that. I'm sure there's been some misunderstanding. Pal had his faults, I know, but basically he was a good man . . .'

'Good man! Jesus! Good for you, maybe. Don't play the innocent with me, Vinnie. He came out to see you last week for the first time in God knows how many years and you're trying to tell me it wasn't to talk about the will? I'll get it overthrown on mental incompetence. I've got someone working on it. And if the powers that be want more evidence than father and son topping themselves in exactly the same way, I'll send them out here to take a look at you and all those fucking birds!'

She reached the Spider, dragged open the door and slid inside. She didn't even look at Hat, but the Crunch Witch did, giving him a welcoming smile as if she'd been expecting him, and murmuring, 'There you are, Mr Hat. Go through into the kitchen. Make yourself at home.'

Then she stooped to the window of the Spider, which the other woman seemed to be having difficulty starting, and said, 'Believe me, my dear, I have no interest in depriving you of what is yours. As for Pal's visit here, I assure you money wasn't mentioned. All I can say is I detected something peculiarly valedictory about it. He was never a great one for wildlife, you'll know that, but this time he seemed to take a real pleasure in watching the birds and I recall he said to me, "Maybe you got it right after all, Vinnie, opting for the birds." And the birds too, they seemed to feel something. They usually don't much care for people who don't much care for them. Like yourself. But they fluttered around him almost as if they sensed something . . .'

Hat, obediently heading down the track to the cottage, heard the woman in the car screech with laughter that had little amusement in it.

'You talk like that in court, Vinnie, and I can't see me having any bother proving you've all got a screw loose!'

Miss Mac started saying something else but Hat was now entering the cottage and as he passed down the corridor he was out of earshot of both women.

Through the open kitchen door he could see on the table the teapot, the butter dish, the marmalade jar and half a loaf of bread covered with a tea towel that a pair of ingenious bullfinches were trying to drag off under the expectant gaze of perhaps another half-dozen birds. As he entered, a fugue of warning notes and flutter of wings signalled possible danger, but he was flattered to see that only a couple fled outside, the others merely retreating to perches on the ceiling beam or the curtain rail.

He poured himself a mug of tea, removed the tea towel and sawed himself a thick slice of bread.

Miss Mac had said make yourself at home. He replaced the towel but left the crumbs of his sawing scattered on the table surface and even before he'd finished adding layers of butter and marmalade to his slice, two or three tits were competing for this largesse.

He was on his last slice (last because there was no more) when he heard the Spider's unmistakable roar as it took off at speed which merged with the sound of another engine coming near at a more sedate pace. A Jag, his well-tuned ear judged, and a few moments later he was able to compliment himself on his audile acuity when Miss Mac came into the kitchen followed by Mr Waverley.

Hat nodded, unable to speak through his full mouth and Mr Waverley smiled as he took in the scene – the empty breadboard, the scavenging tits, Scuttle sitting on Hat's shoulder investigating his hair.

'I have this sense of *déjà vu*,' he said. 'But I'm glad to see it's not all gloom and doom, despite the sad circumstances.'

Hat, feeling this as reproach, swallowed hard and said, 'Miss Mac, I'm sorry, I shouldn't have stopped when I saw you had a visitor . . .'

'Oh yes, Sue-Lynn, my poor nephew's wife. She seems to think I'm part of some plot to deprive her of her inheritance.'

Oh God. Ignoring the fact that she was in the middle of some family bereavement was bad enough. Interrupting a meeting with the widow – no wonder she looked wrecked – was even worse.

'But I presume that at least she has her facts right as regards the will,' said Waverley.

'She said she'd spoken to their solicitor, who confirmed there had been changes, and not to her benefit.'

'Now why would your nephew have done that, do you think?'

'I don't know. Sue-Lynn did go on rather wildly about Pal having set some private detective to following her, so perhaps she was involved in some naughtiness,' said Miss Mac with slight distaste.

If they wanted to discuss intimate family matters, it was certainly time to go, thought Hat.

He began to rise, saying, 'This is really rude of me, turning up when you've got family troubles . . .'

'And you don't think that rushing off now you've scoffed all the loaf will be even ruder? Tut tut, where were you brought up? Mr W, please join us.'

Before he could answer, a mobile phone shrilled in the inside pocket of his overcoat causing alarm in the birds and a moue of disapproval from Miss Maciver. Or maybe it was a wince of pain. She seemed to have aged several years since yesterday.

'Forgive me,' murmured Waverley, heading

through the kitchen door into the garden as he pulled out his phone.

Hat said, 'Miss Mac, are you OK?'

She said, 'I've been better. That's how it is with MS, good days, bad days.'

She saw his blank expression and glossed, 'Multiple sclerosis. You didn't know? Why should you? Don't look so shocked. It's not going to kill me. Not for a long while yet. Excuse me a moment.'

She went back up the corridor, turning into one of the front rooms. A moment later he heard the strike of a match. Perhaps she was lighting a fire against the chill morning air. It was warm enough here in the kitchen but perhaps if you had MS you felt the cold. He knew very little about the illness. Except that there was no cure.

Unable to rest in his chair he stood up and looked out of the window. Waverley was standing in the middle of the garden, taking his call. With his smart town clothes, he should have cut a slightly ludicrous figure but he didn't. Snatches of his conversation drifted through the open window. *Good day . . . yes, yes, I see . . . yes, that I can do immediately . . . no problem, if it comes to it, which I hope it won't . . . yes, as for the other, a little assistance would be helpful there just for the heavy work . . . I'll wait till I hear from you . . . oh and there's one more thing . . .* At this point he glanced round, caught Hat's eye, smiled, and moved further away out of earshot.

Hat sat down again and a couple of minutes later Waverley re-entered the kitchen, followed shortly by Miss Mac. To Hat's relief and pleasure she looked a lot better and said, 'That tea must be cold and stewed by now, let's get some more on the go, shall we?' and set about refilling the kettle.

Waverley said, 'Sorry, Miss Mac, but I won't be able to accept your kind invitation. In any case I only called to confirm that you were well, which I see you are, and in good hands too. So I shall say good morning. Nice to meet you again, Mr Bowler.'

He turned and moved away swiftly, his slight limp masked almost completely by the use of his hawk-headed stick.

Miss Mac didn't see him out but sat herself down at the table and said, 'Now, Mr Hat, it's only thee and me, as they say in these parts.'

'Yes. I'm sorry to . . . look, I really only drove out here because . . .'

She smiled encouragingly at him and said, 'Because . . . ?'

He reached for a reason, found one.

'Because I noticed your kitchen garden needed a bit of digging over to get it ready for planting and I wondered if you might need a hand . . . I'm sorry, I didn't mean because you can't do it yourself . . . I mean, I didn't know about . . . and maybe you can . . .'

She laughed out loud at the tangle he was

getting into and said, 'If we're to be friends, you'll have to stop being embarrassed by my state of health. Yes, you're quite right, my MS does make it much harder for me to look after my patch of garden. On the other hand, I'm rather particular who I let loose in it. I've got friends living out there, you see. So before I give you a spade, and while we're waiting for the kettle to boil, why don't you tell me something about yourself?'

'I don't know . . . what is it you'd like to know?'

'Anything you'd care to tell.'

He inhaled a deep breath, not sure what words it was going to carry when it came out.

'First off,' he said, 'my name's not actually Mr Hat – Hat's just something friends call me, because of my surname, which is Bowler . . .'

He paused, recollecting that Waverley had just used his name in farewell, and trying to remember when he'd mentioned it to him. Miss Mac didn't seem to notice the pause but came in, smiling, with, 'Hat Bowler! How very droll. But Miss Mac is equally droll in its own way, and I am content to remain Miss Mac so I hope you'll be happy to remain Mr Hat. Names make things real, which is why it's best only to name the things you love or at least like. I know Scuttle is Scuttle. I am completely unable to name my Member of Parliament.'

They shared a smile, then Hat recommenced, still with some uncertainty.

'OK. I'm Mr Hat and if I seem to have been

behaving a bit odd both times we met, it's because . . .'

He paused again, uncertain how detailed an explanation he was expected, or wanted, to give, and again she came in.

'Because you have been very unhappy, doubtless through some deep personal loss which you will never forget but are beginning to get over. I haven't learnt a lot about human beings during my life, Mr Hat, or not a lot that I care to remember, but what I do know is that where the appetite is healthy, the hurt body or mind is healing. I am not so impertinent to be curious about the details of your loss, but I am delighted to note how much bread you have put away. Talking of which . . .'

She stooped to the oven, pulled open the door and, using a tea towel to protect her hands, took out a huge cob, brown as a chestnut. As she set it on the table she said, 'While this cools, what I'd really like to hear about yourself is how you came to get interested in birds.'

Hat smiled.

'The important stuff, you mean.'

'That's it, Mr Hat,' she said gravely. 'The important stuff.'

She sat down opposite him once more. The two blue tits, Impy and Lopside, fluttered down to sit one on each shoulder, and looked at him expectantly. He knew it was food they were hoping for, but they felt like an audience.

He said, 'I think it really began when I was six

and we were on holiday on the Pembrokeshire coast and one day I was sitting on the beach and the sea was quite rough and I saw this pair of cormorants hurtle along, only a foot or so above the waves. I remember trying to be them, trying to feel in my imagination what it must be like, moving through the air at that speed and every time you look down, seeing that wild ocean surging and frothing and foaming beneath you, so close that whenever a wave breaks, it must seem like it's reaching up to pull you under and you can feel the spray spattering cold against your belly . . .'

'And did you succeed in finding out what it must feel like, doing that?'

'I think I just about imagined it physically,' he said slowly. 'But since I grew up, I've come to know exactly what it's like. It's like living. That's what it's like.'

Like living.

She looked at him compassionately for a moment then said, 'And then, Mr Hat? Back in Pembrokeshire. What happened next?'

'I suppose I went paddling with my brothers, or we went to buy an ice-cream. But I never forgot. And after that whenever I saw a bird, any kind of bird, I tried to see things as it saw them, and after a while I got interested in what they were really doing rather than just what I liked to pretend they were doing. And that was great too, learning all that stuff. But I've never forgotten the cormorants, never forgotten that when I was six I flew with them for a little while. Does that make sense, Miss Mac?'

On the hob the kettle began to sing and the tits, as if recognizing this was a signal for renewed feasting, joined in.

'Oh yes, Mr Hat,' said Miss Mac, standing up to make the tea. 'It makes more sense than almost anything else I've heard in the last few days. Much more sense.'

3

going with the flow

'A poem?' cried Dalziel, infusing the word with an astonishment that made Edith Evans' *handbag* sound like polite enquiry. 'You want me to read a poem? What comes next? Listen to a sonata for two kazoos and a flugelhorn?'

But he read it, and examined the envelope, and checked out the PM report, and listened with nothing more than a steady volcanic rumbling to Pascoe's account of the other things that bothered him.

Then for a space there fell between them that silence where the birds are dead yet something pipeth like a bird, which in this case was the Fat Man's fingernails being dragged along his trouser gusset.

Finally he said, with menacing softness, 'Twenty-four hours. That's what you've got. To the sodding second.'

'Thank you, sir,' said Pascoe, making for the door.

'Hang about. I've not said what I expect you to do in them twenty-four hours.'

'Sorry, sir. I assumed it was to discover whether or not there was any criminal element in Pal Maciver's death.'

'Nay, lad. Nowt you've said makes me change my mind about that. Suicide, plain as the face on your nose, and that's penny plain. What I need you to do is find me the skulking bastard who sent that letter. There's someone out there trying to stir things up and I want the pleasure of seeing them face to face.'

'Yes, sir. Then I'd better start at Cothersley, I suppose.'

'Cothersley? Why?'

'Because that's where Maciver lived.'

Also where Kay Kafka lived. He'd spotted the Fat Man reacting.

'Then it would be bloody funny if you didn't go there to chat to the grieving widow. Shouldn't bother with the pub, but. Dog and Duck. Used to serve a decent pint, still came in a jug first time I went there, but it's all been fancified like the rest of the fucking place. Six kinds of foreign lager, all so cold they taste like penguin piss, and not a pork scratching in the house. So take heed.'

'Engraved on my heart, sir,' said Pascoe. 'Any other tips?'

'Aye, just the one. Don't get carried away. It's a lot easier to stir crap up than to get it to settle.

293

You might like to engrave that on your arse so every time you sit down, you'll remember.'

'I surely will, sir. And if I need expert advice on sitting on anything else I might find embarrassing, I'll certainly know where to come.'

The not very subtle reference to the Maciver tape popped out like a blown fuse button before he could control it.

Far from being provoked, Dalziel reacted as if this were merely confirmation of some course of action he'd been undecided about.

He reached into his pocket, pulled out a cassette and tossed it to Pascoe.

'Two sides to every tale, Peter. Have a listen to this when you've got a spare moment. Which you don't have. Twenty-three hours fifty-eight minutes, that's what you've got. Now sod off.'

Pascoe looked at the cassette in his hand as he left the room. It was brand new, so probably a copy of . . . what? Two sides, he'd said, so this had to be Kay Kafka, which made it very interesting, but it could be very dangerous too. Putting the Maciver tape into his mental recycle bin hadn't been too hard on his professional conscience. But what if this new tape revealed even more serious breaches of procedure . . . or worse . . . ?

In any case, he had no time to spare for it now. When the Fat Man gave you a time limit, you took it seriously.

He thrust the cassette into his pocket and

bellowed Wield's and Novello's names as he passed through the CID room. A Pascoe bellow was a phenomenon unusual enough to make people jump, but by the time the sergeant and DC appeared in his office, he was already on the phone, despatching the SOCO team back to Moscow House with orders to give the whole house a thorough going over, and get everything moveable out of the study down to the lab.

Replacing the phone, he filled them in on the new situation.

'It may still be nothing,' he said, 'but I want to be sure everything's been covered. Let's give Maciver the full treatment: bank and phone records, credit rating, business deals, the lot. Shirley, you get on to that. Wieldy, that Harrogate PI, Gallipot, check him out, find what that was all about. And get someone talking to the Avenue working girls tonight just in case anyone noticed anything. Oh, and Joker Jennison mentioned one in particular – Dolores, she called herself – who seemed very interested in what was happening in Moscow. I told him to track her down. See what he's done about it and kick his arse if it's not enough.'

Novello, looking as if she'd gladly volunteer for the last job, went out.

Pascoe said, 'And ring the lab, too, Wieldy. Tell them that everything to do with Moscow House is a priority. Tell them the super wants it done yesterday or he'll be down there himself to see what's holding things up.'

'Right,' said Wield. 'Any hint what you'll be doing while me and Novello are working ourselves into a muck sweat for you?'

'Coming on a bit strong, am I, Wieldy?' said Pascoe. 'Sorry, but the fat sod's given me twenty-four hours and I suspect he's using a stopwatch. Me, I'm off to Cothersley to talk to the widow. And this time, I don't care how many clerics or medics get in the way, I'll gallop right over them if I have to!'

Wield watched him go with a fond smile. Pascoe with a bit between his teeth was as formidable in his way as the Fat Man; not quite so hot at breaking down brick walls perhaps, but certainly better fitted for slipping through narrow gaps.

Novello he was pleased to see was already talking to the phone company.

'No,' she was saying. 'This is urgent. I thought people in your line of business might have heard of things like computers and fax machines. Yes, thank you. And some time this morning if it's not disturbing your social life too much.'

Good telephone manner! he thought.

He went to his own phone and rang the lab. The use of Dalziel's name got a cheeky reply, but when he offered to bring the Fat Man to the phone in person, the tone changed. Then, being a thorough man, he double-checked that the SOCO team had taken Pascoe's exhortations as to speed and thoroughness to heart.

Next he found the card with the name Jake Gallipot on it and rang the number.

The phone rang five times before it was answered. Good technique. Never let them think you've nothing better to do.

'Gallipot,' said the kind of dark brown baritone that sells things on the telly.

'Jake,' he said. 'This is Edgar Wield. Mid-Yorkshire. We met way back when you were in the job . . .'

'Wieldy! How're you doing? Great to hear from you, old son. I was just sitting here thinking about the good old days, and how I'd been silly to lose touch with so many old chums, then the phone rings and it's you! Psychic or what?'

Or what, thought Wield. Old chums? He'd never aspired to such a standing. He recalled him as a tall craggily handsome man with the sort of reassuring smile that could have sold a lot of insurance if he hadn't opted for a police career that looked set to spiral onwards and upwards. Rumour and gossip had provided a plenitude of explanation for its abrupt termination, ranging from slipping one to the Chief Constable's wife to difficulty in explaining a wardrobe full of designer suits and a second car which, as asserted by the comic sticker in the window of his old Ford Prefect, really was a Porsche.

'Nice to talk to you as well, Jake,' he said. 'But it's business, I'm afraid.'

'Private or official, Wieldy?'

'Official. Nothing to worry about. A man called Maciver, Palinurus Maciver, killed himself the night before last. We found your card in his wallet. I'm just tying up loose ends and, when I recognized your name, I thought, nice to give old Jake a ring, see how he's doing, kill two birds with one stone.'

'Glad you did, Wieldy. I read about Maciver. Tragic.' A pause. For reflection on the mutability of things? Or . . . ? 'Any idea what drove him to it, Wieldy?'

Keeps on saying my name like we're old drinking buddies, thought Wield.

'That's why I'm ringing, Jake. We just wondered if anything in the work you were doing for him might throw some light on his state of mind.'

Another pause. There's someone there, guessed Wield. Perhaps just his secretary. Then why hadn't she answered the phone?

'Sorry, Wieldy,' said Gallipot. 'I was just trying to run my mind over my responsibilities re client confidentiality. Not sure how death affects things.'

'Depends whether it's his or yours, I should have thought,' said Wield drily.

Gallipot's infectious laugh boomed out.

'Finger right on it as always, Wieldy,' he said. 'Hang on. I'll get the file.'

The phone went quiet, too quiet. He's not getting a file, thought Wield. He's sitting at his desk counting up to ten.

He joined in mentally and spot on ten Gallipot

said, 'Here we are. No, don't think it's going to be any help. Some stuff he got offered for his business. He's in the antiques trade, but you probably know that. Thought it might be a bit iffy and wanted me to check it out. That was a couple of months back.'

'And was it iffy?'

'Not that I was able to find out. I gave him my report, he paid me, end of story. My card must have just got stuck at the back of his wallet.'

No way, thought Wield. It looked pretty new, almost pristine.

'I suppose so. Thanks anyway, Jake. Oh, by the way, how did Maciver come to choose your firm? Yellow Pages job, was it?'

Wield was so casual an old CID man like Gallipot would be on to him like a shot. Slipping in an apparently unimportant question at the end of an interview when the guard was down, a question to which the interrogator already knew the answer, was an old technique. Difference here was Wield didn't know the answer and hadn't the faintest idea if it were important or not. But it was slightly curious that Maciver should have opted for a Harrogate PI rather than one closer to home.

Again the pause while Gallipot weighed the risk of giving unnecessary information against the risk of being caught in a lie. Not a risk worth taking, Wield guessed he'd decide. But the hesitation was interesting.

'I did a job for his father many years ago, not

long after I went private. I think Mac Junior said he came across my name in his dad's papers and, being a bit out of the ordinary, it stuck. So after all those canteen jokes about Pisspot and Tosspot, it came in useful, eh?'

'Certainly looks like it, Jake. Thanks for your time.'

'My pleasure, Wieldy. You ever get over this way, give me a ring and we'll get together and chew over old times. Cheers now, old son.'

Wield replaced the receiver and sat looking at it for a full minute. There was something there, but what? He'd forced Gallipot to give him the truth about how Pal Junior got on to him, but it merely transferred the question back ten years. Why had Pal Senior chosen a Harrogate PI, rather than one located in Mid-Yorkshire? Was this, or anything, worth a trip to Harrogate for a face to face? He weighed time spent against possible gain in the logical balance of his mind. It was no contest. His place was here, doing what he did best, holding things together.

Novello put her phone down, stood up and came towards him.

'That's that fixed, then,' she said.

He looked at her in slight dismay. If she'd already done all she'd been asked to do, then maybe it was time for him to move over and let the new generation in.

'So what have you got?' he asked.

'Nothing yet,' she said. 'Except an appointment

in twenty minutes with Maciver's bank manager. Got his lawyer's name too, so I thought I'd have a word with him about the will. Better to do it face to face, harder for them to pull any client confidentiality crap. Will you be here if I need to check back to you, Sarge?'

He felt a rush of relief. So, not superwoman after all, but she had the makings of a very good detective. Why hadn't he thought of the lawyer? And she was right about face to face, like Pete was right. If you wanted to be sure you were getting the truth, there was no other way.

Every so often granny really needs to be reminded how to suck eggs!

He said, 'No, I'll be out, so you'll need to ring me on my mobile.'

He picked up his phone, dialled Harrogate Police, and asked for DI Collaboy.

'Jim? Ed Wield here . . . Aye, it's been quite a time. Everything OK with you? . . . Grand. Me too. Listen, Jim, this is a courtesy call to say I'm going to be on your patch later today, visiting an old chum of yours. Jake Gallipot . . . No, that's not a courtesy call! It's just he were working for some guy here who's topped himself and I'd like to know what exactly he were doing . . . Just a hunch, probably a waste of time . . . Owt interesting, you'll be the first to know . . . Promise! See you.'

He put the phone down. Collaboy had been the DI with supervisory responsibility for Gallipot at the time of his resignation. Even though there'd been no specific charges against the sergeant, Collaboy always reckoned it was the fall-out from that affair which had kept him stuck at his current rank. The thought that someone was sniffing around his former colleague would not be at all displeasing to him and, knowing Wield's reputation, he'd pay little heed to his claim that he was coming all the way to Harrogate on a hunch.

But a hunch was all he had.

So what?

Sometimes you had to say *Stuff logic!* and go with the flow.

4

the lily and the rose

The flow Pascoe was going with took him past the Central Hospital on his way out to Cothersley.

It occurred to him that a man on his way to trample on the susceptibilities of a grieving widow need hardly feel inhibited by interrupting the joy of a newly delivered mother and he pulled into the visitors' car park. It was crowded. There must be a lot of sick people in Mid-Yorkshire. Of course the majority of people visiting the sick are not too displeased to have an excuse for turning up late, but to a man given twenty-four hours by Andy Dalziel, seconds are precious. He turned towards the main reception area, ignoring a sign which read *Staff Parking Only*, and slid his Golf between a BMW and a Maserati.

When he got out, he stood for a while looking at the Maserati, not enviously, though it was a beautiful thing, but because it brought something to mind. Then he recalled Ellie mentioning her discussion with Cress Maciver about the problems of sexual congress in the machine. He could see what she meant.

There couldn't be many Maseratis in Mid-Yorkshire, he thought. Curiously he checked the parking slot name. V. J. R. S. Chakravarty, Neurological Consultant. Well, there was no law against it. As long, of course, as Cress wasn't a patient.

As he strode down a long corridor en route to the maternity unit, he saw two figures coming towards him, deep in conversation. One he recognized immediately as Tom Lockridge. The other was a tall, slim, extremely handsome Asian.

So engrossed was Lockridge in his conversation, or rather his monologue as he seemed to be doing most of the talking, that he didn't spot Pascoe till they were almost face to face, and didn't look too pleased when he did recognize him.

'Dr Lockridge,' said Pascoe. 'Could you spare a moment?'

'I'm rather busy,' said Lockridge, looking as if he wanted to keep going.

But the other man had paused too and appeared, if Pascoe read him right, not unhappy at the chance of separating himself from his companion.

'Don't worry about me, Tom,' he said. 'Things to do before rounds. Sorry I couldn't be of more help.'

Flashing a smile at Pascoe which might have

set a more susceptible heart racing, he strode away. He was a lovely mover. Pascoe had one of his intuitions.

'Who was that?' he asked.

'Vic Chakravarty.'

'The neuro-consultant?'

'That's right. You've heard of him?' said Lockridge. He sounded genuinely interested.

'Only obliquely,' said Pascoe, smiling inwardly at the hidden aptness of the adverb.

For a second Lockridge looked as if he might be about to say something else then changed his mind. 'So what do you want with me, Inspector?'

'I'm looking into Pal Maciver's death,' began Pascoe, ignoring the demotion. 'And I was wondering . . .'

'Sorry, I really can't talk about Mr Maciver,' interrupted Lockridge.

'Why on earth not?' said Pascoe, surprised.

'Doctor–patient, you know.'

'But that's absurd. I recall you said yourself he was no longer your patient, so your only relationship with him is as the attending police doctor. So if you can't talk to me, how do you justify taking your fee?'

'Yes, of course, sorry. Different hats, it's easy to get confused. But I did put everything I observed into my report,' said Lockridge, on the defensive.

'And a very good report it was,' said Pascoe. 'Why did he cease to be your patient, by the way? His choice, or yours?'

'His. He was a private patient, you understand, so the relationship was pretty flexible, none of all that NHS form-filling stuff. Didn't see a lot of him professionally anyway, so when he announced he thought he'd take his business elsewhere for a change, it was no big deal. In fact we used to see each other more often socially, and I think maybe he liked to keep the two areas separate. A lot of people do, you know.'

'But not Mrs Maciver?'

'No. Didn't bother her. She stayed. What's all this got to do with anything, Pascoe?'

'Nothing really, except it's Mrs Maciver I wanted to ask about. I need to talk to her soon and I was wondering whether you felt she was in a fit state to answer a few routine questions.'

'Oh yes, I should think so. Still a bit upset, naturally, so I'd go easy. But she's a strong personality, very resilient. How's the investigation going? Any sign of a note, anything like that?'

'A suicide note, you mean? Not as such,' said Pascoe, interested that after his initial reluctance the doctor now seemed happy to stand and chat.

'Not as such? But there was something on the desk, I recall. A book.'

'Yes, your memory is good, there was a book.'

'And people are saying that everything was done in pretty much the same way as his father killed himself ten years ago. Any truth in that?'

'Perhaps. What's your interest, Doctor?'

'Just professional. It all suggests a severely

disturbed state of mind, don't you think? Very severely disturbed.'

'I suppose it does. But I imagine some degree of mental disturbance is in fact the norm in most suicides,' said Pascoe. 'Thank you for your help.'

He moved away. At the end of the corridor he glanced back. Lockridge was still standing where he'd left him. It occurred to Pascoe that while he didn't look suicidal, he certainly gave the impression that his own state of mind was far from undisturbed.

On arrival at the maternity unit, he was directed away from the ward to a private room. Nice going for a PE teacher's wife, he thought. Though of course she did have money of her own. And well-heeled friends, one of whom was sitting at the bedside with a baby crooked in either arm.

'Good morning, Mr Pascoe,' said Kay Kafka. 'How nice of you to come. But you were in at the birth, so to speak. Aren't they just gorgeous?'

Her words were unambiguously friendly and spoken with a smile, but he felt warned. Start hassling Helen and you'll have me to contend with.

He poked a finger in turn at the sleeping babies and made token cooing noises. He tended to be rather satirical about what he called baby-gush in order to conceal a powerful impulse to pick small children up and hold them tight and possibly burst into tears at the thought of the long haul that lay ahead for them and their parents.

'How are you Mrs Kafka? Mrs Dunn?' he said, seating himself on the other side of the bed.

In fact the woman in the bed looked a lot better than her visitor. Sitting upright against plumped-up pillows and surrounded by a scatter of glossy magazines, expensive chocolate boxes and exotic fruit baskets as well as enough flowers to keep Eliza Doolittle going for a fortnight, she could have sat for an allegorical portrait of bountiful summer. Kay Kafka by contrast was definitely autumnal, and not the mellow fruitful end either but the frost-on-lawn, burning-of-leaves, drawing-down-of-blinds end. Yet in her way she was just as lovely as the radiant English girl; the lily and the rose, the moon and the sun.

Pascoe shook the fancy from his head and turned to the business at hand.

'Mrs Dunn,' he said. 'I'm sorry to trouble you with reminders of family sorrow at such a joyful time, but I'm sure you'll understand how important it is for the coroner to have as full a picture as possible of what it was that led up to the other night's tragedy. Of course, I'll quite understand if you don't feel up to talking just yet and would prefer to wait till you got home. When will that be, by the way? I bet you can't wait.'

In fact it wasn't a bet he'd have cared to risk loose change on. He had a feeling that the sense of contentment radiating out of Helen Dunn had more to do with lying at her ease, the centre of attention, receiving gifts and congratulation, than with the prospect of getting home to start the long haul of parenthood.

She said, 'Oh that will be a day or two yet of course I can't wait but I've got to think of Jase he's got his work and I don't want him worrying about me while he's at school.'

'He's back at school already?' said Pascoe, mentally punctuating. 'I thought these days you got paternity leave.'

'I don't know I'm sure they'll be very helpful the headmaster's really nice but today there's a really important match I think it's the inter-house final or something and Jase is the only one who's got a proper referee's qualification and they need them nowadays otherwise if something goes wrong they could sue the school. Anyway Mr Pascoe please don't be afraid to ask your questions though I'm not sure how I can help you Pal and I were never close I can't recall the last time I actually saw him though since he started playing squash with Jase we sometimes spoke on the phone and I said to Jase that maybe we should have him and Sue-Lynn over to dinner sometime he was my brother after all and it was silly that we should let that old stuff stay between us after all this time but Jase said OK sometime soon but let's not rush things and Kay seemed to agree with him didn't you Kay . . . ?'

Slightly shell-shocked by this verbal barrage, Pascoe glanced at Kay, who said, 'You're quite right, dear, it's never wise to rush things. Now

I'm going to have to leave you two to your little chat. I hate to abandon these two darlings, but Tony's flying to the States first thing tomorrow so he's staying at Heathrow tonight and I promised to drive him to the station this afternoon.'

'To the States? Oh isn't he lucky? I just love it over there!' exclaimed Helen.

Her stepmother gave her a smile in which Pascoe thought he detected more than a touch of wry irony, then said, 'Don't tire her out, Mr Pascoe. She's going to need to get back to full strength pretty quickly to deal with this gorgeous pair. But I'm sure your business won't keep you long.'

She's wondering why I'm still on the case at all, thought Pascoe. Fat Andy assured her yesterday this wasn't a CID investigation and he's not had time to bring her up to speed yet. She'll probably be on her mobile to him before she gets to her car.

She placed the twins gently in their bedside cot, breathed a kiss over each in turn, then stooped to plant a firmer kiss on Helen's forehead.

'Goodbye, dear,' she said. 'See you later.'

He watched her move out of the room with athletic grace then turned his attention back to Helen, who was checking her hair and make-up in a hand mirror. Was she really as air-headed as she appeared? Kay seemed genuinely fond of her and the American didn't strike him as a woman who'd have much time for the intellectually challenged.

Whatever, close questioning of Helen wasn't really an option, he decided. Simplest thing was to turn her on and give her a direction and hope that later he could hook something useful from the ensuing verbal torrent.

He said, 'Mrs Dunn, what I'm really trying to get a line on is your brother's state of mind, and it would help a lot if I could see him in the context of your father's tragic death which he so closely imitated. Would this be too painful for you?'

She shook her head emphatically and said, 'No, that's fine. Where shall I begin?'

Pascoe produced his cassette recorder and pressed the 'start' button.

'Ten years ago would be fine,' he said.

5

Helen

*I was nine when Daddy died so I was old enough to
know what it meant when Kay told me in America
which was where we were when she got the news and
it was awful and I was shocked but I remember throwing my arms around Kay and crying and saying
something like I'm so glad it wasn't you which must
have been because when Mummy died even though
she'd been ill and even though I understood a lot less
about death then I was only three it was like someone
had switched the little night-light off in my bedroom
and left me in the dark.*

Then Kay came and the light came on again.

*So I was nine and I could bear losing anything except
Kay and hearing about Daddy was awful but like I say
there was that weird feeling of relief too because this
time the light didn't go off because I still had Kay.*

But it's Pal you want to hear about not Kay, isn't it?

*There's ten years between us and that's a lot he
always seemed more like a sort of uncle to me than a
brother oh he was kind enough but not really bothered*

except if I referred to Kay as mum she never would let me call her mum just Kay but that's how I thought of her and sometimes it would slip out and then Pal and Cress too would get awfully angry and tell me she wasn't our mother she was just a conniving foreigner who'd got her talons into Dad and one day he'd see her for what she was and that would be the end of it she'd be out on her neck.

Sometimes they made me cry so badly I was almost hysterical and Kay would come and comfort me and I'd tell her what they'd said and she never got angry with them but just said it was true she wasn't our mother but she'd be like a mother to me and to all three of us if we'd let her and I said yes I'd let her it was what I wanted more than anything in the world but the others never said anything like that.

Cress was nearer my age but still eight years older and if anything I got on even worse with her than I did with Pal or maybe it felt like that because he was a man while she was a girl and my sister so it hurt more when she got irritated with me and called me things like Goodie Two-Shoes or Pollyanna but I had Kay and that was enough for me.

One thing worried me and that was when I got to eleven Kay might want me to go away to school like Cress had done but when I told her this she laughed and said not to be silly Weavers was a perfectly good school and would I like to go there? Of course I said yes and once I got used to it I liked it a lot and made a lot of friends there too and of course that was where I first laid eyes on Jase.

He came to teach the boys PE when I was thirteen it was his first job and all us girls used to drool over him because he was such a hunk and dream of going out with him but he never showed much interest in any of us and of course I never dreamt that barely five years later I'd be married to him!

But I'm getting away from Pal though not really as I hadn't seen him since Daddy's funeral and not even then really as he and Cress stood away from us and wouldn't even look at us.

We were living at the Golden Fleece Hotel then because when we came back from America we couldn't get into Moscow House which Kay explained was because the law didn't allow it when someone had died suddenly but later I found out it was really because Pal had changed the locks which he had no right to do seeing as the house was as much mine as it was his and Cress's.

First of all we went to stay with Tony in Cothersley that's Tony Kafka that Kay worked for but only for a couple of days because I think he said it didn't look right so we went then to the Golden Fleece where Ash-Mac's that's what they call the firm had a suite for important visitors and that's where we stayed for several weeks till we moved to a flat in town and then nearly a year later Kay and Tony got married and we moved back to Cothersley Hall.

As for Moscow Pal and Cress lived there for a bit but really it was too big for them and it would have made sense to sell it which was what Kay wanted she was my guardian it said so in Dad's will which meant she acted for me legally till I got to eighteen but Pal and Cress said no I heard Pal and Kay arguing on the telephone once I eavesdropped on another phone in the Hall and Pal said things like he wasn't selling his family home just so she could get her hands on my money and in the end Moscow was advertised as to let furnished but it was too big for most families and businesses didn't want it not unless they could convert it properly which of course Pal wasn't going to permit so all that happened was from time to time it went on a short lease with some of the rooms like the study in particular locked up till some students took it and they broke into the study and Pal was so furious that he wouldn't let it be let anymore and that's the way it stayed till I got married.

I left school at seventeen I'd gone into the Sixth but when I saw my results at the end of the first year it was plain it wasn't worth staying on to finish my A levels so I told Kay I wanted to leave and she said OK what would I like to do and I didn't really know so she got me a job at Ash-Mac's working in the office there God it was deadly dull but I stuck at it for Kay's sake and things started looking a lot brighter when I ran into Jason when we were clubbing one night and we got together.

Three months later we were engaged and not long after that we got married and not long after that I found I was pregnant.

Pal and Cress didn't come to the wedding but they did send me a present which was something and then six months ago Jase ran into Pal at the Squash Club and they got talking and Jase who's a big softie and hates rows of any kind said look why don't you come home with me and say hello and he did!

It was a real shock seeing him up close after all this time but once I got past that it was fine he really did seem keen to put all the unpleasantnesses of the past behind us and he even asked after Kay without saying anything nasty which was a first.

I thought Kay might be unhappy when I told her but she just said it was good that families shouldn't stay apart and I said I thought I'd ask Pal and his wife and Cressida round one night and would she like to come as well with Tony but she said not yet perhaps later it was important for me to get back on terms with my brother and sister first.

So they came it wasn't a great success but not a disaster either and Pal and Jase seemed to get on very well and they started playing squash together regularly plus Pal said that he and Cress thought maybe it was time to forget the past and put Moscow on the market which was good as with the baby sorry babies coming we were going to have a lot of extra expense.

So while I haven't seen too much of Pal these past few months I've heard a lot about him from Jase and of course we kept in touch about the house sale which wasn't going as fast as we'd hoped so we had to do a couple of price adjustments which required all three of us to agree and sign.

Naturally I asked Kay's advice in all this as I never do anything without checking with her first she's really great but she said she'd rather not get involved with money matters between me and Pal and Cress now that *things seemed to be going better between us and she kept right out of the way if she knew I was meeting with them which was just what you'd expect from someone as considerate and thoughtful as her.*

But what you want to know is whether I noticed anything in Pal that might tell us why he'd do this dreadful thing and in fact I didn't no nothing like I say we didn't talk all that much but when we did he seemed just the same as ever and now we'll never talk again . . . it's only just beginning to sink in really and . . . I'm sorry I really didn't think I was going to cry but I can't help it thinking of poor Pal in that room where Dad . . . I'm sorry I'm sorry . . . oh God now I've set those two off as well can you call a nurse?

6

Big Maggie and Crazy Jane

The Avenue by daylight was not as impressive
as the Avenue by night. Spring sunshine whose
loving glance lights a respondent glow in all that
is young is not so kind to the old; and where man
has built, nature's exuberance is evidence of
decline and decay as telling as flaking paint and
missing tiles. Riotous hedgerows, unpruned trees,
lank lawns, all support the message traced on
unpointed walls by fingers of whitlow-grass – let
the rest of the world prepare to don its Easter
finery; here the best you'll get is shabby genteel.

It didn't help that the Avenue was empty of
human life. Or at least it appeared so, as if the ladies
of the night had decreed that the sins of darkness
should only be enjoyed in the hours of darkness.

But Shirley Novello knew that sex has no
timetable, and the lunch hour finds some men
hungry for more than a cheese sandwich.

She also knew how to make fish rise.

She'd parked around the corner, adjusted the

rear-view mirror so she could see her face and applied enough vibrant red lipstick to stop traffic. Next she slipped off her baggy combat trousers with the practised ease of one to whom the confines of a Uno presented no problem, changed her trainers for a pair of platform heels, and pulled on a red-and-green cagoule. Then she got out and studied her reflection in the car window. While aesthetically the outfit left much to be desired, it also, she told herself complacently, showed even more. The muscular brown legs on display beneath the cagoule might not come up to the dreamy description Jerker Jennison had given of the disappearing Dolores, but what they lacked in length they made up for in strength. Men, in her experience, didn't want to be tied with a ribbon, they liked to be held in a vice.

She was here because she felt she was on a roll.

In other parts of the universe, when it came to dishing out information about their clients, bank managers and lawyers made priests seem like blabbermouths. But in Mid-Yorkshire, things were different. Except in a few tyro cases (where wisdom soon came snapping at the heels of sadness) the simple rubric – *Mr Dalziel would be grateful* – was usually enough to unlock all tongues.

At the Mid-Yorkshire Savings Bank, the manager, Willie Noolan, who'd been looking after local cash longer than the Fat Man had been looking after local crime, didn't even put up a token resistance but presented Novello with a detailed statement of Maciver's personal and business accounts almost before she asked.

The business account confirmed Dolly Upshott's assertion that Archimagus was doing pretty well. The personal account had only one element which caught Novello's eye, an in payment of two thousand pounds early each month and commencing three months ago. The payments were made by BACS and came from a deposit account at the local branch of the Nortrust Bank, a demutualized Building Society. Noolan saved Novello the trouble of bludgeoning another pillar of the financial community with Dalziel's name by checking this out himself.

The account, he announced, was an old one, with a balance of twenty pounds and inactive for many years till it received an injection of two thousand pounds three months ago. This had only remained there for a few days before the transfer to the Mid-Yorkshire Savings. The process had been twice repeated. The account holder was a Mrs Kay Maciver of Moscow House, the Avenue.

Ignoring the inquisitive arch of Noolan's eyebrows, Novello had thanked him nicely and moved on to Pal Maciver's solicitor, a nervous young man named Herring who seemed almost to welcome her interest. It emerged that Sue-Lynn must have risen from her couch of grief at some point during the previous day and improved the shining hour by going through her late husband's papers and, from the sound of it, her late husband's cellar. Unable to lay hands on the most sought-after document, a copy of his will, she had rung Mr Herring at home during the course of the evening, demanding that he produce the original forthwith and bring it round to Casa Alba.

'I explained this wasn't possible. I was at home, I had guests, upon which she became rather abusive, and threatened to come round to my house unless I confirmed the will's contents over the phone. Which I did. She was entitled, and, to be honest, I was rather relieved to be giving it at a distance rather than face to face. You see, about six weeks ago Mr Maciver had come to see me to change his will. In it, after a few small bequests, he leaves the residue of his estate to be divided between his sister Cressida and his aunt, Miss Lavinia Maciver.'

'Nothing to the wife?'

'She was one of the bequests. Fifty pounds, with the rather cryptic comment that it should be more than enough to pay any outstanding bill to her medical advisor for services received.'

'How did the lady take this?' asked Novello.

'How do you think? With more abuse and threats. It really spoilt my evening. I kept expecting her to come banging on my door.'

'Will she contest the will?'

For the first time Mr Herring looked cheerful.

'Oh yes, I'm sure. Should make an interesting case. Could drag on for ever.'

Whether any of this new information was pertinent to the enquiry – whatever that was – she didn't know, but she felt things were going well. Her mind turned to the mystery of Dolores. Even if, as she half expected, it proved to have nothing to do with the case, it would be pleasant to show Joker Jennison that CID could get places fat plods couldn't hope to reach.

Swaying her hips like a howdah, she set off round the corner into the Avenue and took up a position leaning against a tree within thirty yards of the Moscow House entry.

Two minutes later she was being confronted by a pair of women. She recognized them both. The older of the two, a large square-built woman with day-glo hair, was known as Big Maggie. She'd appeared on local television as a self-appointed shop steward in a recent flare-up of the perennial war between the Avenue's residents and the prozzies. The other was a young woman known as Crazy Jane, anorexically thin, with bad teeth and a nervous eye whose ungoverned rollings were the source of her sobriquet.

'What the fuck's your game?' demanded Big Maggie.

'Thought I might put you two out of business,' said Novello.

The attack took her by surprise. She was ready for the traditional open-handed long-nailed stab at her eyes, but this woman broke the mould with a pro-boxer's pile-driving punch to the solar plexus. Not even those muscle-strengthening hours in the gym could stop it hurting but they did prevent it from being disabling. She grunted, absorbed the pain, focused, and when her assailant reverted to type and made a grab at her hair, she moved lightly out of the way and used Big Maggie's own momentum to send her crashing into the tree.

Crazy Jane looked on with an expression of incredulous terror, which by rendering both eyes equally nervous improved her appearance considerably. All she needed was a little dental work to be quite attractive. She showed no sign of wanting to join the attack.

Novello gave her a quick smile and said, 'You saw that, did you, Jane? Unprovoked assault on a police officer.'

'Eh?'

Leaning with her right hand on Big Maggie's back to keep her pressed against the tree, Novello pulled out her warrant card with her left and showed it to the thin girl. Then she pulled the other to face her and held it before her eyes.

'Right,' she said. 'Let's talk.'

Novello knew that in the politically correct police soaps she tried to avoid on the telly, female cops and prozzies often found they were sisters under the skin and established good feminist relationships based on mutual respect and a shared contempt for men.

She reckoned the scriptwriters ought to get out more. They certainly ought to visit Mid-Yorkshire and take a walk on the wild side. In her experience, most prostitutes regarded police of all sexes as their natural enemy and only ever co-operated with them out of urgent self-interest. Novello's attitude had nothing moralistic in it. She didn't judge, but she wasn't a social worker either. It was pure pragmatism.

She regarded the men who used them as sad beyond redemption. In her own relationships, if she got the slightest hint that a current partner had ever been with a pro, she elbowed him with no appeal. 'If I give him for free what the bastard in the past has paid for,' she explained to her confessor, Father Kerrigan, when he expressed disappointment that she'd dumped another parishioner whom he regarded as a good Catholic boy, 'what kind of a loser does that make me?'

Father Kerrigan groaned and thought, as he often did after a close encounter of the ethical kind with Novello, that things had never been the same since the Vatican had turned its back (so to speak) on self-flagellation. Given the choice between a good old-fashioned scourging and dealing with a modern young woman, he had no doubt about his preferred option.

'Right,' said Novello. 'Here's the deal, Maggie. I can take you down the nick and charge you with assault on a police officer and you, Jane, with aiding and abetting, or you can tell me in great detail what you heard or saw last Thursday night when the guy topped himself in Moscow House, plus you can tell me where I'll find a tall well-stacked girl with long black hair called Dolores.'

Big Maggie was recovering.

'That's easy,' she said. 'Tell you same as I told yon fat pig who thinks he's Eddie Murphy. Saw and heard nowt last Thursday except you buggers scaring off the trade and there's no one called Dolores works the Avenue or anywhere else local, so far as I know.'

So Jennison had put in the effort.

Novello frowned.

'Nowt gets nowt,' she said. 'Think harder. But make something up and you'll be cancelling your summer holidays.'

'Not going anywhere I want to be anyway,' said Big Maggie indifferently.

'Jane?'

The younger woman stammered, 'There's a car sometimes . . .'

'Doing what?'

'Going up to Moscow House, I've seen it.'

'Last Thursday?'

'Mebbe. Can't be sure of the days.'

'What kind of car?'

'Don't know the make. One of them estates. Blue, I think.'

Sounded like Maciver's Laguna. Hardly mattered

that sometimes he'd come round to what after all was partly his own house, did it?

She frowned in thought, and Crazy Jane must have felt threatened by the expression for she suddenly added, 'But there were a car on Thursday. A white one. Came slowly by a couple of times. Looking for business, I thought, but there were a woman in the passenger seat already.'

'One of the girls, you mean?'

'Might have been,' she said. 'But I didn't recognize her. Black hair, though, I think she had black hair.'

'And the man?'

'No. Too far off. Never look at their faces more than I can help anyway.'

Novello gave her another smile. This time she smiled back. As she talked, the non-nervous eye had relaxed into steadiness, restoring her half-crazed look. Dark glasses might help, thought Novello. But presumably her clients weren't paying much attention to her face either.

She said, 'Thanks, Jane. You can bugger off now.'

The thin girl hurried away.

Big Maggie said, 'Hey, what about me?'

'You? I've had nothing from you, have I? Come on, you're the one shouts her mouth off about prozzies' rights. You must know this Dolores. Maybe one of the girls has changed her name to try a new line.'

'I've told you, I know nowt about her. Could have been fetched in from one of the big agencies mebbe. Or could be she's an amateur, pocket money and kicks. Surprising how many of them there is. Ever thought of trying it yourself, luv?'

'I get my kicks banging up lowlife. Talking of which, fancy a trip down the station? Bit busy there just now, probably won't get you processed till tomorrow.'

When dealing with prozzies, always make your threats short-term. Court next month means nowt to most of 'em. They live day to day. Losing tonight's earnings and pissing off their pimps, that's what bothers them.

The Gospel according to St Andrew.

Big Maggie got the message. She said, 'I did see someone Thursday night.'

'Who?'

'A woman. She walked past me down the Avenue.'

'A working girl?'

'Definitely not. Didn't know her and if I thought she were trying to muscle in, I'd have had a word.'

'Like with me, you mean?' said Novello. 'So you saw a pedestrian. Big deal.'

'I saw her twice. Once she went past me heading that way, ten minutes or so later she came back.'

'Pedestrian walking her dog.'

'Didn't have no fucking dog!'

'So make me interested in her, lady, or we're taking a trip.'

'She were heading down to Moscow House where that guy topped himself.'

'You saw her turn up the drive, did you?'

A hesitation while she contemplated a lie.

'No. It were misty, remember. Anyway, no reason for me to pay her any heed, was there, not till she came back.'

'And why then?'

'Same person passes you twice in short order, you wonder if they're looking for trade, don't you?'

'A woman?'

The prostitute shrugged.

'You get all sorts, luv. You ever try it, you'll be surprised.'

'Describe her.'

If the woman had started talking about big tits and long black hair, Novello would have discounted everything she said as a blatant attempt to get off the hook, but her reply carried conviction.

'Tall, thin, moved like a dancer. Classy gear. Lovely sheepskin jacket with fur round the collar and cuffs.'

'Hair?'

'Couldn't see it. She had a silk square wrapped round. Looked expensive too.'

'Age?'

The woman shrugged.

'Would have needed to see her with her kit off to tell that, luv. No teenie, but could have been owt from twenty-five to forty-five. You got the bones and the money, you don't need to let it show. I reckon she had both. And that's it. Can't tell you owt else. Can I go now?'

Novello said, 'What did she sound like?'

'Eh?'

'Come on, Maggie. You thought she might be after trade. You'd speak to her, give her an opening in case she was nervous.'

'You sure you've never been on the game, luv?' said the woman. 'I did speak. Asked her if she'd got a light. She said, "Sorry, I don't smoke," and walked on.'

'So what did she sound like?'

'How do you mean?'

'Yorkshire? Posh? Husky? Nervous? Drunk? Everybody sounds like something.'

'Not Yorkshire, that's for sure. Not posh either. Not nervous, Certainly not drunk.'

'Not posh?' said Novello, seizing on the significant negative. 'If not, what?'

'I mean she didn't have one of them fancy accents like the Royal Family, that gang. She sounded, I don't know, sort of American, I suppose.'

She looked slightly surprised at her own conclusion.

Novello got a name and address out of her, assured her if either turned out to be false she'd come looking with dogs, and sent her on her way.

LEEDS COLLEGE OF BUILDING
LIBRARY

Was this good news? Bad news? Was it any kind of news at all?

Only way to find out was to offer it to old Broken Face and see if she could detect a glimmer of appreciation somewhere deep down in those Cracks of Doom.

7

a tool of the devil

Jake Gallipot was doing well. Or at least, looking up at his office building from the outside, you got the impression he must be doing well, but from Wield's recollection of the man, he'd always known the value of appearances.

The building was in a quiet but far from mean street within walking distance of Harrogate's Majestic Hotel. A nervous client could take tea or something stronger there, then stroll round for his consultation without much fear of drawing attention. All the spaces in front of the elegant four-storey terrace had been taken, so Wield had parked the Thunderbird illegally on the other side of the road. Removing his helmet, he identified the door with Gallipot's number on it and let his gaze drift up the façade. It looked freshly painted and well maintained. He caught a shadow behind the Venetian blind in one of the top-floor windows. He hoped it wasn't Gallipot. This was meant to be a surprise.

And now he was where the flow had brought him, feeling it was probably a complete waste of time and glad that with luck he'd only have to explain it to Pascoe and not to the Fat Man.

Tucking his helmet underneath his arm, he walked across the road.

A column of plaques by the front door confirmed that Jake was keeping very respectable company. Insurance Broker, Catering Supplies, Secretarial Agency, Marine Engineer. Not a Personal Masseuse or French Tutor in sight, though maybe, as there couldn't be much call for marine engineering in Harrogate, that was a cover for some other activity popular amongst mariners.

Gallipot's shingle simply read GALLIPOT (Top Floor), nothing about investigations or enquiries. Very discreet.

Wield pushed open the door and stepped into a small but well-lit hallway which offered the choice of lift or steep stairs. The lift looked antique. Wield chose the stairs.

Arriving at the top floor only very slightly out of breath, he found himself facing a door with JAKE GALLIPOT stencilled in gold across the glass panel. He tapped on the glass. There was no reply, so he pressed the handle and pushed the door open.

It was a small but very smart modern office, light years away from the studied untidiness of the traditional hard-nosed private eye's den. Jake had been a hi-tech cop before many senior officers had learned how to use the redial button on their telephones. It was reported that when a search was made of his flat after his initial suspension, they'd found a computer system that made the one down the nick look antique. It was also reported they'd found nothing remotely incriminating on it, not even a bit of straight porn.

Here in his office, a fully kitted work station occupying half the left wall confirmed he was still at the cutting edge. Only two things disturbed the reassuring impression of order and efficiency.

One was the fact that the computer tower was twisted round with its rear panel unscrewed.

And the other was the presence on the floor alongside the tower of the body of a man.

Neither the passage of years nor the angle of view prevented Wield from instantly recognizing Jake Gallipot. Even supine and unmoving with his lips set in a grimace that revealed perfect white teeth, he still looked solid and dependable, a man you could safely buy a used car or a used alibi from.

In his outstretched right hand he held a screwdriver with its end melted by heat.

Pausing only to check that it was no longer in contact with any part of the computer, Wield knelt down and checked for a pulse. There was none. Immediately he went into the resuscitation procedure. His mind ticking off seconds and counting sequences of fifteen chest presses and two mouth-to-mouths. After four sequences, he checked the carotid pulse again. Still nothing. Another four sequences. Still nothing. Another four.

Nothing.

He stood upright, took his mobile from his pocket, dialled 999 and asked for the ambulance service and the police.

An hour later he was standing in the empty office with DI Collaboy.

Gallipot had been rushed off to hospital in an ambulance but Wield knew that not even the wonders of modern technology could bring him back to life.

'So what's this all about, Wieldy?' said the DI.

'What's it look like to you, Jim?'

'Looks like Jake decided to change the hard drive on his computer, got careless, and forgot to switch off at the mains.'

They had found the packaging for a new hard drive in the waste bin.

'That's how it looks to me too.'

'But?'

'You'll recall Jake and computers. He were playing around with them when folk like Andy Dalziel still thought the abacus was a tool of the devil.'

'Familiarity breeds carelessness,' said Collaboy.

'Where's the old drive, the one he were replacing?' asked Wield.

'Packed up, got wiped, so he took it out to have a look, decided it were knackered and dumped it when he went to buy a new one.'

'Then where's his back-up disks? You knew Jake. He'd have everything backed up.'

'Could be anywhere,' said Collaboy, looking round the office.

'Let's look, shall we?'

It was a pointless search as Wield had looked already. In the drawers and cupboards he'd found all the tools of Gallipot's trade – various bugging devices, a digital camera, a set of pick-locks, a bunch of dodgy-looking keys, a collection of business cards with a variety of names and businesses – but no trace of any back-up disks. He'd also checked the filing cabinet. There was a wallet marked *Maciver*. It was empty.

'I think you'd best tell me what this is all about, Wieldy.'

Wield looked at the DI. Time had not been kind to him. Since last they met, his hairline had receded and turned grey in retreat, while his face had – in one of the phrases Andy Dalziel claimed to have learned from his old Scots grandma – enough wrinkles to make a cuddy a new arsehole.

He told him the story, explaining his own presence there by the truth, more or less.

'I didn't think he was being straight with me,' he concluded.

'Because he talked to you like you were his best friend in the world?' said Collaboy sceptically. 'You know Jake. That's how he talked to everybody! The bugger still used to ask me for

335

favours long after I'd made it clear I didn't want owt more to do with him. Come to think of it, you mentioning the name Maciver reminds me, long time back, can't have been long after he got his cards, he asked me if I'd give him a reference for a job on the security team at some outfit in your neck of the woods that had Maciver in its name . . .'

'Ashur-Proffitt-Maciver's?' asked Wield.

'That could have been it. Any connection with this dead guy?'

'It was the family firm till it got took over. Did you give him the reference?'

'Aye, I did, oddly. Just said he'd been a serving cop for however long it were and that he'd retired as a sergeant. Don't know why I bothered . . . no, that's a lie. I knew he'd set up as a PI and I thought this meant he hadn't made a go of it and I've got to admit the thought of Jake wearing a peaked cap and wandering round a factory site in the early hours of a winter morning didn't displease me. Looks like I were wrong, but. Bit of money went into this set-up.'

The two men looked around the office, both of them perhaps wondering what the future held for them when their time came to hand in the badges.

'Right,' said Collaboy. 'I'll need a statement, Wieldy, and I'll get a SOCO team in here just in case, but unless they or the medics come up with something significant, I can't see I'm going to be able to tell my boss this is anything but accidental death. Not unless you've not told me everything you know?'

This is what working on a hunch gets you into, thought Wield.

He said, 'I can just give you the facts as I know them, Jim. How you move forward from there is down to you. Anything else comes up, you'll be the first to know.'

He hoped he sounded sincere.

8

a bloody great splash

Back in the Penetralium of Mid-Yorkshire CID, Dalziel stood by his window apparently staring out into the bright spring air but it might as well have been a-swirl with smoke for all that his unblinking gaze was seeing.

He was listening to a tape. Not the one Pascoe had tossed on to his desk with a casualness more cutting than accusation. How that had come to be stored with the Pal Senior suicide stuff he didn't know, which bothered him. Pascoe in prissy mode liked to quote one of them foreign psycho-wankers – *there's no such thing as accident*. Mebbe some imp of uncertainty dwelling deep in that darkness which lies at all our centres had made him leave the tape there. He didn't like the feel of that, which was why he was listening to this other tape now, the original of the one he'd tossed back at Pascoe.

The voice on the tape, a woman's voice, its soft American accent melodious on the ear, fell silent.

It had worked its magic. He felt reassured. The imp was back in its dark cave. His sight cleared and took in the blue sky, the golden sun, the budding lime tree overhanging the corner of the car park. Once more he was Andy Dalziel, monarch of all he surveyed. In his mind's eye he beheld the towns, villages, fields, woods, and rolling hills of Mid-Yorkshire, his proper dominion, and he saw that it was good; and the reason it was good was that behind him on the CID floor the massed ranks of his minions waited with bated breath for the commands which would send them galloping forth to defend the persecuted and bring the wrongdoer to justice.

His phone rang.

He picked it up and pronounced, 'Dalziel,' with more than usual authority.

'God, Andy, that hurt! I'm on the phone, man, not standing on the next mountain top!'

He recognized the voice of Chief Constable Dan Trimble.

'Sorry, sir. And what can I do for you?'

'I just want to confirm a staffing detail. Your DC Bowler is still on sick leave, is he?'

'Yes, sir. He is. Leaving us short-handed and overstretched, as usual,' said Dalziel with only ritualistic force. His mind was too busy looking for the reason behind the query.

'Good, yes, I see. So there's no way he could be operationally active, on say DCI Pascoe's behalf? Without your knowledge, I mean.'

'No way,' said Dalziel firmly. He meant it. Pascoe was capable of pulling many clever strokes, but not this. In fact in the case of young Bowler, he'd got up Dalziel's nose a bit, the way he clucked around like a mother hen, insisting that it might be a good six months before the lad was fit to return.

'Good, fine, didn't think so,' said Trimble. 'Thank you, Andy.'

The phone went dead.

Dan Trimble hailed from Cornwall, a county much admired by Dalziel for the unflinching brutality of its rugby players, the subtle ingenuity of its entrepreneurs, the vibrant beauty of its womenfolk, and the deep distrust of London shown by all its natives. After an initial sniffing-around period, he and Trimble had come to a series of mutually beneficent working understandings, and the Chief was looked up to with considerable respect by his fellow high-fliers as the man who could handle Fat Andy.

But though he had learned much, he had not yet learned that if you wanted to avoid awkward questions from Dalziel, it wasn't enough to ring off quickly and order your secretary not to take the Superintendent's calls, you must also pack a suitcase and flee the country.

'Mr Trimble's office,' fluted his secretary when the phone rang a few seconds later.

'Bishop's chaplain here,' said a high, faintly Welsh voice. 'Could His Grace have a word?'

A moment later, Trimble said, 'Good day to you, Bishop. How can I help you?'

'Sorry, sir, must be a crossed line. We got cut off. I were just going to ask you, what's all this stuff about Bowler about?'

Now Trimble showed his quality by hesitating only a split second before admitting the inescapable.

He said, 'Andy, I don't know, and what little I do know I'm not supposed to tell you. I had a query from an old Hendon chum at the Yard saying he'd been asked to check unofficially with me if we had some operation going involving DC Bowler in a covert surveillance role.'

'Asked who by?' demanded Dalziel.

There was a pause and he went on impatiently, 'Come on, sir. I know you. You're like me, you'd want to know the why's and wherefore's.'

Feeling obscurely complimented, Trimble said, 'Some chap by the name of Gedye. Works out of the Home Office, my chum gathered, whatever that means.'

'I know what it means and it don't mean he's a cleaner,' said Dalziel. 'And what did you tell your chum? Sir.'

'I explained that Bowler was on sick leave but I'd double-check just to be quite sure. He said fine but the word was I must be very careful to create no ripples. I am on the point of reporting back negatively, and that I assume will be the end of the matter. Clearly been an intelligence snarl-up, which is par for the course in those misty regions on the edge of government. So no harm done. And I hope, Andy, this is going to be the nearest we get to a ripple from your direction.'

'Of course, sir. Thanks for being so forthcoming. Cheers, now.'

Dalziel put the phone down.

'Aye, Dan,' he said to the air. 'No need to worry, my little pixie. I don't do ripples. But I've promised nowt about bloody great splashes.'

Not that there was anything to splash in. Like Trimble said, probably a simple snarl-up. Them buggers down south made things so complicated that when they unzipped their flies they never knew whose cock they were going to pull out.

So why was that imp so recently repulsed twitching around in his gut once more? He poured himself a scotch and tossed it down. The imp received it gratefully. It was to be expected that any entity inhabiting the Dalziel frame would have developed a taste for old malts.

A phone was ringing close by. Pascoe's he guessed. It stopped. Then another phone started up in the main CID room. After five rings he flung open his door and strode down the corridor to demand to know why his minions with their bated breath weren't rushing to answer it.

The answer was clear. Not a minion in sight.

No. Wrong. There was one, by the fax machine, trying to conceal himself behind a sheaf of printouts.

'Bowler. What the fuck are you doing here?' demanded Dalziel.

He did not pause for an answer but went to Wield's desk and picked up the ringing phone and gave a noncommittal grunt.

'Wieldy, I was trying to get hold of Pete Pascoe. He's not around, is he?'

The voice was Paddy Ireland's. Dalziel gave another grunt, negative this time.

'Maybe you can help. It's about this Moscow House business. Fat Andy was really keen to dump it on me – God knows why when you think of the speed he came running to stick his big nose in – but I managed to toss it back in the DCI's lap. Now one of my lads has just mentioned that young Bowler has been asking questions about it down here, like he thought we were still dealing, and I wondered what that was all about. I thought he was off sick. Didn't realize he was back.'

'Oh, he's back, but he still looks pretty sick to me,' said Dalziel grimly. 'Thanks, Paddy.'

He registered the shock at the other end, put the phone down and glared at Bowler, who was still crouching by the fax machine like a down-hill skier who has felt a tremor in the ground and longs to fly away but fears a very slight move could bring the whole mountain crashing down.

Then suddenly, to the DC's amazement, that great slab face fissured into a broad grin.

'Whatever you're up to, it's good to see you

back, lad,' said Dalziel. 'Come into my office and let's see if we can't find you some medicine.'

A few moments later, Hat found himself seated in front of the superintendent's desk with a tumblerful of Highland Park in one hand. In the other he was still clutching the fax sheets in a grip which the shock of seeing the Fat Man had locked tight.

Dalziel had learned through a lifetime of interrogations that scaring people shitless wasn't always the quickest way to extracting information. In addition, after a dicey start to their relationship, he had come to feel quite fond of Hat. As he said to Pascoe, 'You can do a lot with a poncy graduate if you catch him young. Look at you.'

'So, tell us all about it,' he said now. 'Off the record, like, seeing as you're still officially on the panel. And no editing. The full monte.'

So Hat told him all about it. Or nearly all.

When he'd finished, Dalziel said, 'Sounds like you've taken a real fancy to this bird lady. I met her way back, when her brother topped himself. She made a statement. Routine, nowt important. But I recall she struck me then as being a bit original. Mind you, they all are, the Macivers. No two of them the same.'

'I've not met any of the others, sir, and I've only met Miss Mac twice, but she's really great, and she's so brave with her MS . . .'

'Aye, I didn't know about that. Feel sorry for her, do you?'

Hat didn't have to consider that.

'No way,' he said. 'She'd hit anyone with her stick if she thought they felt sorry for her. No, I just like her and she seems to understand me, what I feel, I mean. And because of that I don't seem to feel it so much, I mean I still feel it, but I feel better too, as if things are still possible, if you know what I mean, sir . . .'

He regarded the Fat Man uneasily, fearful that this descent into incoherence might signal the end of this period of rapprochement, but his response was to nod and say, 'Aye, lad, we've all had shocks and losses and it's never any use anyone telling you you'll get through it, not till you find out for yourself.'

But now his tone became more businesslike.

'Right, then. You like the bird lady and because you can see her nephew's death's upset her, you thought it 'ud be a kindness to check out what the state of play is in the investigation?'

'Yes, sir. But I thought it was just a straightforward suicide, sir. It wasn't till I started asking downstairs that I realized we were still investigating it as a suspicious death.'

'And that changed everything, of course. You thought, *Oh dear, this changes everything, I can't go shooting my mouth off about an active case, I'd best keep my neb out of this.* Right?'

As he spoke, the Fat Man's eyes were fixed on the faxes in Bowler's hand.

'Yes. Sir. Really, sir. I came upstairs to say hello

to everyone, and OK, maybe I'd have asked a few questions, but there wasn't anyone here and then this stuff started coming through the fax and when I looked I could see it was details of Mr Maciver's phone calls. But I was just looking, sir. I mean I wouldn't have said anything. I don't know anything, do I? Sir, what is going on?'

'If I tell you, then you will know something, won't you? Will it go straight back to the bird lady?'

Hat looked him straight in the eye.

'No, sir. No way.'

'Glad to hear it. And this idea of checking up on the state of play, that was yours alone, was it? She didn't suggest it to you when she found out you were a cop? She does know that, does she?'

'Yes, sir. I told her this morning. I told her all about me. No, she never suggested anything. She wouldn't.'

'I'll take your word for it. So, lad, what shall we do with you?'

'Sir?'

'I mean, how are you feeling? Do you want to go home and take a rest after all your exertions, lie in bed with some soft music on the gramophone, feel sorry for yourself. Or are you fit enough to do some work?'

Hat downed his whisky.

'What had you in mind, sir?' he said boldly.

'Good lad! Well, seeing as you seem to have

got very attached to them telephone records, why don't you start there? I'll get the file from Mr Pascoe's room so we can see the full picture.'

'Yes, sir. What exactly are we looking for, sir?'

'I haven't got the faintest idea, lad. And as there's no bugger around to give us a hint, we'll just have to play it by ear. But I'll tell you one thing. If we find nowt, this is one time I won't give a toss!'

9

blue beer

Most Yorkshire villages, even those most famed
for their attractiveness, have retained a comforting workaday ambience. The sixteenth-century
cottages may be painted in twentieth-century
pastels and festooned with Mediterranean-style
window boxes, but there's cow shit on the main
street to show that the true bucolic still persists.

Not so with Cothersley. Any cow entering here
had better wipe its feet and keep a tight ass,
thought Pascoe. Even the speed bumps seemed
to have been designed to wreck any suspension
less sturdy than a Range Rover's, though they
didn't seem to be inhibiting the desire of a convoy
of mini-buses to shed the Cothersley dust from
their tyres.

In the centre of the village the road furcated
on either side of a manicured green across which
the rather severe façade of St Cuthbert's church
frowned at the Dog and Duck, apparently dis-
approving its dazzling whitewashed walls and

cute new painted sign as much as Andy Dalziel. Outside it stood a police car.

Pascoe drew up behind it, got out, and, not wanting to risk interrupting serious police business at a critical stage, peered through a window. His view was partially blocked by a menu promising bar meals in which goujons and rocket garnish figured largely. Beyond this he could make out a deal of tartan upholstery and walls festooned with enough horse brass to refurbish the Household Cavalry. He shifted his angle of view and finally glimpsed Mid-Yorkshire's Finest at their dangerous and demanding work.

Constables Jennison and Maycock were standing side by side at the bar with their heads tipped back to extract the last drop of liquid from their pint glasses, observed by a military moustached man in a blazer and regimental tie.

The glasses were then set on the bar with something of reluctant finality and Pascoe retreated to lean against their car, facing the pub doorway.

It was a fairly wide door but not wide enough to permit the pair to exit abreast. Maycock came first, stopping suddenly when he saw Pascoe, with the result that Jennison bumped into him.

'What's up, you daft sod? Good job I weren't excited else you might have had to marry me,' cried Joker. 'Oh shit.'

The last was sotto voce, caused by glimpsing Pascoe.

'Hello, sir,' said Maycock, recovering. 'Didn't think this would be important enough for CID.'

'What is *this*?' enquired Pascoe.

'Got a call from the Captain . . .'

'Captain?'

'Captain Inglestone, the landlord. Little bit of bother. Seems some joker circulated several care-homes in the area to say that the Dog and Duck was offering special pensioner discounts this lunchtime, eighty per cent off all drinks and meals. A lot of them made a special effort to get out here.'

'I think I saw them leaving.'

'Aye, we persuaded them, but it were a close-run thing,' said Jennison. 'There was a popular motion to drown Captain Inglestone in his own slop tray. If he hadn't agreed to dish out free half-pints all round, I don't know what might have happened.'

'And as old age pensioners, that was your free beer you were drinking just now, was it?'

'No, sir,' said Maycock. 'That was by way of experiment. Seems some joker had doctored one of his kegs so that when he put it on yesterday, the beer came out blue. Had to dump the lot and flush out his pipes and we were just making sure the new lot were fit for human consumption. Sir.'

'Not a very popular man, this captain, by the sound of it,' said Pascoe.

'Probably his mother loves him,' said Jennison. 'Specially if she lives a long way off.'

Pascoe turned away to hide a smile. Across the green, a dusty hatchback pulled up in front of St Cuthbert's. The driver got out, looked across at the three policemen and gave a wave.

It was Dolly Upshott, Pal Maciver's assistant and the vicar's sister.

She'd abandoned her Archimagus outfit and looked much more at home in full country-girl kit, green Barbour sweater straining over her bosom, cord breeks doing the same over her bum, long shapely legs plunging into green wellies. The crown of unruly brown curls remained the same. Curate's fiancée in a Wodehouse short story, thought Pascoe. Better than him at golf and her parents object.

Though Wodehouse had never observed, to his knowledge, just how sexy green wellies could be.

She opened the hatch. The back of the car was filled with cardboard boxes and she bent forward to lift the first of these out. The resultant seam-popping curve of cord over shapely buttock was something to make gods grow languid and mortals feel godlike.

Now she straightened up with the box in her arms and headed into the elegant brick-built village hall which stood next to the church.

'Right, lads,' said Pascoe. 'I'm sure you've got better things to do. By the way, Joker. Any progress in tracking down that Dolores tart?'

'Eh?' said Jennison, who seemed completely rapt.

'Come on, lad. Snap out of it. Dolores, the woman you say chatted you up outside Moscow House.'

'Sorry, sir.' With a visible effort Jennison brought himself back from whatever land of sweet content his febrile imagination had conveyed him to. 'No, no sign. Your lass Shirley got on to me earlier. I told her I'd checked the phone boxes and such. She's left no cards anywhere, none of the other girls know owt about her, or else they're keeping stumm.'

'All right,' said Pascoe, pleased to hear that Novello was on the ball. 'Keep trying. Now off you go.'

Dolly Upshott came out of the hall, returned to the car and stooped to pick up another box. Jennison looked as if he wanted to stay and see the view again but Maycock drew him away by main force. Pascoe set out across the green towards the hatchback.

'Hi, there. Need a hand?' he said.

'Hello, it's Mr Pascoe, isn't it? Yes, that would be awfully kind. It's stuff for our bring-and-buy sale. Trouble is, most people just bring it to the vicarage and leave it for me to sort out then ferry it down here.'

'All by yourself? I always thought our village churches were brimming over with helping hands.'

'Most of ours are pretty good at dipping into their pockets but not so hot when it comes to flexing their muscles. Anyway it's my own fault. I've been neglecting parish stuff a bit lately, particularly these past couple of days, since . . .'

'In the circumstances, very understandable,' said Pascoe, picking up a box which turned out to be a lot heavier than it looked and trying with a machismo Ellie would have mocked not to stagger as he followed her up the path to the hall. 'You said that the Macivers were rather more generous with their money than their time, I recall.'

'Yes, that's right. Just put it down here, will you? David, that's my brother, he says he'd rather have bums on pews than cheques in the post, but he doesn't pay much attention to the accounts, that's my job. I don't know where we'd be, the parish I mean, without people like Pal to turn to when we need them. Even with something like this sale. It was only last weekend he turned up with a whole carload of stuff. I thought some of it looked good enough to put in the shop but he said no, he wanted it to go on our stalls, picking up bargains was part of the joy of being in the antique business and he'd be delighted to think some of his fellow villagers were getting a chance to share his pleasure. Only last weekend . . .'

Her voice broke slightly.

Pascoe said briskly, 'And how about the Kafkas at Cothersley Hall? Mrs Kafka is, or was, Mr Maciver's stepmother, I believe. But I daresay you knew that. How do they rate as churchgoers?'

'Mrs Kafka attends services sometimes, and I've often seen her in the church at other times, just sitting there peacefully. Mr Kafka hardly appears in the village at all. But, like Pal, he's very generous when it comes to appeals.'

They were walking back to the hatchback now. To his irritation he saw the police car was still parked outside the pub with Jennison's broad face at the open passenger window, as if hungry for another helping of curvaceous corduroy. He glowered towards him and a moment later Maycock started the engine and the vehicle drew away.

'Something happening at the pub?' enquired Dolly.

Pascoe told her and she laughed so joyously it was impossible not to join in.

'Pal would have loved that,' she said. 'He hated Captain Inglestone. Always called him corporal.'

'Why didn't they get on?'

'Mutual antipathy, I think. Also the Captain let Sue-Lynn run up a pretty hefty slate then had the cheek to present it to Pal for payment when he was in there with some friends one night. I gather the air was pretty blue by the time they finished.'

'Like his beer,' said Pascoe, and was rewarded with another infectious laugh.

'Did Pal and the Kafkas socialize much, do you know?' he asked as they made their way back into the hall with two more boxes.

'Oh no,' she said, then qualified, 'Not to my knowledge, I mean.'

'No? Bit odd, given the relationship,' he probed, curious to know how current rumours of bad blood between stepmother and stepson were. In his experience there was no such thing as private business outside city limits.

'What people do in their personal lives is no affair of anyone else's,' she said rather brusquely.

'Really? I think your brother might give you an argument there,' he said pleasantly.

He set his box down. It contained books. One of them slipped off the top of the pile and fell to the floor. He stooped to pick it up. It was a tiny volume in a marbled binding. He opened it at the title page and read *Death's Jest-Book or The Fool's Tragedy*, London: William Pickering, 1850. There was no author's name but he didn't need one.

'Are you all right, Mr Pascoe?' asked Dolly anxiously.

'Yes, fine. It's just this book, the man who wrote it, I've a . . . friend who's very interested in him and he's rather ill at the moment . . .'

'I'm sorry about that,' she said. 'Look, if you'd like to buy it for him, it's only a pound . . .'

'A pound?'

'Yes. All hardbacks are a pound, paperbacks twenty pee. It makes things so much simpler. That's one of the ones Pal donated, probably worth a bit more but he was so insistent. A pound each, he said. So, give me a pound and it's yours.'

Pascoe produced the coin and slipped the book into his pocket.

'Thank you,' he said. 'Now, let's get on. Can't be much more.'

'No, there's not and I can manage,' said Dolly smiling. 'I'm sure you haven't come out to Cothersley just to act as a beast of burden.'

He noted the implied question and saw no reason not to answer it.

'That's true. In fact, I'd be grateful if you could help me with some directions. I'm on my way to see Mrs Maciver at Casa Alba. How's she bearing up, by the way?'

Dolly made a wry face and said, 'Not very well, I gather. I haven't seen her myself. She's not very keen to have company. Almost chucked David out of the house.'

'Let's hope I have better luck,' said Pascoe. 'Now if you could point me in the right direction . . .'

She led him outside and gave him his directions with an admirable succinctness, then, as he thanked her and made to leave, she said, 'Yesterday you sounded pretty certain Pal shot himself. Is there some doubt now? I mean, with you coming here and asking questions . . . I only ask because, naturally, there's all kinds of rumours flying round the village and I know my brother would be grateful if he could scotch the wilder ones with a bit of authority.'

'Yes, I can see that. But my job's just to get

information to pass on to the coroner and to do that I've got to ask questions,' Pascoe prevaricated. 'Best way to deal with rumours is to ignore them and wait for the inquest.'

'But what do you think, Mr Pascoe? I mean, do locked-room mysteries really happen outside detective novels?'

'Believe me, real life is infinitely more incredible and unpredictable,' said Pascoe. 'Good day, Miss Upshott.'

As he drove away, he could see her in his mirror still standing by the church gate, looking after him.

Nice woman, he thought.

And she gave good directions too, he acknowledged as after a pleasant two-mile drive through rolling English countryside, liberally wooded with oak and elm and lightly dotted with properties, some old, some new, all substantial, he spotted what had to be Casa Alba.

The name had conjured up a picture of some version of Costa del Holiday villa, but its style, though distinctly Spanish, was the kind of Spanish that acknowledges winter and rough weather. It was a solid-looking two-storey building, burnt umber in colour, with balconied bedrooms and what looked like serviceable shutters, and a shallow pitched hip-roof of richly ochrous tiles. In front of it was parked a car.

Gotcha! thought Pascoe.

As he drove slowly up the long gravelled drive,

it occurred to him that a good socialist should be feeling the odd pang of indignation that such a deal of space and building was squandered on two people, but all he could manage was a twinge of old-fashioned covetousness. Ellie would have done better, but then Ellie wouldn't have liked the house anyway. Surprisingly for one so determinedly contemporary in outlook, her architectural tastes ran to ivied brick and ancient beams. She would have thought Casa Alba with its green shutters, its curved balconies, its blue tennis court and its kidney-shaped swimming pool, was discordant here and vulgar anywhere.

To Pascoe however it looked just the job. Ivied brick and ancient beams in his experience usually went hand in hand with icy draughts, uneven floors, deficient damp courses, smoking fireplaces, and an ambience more suited to rodent than human life. Happily, unless he won the lottery, this division of taste was unlikely to put much of a strain on his marriage.

The parked car, he saw as he got nearer, was a BMW 3 Series hatchback, and there was someone sitting in it, a woman he didn't recognize. He drew up behind her, got out and stooped to her window, smiling.

She didn't smile back. She didn't do anything.

After a moment he tapped gently on the window.

The woman lowered it an eighth of an inch.

'What?'

'Mrs Maciver's out, is she?'

'Yes.'

'Any idea when she'll be getting back?'

'No.'

The window closed.

She was a well-made woman in her thirties, not overweight but with the athletically muscular look of a tennis or hockey player. She was probably quite good looking but unfriendliness didn't do her any favours, emphasizing the strong jaw and shrinking the full lips to a tight line.

He had a wander round the house, glancing through the windows. It looked cool and comfortable inside, big chairs and sofas in soft white leather, just the job for relaxing in with a chilled San Miguel when your throat felt dry as an old don's wit. Should have taken his chance with the blue beer at the Dog and Duck.

When he got back into his car, he was still undecided what to do.

He would like to talk to Sue-Lynn, but he didn't want to waste any more time hanging around waiting. The day Dalziel had given him to check things out was running away fast and he was still as far as ever from having any coherent reason for keeping this investigation going. All he'd discovered was that Maciver relationships were marked by divisions, disloyalties, dislikes and distrusts. Bit like the Balkans. Stretches of fragile peace beneath which the old hostilities and hatreds gently simmered, waiting to burst out.

But was there anything unusual in this? What family didn't have its scar tissue? His certainly did.

With the Macivers, however, there was a focal point. Kay Kafka. You were either with her or against her. You either worshipped or reviled.

No question which camp the Fat Man was in. The woman seemed to have him, in Pal Junior's phrase on the tape, deeply magicked. Ten years ago it was clear he'd taken over the case of her husband's suicide to make sure she was protected. And somehow he'd made all the venomous accusations contained in the son's tape go away.

But so what? Did any of this raking over of ten-year-old ashes have anything to do with today's case? Pascoe couldn't yet see how, hoped he never would. Perhaps the answer was in the cassette that Dalziel had given him, but he still felt reluctant to listen to it. All he wanted now, he told himself, was to be able to say, *Yes, it was definitely suicide,* and get back to his statistical analysis without having to follow the trail any deeper into the caverns measureless to man of Dalziel's psyche.

But he couldn't deny the denizens of his own caverns, particularly that insatiable curiosity about human motives and make-up which had led him into the police force in the first place. Who really was the abuser here and who the abused? Which was the more important spoor to follow – that mesmeric quality which Kay seemed to bring to bear on most men, or the obsessional element clearly present in Pal Junior's statement?

Only one way to find out, and after all he couldn't think of anything else to do.

He ejected *Charles Trenet's Greatest Hits* from the car tape deck, took Dalziel's cassette from his pocket, inserted it, and sat back to listen.

10

Kay (1)

I was born Katherine Dickenson but I always got Kay.

I was an only child, I think. I seem to recall a baby when I was still very small, but it went away and nothing was ever said about it.

Maybe it was just some neighbour's child my mother looked after for a while.

I never dared ask in case I found myself disappearing the same way.

My birth certificate says I was born in Milwaukee but we must have left there long before I started registering places. We seemed to move around a lot. Going where the work was, my mother told me when I was old enough to ask. But it always felt like we were leaving some place fast rather than going some place else we wanted to be.

My father was a sudden man; not bad tempered so's you'd notice, and not violent, at least never to me. But sudden. And unchangeable. No debating. He'd make up his mind and that was it. I think this happened at work a lot. He'd do his job well enough till one day someone would ask him to do something he didn't care to do, and he'd say no. No reason given. And if his boss said do it or leave, he'd leave. Then he'd come home and say, 'Pack your bags, we're moving on.'

I got to hate it if ever Pa showed up early. Ma and I would hear the door and whatever we were doing, we'd freeze.

Place we stayed longest was Springfield, Massachusetts. We were living in a trailer park. 'Just temporary,' Pa said, 'till we find something better.' That was Pa. First place he called temporary was where we got closest to being permanent.

I was fourteen when we moved to Springfield. I did well at school but always thought I'd be out of there soon as I was able and getting a job. Then one day Pa told me I was staying on and going to college. No explanation, no argument. Like I said, sudden.

That's the way he died too. And my mother. I was seventeen, going on eighteen, all fixed to start college in the fall, down in Hartford. That's in Connecticut, next state south. Pa's choice. He said there was plenty of work in Hartford and he was planning to move us there anyway. Planning! Maybe after a life of suddenness he'd decided to try forethought. Maybe that was what distracted him, starting to think ahead at last, and he stopped paying attention to what was close up, like the truck he pulled in front of, joining the interstate.

They were killed outright. When I got the news I must have gone into some kind of trance because I don't remember much else till the funeral was over and suddenly I found I was surrounded by strangers, all concerned for my future. I heard myself telling them it was OK, I'd been going to stay with my aunt in Hartford when I went to college, so now I would just move in with her permanent. Someone asked why she hadn't been at the funeral and I said she'd been on vacation in Europe and by the time she was contacted it was too late, but I'd spoken with her on the phone and she was expecting me in a couple of days.

What made me do this, I don't know. Maybe it was Pa in me, not caring to be told what he should do.

They all bought it, everyone thinking someone else knew more of the details, and all of them probably glad to be rid of a problem that wasn't really theirs.

There was a bit of money, more than I'd expected, enough to get me settled in Hartford but a long way short of enough to get me through college. I'd been going to get some work anyway, but now I really needed it.

That's how I first got involved with the Ashur-Proffitt Corporation. A-P's main plant wasn't too far from the house where I boarded and my landlady told me they were always looking for canteen staff for the night shift, which suited students, long as they didn't need much sleep. Well, I've never been a bed-bug, three hours a night does me and anything extra I can make up by cat-napping.

I started in the kitchen but soon I was waiting on tables. They looked after their people at A-P and that canteen was like a good-class diner, with the execs using it as much as the line workers. Not so many of the suits around at night, of course, but always some.

The man in charge of the whole corporation was Joe

Proffitt. His grandfather had started the business way back. Like Maciver's it had grown, but much faster and further, and the Proffitts had kept a controlling interest through all the development. He moved in pretty rarefied circles so we didn't see much of him though I got to know him later. His man on the spot was Tony Kafka, still young but definitely the kind of guy stopped you talking when he came into a room. He often dropped into the canteen at night. I was told exactly how he liked his coffee served.

Funny in view of what happened later, but to start with I didn't care for him much. He was friendly enough, but not really seeing me as anything but a skinny waitress. He used to make jokes about my figure, saying someone ought to feed me up, how did I expect to keep a man if I didn't give him something to get a hold of?

The one I liked was Frank Phillips. He was a computer whizz in Accounts, so not much cause for him to be around nights, but soon he started showing pretty regular.

He wasn't much older than me, still in his early twenties, but a real high-flier and he seemed to know everything. The word cocksure was made for him in any and every sense. Gorgeous to look at and I guess he knew it. Never short of admirers so when he started admiring me, I was flattered. He seemed genuinely interested in me the way I was, asking about my family background and what I was doing at college. Deception's habit-forming and I'd got used to answering family questions vaguely. But when he said, 'Dickinson, from

Massachusetts . . . not related to Emily by any chance?' –
instead of telling him I wasn't really from Massachusetts
and spelt it with an 'e' anyway, I heard myself saying,
'Distantly, I think. But we don't exchange Christmas
cards.'

I don't know why I said that. Yes, I do. I was a
skinny no-account waitress and I wanted to make myself
interesting.

We'd looked at some of Emily's poems in the
American Literature module on my course, but after
that I really started to get into them. Stupid, eh? All
because of something some cute guy says.

To cut to the chase, what was always going to happen
happened. We went out a couple of times. He said he
was crazy about me, I was certainly crazy about him.
When we went to bed he produced a skin. I took it off
him and threw it aside. He said, 'You sure?' I said,
'No problem.' I guess he thought I meant I was taking
care of things. What naïve little me meant was, this is
for life, isn't it? What need to take precautions?

And when I found I was pregnant, I really believed
the news would have him lighting cigars and jumping
for joy.

Well, the only thing he jumped for was the door and
the only thing he lit was out.

I didn't see him for a week and when he did make
contact with me it was to offer to pay for a termination.

I told him, no way. By this time I'd learned he was
the company stud, but it made no difference to the way
I felt. I just thought that once he got used to the idea
of being a father, he'd see it was time to settle down.

Days of complete silence followed, became weeks. Finally after a month I sank my pride and made enquiries. That's when I learned he'd got a transfer to one of A-P's overseas subsidiaries.

I was devastated. Then I thought, To hell with him! I can do this alone.

Maybe I could have done, but I didn't have to find out. This was where Tony came in. I'd have expected him to come on hard with heavy jokes about how he was pleased to see I'd decided to put on some weight after all. Instead, as my waistline thickened he seemed to start seeing me as a real person, not just some part-time waitress passing through. Could be he felt responsible when he found out it was one of his own people who got me in this fix. I heard later that he put it around that after Frank left Hartford they found he'd had his hand in the till, with the result that not only did he get dumped from A-P but he was going to find it hard to get work anywhere serious.

So my time came. I even got maternity leave under the A-P welfare scheme, not something I was entitled to as a part-time casual, but Tony had given the nod. When my time came it was hard. You name a complication, I had it. By the time they finished with me, I wasn't in a state where I was going to be able to have any more kids, but that didn't bother me, not then, not when I found myself nursing my little girl.

She was enough for me. She was my world, my meaning, my future.

If that sounds big for a little girl, let me also say that she was lovely in the most conventional ways – big blue

*eyes, blonde hair already growing at birth and blos-
soming into a mass of curls within a couple of weeks,
and a skin white as a pearl touched with the pink of
a new day.*

Maybe that's why I called her Alba. The dawn.

*The next few months were the happiest of my life.
Money was tight but sufficient. With my own little bit,
plus (thanks to Tony) my maternity leave 'entitlement'
from A-P, I was able to look after Alba and even keep
my college work ticking over. Eventually I had to commit
myself fully to my course, and also get back to earning
some money. Fortunately there were good crèche
facilities at the college and even better ones at A-P, so
wherever I was I was never far from Alba.*

*In the canteen, Tony treated me like a friend and I
noticed that all the other execs were polite and courte-
ous. No wisecracks or jokey flirting. I didn't know then
that Frank's career had suddenly gone into a tailspin,
but I guess word had already reached the A-P executive
locker room, making everyone aware I was somehow
under Tony's protection. Not that he ever came on. It
was like having Pa around to look out for me. Pa
without the suddenness. Pa as he might have become.*

*At college I was doing OK, considering I was getting
even less sleep now than before. Like I say, thank God
I don't need much! When I thought of Frank I couldn't
feel bitter. Hadn't he given me the best thing in my life,
my daughter?*

Also, indirectly, he'd given me Emily Dickinson.

*For my main course project I'd opted to do a study
of her. A fine poet, odd, weird even, but she spoke directly*

to me. Sometimes I felt I was eavesdropping on my own thoughts. All those tiny poems. Reading them was like dipping my fingers into a casket of gems; I never knew what I was going to come up with but I knew it would be precious. Sometimes more than precious. Prophetic. For when the mood came on me, I even started using them as a kind of Sortes, opening my collection at random and rarely being disappointed in my expectation that something on the page before me would speak to me in a special way.

But the casting of lots is not always a source of solace.

I was working on my paper in the college library one day when I felt the urge to delve.

I opened the volume casually and read the first poem my eyes lit on.

> Good Morning – Midnight –
> I'm coming Home –
> Day – got tired of Me –
> How could I – of Him?

And as I read that first stanza, a bitterness filled my mouth like I'd bitten on a suicide ampoule and I felt a paralysing numbness coursing along my veins.

'Miss Dickenson,' said a voice behind me.

It was the librarian, his face a blank more expressive than concern. He said, 'Just had the crèche on the phone. Could you get down there?'

As I ran along the corridors, my feet beat out the rhythm of the second verse

Sunshine was a sweet place –
I liked to stay –
But Morn – didn't want me – now –
So – Goodnight – Day!

In the crèche I found alarm and confusion centred on Alba. She had had some kind of seizure and was now breathing shallowly, her face flushed, her eyes open but unfocused. An ambulance was on its way.

As it bore us to hospital, the last two verses of the poem beat through my mind. They sounded at the same time valedictory and menacing:

I can look – can't I –
When the East is Red?
The Hills – have a way – then –
That puts the Heart – abroad –

You – are not so fair – Midnight –
I chose – Day –
But – please take a little Girl –
He turned away!

And that was it. The next few hours were filled with nurses and doctors and I could quote you every syllable of every sentence they spoke to me. But from the start, no matter how desperately I riddled their words, I could find nothing in them to show me a prospect more hopeful than that which Emily's poem had already laid out.

It was midnight for Alba, midnight for me. The doctors spoke of cause. Acute viral encephalitis. But I could see only effect. My bright, beautiful, laughing, loving baby was now an unresponsive bundle of emptiness. I looked into those dull eyes and told myself my Alba was in there somewhere. But she was already far beyond my feeble outreach.

She still had all of my love but it wasn't enough, and I felt it was my fault it wasn't enough.

In the end they told me she was gone beyond all hope of recovery. Only the machines kept her breathing. They needed my say-so to switch them off.

It was like they were saying, you've already managed to lose your child, now we want you to kill her.

So I did.

Goodnight – Day!

11

a feminist hook

The tape hadn't finished – Pascoe could hear the woman's breathing, short and harsh at first then modulating into a softer, longer rhythm, as if she were pausing to get herself under control.

He needed a pause too. He switched the machine off and sat staring sightlessly out of the window.

A lost child. A lost daughter. He had been very close to that. And in this, being very close meant going all the way and beyond, as no matter what others told you of hope and urged on you of strength, you were already over the threshold and into the grey land of loss, of grief, of living death. He recalled his feelings on being dragged back from that land. Oh there was joy, and gratitude, and happiness almost painful in its intensity. But before that there'd been what later analysis made him think of as a Lazarus moment, compounded of bewilderment; and resentment almost, at being returned to a state where crossing that dreadful threshold still remained a possibility.

This woman had been over that threshold. And hadn't returned.

He shook his head and forced his gaze to focus on the reality of the handsome Spanish-style house.

Casa Alba.

Oh shit.

Casa Alba. Meaning, if his small Spanish served him, the house of dawn.

Alba Dickenson. Named after the dawn. Whose death sent her mother leaping over the intervening day into midnight.

Could it be simple coincidence that Pal had built his house in the same village where his stepmother lived and given it a name that must remind her every time she heard it of her dead child? Could he have been capable of such a piece of cruel mockery?

And in relation to his own death, did it matter anyway?

He was drawn out of this painful speculation by the sound of a car engine being driven very fast. He twisted in his seat to look towards the narrow country road, along which a bright red sports car was hurtling as if driven by one of the Schumachers with the other in hot pursuit.

A red Alfa Romeo Spider. Hadn't Sue-Lynn been driving such a car the other night at Moscow?

The question was answered as, with a screeching of brakes of the kind which is usually followed by a very loud crash, the Spider span off the road and through the gateway with no more than the merest clipping of a wing mirror.

It was a fine or fortunate piece of driving but it looked like it might all go to waste as the car came screaming up the drive as if its driver's intention were to enter the house without bothering to knock. He could see Sue-Lynn's face through the windscreen, so devoid of emotion it might as well have been a mask, and just when he was convinced that in an unlikely act of suttee she had decided to follow her husband at speed into the next world, she hit the brake.

In a second manoeuvre worthy of a stunt artist, the car skidded to a halt, its back end slewing round and sending a machine-gun spatter of gravel against the bonnet of the BMW.

Sue-Lynn didn't even glance towards the other two vehicles as she slid out and headed up to her front door, almost as fleet of foot as she was of machine.

And the woman in the BMW was no slouch either, observed Pascoe. She was out and heading towards Sue-Lynn, shouting something as she ran. He couldn't make out the words but the tone was unmistakably hostile. He began to get out of his car.

Sue-Lynn turned and looked at the approaching woman, decided she didn't like what she saw or heard, and continued inserting her key in the lock, presumably with a view to putting the front door between herself and her visitor.

It would have been a wise move. The well-built woman was alongside her now, still yelling incoherently and thrusting a sheet of paper in her face.

Sue-Lynn looked at it and spoke.

Whatever she said didn't go down too well. The other woman said, 'Bitch!' Pascoe was close enough now to make this out quite clearly, but not yet close enough nor indeed psychologically prepared enough to intervene when she drew back her right hand and launched a blow at Sue-Lynn's head. No open-handed feminine slap, this, but a full-blooded feminist right hook that landed with audible ferocity on the side of Sue-Lynn's jaw.

She crashed back against the door and slid down it with an expression that seemed to have as much of surprise as pain in it. Her attacker loomed over her for a moment as if contemplating giving her a kicking, then ripped in half the paper she'd been waving in her left hand and scattered the halves over the recumbent woman.

Pascoe said, 'OK, that's enough.'

She turned, glared at him and said, 'You think so?' then shouldered him aside and headed back to the BMW.

He knew he ought to arrest her. Senior policemen couldn't be witnesses to assault without doing something. On the other hand with a punch like that . . .

Too late now anyway. The BMW's engine

roared, its rear wheels span in the gravel and it was his car's turn to get the fusillade, then it found traction and set off down the drive as if bent on breaking the Spider's recently established record.

Sue-Lynn was trying to stand. He said, 'Are you all right?' and offered his hand. She ignored it and pulled herself up by the door handle.

He said, 'Mrs Maciver, I'm Detective Chief Inspector Pascoe. We met at Moscow House.'

She turned the key in the lock and opened the door just sufficiently to slip inside.

He said, 'I'm sorry to trouble you so soon after your sad loss, but I wonder if we could talk . . .'

She said with some difficulty – her jaw visibly swelling – 'My sad loss? You mean my house and my income? That's the only fucking sad loss I've had. But the bastard's not going to get away with it, believe me! So why don't you just piss off?'

She slammed the door in his face.

What's happened to the old Pascoe charm? he asked himself.

He turned away, then paused and bent down to pick up the two pieces of what appeared to be a computer-generated photograph printed on ordinary bond paper.

He joined them up.

It was a picture of a ruffled bed with on one side of it a woman in her panties wrestling with her bra, and on the other a man apparently having a problem zipping up his trousers over a semi-erect penis, both staring pop-eyed into the camera as if it were (and indeed as in the circumstances presumably it was) the last thing on earth they wanted to see.

The woman was Sue-Lynn, the man was Dr Tom Lockridge.

And it didn't take more than a small proportion of Pascoe's detective skills to guess that it was probably Mrs Tom Lockridge speeding away in the Beamer.

There was a date and time registered along the bottom of the photo.

The same night as, and not very long before, Pal Maciver's suicide.

He returned to his car and sat down to review the situation.

So far, he concluded, all he'd got was a mixture of doubts and whispers, sound and fury, none of it signifying enough to make a coherent report.

What next?

While he was trying to reach that important decision, he might as well hear the rest of this tape which Dalziel clearly believed was important to his understanding of . . . what?

He pressed the 'start' button.

12

Kay (2)

After Alba died, there were those who began to talk of 'a blessed relief', but my reaction was so savage, the banalities rarely emerged complete from their lips.

Only Tony got it right.

'Life's shit,' he said. 'Be strong. It won't get better. But you'll get stronger.'

I don't know what I would have done without Tony so many times in my life.

At the college they were kind and understanding but I had no energy for that stuff any more and I dropped out. I needed work and took the easy route of applying to go full-time in the A-P canteen. Easy routes were my preferred option then. I don't recall much of that time, but I suspect I was such a lousy miserable waitress people were put off their food. I must have come close to being fired. Again it was Tony who saved me. One day a woman from personnel told me I was starting in Tony's office the next day. I didn't ask, Starting what? or offer any objection. I just turned up, sat down, did what I was told. And that was how I spent the next eight, nine, ten months – simply doing whatever the office supervisor told me – word processing, filing, making coffee – all she had to do was ask.

Slowly I began to emerge from my shell of grief. Very slowly. Some time in all this, I became aware there was important stuff going on – big shake-ups, crisis meetings, worried faces all over the place – but my awareness never got close to interest or understanding. Maybe my indifference somehow got confused with loyalty and dependability, for at the end of it all, I found Tony's PA inviting me to work as her gofer. She was good, so good she got head-hunted. I'd been working with her nine months when she said she was leaving. I expected the job to be advertised and even wondered if I dared apply, but not very seriously. Then I came to work one morning and found my name being stencilled on her office door.

I was so knocked over, I didn't think of Alba for over an hour.

And when I did, for the first time since she died I found I was totally aware of who I was, where I was, and what I was doing.

Still no men in my life. Understandable, as anyone who gave me the eye I automatically hated. Not that there were many. Under Tony's watchful eye, I could probably have walked round the plant naked carrying a sackful of gold without fear of molestation. As for elsewhere, there wasn't really any elsewhere.

Then we came to England for the Maciver takeover negotiations and I met Pal.

I could see he was interested from our first encounter, and he didn't give a damn if Tony approved or not.

Me, at first I was amused. Twenty years older than me, a widower with three kids, a Brit – nobody needed to rehearse the strikes against him. And even if I'd fallen madly in love with him at first sight, my first sight of Pal Junior and Cressida would probably have nipped that in the bud. I don't know in what terms their father had prepared them for my appearance, but they were on full security alert, all systems armed. I was the enemy, their mission was to destroy. I couldn't blame them. Young Pal was fifteen, Cressida twelve, not the most rational of ages. And nine months earlier they'd lost their mother.

I would have signalled no-contest and got out of there if it hadn't been for Helen. She had big blue eyes and blonde curls and she was just turned four, the same age Alba would have been. A kid that age loses her mother, it must leave a gap of instant unquestioning love no amount of sympathy and concern can fill. It was sympathy and concern I felt for the older children, but not for Helen. I saw her and all the love I'd had for Alba came surging through. She must have felt it, for there wasn't even a moment when we were strangers.

And Pal watching us together at that first encounter must have known he'd got himself a wife.

I'd expected if not objection at least reservation from Tony but once more he surprised me. He was more than encouraging, he was enthusiastic. 'The kid needs a mother,' he said, by which at first I thought he meant I needed a kid. But thinking about it since, I don't recollect ever hearing Tony say something he didn't mean.

Anyway, the marriage went ahead, the takeover went ahead, everyone was happy.

Except Pal Junior and Cressida.

They set out to make my life hell. Not too obviously and never in front of their father. But they worked at it, oh yes, they really worked at it. And they might have succeeded if it hadn't been for Helen. She was my antidote. She made my life a heaven their feeble attempts at hell couldn't touch. Naturally they tried to get to me through her, but I let them see that here was the line in the sand. Step over that and I'd go nuclear. They backed off, but the guerrilla war continued. There's no defence against a guerrilla war; all you can do is tough it out and hope that at last simple fatigue will bring them to the conference table. I did try to talk to Pal Senior, but it was hard. He'd got himself the family grouping he wanted and he didn't care to see any cracks in the plaster. I tried to get to him through his sister, Lavinia, but she was right off the map, both mentally and physically. I called in to see her once and it was like stepping into that Hitchcock movie The Birds.

So I just had to play the waiting game. I thought things might get better when Cressida went away to school. It was her own idea and her father was keen. Me, I'd never have wanted any child of mine to spend so much of those formative years away from home, but I wasn't about to object in Cressida's case. With Pal Junior out of the house for much of the time doing whatever teenage boys do, it meant I'd have lots of quality time with Helen. And I was still naive enough to hope every time Cressida came home for the holidays, that she'd have grown up a bit and grown out of her petty resentment. Certainly for a while I began to feel that maybe her brother had made this progress. He had gone into the sixth form and there'd been some friction between him and his father about his choice of subjects. Pal Senior had been the active outdoor type in his younger days, I gathered, climbing, shooting, that stuff, and later he'd channelled all those energies into the business, which made giving it up so hard. Pal Junior had never shown any interest in outdoor activities and now he announced bluntly that he certainly didn't want to follow his father into a business career, instead it was his ambition to go to university and study art history. If the family firm had still existed as an entity, I dread to think what a schism this might have caused. Even without the inheritance factor, his father was seriously pissed, but I stuck up for the boy and acted as mediator and I guess I hoped that this might have helped him see what an asshole he'd been over the past couple of years. Certainly to start with he seemed much less surly towards me. In fact on occasions he was positively attentive. Then gradually I began to feel he was being over attentive. He always seemed to be around, bringing me drinks, checking that I was comfortable. If I sat on a sofa, he'd flop down next to me. And, even more worryingly, whenever I lay around the garden sunbathing in my bikini, he'd turn up too. Or if I went to have a shower, when I came out of the shower room with my towel draped around me, he'd just happen to be strolling along the corridor. I began to feel stalked. This was just a new technique to get at me, I decided. The bastard knew how hard it would be for me, after complaining for so long that he took no heed of me, to start protesting he was over-attentive!

But maybe I should have spoken up instead of just taking steps to keep out of his line of sight . . . Maybe he took my lack of open complaint for encouragement.

I'm being charitable here. I don't really feel it.

It was towards the end of his last term in the sixth, exam time. I had the house to myself one afternoon. My husband was at the works – he still insisted on going in most days, even though it was clear to everyone else that his so-called advisory responsibility was merely a face-saver. Cressida was away at school, Helen was at a friend's birthday party and Pal Junior, who was doing his last exam that morning, had announced he and his friends were going to spend the rest of the day celebrating. I took the chance to do some work in the garden. I love gardening but didn't get much encouragement from my husband, who hired a man to come in two or three times a week and, like a true Yorkshireman, didn't see why I should do work he'd paid someone else to do. Today wasn't one of the gardener's days, so I was able to really sort out a couple of the beds that had been irritating me for some time.

It was funny. From time to time I felt like I was being watched but whenever I looked up, I could see no one. After a couple of hours I'd worked myself into a good sweat and my back was beginning to ache so I went into the house for a shower. It was heaven just to stand there under the hot jet and feel the water washing the sweat off my body and the aches out of my muscles. I stood there I don't know how long with my head back and my eyes closed.

And when at last I opened my eyes I saw through the

steamed-up glass of the shower cubicle a figure standing outside.

I said, 'Pal, is that you?' and opened the door.

It was Pal all right, but Pal Junior. He was standing there naked, jerking off.

We just looked at each other for a long moment. Then he flung himself at me, forcing me back into the cubicle.

What would have happened then I don't know, but fortunately he was already so roused that his efforts to force himself between my legs brought him to climax. I felt him go into spasm against me. He was screaming out my name, whether in pleasure or frustration I don't know. I pushed him away with all my strength and he stood there, still firing come at me like he wished it were bullets.

I lost it then for a while and began to yell at him, incoherently at first, but eventually I got back control. I grabbed a towel around me and I told him he was a disgusting little shit and this was one piece of behaviour his father wasn't going to be able to ignore. I'd stopped being frightened now – he certainly wasn't a sexual threat any more – and even as I spoke I found myself thinking I sounded like some outraged doyenne of the League of Purity. But I didn't know how else to deal with the situation.

Pal was much more self-possessed.

He just stood there smiling and said, 'You do that and I'll tell Dad that what really happened is you've been coming on to me and you got pissed because I turned you down.'

'And you think he'll believe that?' I demanded.

'Why not? I'm a lot nearer your age than he is, aren't I?' he replied. 'In fact, come on, admit it, there's a bit of truth in there somewhere, isn't there? Don't pretend you've never wondered how it would be with me. So how about it some time? Keep it in the family, eh?'

I ran at him then, wanting to scratch the sneering complacency out of his face. It was probably a stupid thing to do, but he didn't retaliate, just ducked out of my reach and turned and left. A few minutes later I heard him go down the stairs and I ran to the bedroom window and watched him stroll off down the drive. He even turned to wave at me!

At that moment I was absolutely resolved to tell Pal Senior everything, but by the time he came home that evening, I had weakened. Faced with such a conflict of stories, how would he react? Would he recall the way I'd taken his son's part against him in the matter of the university course and let this sow the seed of doubt? Anything but total belief on his part I couldn't tolerate.

He was in an angry mood when he got home, which made my silence the easier. After years of being master of all he surveyed at the plant, and first mover of all activity there, he grew increasingly frustrated each time he found himself being cut out of the loop. This was driving a wedge between us too. Tony had stayed on in Mid-Yorkshire to oversee the transition period at A-P's new acquisition and I'd carried on as his PA after my marriage, thinking it was short term till he went back to the States. But for one reason or another after a couple of years Tony seemed to have settled into the job of head man at Ash-Mac's on a more permanent basis and had

385

even got himself a house out in the sticks at Cothersley. I carried on working for him but only after I made it quite clear looking after Helen was my first concern. Tony said no problem, he'd have sacked me if he thought I wouldn't put Helen first, which was sweet. And for a while, Pal had seemed cool with the idea, but as his frustration with being side-lined as he saw it grew, I think he started resenting his feeling that I was a lot closer to the action at Ash-Mac's than he was.

So all in all it seemed better to keep my mouth shut and take even greater care to avoid letting Pal Junior in striking distance.

This proved easier than I'd hoped. He announced he wanted to spend most of his pre-Cambridge vac doing a modern version of the Grand Tour with some chums. His father fulminated about the expense but I chipped in that, in view of his degree course, this could be regarded as useful preparation.

So he disappeared, Cressida went off to stay with a schoolfriend, and I had a lovely summer with Helen.

For the next eighteen months, with Pal Junior up at Cambridge and Cressida in her school sixth form, things got a bit easier, but only because they spent less and less time at Moscow House. When they were home, their campaign against me was pretty unrelenting. Its form had changed. No malicious practical jokes. In their father's presence they were coldly polite. Out of it they treated me as an ignorant foreigner untouched by either learning or culture who needed to be talked to in words of one syllable and who nursed an illicit passion for Pal Junior.

But familiarity breeds indifference even to offence, and I let all this roll off me, helped, as I say, by the knowledge that I never had to put up with it for long.

Then came last Christmas. They were at their worst. Their father was immersed in one of his deepest bouts of resentment at what he called the mismanagement of Ash-Mac's, which, in my view, amounted to little more than a pig-headed refusal to admit he'd sold the company and finally moved on. Some of this resentment seemed to spill over on to me and the children, sensing the barrier his presence normally created was lowered, were merciless. Even when they went back to college and to school in January, things didn't get much better. My husband too now treated me with a cold reserve which made life very uncomfortable. So when Tony told me that Ashur-Proffitt were having a big party in Hartford at the end of March to celebrate fifty years of trading and invited me to attend, I jumped at the chance to get away. It seemed silly to fly all that way just for a weekend, and in any case I really wanted a longer break from Moscow House. The only trouble was Helen, who got deeply upset when I told her I might be away for a couple of weeks, so in the end I got this great idea of taking her with me and showing her a bit of the States. It meant taking her out of school but with the Easter holiday not far ahead, it wasn't going to make very much difference. Pal Senior reacted with indifference. He seemed to be totally immersed in some scheme he was hatching to get back some of his old power at Ash-Mac's. What he thought he could do, God knows. I tried to remind him that legally he was out of the loop with no way back in, but he wasn't listening. A couple of weeks ago he took off on some mystery trip to London, and that same afternoon I heard the front door open and when I went to see who it was, I found myself looking at Pal Junior.

He pretended to be surprised that his father wasn't there. Maybe he was. But I was taking no chances. Helen, who had a bit of a cold, went to bed early and I followed her not long after, locking my door behind me.

Helen's room was next to mine and I could hear her coughing. I must have fallen asleep for I awoke just as the clock on the landing struck midnight. There was no sound of coughing from Helen's room but I thought I heard her door close. After a while I got up and went to check. Her bed was empty. I went out on to the landing thinking she'd probably gone to the bathroom when I heard a noise downstairs. I went down the stairs cautiously – I hadn't forgotten Pal Junior was home – but when I heard the piano in the music room, I was sure it must be Helen. She was the only one in the family with any real musical talent and the notes being picked out were the opening bars of her party piece 'Of Foreign Lands and People' *from Schumann's* Childhood Scenes. *So I just walked straight into the darkened room, saying something like, 'Hi, darling, it's only me. Couldn't you sleep then?'*

And Pal Junior's voice replied, 'With you in the house? No way, darling.'

He'd been drinking, but not enough to affect his movement. He was off the piano stool and round behind me, shutting the door, before I could even feel concerned. But when he grabbed hold of me, I felt concerned. I was only wearing the short T-shirt I sleep in and he pushed this up and pulled me to him. He was fully clothed but that didn't stop me feeling his huge excitement. He was trying to kiss me. I wanted to shriek but with only Helen in the house, what good would that do? I tried to talk to him, but he was beyond reach of words. He released his grip with one hand so that he could undo his belt and push his trousers down. I twisted out of his other arm and scrambled away from him but I fell over the stool and crashed down on the open keyboard. The noise was tremendous. It seemed to excite him even more. He threw me to the floor, face down, and straddled me, saying something like, 'Prefer it this way, do you? Suits me!' And he'd got his pants undone by now and God knows what would have happened. But just then I heard Helen's voice calling, 'Kay? Kay? Is that you?'

She had been in the bathroom, I realized later, and now she was descending the stairs, attracted by the discord from the piano.

Pal paused. I said, 'For God's sake, it's your kid sister. You want her to see you like this?'

He rolled off me.

As I got up and headed for the door, he said, 'Another time then, Kay. Third time lucky, eh?'

I got out of there and pulled the door shut behind me just as Helen reached the foot of the stairs.

I turned her round and hurried her back upstairs, scolding her for wandering around in the night draughts, and insisting she came into my room for the rest of the night, which she always loved doing. She lay beside me and chattered herself to sleep but I never closed my eyes, *listening to every noise in the darkness and wondering how I was going to deal with this.*

In the morning I found that Pal had gone.

His father didn't return till a couple of days later, the day before I was due to fly to the States with Helen. Whatever he'd been doing, he seemed very pleased with the way things had gone and this spilled over into the way he regarded me. It didn't seem a good time to say anything. When would there be a good time? I didn't know, but with my trip back home so close, it was easy to postpone my problem. In fact I decided to take my leave of him while things were so good between us. Does that seem contradictory? My thinking was how much better it would be for both of us if we didn't separate for what was going to be our longest period apart since the wedding on a sour note. So I told him that, rather than heading off first thing in the morning, I'd decided to book me and Helen in at an airport hotel that night. He said fine, it made much more sense, it's what he always preferred to do. And we kissed like a fond old married couple and off I went.

Would it have made a difference if I'd stayed? I don't know. I can't say whether the lying letter Pal Junior says he sent him was already in the pile of mail which he hadn't yet opened when I left or whether it came next morning. Maybe if those dreadful accusations were what drove him to kill himself, I could have refuted them. But only at the expense of showing him the kind of son he had, and that might have been worse.

Of course it could be Pal Junior never sent a letter at all and has just made that up because he's genuinely convinced that I'm indirectly to blame for his father's death. Which would mean there's some other reason for the suicide.

I don't know. All I know is we kissed goodbye then off I went, first to Florida to give Helen a look at Disneyland and get the English chill out of our bones. Then I hired a car and we headed north. No plans. I had ten days to get to Hartford and I just wanted Helen to have fun and see as much of my country as we could. That's why it took the cops so long to track us down.

I wish I'd been here. In the long run it might not have made any difference, but at least I'm sure he wouldn't have done it with me and Helen in the house. And I wish I could have got back quicker. Young Pal and Cress were always going to blame me. There'd have been bitter words, I don't doubt. But words are only a vibration of the air. However bitter, they leave no trace. My delay gave them time for deeds, however. They changed the locks, shut me out of my house because it was now their house. And that first deed was a step which has set them on a path it was always going to be hard to retreat from.

Like I say, I don't know exactly why my husband killed himself. Perhaps he didn't really know either. Perhaps that's why he seems to have started writing a note then burnt it, because if he could have expressed the darkness inside him, he could have brought it under control. Maybe it was Pal Junior's letter he burnt. Maybe. Certainly, the way Pal's been behaving, the things he's been saying since it happened make it sound like he's got something on his conscience and is trying to offload *his guilt on to me. I wish you could assure him it's not worth the effort, Andy. I sure as hell feel guilty enough without his help. Much as I'd like it, there's no way I can put my hand on my heart and swear Pal's suicide had nothing to do with me. It had something to do with all of us because none of us could offer him enough to stop him doing it. But was I to blame solely and specifically? I don't believe so. I can't believe so. Having Emily Dickinson's poems open on the desk before him, the same volume I had given to him in token of love, might seem like a kind of accusation. I'm sure the kids are going to think so. In a sense they're right. I'd told him about the way I used the poems as a form of Sortes. So maybe he'd followed my example and hit upon 1062 . . .* Caressed a Trigger absently and wandered out of Life . . . *Could that have tipped him over? Maybe. But when you're ready to be tipped, even the sun shining bright and daffodils dancing in the breeze must look like a message telling you it's time to go.*

That's what I'm telling myself anyway. I loved my husband. OK, maybe I loved him more for being Helen's dad than for being Palinurus Maciver. But that made him even more precious to me. Sexual love is selfish. As well as great pleasure it can be the occasion of great pain, sometimes given carelessly, sometimes with malice aforethought. But I loved Pal through Helen. No way I could hurt one without hurting the other. If I seem cool and collected now it's not because I'm not in pain myself. It's because all my strength now has only one task.

To protect Helen and bring her through this pain.

I can't find it in me to condemn Pal Junior for the

*way he's reacting. Finding his father like that must have
been terrible beyond belief. However badly he's behaved
in the past, the way he's acting now is completely understandable. But he's got to stop. Not for my sake, I'm big
enough to take it. But for his own sake, and for Cressida's,
and above all for Helen's.*

*She's got her life ahead of her. With me by her side,
I believe that can be a good life, the kind of life her father
would have wanted for her. No way should anything be
allowed to get in the way of that.*

That's what I owe to my husband.

That's what I owe to myself.

*Andy, I'm sorry, you asked for a brief statement and I
seem to have given you a life history. Once I got started . . .
well, it's probably not much use to you, but it's done me
a lot of good, I think, just getting it all said. I could just
scrub over it, I guess, but I'd like you to hear it, because
I want you to understand why I want all this tidied up
as quietly as possible. Like I say, Helen's the only person
who matters in all this. I don't much care what the other
two do or say, so long as it doesn't turn into a public
screaming match that Helen can't help hearing about.
Time will sort everything out, I'm sure of that, but to get
that time we need a truce.*

*Andy, I'm sure that if any man can fix that truce,
it's you.*

13

not the Beverley Sisters

After the tape had finished Pascoe once more sat staring at the windscreen, his gaze going no further than the insect-smeared glass.

No question, it was a powerfully moving statement. Even without anything but a superficial knowledge of the woman, he could feel himself being magicked by her.

But was it enough to explain Dalziel's relationship with her? He thought not.

The Fat Man was beyond simple enchantment. He wouldn't have needed to be bound to the mast to listen to the sirens singing. He'd have sat in a deck chair with a pint in his hand, applauded politely when they finished and said, 'Aye, very nice, but they're not the Beverley Sisters, are they?'

No, though the statement may have reinforced his feelings for the woman, their relationship predated it. Wield had spotted something between them from the start, and the way she addressed him and the things she said in the tape's little coda confirmed a relationship already established, a judgment already made before Pal Senior's suicide brought Kay into his life professionally.

And here he was again ten years on, the perfect gentle knight riding to his lady's aid.

'God help the horse!' said Pascoe out loud, and smiled.

Conclusion: the only thing he was certain of was that if the Fat Man believed hearing the tape would make him steer well clear of Kay Kafka, he was wrong. Their brief encounter at the hospital hadn't told him much, but then he hadn't been asking much. He was still a long way from seeing how the link between stepmother and stepson could have any bearing on the latter's death, but after listening to the tape he knew he would like to confront the enchantress again and make up his own mind about her.

And why not now? Cothersley Hall was only a few miles away. He'd noticed it on his map when he'd been looking for Casa Alba, which didn't figure. You needed more than money to get your house name on an OS sheet, you needed antiquity.

So, he was resolved. Like the tinker in the ballad he would ride boldly up to the hall. But not quite straightaway. It was a long time since breakfast, which as a result of his late rising (oh, the sweet memory) had consisted of a mouthful of coffee and a gobbet of bread. Now, despite the

Fat Man's warning and his own observations, the fripperies of the Dog and Duck were seeming quite attractive. In addition there were a couple of things he'd like to check out with the Captain.

As he turned on the engine, he glanced up at the house.

Sue-Lynn was standing at an upstairs window watching him. She was holding something to her jaw, probably a bag of frozen peas.

No, he corrected. Not peas. Dublin Bay prawns, or Beluga caviare. She looked like a woman with expensive tastes.

Which from the sound of it she wasn't going to enjoy for long.

He gave her a wave, resisted the temptation to gun his engine and dig up more gravel as he tried to break the records so recently established by the two women, and set off down the drive at the speed of a cautious cortege.

14

Mohawks

As Edgar Wield drove back from Harrogate, he thought of diverting to the Golden Fleece once more in the hope that Edwin might be free for lunch. Mature consideration made him decide this was unlikely and to expect his friend to break off some learned confabulation with his dusty colleagues would be as unfair as the bookseller calling him out of a CID meeting.

Instead he turned the bike in quite the other direction and headed for the Blesshouse Industrial Estate which sprawled to the south of the city.

It was clear as he got nearer that even with New Labour's promised recovery, the working week ended at Friday lunchtime for a lot of workers. A steady stream of cars and buses flowed out of the estate and probably some of them wouldn't be flowing back in until the following Monday lunchtime or even Tuesday.

He paused to study a billboard diagram and

located Ashur-Proffitt (with Maciver's printed after it in smaller letters). When he arrived at the barrier that blocked his entrance to the plant, a uniformed man appeared from the kiosk and said, 'How do, mate? And what can we do you for?'

As he removed his helmet and goggles, Wield said, 'Bet if I'd turned up in a suit and a BMW you'd not have talked to me like that, Bri.'

'Bugger me, it's you, Wieldy!' exclaimed the man. 'I should have recognized the bike. How're you doing? Long time no see.'

His name was Brian Edwards, he was a broad red-faced man in his fifties, and he'd been a DC till a problem with stomach ulcers brought on by the usual CID mix of stress, fags, beer and fatty take-aways had got him invalided out.

'I'm fine,' said Wield. 'Didn't know you worked here.'

'Oh aye. More than ten years now.'

'And is this all you do? I mean, are you on the security staff?'

Edwards grinned.

'You're thinking, is this the best the poor sod could get, being a gate-man? No, don't deny it, Sarge. Aye, I could have done better, might even have been wearing a suit and sitting in an office now. But I told 'em, I don't want owt that means wandering around at night and risking getting banged on the head and having to chase some thieving scrote who'll likely pull a blade if I catch him. No, checking folk in and out of the gate will do me fine. Regular hours and I've not had any trouble with me belly for years.'

'You're looking well,' agreed Wield. 'You don't recollect another ex-job guy, name of Jake Gallipot, who worked for Security here about ten years back?'

'Gallipot? DS from Harrogate? Him there used to be the stories about? Aye, I remember him. I recall thinking, if retired DSs are reduced to wandering around in peaked caps with a big stick, then mebbe I'm not doing so bad. He didn't last long, though. Couple of months at the outside, could have been less.'

'Did he leave or was he pushed?'

'Think he just handed in his cards. Never heard nowt to the contrary. He were pretty popular, always ready to stand and have a chat with anyone. Aye, everyone liked Jake. I heard later he'd got his own business, security or investigation or something, is that right?'

'Yes, that's right.'

'Good luck to him. Wouldn't have done for me. Start sticking your nose into other people's business you never know what they'll end up sticking into you.' He regarded Wield shrewdly and asked, 'Is it Gallipot you're here about?'

'If it was, who'd I want to speak to?' said Wield.

Edwards laughed.

'You don't change, do you? Give nowt that's not paid for and then ask for change. It 'ud be Tom Hoblitt. He does the hiring and firing. If this were the army, he'd be the RSM or top sergeant, him being a Yank.'

'Mr Hoblitt it is then. Where do I find him?'

'Nay, I'll take you across to Admin myself,' said Edwards. 'Can't have suspicious characters wandering around the plant unaccompanied, got strict instructions about that. Leave your bike here, it'll not get nicked.'

He spoke briefly to another man in the kiosk then led the way towards the plant at a brisk pace as though determined to demonstrate how fit he was.

You didn't have to be an industrial archae-ologist to plot the history of Ash-Mac's, thought Wield. The story of the firm was written quite clearly in the ugly sprawl of buildings that lay before him. The initial basic workshop where Liam Maciver had started all those years ago was still there, with around it all the brick-built devel-opment that marked the company's rapid expan-sion in the late thirties and forties. A keener eye might have been needed to detect the point where consolidation finished and decline began, but the reversal of that decline was unmistakable in several brand-new concrete-and-glass structures including a small office block over which flew both the Stars and Stripes and the Union flag.

Edwards led Wield in here. An unwelcoming receptionist wearing more paint than a bellicose Mohawk listened as the gate-man explained the sergeant's purpose, her gaze running over his leathered body as though assessing where best to place her tomahawk. She then picked up her phone, pressed a button, spoke rapidly in what might as well have been Iroquoian, listened, then said, 'Thank you, Mr Edwards. Sergeant Wield, will you come this way?'

She rose and set off rapidly up a flight of stairs.

Wield looked at Edwards, who made a face, murmured, 'I think she likes you,' and left.

The woman, as if unable to conceive her instruction would not be instantly acted upon, was already out of sight but Wield was able to detect her progress by the sonar click of stiletto heels and soon fell into line astern. On the second landing she passed through a door without knocking, said to another woman, whose face differed from hers only in that the tribal artist had painted a smile on it, 'This is Sergeant Wield,' and left.

The smiling woman went to an inner door, tapped once, opened it, and said, 'Sergeant Wield.'

He went through. A man was sitting behind a desk. He was in his forties, stockily built, with vigorous hair on the turn from black pepper to sea salt. He rose, extended his hand and said, 'Tony Kafka. How can I help you?'

'Must be a mistake, sir,' said Wield, shaking the proffered hand. 'It was Mr Hoblitt I wanted to see.'

'So I understand, but this time you got on a fast track to the organ grinder himself. Hoblitt's around the plant somewhere, so maybe I can clear up whatever it is you want clearing up.'

'Just a routine enquiry, sir. Hardly worth bothering you with.'

This was his first encounter with Kafka. There'd been no reason to have any direct contact with him when Pal Senior topped himself and less reason since. But he'd often wondered what kind of man it was that had taken on the enigmatic Kay Maciver and her stepdaughter after the tragedy.

The room itself gave little clue to character. Hanging on the wall was a photograph of the rock carvings of the heads of some American presidents which Wield recalled seeing in an old Hitchcock movie. On the clutter-free desk stood another photo in a silver frame, this one of a smiling soldier with a medal on his chest. He had to be some close relative of Kafka. The cheekbones and the nose were unmistakable. Nothing else which could be called personal was on view.

'You won't be bothering me, Sergeant,' said Kafka in a tone which clearly implied, *How could you?*

'Just an old employee we're interested in,' said Wield. 'Man called Gallipot. He worked for your Security people about ten years ago.'

'Gallipot?' said Kafka. 'Doesn't ring a bell.'

But it did. And not a very sweet chime either, thought Wield. The guy was good but it took best actor Oscar ability to deceive this critical gaze.

'No reason it should,' said Wield. 'Maybe I should talk to Mr Hoblitt . . . ?'

'Of course. Sorry. Let's see if we can find him for you. I'm just on my way out. Off to the States first thing tomorrow so I'm heading down to London tonight. And I'm still not packed.'

This sudden flood of information affably expressed was a natural reaction, often observed by Wield, in a witness who has decided to move swiftly away from an area he's not comfortable with. Kafka was a man more at home with direct-ness than deceit, which did not necessarily mean he was not deceptive.

He picked up a briefcase and led the way out of the office block. A man in a rather Ruritanian uniform was walking toward them with a huge German Shepherd whose expression reminded Wield of the receptionist.

'Seen Hoblitt, Joe?' said Kafka.

'In Despatch,' replied the man.

No, *sir*. Was this American democracy at work?

Kakfa glanced at him amusedly and said, 'What do you think of the uniform?'

Perceptive as well as deceptive.

'Love the tunic,' said Wield. 'Not very practical though.'

'Very visible though, which is the point, like those tall pointy hats your lot used to wear before they stopped pounding the beat. In Security, deterrence is the name of the game. In your busi-ness too, I guess.'

'Not my end of it, sir. Some folk you can't deter, you've got to catch 'em.'

'And some don't even give a damn about being caught. What do we do about those, Sergeant?'

'Suicide bombers and the like, you mean?' Wield shrugged. 'Build thicker walls. Retaliate. Persuade. No simple answer, sir. Hope the politicians find a way through, like they did in 1918.'

Kafka frowned.

'1918? There weren't any suicide bombers back then, were there?'

'Oh yes, sir. On both sides. Only they called them infantry and didn't give them a choice. You closed down for the weekend?'

'More or less. It's the way of the world. Recession, competition and automation. Fewer orders harder to get, and we don't need so many bodies around all the time anyway.'

He led the way into a long low windowless building from which the hum of machinery was still emanating, up a short stair and out on to a narrow catwalk overlooking a central area divided into several glass-enclosed sections joined by a heavyweight version of the moving belt used on an airport carousel. A piece of machinery – some form of lathe, Wield guessed – appeared at one end and began to move forward.

'This is A-P's own prep system,' said Kafka proudly. 'Some very clever guys back in the States devised it. Four separate stages, all fully automated. First there's the *oiler*, except of course its not oil but a polymeric silicon compound that coats the machine completely, then the *wrapper* where it's wrapped in a sheet of modified polyethylene which is then seam-sealed so that the *vaccer* can suck every molecule of air out before the final seal is completed. After that it will be suspended in an aluminium crate and completely enclosed in a polyurethane foam shell. When that hardens, you could drop the crate from a third-floor window and not do the contents any harm, and even if the machine's left lying around some damp or freezing or sandy or red-hot storage area for the next several years before being put into use, it will stay in perfect working condition. And all this requires just one guy to operate it.'

And a dozen guys to collect the dole, thought Wield.

He said, 'Do you have a lot of customers who'll pay a small fortune for goods they're going to leave lying around to get dusty and rusty?'

Kafka frowned and said, 'Once they pay, what they do with it is their business. We just guarantee it reaches them in the same condition it leaves here. There's Hoblitt. Hey, Tom!'

They had walked slowly along the catwalk keeping pace with the processes below. At the far end, a single silhouette against a strip light, stood two men deep in conversation. They looked round at the sound of Kafka's voice, then the silhouette divided, revealing one of the pair to be of almost Dalzielesque proportions. He came towards them, his bulk blocking sight of the other

405

who vanished down the stairs leaving only the impression of conventional proportions and a hat.

'Hi, Tony,' said the large man with an American twang that made Kafka sound like Noel Coward. 'You still here?'

'Evidently,' said Kafka. 'This is Sergeant Wield from the local CID. Something he wants to ask you about some old employee of ours. Name of Gallipot, was that it, Sergeant?'

'That's it, sir,' said Wield, who would have preferred to start from scratch with Hoblitt.

'I'll leave you to it then. Goodbye, Sergeant.'

'Goodbye, sir. Thank you.'

Kafka turned away then turned back.

'Tom, just to be sure there's no confusion, I've left instructions this order's to be put on hold till I get back.'

'Yeah, I was there when you said so, Tony. You just go and enjoy yourself. Lucky bastard. Wish it was me. Give my regards to the folks back home.'

'It's business, Tom,' said Kafka sternly. Then he smiled and added, 'But I've got to admit it will be good to see the old place again.'

He strode away and vanished down the stairway.

'Right, sergeant,' said Hoblitt. 'You want to come to my office and tell me what this is all about?'

Which proved to be a great deal harder than it sounded, and Hoblitt, though almost parodically

American, turned out to have absorbed enough of Yorkshire to be determined not to give anything without getting something in return.

'Look, Sergeant, before I go digging through old records, which will cost me time, and give you personal information about a former employee, which may itself be an offence under the Data Protection Act if not Human Rights legislation, you'll need to give me a hint. At the very least I'm entitled to know if this has got anything to do with anything that could affect the reputation or integrity of the Ashur-Proffitt Corporation.'

Wish to hell I knew! thought Wield.

He said, 'Not that I'm aware, sir. I'm sorry to tell you that Mr Gallipot is dead. Can't go into details, you understand. This is just in the nature of gathering background information. It's pretty routine in such circumstances.'

'Gathering information about a job a dead guy had for a couple of months ten years back is routine? No wonder you guys moan about being overworked!'

'You do remember Mr Gallipot then, sir?'

'Why do you say that?'

'Well, you recall he only worked here a couple of months.'

'Didn't you say that?'

Wield pursed his lips in a parody of attempted recollection.

'Don't believe I did, sir.'

'No matter,' said Hoblitt, making a visible decision to relax and be jolly. 'Yeah, I remember Jake. Ex-cop wasn't he? Kind of guy could sell rubbers to a eunuch. I tried to get him to apply for a job in our Sales department, that's how I remember him. But he said he wanted to stick with what he knew. Didn't stick with it long though, if I recall aright. Let's see . . .'

He put a floppy into the computer on his desk, hit a couple of keys, then said, 'Yeah, there he is. He came, he saw, he went. Of his own accord, no problems. Two months almost to the day. Nothing remarkable. You want a printout of this?'

'Thank you,' said Wield.

He could think of no reason to extend his visit and a few minutes later he was walking towards the gate. A car went by him driven by Kafka, who gave him a friendly wave. It paused by the kiosk and Edwards came out. Kafka spoke to him for a moment then drove on. Edwards waited for Wield but as he reached him a phone rang in the kiosk and the gate-man made an apologetic face and went inside.

He re-emerged as Wield geared up for the bike.

'Wish they'd make their minds up,' he grumbled. 'First one tells me the pick-up this afternoon's been cancelled, then t'other says it's back on again. I should have stopped in the job, Wieldy. At least when Fat Andy said owt, you knew it were carved in stone and it would take a sledgehammer to change it.'

'Don't know,' said Wield. 'You can do a lot of damage with a chisel if you just keep chipping away. Good to see you, Bri.'

'You too. Hope it's not so long next time. Any chance you'll be back?'

'Who knows?' called Wield over his shoulder. 'Who knows?'

LEEDS COLLEGE OF BUILDING
LIBRARY

15

our Lady of Pain

Dalziel at a case file was like a hyena at a carcase – he usually got to the heart of the matter but he didn't half leave a mess.

Hat Bowler, schooled by that most methodical of policemen, Edgar Wield, looked uneasily at the spoor of paper which ran from the Fat Man's side of the desk and ended accusingly at his own feet. Surely there was far more here than when they started?

The super himself seemed to have gone into some kind of trance. Perhaps his astral body was floating somewhere near the ceiling looking down on the chaos and detecting patterns not visible to mere mortal eyes.

Well, two could play the absence game, thought Hat. Officially he himself wasn't there at all, so none of this could be his responsibility.

He returned his attention to the telephone numbers. So far they'd revealed nothing of interest, though there was one number, a pay-as-you-go mobile, no subscriber name and address attached, which occurred a few times, both in and out, and most significantly on the evening of Pal Maciver's death.

He took out his own mobile, entered the number, got a message.

When he'd listened to it he switched off and checked the number on the sheet. Then he entered it again, very carefully, and listened to the message once more.

'Sir,' he said.

It took three more sirs *crescendo* before Dalziel descended to the terrestrial plane.

'Eh? What? You got something, lad?'

'This number, sir. Round about the likely time of Mr Maciver's death, someone rang his mobile, then his shop, and then his home, in that order.'

'Let's have a look. Oh aye,' said Dalziel, plucking a sheet of paper apparently at random from the scatter. 'That 'ud be Jason Dunn, the brother in law he were supposed to be playing squash with. So?'

'Think you should listen to this, sir.'

He pressed redial on his mobile and handed the phone to the Fat Man, who listened.

'Well well,' he said. 'Well bloody well.'

He switched off, and studied the list of telephone numbers. Finally he nodded, smiled the smile of a cannibal who sees several courses of lunch rowing towards his beach, and stood up.

'Nice one, Hat. That little holiday of thine's

clearly sharpened you up. I'm off out. You hold the fort here, in case any other bugger condescends to show his face. Keep sorting through this stuff, but try to be a bit tidier. You've got in a right scrow.'

'Yes, sir,' said Hat. 'Sir, if anyone asks, where shall I say you've gone?'

'I'll be down at the sports centre for starters. You play squash, lad?'

'No, sir.'

'Very wise. I once gave it a try but there weren't room to swing a cat and the other bugger kept bouncing off me and claiming the point. Told everyone later he'd whupped me, but he were the one had to be helped into Casualty, so it were one of them lyric victories Mr Pascoe keeps talking about.'

'Think maybe that would be Pyrrhic,' said Hat boldly.

'Correcting me as well? You must be good and ready to be signed off, lad.'

And whistling a tune which Hat, if he'd been a musical comedy fan, might have recognized as 'Goodbye' from *The White Horse Inn*, the Fat Man strode out of the office.

The young man on reception at the sports complex was a walking piece of physical geography, his biceps and triceps swelling like the Cotswolds and his tight-fitting gold singlet displaying a finely detailed relief map of his pectorals.

Unfortunately his devotion to muscular development seemed to have extended to his brain and neither the flashing of Dalziel's warrant card nor the baring of Dalziel's teeth could persuade him to co-operate with the superintendent's request.

Magnanimously putting this down to natural stupidity rather than wilful obduracy, Dalziel leaned over the counter and said very slowly, 'Take – me – to – your – leader.'

He also said it very loudly and the leader in question, the complex manager, emerged from his office. Name of George Manson, a native of the town and a long-time supporter of the rugby club bar, he recognized Dalziel immediately and two minutes later the Fat Man was sitting at a desk with a glass of scotch at his elbow and the squash court booking ledger open before him at the current page.

He went slowly back through it, making the occasional note, till he reached a point in December of the previous year. Then he reversed the process till he was back at today's date. Then he went back again, further this time, before returning once more to the present. In a rhythm approximately matching his temporal progress, the level of his scotch sank only to rise again as Manson kept a waiter's eye on his unexpected guest.

'Crossing out and another name being put in means a cancellation, right?' said Dalziel.

'Right.'

'And all the courts are here? I mean, there's not another court put aside for folk who just turn up?'

'No way. Most of the time, evenings and week-ends anyway, we're fully booked.'

'Oh aye? No wonder the intensive care units are overstretched,' said Dalziel. 'Thanks a lot.'

'My pleasure. Owt else I can help you with, Andy?' said Manson, curious as to what it was his visitor was looking for.

'Aye,' said Dalziel. 'A wee deoch an doris wouldn't go amiss. Good stuff this, George. Long time since I had a malt at export strength. Thought it all went to the States. Not been buying off the back of a lorry, I hope?'

'Cousin in the trade,' said Manson blandly. 'Get you a box, if you like. Trade price.'

'You're a kind man, George,' said Dalziel, drinking up. 'But no thanks. Small gifts I can accept, but owt that smacks of commercial advantage is right against the rules.'

The manager sighed and said, 'Remind me, when's your birthday?'

Half an hour later Dalziel was standing on the touchline of Weavers School rugby pitch on which thirty boys reduced to anonymity by several layers of mud were trying to prove their aptitude for the professional game by knocking hell out of each other. On either side of him stood parents, exhorting their offspring to greater excesses of brutality.

'Ever think of just teaching the lad to run with the ball and pass it?' he observed to the particularly vociferous father next to him.

'What the hell do you know about it, fatso?' came the snarled reply.

Dalziel turned his great head and looked directly into the man's eyes.

The man fell silent and after a moment moved away.

A few minutes later the whistle blew for no side.

As Jason Dunn trudged off the field with the match ball tucked underneath his arm, he found his way blocked.

'In my day, lad, a ref were supposed to control the game,' said Dalziel.

Whatever retort was forming on Dunn's lips died as he identified the obstacle.

'These days it's a hard game,' he said.

'Always were. Ref needs eyes in the back of his head. You weren't even seeing what you were looking at. They could've started gang-banging each other in the scrum and you'd not have noticed. Summat on your mind, Jason?'

He stood aside and fell into step beside the young man as he made his way towards the changing rooms.

'I've just become the father of twins, Mr Dalziel, or have you forgotten?'

'Nay, I recall. And mother and babbies doing fine they said when I rang the hospital just now.

I'd tried your house first. Thought the family might be home by now, the way they like to clear hospital beds these days. But she's private, isn't she? Nice. Might as well enjoy the benefit while you can, eh? Did think you might be there by her side, getting used to the idea of being a dad.'

'I'll be along later,' said Dunn. 'I had this match to see to. Hard to get cover these days.'

'So I understand. Back in my day every poor sod of a young teacher who could summon up enough breath to blow a whistle were expected to run around a playing field at least once a week. But you're not like that, Jason. You're a pro. And you know the game, I've seen you play, remember? But your mind weren't on it today. Just the responsibility of fatherhood is it, lad? Or is there summat else?'

'I don't know what you mean. Now if you don't mind, I need to get showered. And we don't allow strangers in here, for obvious reasons.'

They had reached the changing-room building.

Dalziel pushed open the door saying, 'Nay, lad, no need to worry on my account. I've seen bums and cocks, all ages and all sizes, and they do nowt for me. You go ahead. I'll just sit around and wait till you're ready to talk.'

'I don't understand. What is it you want to talk to me about?'

'About sport, what else? Specifically about squash. Now I don't play myself, but I always understood it were a game for two people, played in a court like a glass coffin?'

'That's just about right.'

'So there isn't another more advanced version that's played in a double bed with three players, one lass, two lads, all bollock naked? Let's help remind you.'

He took out his mobile, dialled a number and held it up so that the recorded message could be heard by both of them.

It was a woman's voice, husky, sexy, foreign.

''Allo, 'ere is Dolores, your Lady of Pain. Sorry, got my 'ands and maybe my mouth full at the moment, so leave a message and I'll get back to you soon as I am free and rested. And remember – anticipation can be part of the pleasure also.'

Dalziel switched off and said, 'Is she right, do you think, Jase? Me, I never cared to be kept waiting.'

'I don't know,' blustered Dunn. 'What's this got to do with me anyway?'

'That's what I want to know. You told Mr Pascoe that when Maciver didn't turn up, you tried ringing him on his mobile, at his shop and at home. This is the only number which is recorded on those three phones at that time.'

It is a cliché of the horror movie that at some point the hero sees his worst nightmare take shape before him and realizes that this time he isn't going to wake up. Getting actors to produce the right reactive expression can be a real problem. Too little and you lose the moment. Too much and it's ham.

They should have hired Andy Dalziel. He'd seen it again and again in big close-up.

'Oh Christ,' said Jason Dunn. 'Oh Christ.'

'Sorry, lad. For the time being you're going to have to make do with me,' said Dalziel kindly. 'Why don't you go ahead and get your body nice and clean. Then we can have a go at your soul.'

16

Jason

It wasn't me, it was all down to Pal, you've got to understand that. I know it sounds like I'm blaming the guy because he can't answer back, but it's true. OK, it takes two to tango, but he got me at a bad time and I thought it would be just a one-off and it was just a fill-in anyway until . . .

But you want this laid out plain and clear. Like a lesson plan. Right?

OK. Here goes.

When I married Helen, I didn't know Pal. I knew she had a brother, of course, and there'd been this bother between them, but I'd never laid eyes on him.

Then after we got married, things got better between them, something to do with her wanting to sell Moscow House which belonged to all three of them, her sister too who I didn't know either. Cressida. She's a bit weird. Tasty but weird.

Anyway.

After a while I met Pal. I quite liked him. A bit of a smoothie, knew his way around, but he came across as the kind of guy you could have a drink with, not the monster I'd been half expecting. Then I ran into him again at the sports centre. He'd been playing squash with Chak, that's Dr, sorry, Mr Chakravarty, he's a consultant, you know, one of them doctors who are too high-powered to call themselves doctor. He's also greased lightning on the squash court, so I knew that if Pal had been playing with him, he had to be pretty hot stuff himself. He was really pleased to see me and we had a drink and when he suggested we might have a game some time, I said why not?

That's how our regular Wednesday-night games started. It suited us both. Kay, Helen's stepmother, always dropped by on Wednesday, so it gave me an excuse to leave them to themselves – they're as thick as thieves, those two.

Then I turned up one Wednesday and I met Pal in the foyer and he said, 'Major cock-up, I'm afraid. They've got us double-booked with someone else, and they got here first.'

Well, I was pretty disappointed and I suppose it showed. By contrast he seemed laid back about the business. I suggested we might as well have a drink, he said, thanks but no, when he realized what had happened he'd made other arrangements. Then he looked at me, hesitated, and said, 'I don't know if you'd be interested . . .' 'In what?' I said. He said, 'It's just that I need some sort of exercise and there's this girl I sometimes see, so I gave her a bell . . .' 'A tart, you mean?' I said, a bit taken aback. 'I suppose so,' he said. 'But she's something rather special. Rather choosy. But

I know she doesn't mind doubling up if she likes the look of a guy.'

Now I was just curious to start with. OK, and also a bit randy. Helen had gone funny about sex pretty soon after she got pregnant, and it was getting to the point where the result wasn't worth all the hassle. I've always been used to . . . I mean, it's been pretty regular with me . . . well, you get the picture.

So Pal went off to the car park to see if his woman had turned up. Then he came back in and called to me. I went out and she was sitting in the back seat of his car. She looked a bit like an advert for a vampire movie, very pale with long black hair, but she was certainly a looker. She gave me the once-over, then nodded. Pal opened the back door. I said, 'Not in the car park, for God's sake!' thinking that even though we were in the darkest corner, a steamed-up car rocking around on its springs would soon attract attention from some of the young bucks who use the centre. He said, 'Don't be silly,' and he drove us to Moscow House while Dolores – that was her name – and me started to get acquainted in the back.

Well, she really was something else. I was a bit worried at first that Pal might turn out to be AC/DC and set his sights on me too, but thank God he played it straight hetero, and though you can't do a threesome without there being some contact with the other fellow, there was never anything kinky in it.

So it became a regular thing on Wednesdays. We'd meet in the centre car park, get into Pal's car, keep our heads down as we reached the Avenue, enjoy ourselves in Moscow House for an hour or so, then back to the car park and home. No harm done to anyone. It kept me happy and indirectly it kept Helen happy, because I didn't bother her any more. Or not much. Giving up altogether might have made her suspicious. But I knew once she had the twins and things got back to normal that that was the end of this fling with Dolores.

I never thought it would end like this.

You can imagine what I felt like that night. Or maybe you can't. I sat in the car park at the centre waiting for Pal. After a while Dolores got into my car. She said something must have happened. She had her mobile with her and tried ringing Pal's but it was switched off. Then she tried his shop. No answer. I borrowed her mobile and rang Pal's home and spoke to his wife, who hadn't heard from him.

Using Dolores' mobile was stupid, I see that now. I should have gone into the centre and used the payphone there. But I never dreamt that . . . Oh shit.

Finally we drove down the Avenue past Moscow House and started to get really worried when we saw a police car turning into the drive. We came back to the car park and split up. After that, well you know what happened after that. I couldn't believe it, everything just seemed to be falling apart.

These past couple of days, I've just been keeping my head down and hoping nothing would come up that would lead you people to me. Does that sound selfish? I suppose it must in view of what happened to Pal, but he's out of it now, nothing I can do to help him, is there? Honestly, I knew nothing about what he was *planning. He gave no hint. The poor bastard must have had a brainstorm or something. Ask Dolores, she'll tell you the same. We both just thought it was going to be another straightforward Wednesday-night session.*

Look, Mr Dalziel, I'm being completely straight with you. Does any of this have to come out? I've been falling apart worrying about what it would do to me and Helen if she found out. Please, Mr Dalziel, I'll do anything you want me to do if only you'll help me to keep this from Helen.

17

lunch at the Mastaba (2)

If Tony Kafka could have seen the dining room of the Mastaba Club this lunchtime, his suspicions about the unreal nature of the place would have been confirmed. The same Mastabators occupied the same places, the same waiters soft-shoed along the same routes between the same tables, and even their trays bore platefuls of the same soup. Put on a looped tape to play endlessly, it would have been a hot favourite for the Turner prize.

'I often wonder what the vintners buy,' said Warlove, pouring the wine, 'one half so precious as the goods they sell.'

'So you say, Victor. So you always say,' replied Gedye in his dry lifeless voice.

'Do I? You sound a little tetchy, Timothy. Has something happened? Indeed, to have the pleasure of your company twice in two days makes me suspect that something must have happened. Not bother, I hope. I don't have the temperament for bother.'

'There were developments. Action had to be taken.'

'Oh God. Action. I hate it more than bother. And on your lips the very word is like a knell. What happened to good old pressure? Surely the authorities up there are as susceptible to pressure as anywhere else.'

'In this case, no.'

'Come, come. Policemen are like politicians, very few of them can pass the three vee test unscathed. You recall the three vee test?'

'You have mentioned it before,' said Gedye.

'Venery, venality, vanity. If they flunk out on one you always get them on another. I cannot believe Mid-Yorkshire is any different from the rest of the world. And doesn't a Special Relationship exist between our Yankee lady and our Yorkshire tyke?'

'Yes, but it's special in a special way. It involves trust. Also this fellow's outward semblance, which is overweight bumpkin, apparently belies his inner nous. You recall Gaw Sempernel? Retired early, ended up as Hon Consul in Thessaloniki? It seems our Northern friend contributed in no small part to his downfall. In addition there is another officer in that northern wilderness who is so sea-green incorruptible, they'll probably dig him up a hundred years from now and make a saint out of him. Action had to be taken, and I fear there is more to come.'

'More action? Oh dear. Oh dear. Tell me then.

I cannot contemplate a mouthful of lunch before I hear the worst, so delicate is my digestion.'

'I have it on good authority that the Securities and Exchange Commission will be launching an investigation into Ashur-Proffitt shortly before the close of business this afternoon, which will be about eleven p.m. our time. I did warn you yesterday, but I admit it's happened somewhat sooner than I guessed.'

'And what is Joe's reaction?'

'It didn't seem worth warning him. That way he won't have to fake shock.'

'Always so considerate, Tim. And this action you are contemplating . . . ?'

'Kafka is due in the States tomorrow to meet with Joe and discuss his concerns about the current activities of Ash-Mac's.'

'Well, from the sound of it, that meeting will be off, so nothing to weep or beat the breast about there. Indeed, it could be a plus, the way Tony was going on.'

'I don't think so. A tête-à-tête with Joe might just have brought him back into line. I fear that when he realizes what has been going on in the Corporation, that pustulating conscience of his may just explode.'

'You think so? He hasn't been party to any of this, then?'

'No. But he'll be investigated along with the others, of course.'

'And no doubt someone will do a deal to get

immunity from prosecution. They always do. So what's the worry?'

'You're right. Someone will do a deal. But what they say will, on the whole, only harm Ashur-Proffitt. What Kafka might say could harm us. All of us. You. Me. Our masters.'

'Oh dear. So you think . . . action? No need to give me details. And then things will be OK?'

'Hoblitt, my man informs me, is sound. You agree?'

'Excellent fellow,' said Warlove. 'Like a rock. All three vee's and I wouldn't be surprised if there were a few more.'

'Good. Let's proceed.'

'If we must. But what about questions . . . this sea-green incorruptible, is he the kind to ask questions?'

'Of course he is. But policemen are the prisoners of their own experience. They never ignore the obvious. Over the next few weeks, I suspect that Ashur-Proffitt executives are going to go missing in droves.'

'You think so? Then I am reassured, my boy. Oh look. Here's the soup. How do they always manage to get their timing so perfectly right? I sometimes suspect that they must have the tables bugged.'

Gedye smiled to himself and began to eat his soup.

18

in the parlour

Arriving at Cothersley Hall was a very different experience from arriving at Casa Alba.

For a start there was no sign of the house from the roadway, just a pair of massive granite columns Pascoe was sure he'd once seen in the British Museum, crowned by eagles with wings outstretched and expressions of pained surprise, as though in the act of laying polyhedral eggs.

On either side of the columns as far as the eye could see stretched a six-foot wall topped by razor wire, and from them hung a double metal gate, apparently designed to obstruct incursion by anything less than a Centurion tank.

He began to get out of the car then paused as a small CCTV camera situated in the lea of one of the eagles turned towards him. It must have liked what it saw for a moment later the great gates began to swing silently open.

Come into my parlour . . .

But spiders offered no threat to a man fortified with what in fact had turned out to be a rather good ploughman's at the Dog and Duck washed down with half a pint of lager. A fondness for lager was a vice he concealed from Andy Dalziel. He admired Shirley Novello's refusal to be intimidated into drinking anything she didn't fancy, but he hadn't yet found the nerve to join her in sitting at the Fat Man's table in the Black Bull sucking some Transylvanian pils called Schlurp straight out of the bottle.

It had been easy to get the Captain talking about his blue beer. In fact once started it had been hard to get him talking about anything else, though reference to the tragic death of Mr Maciver had stimulated a curious melange of what's-the-world-coming-to-I-blame-the government polemic and always-thought-there-was-something-odd-about-him *Schadenfreude*.

He set the car in motion and drove through the gateway into a long curving avenue of ancient beeches, festive with the first bright growth of spring. In his mirror he saw the gates closing behind him, occasioning a momentary feeling of unease which quickly vanished as the car rounded a bend and Cothersley Hall came into view.

Now this, he thought, was much more to Ellie's taste than Casa Alba. It was a solid brick built seventeenth-century manor house, south facing, adorned with but not swamped by gold-heart ivy, not overlarge, just right for a gentleman farmer and his family, and of course a few necessary servants.

He tried to imagine what a seventeenth-century Ellie would have done about necessary servants and smiled.

Twenty-first-century Ellie certainly wouldn't approve the single-storey extension on the western side of the building, with its broad expanses of glass through which he could glimpse a swimming pool, but its architect had done his considerable best to preserve the harmony of the place.

As he got out of the car, the house door opened and a man came out. He was in his forties, stockily well-built, with greying black hair just short of a crew cut and a leathery high-cheekboned face.

He came down the steps and said, 'You the dick?'

'Some people have called me such,' said Pascoe. 'I prefer Detective Chief Inspector Peter Pascoe.'

'Yeah. Thought I recognized you from Kay's description. I'm Tony Kafka.'

He shook hands with a firm but non-competitive grip.

'So what's the word on Pal?' he asked. 'Suicide, or is there more?'

'What makes you ask that?' said Pascoe.

'Ranking cop coming out of his way to interview the dead man's former stepmother don't strike me as routine procedure.'

He set off up the steps towards the door. He walked with a rolling gait like a traditional sailor.

'You're conversant with routine procedure, are you?' said Pascoe following.

'I read a lot of crime crap,' said Kafka over his shoulder. 'And I've been in business long enough to know a guy ducking a question when I see one. That guy who came out to the plant was just the same.'

'I'm sorry?'

'Guy with a face to sink a thousand ships. Detective Sergeant I think he was. Turned up just as I was leaving an hour or so ago. God knows what he wanted and neither of them was sharing the info with me.'

Wield had gone to Ash-Mac's? What the hell for? wondered Pascoe as Kafka led the way across a shadowy heavily wainscoted hall. On a table by the door stood a well-used leather grip.

'In here,' said Kafka, pushing open the door into a long airy reception room where Kay Kafka was sitting on a chaise longue as gracefully as any character in a Jane Austen movie. 'Honey, you got a visitor.'

'Mr Pascoe, how nice to see you again,' she said. 'Please, sit down.'

'Yeah,' said Kafka. 'Over there with your back to the light, that's the best interrogation position, right? And do you want to grill us both at once or separately?'

'It's Mrs Kafka I'd like to speak to,' said Pascoe.

Kay said, 'You must forgive my husband, Chief Inspector. Tony, if the cabaret's over, maybe you'd like to organize some drinks? Coffee? Tea? Or something stronger?'

'That's to check how serious this is,' said Kafka. 'If you say, "Not while I'm on duty, madam," we know we're in for a rough ride.'

'I think you may have been reading the wrong crime crap,' said Pascoe courteously. 'Coffee would be nice. Espresso if at all possible.'

'If at all possible!' echoed Kafka as he left the room. 'Only in England . . . !'

Somewhere a phone was ringing.

Kay said, 'Excuse Tony. He thinks he's putting you at ease.'

'No problem. I love a wag,' murmured Pascoe, sitting down at right angles to the window. 'And I'm certainly at ease. Nice house you've got, Mrs Kafka.'

'Yes, I suppose it is,' she said. 'Though not precisely to my taste.'

'No?' said Pascoe, surprised.

'No,' she said firmly. 'Tony bought and renovated it long before I married him. I've made some adjustments since, but the main structure's pretty obdurate. As indeed is Tony.'

'My wife would like it,' said Pascoe.

'She would? How is she, by the way? We only met briefly the other night, but she struck me as a pretty capable lady.'

'She's fine,' said Pascoe. 'Look, I'm sorry to be troubling you, but there are a couple of uncertainties surrounding the sad death of your stepson which I thought you might be able to help with.'

She said, 'Uncertainties? Yes, I should imagine that when someone chooses to kill himself in such a macabre fashion, there are bound to be uncertainties.'

'Macabre?' said Pascoe. 'Shooting yourself is, alas, pretty commonplace.'

'But doing it in a manner which almost exactly replicated his own father's death seems pretty macabre to me,' she replied.

'I suppose it was,' said Pascoe as if this had never occurred to him. 'What do you think was going on in his mind when he chose to do that? Was he making some kind of statement, perhaps?'

'I doubt it. Striking a pose, perhaps.'

'A bit extreme, don't you think? I mean, people strike poses to draw attention to themselves, but there's not much point if you can't enjoy that attention.'

She shook her head and said, 'I'm sorry, I wasn't suggesting that as his reason for killing himself. God knows what that was, but once he'd decided to end his life, then, being the way he was, naturally he'd look for some specially dramatic way of making his exit. In fact, I'm not a psychiatrist, but it must take a lot of will power to carry you through from the idea of suicide to the actual execution, and maybe setting up some kind of formal dramatic structure is a good way of keeping you on track.'

'How would you apply that in your first husband's case?' enquired Pascoe. 'I hope you don't mind me asking.'

'No, I don't mind. It's something I've thought about a lot. Pal Senior was very different from his son. He found the striking of poses offensive. He prided himself on his matter-of-factness. He was a man of business and proud of it, and he believed that once you set your mind to a task, you carried it through, no second thoughts allowed. So he wouldn't need a dramatic structure. He had a shotgun. He used it.'

'Yet there was some artistic presentation involved,' insisted Pascoe. 'The volume of Emily Dickinson's poetry on the desk, the particular poem it was open at. How did it go? *He scanned it – staggered – dropped the Loop to Past or Present . . .*'

'*Past or Period*,' she corrected. '*Caught helpless at a sense as if His mind were going blind –*'

'Doesn't sound very matter-of-fact to me,' said Pascoe dubiously. 'Sounds like a man who feels things slipping out of control. Yet he seemed to do everything very methodically. Why do you think he left the book on his desk?'

This was dangerous ground, he realized. He was questioning a woman about the way her first husband had killed himself with her second about to return any moment. From what little he'd seen of Kafka he didn't seem like a man who'd react kindly if he found someone had reduced his wife to a tearful breakdown.

But Kay didn't look as if she was about to weep. Her expression was gravely compassionate rather than sorrow-stricken. It suited her. She was, he acknowledged yet again, and almost with a shock as if he'd somehow missed it before, a truly beautiful woman.

She said, 'The poem was a message to me. I gave him the book, and because he knew it was important to me, he really worked hard to come to terms with Emily. But often I'd catch him reading it with a look of exasperated bafflement on his face, like a child asked to study what is yet beyond his ken. He once told me it troubled him that such short poems, often just a scatter of lines, a handful of words, should leave him groping after meaning.'

'*Groped up, to see if God was there – Groped backward at Himself,*' said Pascoe softly.

She smiled at him, briefly, then went on, 'I think that what he was saying to me by leaving the volume open at this poem was, *Listen, love, I got this one right in the end. Now I know what this one means.* He was offering the only kind of comfort he could think of. I believe he tried to write me a note explaining what was going on in his mind, saying how sorry he was, but found the only words he could use were inadequate. So he chose instead to let Emily describe how he felt for him and, by using her poem, he said he loved me.'

She fell silent. Pascoe was deeply moved. All

the nasty things that had been said about this woman sounded in his head now like mere snarls of envy and resentment. Oh yes, she was a pretty good magicker all right.

Time to pull something out of the hat himself, if he could.

He produced his wallet and from it took the sheet of paper on which he'd copied poem no. 870.

'I wonder if you recognize this,' he said.

She took the paper from his hand, unfolded it, placed it on the table to smooth it out, then read it without any change of expression.

Finished, she said, 'It's Emily Dickinson, of course. I've read it but I wouldn't say I know it.'

'Sorry, I thought being an expert . . .'

She smiled and said, 'I'm only expert enough to know how hard she can be. What's your reading of it? Andy Dalziel tells me you're a grad, and bright with it.'

He liked the easy way she brought her acquaintance with the Fat Man in and the mischief in her eyes which suggested that what Dalziel had said was something like, *Clever bugger, yon Pascoe. Went to college but he's turned out not a bad cop despite that.*

He said, 'It seems to me it's about delusion, deceit, loss. She seems to be saying that we invent quests for ourselves to give our existence meaning but that the only result of this is to make ourselves as fallacious as the invention.'

She said, 'Wow. I see what Andy meant.'

'But I know so little about her,' he went on. 'Is she the kind of writer whose references need close exploration? For instance, does she want us to be thinking about Ino who hated her stepchildren so much that they could only escape her wrath by fleeing on a golden ram with wings? Or Medea who killed the kids she'd had with Jason after he betrayed her? Or . . . well, you see what I'm getting at.'

'She certainly knew all about the complexities of family relationships,' she said. 'Mother, brother, sister, sister-in-law – enough material for several Greek tragedies there, with maybe the odd comedy thrown in. She had a wry sense of humour, did you know that? It's always worth recalling before you take everything she says too seriously.'

She paused, fixing a wide candid gaze on him, then asked, 'Why are you so interested in this particular poem anyway?'

'I just happened across it,' he said, meeting the gaze unblinkingly. 'You know how it is. Something comes up – some name, some place, something you haven't thought about for years, if at all – and suddenly you happen on references almost anywhere you look.'

'Yes, I know the feeling. Life's all about patterns, I sometimes think. Patterns imposed upon us, patterns we impose upon ourselves. Ah, here's Tony.'

Kafka came back into the room with a tray.

'One espresso-if-at-all-possible,' he said. 'Mr Pascoe, you want to talk to me for any reason?'

'I can't think of any reason offhand,' said Pascoe. 'So unless you can suggest one, then no.'

'Good. It's just that I'm heading down to London shortly. Got a plane to catch first thing in the morning so I'll be staying out at Heathrow.'

'I haven't forgotten I'm driving you to the station,' said Kay. 'But we don't have to go for an hour at least.'

'Hey, I'm not trying to break up your tête-à-tête,' said Kafka. 'In fact it can go on long as you like. Just got a call, I need to get back to the plant. Sod's law, I'm there all morning, nothing happens. Soon as I come away, I'm needed. It's OK, I'll drive myself and leave my car in the station park.'

He spoke perhaps just a shade too casually.

'You sure?' said Kay. 'I can easily . . .'

'No problem,' he said. 'Goodbye, Mr Pascoe. Don't get up.'

He offered his hand again. Then he went to his wife, bent to her, kissed her lightly on the cheek and said, 'I'll ring you from the hotel.'

He went out. After a moment of silence, Kay said, 'Excuse me just a moment, Mr Pascoe. Something I forgot.'

She rose and went out after her husband. Watching her move was worth paying money for, thought Pascoe. A grace so understated you hardly noticed it till you realized you were holding your breath.

Outside, Kay caught up with her husband as he tossed his grip into the boot of his car.

'Tony,' she said, 'is everything OK?'

'It will be,' he said lightly.

'I wish I were coming with you.'

'To the plant?'

'To the States.'

'Yeah?' he said. 'And miss seeing the twins every day?'

'I didn't mean for good. I meant so that I'd be around when you meet Joe and the others.'

'Honey, there's nothing to worry about. Like I told you last night after I talked to Joe, he was OK with the way I felt. He said the time had come for a rethink, this wasn't just about politics any more, this was about patriotism.'

'No. With Joe it will always be about profit, however you spell it.'

'Hey, I thought I did cynicism in this family. I'll be fine. You stay here, make sure Helen turns into the kind of mom you'd have been. Things are going to be OK.'

'And if they're not? If Joe won't listen?'

Kafka's expression became hard.

'Then it's golden handshake time. And maybe I'll crush a few fingers while we're at it.'

She shook her head as if acknowledging that there was nothing more she could say. Then she put her hands round his neck and drew his head down to hers and kissed him long and passionately.

'Goodbye, Tony,' she said.

He drew back and viewed her quizzically.

'Wow,' he said. 'Maybe I should go away more often.'

She turned from him and went back into the house.

Pascoe, who had been watching from the window, hastily resumed his seat.

A moment or two later Kay came back into the room.

'Everything all right?' said Pascoe.

'Why shouldn't it be?'

'No reason. I just thought Mr Kafka seemed a little . . . rushed?'

'Tony is a good man. He wants to be a good American,' she said, as if this answered him. 'Now, Mr Pascoe, where were we?'

'I think somehow we'd got on to critical interpretation of Emily Dickinson,' he said with a smile. 'If we could return to the sad matter in hand, I'll try not to keep you much longer. How would you describe your relationship with your stepson, Mrs Kafka?'

She showed no surprise at the question but after a pause for consideration replied, 'It ended better than it started. Though I'm not sure I understand the relevance . . . ?'

'Just looking for details in a picture,' he said.

'From what I've learned from Mr Dalziel, it seems on occasion to have been a little fraught.'

Let her know that Fat Andy's my colleague as well as her buddy.

'As a boy he resented me taking his mother's place. As an adolescent, I think these feelings of resentment got muddled with the kind of sexual fantasies young men have about any person-able female within easy reach. Guilt feelings after his father's death brought everything to a climax and for several years I think his easiest solution was to condemn me as the cause of everything disturbing and distressing in his life.'

'How did this manifest itself?'

'By barring me from re-entering Moscow House. By making allegations about my conduct which I might have had to answer in the courts if he hadn't been brought to see the foolish-ness, and the danger to himself, of his actions. By instituting legal proceedings to remove Helen from my custody.'

'But that never came to court?'

'Thanks mainly to Tony. Pal's objections were based on me being American and the lack of blood relationship. What, he asked, if I decided to return to the States? His father wouldn't have wanted his daughter brought up out of the UK. Or what if I remarried and my new husband didn't care for the child? With no blood relationship between us, wouldn't it be easy for me simply to dump her? Tony listened to my troubles and said, "Let's get married and officially adopt the kid." That, plus undertakings to have her educated wholly in the UK no matter what happened to Tony in his job, cut the ground from under Pal's feet. But I guess you know most of this already, Mr Pascoe.'

Her smile was ironic.

He said, 'Detective work is all about hearing the same things again and again and looking for new angles, or discrepancies, Mrs Kafka.'

'You spotted any yet?'

'Nothing that can't be explained by forgetfulness, natural bias, or inadvertence. But things got better, you say. Why was that?'

'Time, maturity, perspective. A recognition that the situation as it was now wasn't going to change.'

'The situation being that you had succeeded in bringing Helen up in Mid-Yorkshire, she was now legally of age, not to mention married and pregnant. And he had accepted this, I understand. There'd been a rapprochement as evidenced by his playing squash with his brother in law.'

'So it would appear.'

'Which makes it a strange time to decide to commit suicide. If he'd hung on another day, he would have been an uncle. As it was, he was sounding a new note of family tragedy at the very time when the Macivers should have been popping corks to celebrate the start of the next generation.'

'Pal was never a man to let the needs or wishes of others take priority over his own.'

'You mean he might have chosen this time deliberately to upstage his own sister?' said Pascoe incredulously.

'I don't say that. I just mean that all potential suicides must develop some form of tunnel vision; with Pal the tunnel was always there.'

His mobile rang. Mouthing an apology, he took it out and read the number.

Dalziel.

'Excuse me,' he said.

He stepped out into the hall and took the call.

'Pascoe.'

'Where the hell are you?'

'I'm at Cothersley,' he said. Then, annoyed at his own circumspection he added, 'Cothersley Hall.'

'Oh aye. Best get back here.'

'What's up, sir? Developments?'

'You could say. Meeting, my room, thirty minutes. And that's an order.'

He went back into the room and said, 'Thank you for your time, Mrs Kafka.'

'Does that mean we're done? Or have you merely been interrupted?'

'Who knows?' he said. 'Oh, by the way. Your husband, your first husband I mean, he owned two shotguns, I believe?'

'I seem to recall so.'

'The one he used is still in police hands. The one your stepson used seems to be the other half of the pair. Any idea where it's been for the last ten years?'

'I don't know . . . in Moscow House I presume.'

'Perhaps. Certainly not in the gun case in the study, which only has room for one gun and shows no sign of having had a weapon in it for some considerable time.'

'Then I'm sorry, I can't help you.'

Can't you? he wondered. *I think perhaps you can.*

But he said nothing, took his leave and went out to his car.

As he drove away he glanced towards the window.

And was rather disappointed this time to find no one watching him.

19

confessional

There had been a time in Pascoe's career in Mid-Yorkshire when he would as soon have thought of wearing a dress to the Police Ball as of disobeying a Dalziel order. But those days were long past, though on the whole being caught doing the former was likely to be less painful than being caught doing the latter. So it was not without qualms that he diverted to the police lab on his way back.

Here he handed over an evidence bag with a scribbled note:

You'll find my prints on this and one other set with, hopefully, a palm print. Check 'em out against the prints on the study door at Moscow House.

'How's it going?' he asked the technician he spoke to.

'Very interesting. Why don't you come up and have a word with Dr Gentry?'

Dr Gentry was the head of the lab, a man famous for many things, among which wasn't an inclination to brevity.

'No time. Mr Dalziel's waiting for me. And you might like to tell Gentry he's also waiting for the results.'

There was never any harm in threatening the workforce with the bogeyman.

Not of course that it was an empty threat, as evidenced by his own unease at finding himself already ten minutes late as he entered the station. He found the way ahead blocked by Joker Jennison, which meant it was substantially blocked.

'Sir, I were looking for you,' said Jennison.

'Not now, Joker,' he said, attempting to squeeze past.

'Sir, I think I saw that Dolores.'

That stopped him in his tracks.

'You think . . . ?' he said.

'Well, I were sure at first. It were when she bent down. I may not be too hot on faces but I never forget a nice bum.'

'That's great, Joker,' said Pascoe. 'Have you spoken to her? Is she here?'

'No, sir. Thing is, when you seemed to know her, and her with her hair all different and looking such a bonny girl, not all white like a vampire on short rations, and when I told Alan, that's Maycock, he said I were mad, but the more I've thought about it . . .'

'What the hell are you rambling about, man?' demanded Pascoe, glancing at his watch. 'Come on. Spit it out.'

'That lass you were talking to outside the church at Cothersley,' said Jennison unhappily. 'I'm certain that were Dolores. Like I say, when she bent down . . .'

'Miss Upshott, the vicar's sister, you mean?' said Pascoe incredulously.

'Is that who she is?' said Jennison, looking even unhappier. 'Look, sir, maybe it's mistaken identity, but I felt I had to say summat . . .'

'Yes, yes, quite right. Listen, Joker, we'll talk about this later, OK?'

He was now fifteen minutes late. But at least the mind-boggling improbability of what he'd just heard squeezed the fear out of his system as he tapped lightly on the door to the monster's lair and slipped inside.

It was not often that the atmosphere in Andy Dalziel's office could be described as religious but this was like stepping into a Quaker meeting.

The Fat Man sat behind his desk, head bowed, eyes closed. Sitting in front of the desk were Sergeant Wield and Shirley Novello and Hat Bowler (what the hell was he doing here?). The silence was total, not just the absence of speech but the absence of any sense of relationship between these people and their physical surroundings. Their minds and spirits were focused on something within, as if no one was going to break that silence till the Inner Light guided them to utter what was in their heart.

Like a mourner arriving late at a funeral, Pascoe glided silently to an empty seat.

'He comes, he comes,' said the Fat Man suddenly. 'At last he comes. I feel his presence among us, the one who started all this crap.'

Somehow Pascoe didn't think he was referring to the Paraclete.

'Sir,' he said. 'Sorry I'm late. Traffic.'

'On the high intellectual fast track?' said Dalziel with mock incredulity. 'Is it possible? Right, recap for the DCI. Wieldy, you first. Don't worry I've heard it all before. It might sound better second time round.'

The sergeant glanced at Pascoe ruefully, then with a clarity and brevity so familiar you hardly noticed them any more, gave an account of his visit to Jake Gallipot, concluding, 'Confirmed DOA at the hospital. We'll need to wait for the PM, but nothing at first glance to contradict death by electrocution. Contusion on back of skull consistent with striking head against something sharp, like the corner of a desk, after being thrown there by the shock.'

'But this isn't how you see it?'

'Jake knew his way around computers. He wasn't the kind of guy who goes poking about inside one with the power still on.'

'Overconfidence can kill too.'

'That's what Jim Collaboy said. Like I say, I suggested the absence of back-up disks was suspicious, but he didn't seem much bothered.

One other thing. There was a digital camera in a desk drawer. I checked the images. Meant nothing except the last one. It was a photo of a man and woman caught with their pants down, so to speak. Didn't recognize her, but the fellow looked a lot like our Dr Lockridge. Probably not relevant unless . . .'

'Ah,' said Pascoe. 'You've not seen Mrs Maciver, have you?'

'No,' said Wield.

'Let me introduce you.'

Pascoe produced the evidence bag in which he'd put the ripped photograph.

'Ooh,' said Novello over his shoulder. 'Bet that hurt.'

Dalziel, who'd been quieter longer than anyone could remember, grabbed the picture and said, 'Soft porn, is it now? Right, Pete, fill us in, unless it's a secret.'

'You know me, sir, I don't believe in secrets,' said Pascoe, meeting his gaze unflinchingly. 'A woman, Mary Lockridge, I believe, delivered this to Sue-Lynn Maciver this morning. Along with a good right hook. It's very interesting, but I don't see where it gets us. Now we probably know why Maciver really hired Gallipot. To check his wife out. Not without reason.'

'Found out she were playing away, balance of mind upset, tops himself,' said Dalziel hopefully.

'Don't think so, sir,' said Pascoe. 'Maciver

doesn't strike me as that type. No, I see it as a contra-indication. The time and date indicate this was taken round about the very time Maciver was dying. Frankly I wouldn't imagine a man contemplating suicide would give much of a damn what his wife's getting up to. I can't really see what it can have to do with our case.'

'But it might help in looking for someone with a motive for killing Gallipot,' said Novello. 'Sarge, this guy you said was seen leaving the building, could it have been Lockridge?'

'Which guy was this?' demanded Pascoe. 'You've been doing house-to-house as well, have you, Wieldy?'

'No,' denied Wield. 'Jim Collaboy put one of his lads on to asking questions round the other offices. He reported in when I was at the station. Someone looking out of the window spotted someone leaving the building, description, male, wearing a hat – a trilby, she thought. Didn't pay much heed and looking down from the first floor doesn't give the best view anyway. But no one in any of the offices recalled having dealings with a guy in a trilby that morning.'

'I'm sure I've seen Dr Lockridge in a trilby,' said Novello. 'So maybe . . .'

'Forget Lockridge,' interrupted Pascoe. 'I was talking to him at the hospital this morning, so unless he's got wings . . .'

Novello subsided, looking crestfallen at having her theory shot down so comprehensively.

'Mr Waverley wears a trilby,' said a low and hesitant voice.

It was Hat Bowler. When all eyes turned his way, he looked like he wished he'd kept it a bit lower and hesitated a bit longer.

'Is that a riddle, lad? Or a message from the other side?' asked Dalziel long-sufferingly. 'Who the fuck is Mr Waverley?'

Bowler looked so unhappy that Pascoe took pity.

'He's a friend of Miss Lavinia Maciver,' he said. 'But how do you know him, Hat?'

Dalziel shot Bowler a glance like an Olympic shot-putt and said, 'Well, tell the DCI, lad.'

Hesitantly and ignoring a bit of eye-rolling from Novello, Hat gave an account of his acquaintance with Lavinia. Her he spoke of with undisguised enthusiasm.

'But all I know about Mr Waverley is that he's an old friend. He came to tell her about her nephew's death. Oh, and he's a retired VAT inspector.'

'That's definitely a strike against him,' said Dalziel. 'But we'll need a bit more if we're going to fit him up for murder. Is there more?'

'He got a phone call when I was there this morning, and he left straight after,' persisted Hat.

'Oh aye? And you managed to hear this call, did you?'

'Not really. You see, he was out in the garden and I was eating a bit of toast and Scuttle was chattering away on my shoulder 'cos he wanted a bit . . .'

'Scuttle?'

'He's a coal-tit . . .'

Dalziel hid his face behind his hand and rubbed it as if trying to raze his nose.

'A coal-tit,' he syllabled softly. 'Did you get its address?'

'It lives at Miss Mac's . . .' began Bowler, then let his voice fade away.

'Of course it does. With Noddy and Big Ears. That it, lad? Or do you have owt that comes within pissing distance of suspicious?'

Bowler racked his brain. All the brownie points he'd won with Dalziel by his discovery of the Dolores recording seemed to be sliding away.

'There was something . . .' he said. 'But it's probably nothing really . . . It's just that Mr Waverley sounds ever so faintly Scottish, only when he started talking just for a second he sounded, I don't know, Australian . . .'

'Australian?' said Dalziel, fanning himself with a file as if all this was bit too much for his delicate constitution. 'Having a conversation with a kooka-burra, were he?'

'No,' said Bowler defiantly. 'I heard him say "Good day" when he answered his phone, but it came out the way Aussies say it. *Gedye*.'

For a fleeting moment Pascoe saw the ghost of a reaction drift across Dalziel's face, then it was gone.

'Well, gedonyer, cobber,' he said in a dreadful approximation of Oz-speak. 'Now would you like to flap your wings and rejoin us in the real world? Ivor, your turn.'

Pascoe, taken aback by the force of Dalziel's put-down and irritated by Novello's ill-disguised *Schadenfreude*, said rather sharply, 'Yes, let's hear what entertaining discoveries you've made, Shirley.'

Unfazed, Novello, in a style which attempted with some success to emulate Wield's, told the story of her adventures among the bankers, lawyers and Avenue ladies.

Impressed despite himself, Pascoe said, 'Well done, Shirley. Now that is interesting,' aware that Dalziel's eyes were watching him under a brow louring like a typhoon sky.

He's daring me to make assumptions or even build hypotheses, thought Pascoe. Well, let the old sod wait!

He said briskly, 'Now, where are we? Top-of-the-bill time. Must be your spot, sir.'

Dalziel's gaze modified from threatening to sardonic. He picked up his phone, dialled a number and passed it to Pascoe.

'Have a listen,' he said.

He put it to his ear, heard it ring, then the answer service clicked in.

He listened.

'Allo, 'ere is Dolores your Lady of Pain . . .'

'Pull your tongue back in afore someone steps

453

on it,' said Dalziel. 'It were the only number trying to make contact with Maciver's shop, home and mobile around seven o'clock, which meant it should have been Jason Dunn. It were young Bowler here that spotted it – nice to see that once you shake the feathers out of his bonce, his brain's as sharp as ever. We'll make a real thief-taker of him yet . . .'

This was as near to fulsome praise as you were likely to get from the Fat Man and Novello once again felt the injustice of it. Those phone records had been sent at her behest, she should have been the one to analyse them, she would have spotted the number and rung it, no bother . . .

She was diverted from the treacherous path of might-have-been by her awareness that the DCI seemed to have gone mad.

He had pressed the redial button and this time when the message bleep sounded, he said into the phone, 'Oh hello, Miss Upshott. Peter Pascoe here, DCI Pascoe. Could you drop in to see me at your earliest convenience? Alternatively, I could call round at the vicarage to speak to you there. Thank you.'

The silence that followed was religious in its intensity and breakable only by God.

'What the fuck was that all about?' demanded Dalziel.

'It's about Joker Jennison's highly specialized powers of perception,' said Pascoe.

When he'd completed his explanation, the Fat Man shook his head incredulously.

'And you believe him? You don't think this could be one of Joker's little japes?'

'I don't know if I believe him or not,' said Pascoe. 'But there's a close connection between Miss Upshott and Maciver – the shop, the village – and if it is her, when she gets my message, she'll be round here like a flash rather than risk me dropping in on her and her brother. And if it's not, well, all we've got is one very puzzled Lady of Pain.'

Novello, feeling rather ashamed at her resentment of Hat's small triumph, now compensated by saying, 'I think Joker could be right. There's not much I'd trust his judgment on, but when it comes to female bums, I reckon we should take it as an expert opinion.'

'You reckon?' said Dalziel. Then his face split in a salacious grin. 'Here, it 'ud make a grand identity parade, but. We could sell tickets.'

No one laughed and he grunted, 'Please yourselves,' and continued with the story of his interview with Dunn.

When he'd finished, Pascoe said, 'Oh shit.'

'Eh? Thought you'd have been glad. I still don't know what it adds up to, but it's been you from the start saying there's more going off here than meets the eye.'

'I was thinking of that poor girl in hospital. Does this have to come out, sir?'

'Only if it's relevant to your enquiries into Maciver's death,' said Dalziel.

In other words, if it's suicide, we can sit on it. But if it's murder . . .

There were things to be got out into the open but the open didn't include everyone present. Not even Edgar Wield.

He sought for some courteously diplomatic way of suggesting that the meeting close and he and Dalziel be left to themselves, but before he could speak, the Castiglione of Mid-Yorkshire showed him how it should be done.

'Right, you lot. Bugger off,' he growled. 'Everyone except you, Pete.'

As the other three made for the door, Dalziel called, 'Ivor, you've earned a break, you and young Bowler both. He's still on the panel officially so why don't you ferry him down to the canteen and see if you can lure him back permanent with a mug of tea and a slice of summat tasty? But keep him off the millet. All that ornithology can send a young man blind.'

When they were alone, Pascoe said, 'Nice to see Bowler getting back to normal. Meeting Lavinia's obviously done him a world of good.'

'You reckon? Gives you a warm glow, does it?'

'Well, yes, it does. And I hope it makes you happy too, sir,' said Pascoe.

'Happy? Aye, it might have made me happy if I'd not had a call from Desperate Dan asking if the lad were back on the strength.'

Pascoe turned this inside out looking for hermeneutic clues, gave up, and said, 'You mean the Chief noticed him hanging around and wondered if he'd been signed off the sick list?'

'No, I don't bloody mean that. I mean that some mate of Dan's at the Yard has been enquiring all unofficial like if DC Bowler was assisting in some delicate CID enquiry under the guise of being off sick.'

This required even more consideration.

'Why should the Yard be interested in Bowler?'

'Not the Yard, dickhead. Some other bugger somewhere had enquired at the Yard for someone who was well placed to make a nice chummy call to Dan and put the question.'

'Some other bugger . . . ?'

'Some other *funny bugger* is my guess,' said Dalziel grimly.

In Dalziel-speak *funny buggers* meant anyone working in the shadowy realms of security, whether MI something, or Special Branch, or MoD, or some other area so penumbral it dare not speak its name.

Pascoe was amazed.

'But why on earth . . . I mean, what's Bowler been up to that even the neurotics who run these outfits could misconstrue?'

'You heard the lad. He's been wandering round the woods and having breakfast with this bird lady and her feathered friends. Now it could be that she's a key figure in a pigeon post network

457

that's going to take over after all electronic communication's been nuked out of existence. He did say she don't have a phone or a radio, didn't he? But if it's not that, what are we left with that's set some funny bugger's alarm-bell ringing?'

Pascoe said, 'The only connexion she's got to anything vaguely official is she's Pal Maciver's aunt.'

'Aye. And then there's this VAT man, Waverley.'

'But you just sat on Bowler for even suggesting as a long shot that he could be linked to anything . . . Ah . . .'

'That's right,' said Dalziel approvingly. 'The lad's keen as mustard and now he's getting back to the land of the living, he'll be eager to impress. Plus he seems to have taken a real shine to the bird lady. If this Waverley does have owt to do with the funny buggers' interest, the last thing I want is young Bowler sticking his beak in and getting it snapped off. So, what did you reckon to Waverley?'

'I took him at face value. Retired Customs and Excise, on a decent pension – drives a newish Jag, wears a mohair Crombie – so, fairly high-powered – uses a walking cane, heavy silver top – slightly favours his right leg.'

'What's his relationship with bird lady?'

'Old friend, likes to take care of her. Physically she looked just a touch wobbly, arthritis maybe . . .'

'MS,' interrupted Dalziel.

'Hat told you that? Then maybe Waverley's right, she does need looking after.'

'Is that all? Nowt sexual?'

'Who knows? People like them aren't all over each other. Certainly emotional. They still address each other pretty formally – Mr W and Miss Mac – but that's probably just a habit which helps preserve the equilibrium of a loving friendship. Look, sir, apart from the fact he wears a trilby, is there anything else to make us take a closer look at Waverley?'

'Gedye,' said Dalziel.

'And to you too, sir,' said Pascoe.

'No. It's a name. It's the name of the funny bugger who got Dan's old mate at the Yard asking questions about Bowler.'

'Ah,' said Pascoe.

'Ah so,' said Dalziel. 'Any idea how they met? Not one of them tweeters, is he?'

'Twitchers. Don't think so . . . though she did say . . . yes! I knew there was something!'

Detectives, like Quakers, had their Inner Light too and if you relaxed and didn't fret about it too much, eventually it would bloom and effulge in speech.

'What?'

'It was at Moscow House. She said something about seeing or hearing the green woodpeckers the first time she and Waverley met. And she dragged him off to see if they were still in some beech tree which she said had been quite rotten

ten years ago. Ten years . . . that would be at the time of the first Maciver suicide. That's when she met him.'

'At Moscow House? He never came up in the investigation.'

'Why should he?' said Pascoe, then couldn't resist adding, 'And maybe you were too busy consoling the grieving widow to pay too much attention to irrelevant detail.'

Dalziel gave him a look which reminded him belatedly that kicking some men when they were down could put you in a fair way to breaking your foot.

Hastily he went on, 'Look, sir, I'm still not clear precisely how any of this connects with my investigation of Pal Junior's death, but one thing's for sure, there's definitely something here that needs investigating.'

Dalziel sat silent, chins on chest, contemplating his crotch like some parodic Buddha. He still doesn't want to give it up, thought Pascoe. He's promised his dear friend Kay Kafka that all shall be well and all manner of thing shall be well, and he hates the idea of admitting he's fallible. I know the feeling. But before I start admitting things, I want the facts.

He pressed on, 'One thing I need to know – not because I'm saying it's relevant, but because sooner or later I'm going to have to know whether it's relevant or not – and that's the precise nature of your relationship with Mrs Kafka.'

460

'Kay? You've not listened to the tape I gave you, then?'

'Yes, I have. And it was very interesting. Very moving. But it doesn't explain your attitude to her. Not fully anyway.'

'You think I'm shagging her, is that it?'

'No, I don't,' said Pascoe with some irritation. 'But there has to be something more, that's clear.'

Now the Fat Man smiled, almost approvingly.

'The reason behind the reason behind the reason, eh? That's the name of our game, lad. Always knew you had the real detective nose from the first time I saw you picking it.'

This wasn't altogether true – or if it were, the Fat Man had concealed his knowledge pretty well.

'I'm flattered,' said Pascoe. 'So?'

'Confession time, is it?' said the Fat Man musingly. 'Why not? Always felt there were a bit of the priest in you, Pete. But no sacrament without a noggin, eh?'

He reached into his desk cupboard and produced a bottle of Highland Park and two tumblers. He filled them both, passed one across to Pascoe, half emptied the other.

'Are you sitting comfortable?' he asked. 'Then I'll begin.'

20

Dalziel

Would you like it formal?

Nay, never shake your gory locks at me, lad – I've seen the way you cross your sevens like a kraut – you love formal.

Statement of Detective Superintendent Andrew Dalziel.

Made in the presence of Detective Chief Inspector Peter Pascoe.

I'm definitely not making this statement of my own free will.

Here we go then.

This started a long time back. I were younger then. Not a lot younger but enough. Oh aye, likely looking at me you'd not be able to tell much difference. When you've got the bone structure, you don't lose your looks. But inside, that's where it counts, and to tell the truth these past couple of years I've felt it counting a bloody sight quicker.

I'm not saying I'm getting past it.

No, most of the time I can still feel the old spirit rattling around deep inside.

But it's a ghost haunting a bloody ruin.

If that's sympathy on thy face, best wipe it off else I might scrub it clean with a knuckle flannel.

America, that's where it started.

That's where most things start these days, good and bad.

Linda Steele were one of the good things. At least I thought so to begin with.

I know it's over ten years ago, but don't let on you don't recall Linda. OK, you never met her, but I bet she'd not been in my house five minutes afore all the station wags were running round saying, 'Have you seen yon bit of dusky chuff the super's brought himself back from the States? Wish I'd asked him to get me one!'

Well, like I always say, if you can't take a joke, you shouldn't have joined.

But if ever I get my hands on the sod who wrote that limerick in the bog, I'll shake him till his teeth rattle like his lousy rhymes.

Linda were a journalist who doubled up working for the CIA, which is like a tick hanging out with crab lice. But, you know me, I'm not judgmental, and we came to a working arrangement. I admit I were a bit surprised when she turned up here. Even with my magnetic personality, you don't expect a gorgeous young blackbird like Linda to come flapping across the Atlantic just to get a second helping of nuts. But she came clean, or at least so I thought. Seems she'd told her funny bugger boss she wanted out and was proposing to take a trip to Europe, and he said that were fine, no problem his side, but could she do him one last favour and check up that I weren't going to give anyone any grief shooting off my mouth about what had happened in the States. Me, the arsehole of discretion! Any road, even if I'd wanted to blab, I'd been heavily sat on by our funny buggers soon as I landed. You'll likely recall that. You were there, remember?

So I told Linda she could set her boss's mind at rest. She were really grateful. Also she'd got nowhere to stay till she got her plans sorted, so pretty soon we'd got our old working arrangement going again.

I liked her a lot, even more now she said she'd resigned from the funny buggers. She told me stuff about the CIA would make your hair stand on end. But when I said nowt the Yanks did would surprise me, she said I shouldn't be so goddam superior, our lot were just as bad. Only difference was that over there, they had so much information they kept tripping over it, while over here they had so little they had to make it up.

Aye, we had many a good laugh, and she liked a drink, and in bed she – but a pillar of the community like you don't want to hear stuff like that. I thought me birthday had come every day. I'd wake up and look at that lovely black face lying on the pillow next to me, and think, You're a lucky bugger, Andy Dalziel!

And I'd tickle her ear and whisper summat daft like, 'Good morning, Midnight.'

Then she'd open her eyes and smile and show me all those lovely white teeth and say, 'Hi.'

And it never ever crossed my mind to wonder what

she were thinking when she woke up and the first thing she saw in the morning was me . . .

Good stuff this. You want a fill-up? Please yourself.

Well, I knew it couldn't go on forever but Linda seemed in no hurry to move on and I could see no reason to rock the boat by asking her what her plans were. She said she liked it here, the folk were real friendly and it was the first time in years she'd been able to relax, no deadlines to meet, no bosses snapping at her heels, nobody to please but herself. And me.

Oh aye. She were very good at pleasing me.

Sometimes I felt so pleased, I could hardly get out of bed in the morning.

When I were out at work she'd go wandering off by herself. She hired herself a car and drove around all over the place, sightseeing, shopping, going to a movie. She never seemed to get bored and when I got back home she'd tell me all about it, excited, like a kid, making daft ordinary things sound interesting.

One day she told me she'd almost had an accident. Daydreaming, she forgot she were driving on the left and found herself heading straight for another car. They both hit the brakes and stopped, no damage done. Linda got out to apologize and explain, but far from being narked, the other driver just laughed and said it was OK, she understood, she were American too, and it had taken her forever to get used to driving on the left.

Aye, you've guessed it. The other driver were Kay. Kay Maciver as she was then.

They chatted a bit then went their ways. Couple of days later Linda went into yon Yankee coffee-shop in the High, you know the one, costs a fortune, coffee all tastes like owl piss. Kay were sitting there. Linda said hello, place were a bit crowded so she asked if Kay would mind if she joined her, they got talking, liked the look of each other and the upshot was they arranged to meet again. I knew Pal Maciver, not close, but we'd met, and I knew all about the Yanks taking over Maciver's, of course, and him getting himself a Yankee wife as part of the deal, leastways that's how the jokers down the rugby club saw it, so I were able to fill Linda in with what I knew, and I were dead chuffed she'd found a mate as it seemed likely to make her hang around up here a bit longer.

So everything in the garden were lovely. But it doesn't matter how green the grass grows and how sweet the flowers smell, a man in our line don't stop being a cop just because he enjoys a bit of gardening. That's where some women get it wrong. They think just because they can switch you to any channel they want by pressing the right buttons, they can do the same trick by remote control, but a man's bollocks aren't tuned to a zapper, and once her hands are off the controls, his brain clicks back in.

Two things began bothering me. One was I were pretty sure Linda was doing drugs. She weren't blatant but I'd been in the business too long not to spot the signs. Can't say I was surprised. Back then, recreational drugs weren't a big problem yet in Mid-Yorkshire, but over in the States I'd seen and heard enough to know that if you lived in what they call the fast lane, they were there for the asking.

Second thing was, I'd met Kay Maciver. First time, I came home and found Linda had asked her round. Then we went out for a drink with her a few times. Pal too – old Pal, I mean. He obviously found it hard to understand what a gorgeous bint like Linda were doing shacking up with an old buffalo like me, which I found a bit offensive from a man in his situation. But Kay just took me and Linda in her stride. That's what I liked about her. She saw everything, judged nowt. Having her around was very peaceful. We got on like a house on fire. I could really talk to her. If Linda had been the jealous type, it might have pissed her off a bit. But to get jealous, you need to give a fuck about someone and, while I hope she liked me a bit, I don't think it got close to that.

Any road, this time I were sitting yacking with Kay while Linda were off in the bog probably having a pinch of white snuff, and Kay let drop that Linda had told her she'd once worked for one of the papers in Hartford, which were where Kay came from. This was something in common which had helped them get on so well to start with. The HQ of Ashur-Proffitt was in Hartford, and Linda, being a journalist, thought a nice human interest story about local firm conquering the world might go down well back there, and she'd been on to her newspaper contact and got the go-ahead. Kay, being Tony Kafka's PA as well as being married to Pal, who was still on the Board of Directors, was well placed to smooth the way for Linda to take a close look at Ash-Mac's and talk to people there for her piece.

Linda had mentioned nowt of this to me, plus in all the tales we'd swopped about our backgrounds, this Hartford place had never even been mentioned.

Next day I put in a call to Dave Thatcher. I think I told you about him. Captain Thatcher, this New York cop who'd helped me a lot when I were over there. Lovely man. Looked like Joe Louis's sparring partner. I had a laugh about his name and tried to start a rumour he were Maggie's love-child by Idi Amin . . . Any road, it were Dave who first tipped me off Linda worked for their funny buggers as well as being a journalist. I explained my situation with Linda. When he stopped laughing he said, 'You two have a love-child, hope it don't have your looks and Linda's colour, else it could make Idi Amin look like Miss World,' so he hadn't forgotten. He rang me back a couple of hours later, a lot more serious. His funny bugger contact said that to the best of his knowledge, Linda was still on the books. Her CV had no record of her ever having worked for a paper in Hartford.

And there was something else. You recall back in the mid-eighties there was a big political scandal in the States when it came out there'd been arms sales to Iran with the profits going to the Contra rebels in Nicaragua so they could buy guns to use against the government, who were too left wing for Ron Reagan and his chums? Of course you do. I bet that missus of thine were waving a banner outside the Yankee Embassy in Grosvenor Square. Seems that Ashur-Proffitt, who had a big network of contacts in the Middle East, were seriously involved here. None of their people ever got named, let alone indicted. Not that it would have made much difference if they had. Just about every bugger who was tried and found guilty either had his sentence quashed on appeal or got pardoned by old man Bush when he took over. Who put the mock in democracy, eh? Our own bunch of jokers, past and present, learned a lot from the way the Yanks handled things there.

But the white hats were riding around back then, guns blazing, and it seemed wise to the big nobs at Ashur-Proffitt to keep their heads below the parapet for a bit, and some people said this was why they suddenly got interested in finding outlets in Europe, particularly those bits of Europe with a nice sympathetic right-of-centre Yankophile government.

And it seems their funny buggers weren't all singing off the same hymn sheet either. Not all of them were paid-up members of the Ollie North fan club. Couple of those who were went to jail, but there were plenty of others who'd have been only too delighted to pay off old scores and clear promotion channels by sending a few more to join them. Dave Thatcher reckoned that's why Linda got sent over here to check out Ash-Mac's and see if she could come up with a smoking gun. Me being in Mid-Yorkshire fell lucky for them. Linda must have mentioned how much I'd enjoyed working undercover with her in the States, so it gave her a perfect in to set up shop on Ash-Mac's doorstep and look for a way of getting even closer.

OK, no need to look like that, it sounded like a right load of bollocks to me too, except that I'd met some of these people and I knew most of them had got such a distorted view of reality, they could easily have got jobs working in a telly documentary department.

So when Dave said take care, I said thanks, I would, and I meant it.

Only I forgot one thing. I said that having my head shagged off didn't stop me being a cop. I forgot that it didn't stop Linda being a spook either and she'd learned enough to spot I were getting suspicious of her, plus mebbe Dave Thatcher's enquiries about her back in the States hadn't been as discreet as he thought.

I'd like to think that what happened next weren't her idea, that she took advice and got instructions. But I daresay I'm just fooling myself.

Realizing she couldn't guarantee controlling me through my dick any longer, she had to find some other way of doing it. In fact I think she'd set up a fail-safe plan long in advance of me getting worried about her. I found out later that she'd been using her connection with me to make contact with some of the local pushers. 'Andy Dalziel says give me a good deal or you'll go out of business,' that sort of thing. There were a couple of occasions guys came to my door with packages for Linda, special delivery from the States, C.O.D. I took them in, handed over the money. Later I saw Linda open the packages and they were always what she'd said, items of clothing from some mail-order fashion house, or documents, whatever. What I didn't know was I was on candid camera, taking packages and handing over cash to guys the Drug Squad had a long interest in. But the big sting came when I started feeling dodgy after dinner one night. I thought it were the prawns in this *jambalaya thing she'd done. Everything went pear-shaped, then banana-shaped, then no shape at all. Then I seemed to be drifting in and out of these weird dreams. Only, next day when I saw the pictures, I realized they hadn't been dreams at all. There I was in black and white and technicolour shooting up and I had the puncture marks to go with it.*

These pics were on my pillow when I woke up about four o'clock the following afternoon. I felt like death warmed up. The phone rang while I was lying on the shower floor with the cold tap turned full on. It kept ringing till I got to it. I knew it would be Linda and it was.

She said she were sorry and she sounded like she meant it. She really liked me and believed I really liked her, but would that be enough to keep me quiet? She made it a real question and of course the answer was no it bloody wouldn't, so already I was feeling partly responsible for what had happened. She were good at her job, Linda, I have to give her that. All of her jobs.

She hoped we could stay friends. In fact, she'd like to stay my very loving friend, she'd enjoyed it so much. But just now she thought it best if she took a little break to give me time to consider the situation which was that as well as the still photos, of which I'd seen a small sample, there was a video, plus pics of me handing over money for packages from known dealers, plus they had a sample of my blood, which analysis would prove was awash with drugs.

Then she said she'd be in touch later and put the phone down.

The door bell rang. I were still so out of things I went to answer it without even thinking.

It was Kay. Must have been a shock for her to see me standing there, bollock naked, dripping water all over the hall mat, but she didn't blink an eyelid, just asked if Linda was around.

I think I said some rude things about Linda. Kay asked if she could come in. At this point I realized the state I was in and shot off to get myself dry and decent. When I came out of the bathroom into my bedroom, she were there, looking at the pics. I didn't ask her what she were doing. Somehow all that mattered was she didn't believe what them photos seemed to be saying, so I told her everything.

She didn't seem surprised, but went downstairs. I could hear her on the phone as I got dressed. When I came down she was making a cup of coffee and as I drank that she did me a great mountain of toast and fried me some eggs and half a dozen rashers. I felt better after I got that lot down. I wanted a drink but she wouldn't let me have anything alcoholic, not till she'd done me a repeat order of food. Then she poured two glasses of malt, a big one and a little one. And she handed me the little one.

I'd thought she might be something special from the first time I saw her, but that was when I knew it for sure, when she handed me the little Highland Park and kept the big one for herself!

After that she lit the fire and we sat and talked, not about Linda or anything, just ordinary stuff, and finally I must have dozed off 'cos suddenly I was woken by the door bell and when I opened my eyes it were after nine o'clock.

I heard Kay answer the door, talk to someone, then she came back in to me. She were carrying this cardboard box which she put on the floor in front of the fire. Then she said she had to be going, and that she'd call me in the morning to check I was OK.

And she was gone before I even had time to say thank you.

I sat there for another half-hour before I looked in the box. Truth was I were feeling better and I didn't want to risk losing the mood. Just by sitting around talking with Kay I'd calmed down so much that even though things still looked black as midnight, somehow midnight didn't seem such a dreadful place to be.

Then, only because I began to feel knackered and decided it were time to head for bed, I looked in the box.

That woke me up.

I couldn't believe it. I thought I must be hallucinating again. It was all there.

Photos, negatives, video, even the little vial of blood.

Everything.

I didn't hang around.

I stirred up the fire till it really got going then I dumped everything out of that box on to the flames and I sat there with my bottle of malt watching and occasionally stirring the coals till there was nowt left but a pile of hot ashes.

Then I went to bed.

End of story. End of statement.
Christ, but all this talking makes a man thirsty.
Are you ready for a top up yet, lad?

21

the voice of Death

'No thank you, sir,' said Pascoe. 'So let me get this straight. What you're saying is that Kay Kafka once covered up for you and now whenever she snaps her fingers and asks for help, you come running. Would that be simply because you're grateful, sir, or because she's got enough on you to lose you your job if she talks?'

It was the only time in his life that Pascoe thought that Dalziel might physically assault him.

The Fat Man came round the desk with the speed of a Kodiak bear and put his face so close to Pascoe's, he could smell the Highland Park on his hot breath.

'What have you got in that college-educated, over-heated brain of thine?' grated Dalziel. 'Bird droppings? Have you listened to a word of what I've said? Well, have you?'

'Acu-otically,' said Pascoe.

He doubted if the word existed, but instinct told him that you don't fight an enraged beast, you try to distract it and he knew the Fat Man could rarely resist an opportunity to mock redundant sesquipedalianism.

'Acu-otically?' echoed Dalziel, still just an inch away. 'Acu-otically?'

He barked a disbelieving laugh and withdrew a couple of inches.

'Acu-fucking-otically!'

Also he dearly loved a tmesis.

Slowly he straightened up and backed away, all the way round his desk, never taking his eyes off Pascoe even as he sat down and topped up his whisky tumbler and drained it dry.

Then he slammed it on the desk surface with a crash that made Pascoe jump.

'You think if she'd ever suggested some kind of trade-off, I'd have listened for a second?' he said. 'You think if she'd tried to blackmail me, I'd have put up with it for even half a second? I'll tell you what she asked for, lad. Nothing! Not then, not ever. I rang her up the next day and tried to say thanks and she said, "Andy, I fried you some eggs and made you some toast. What's to thank me for?" Next time I saw her, I tried to thank her again. She looked at me like I was raving. Not then, not ever, has she mentioned any of that stuff. Not a hint. Not even a bloody hint of a hint of you-owe-me-one. When Pal – old Pal, I mean – topped himself, I stepped in to take care of the case because of her, I don't deny it. But I checked every bit of her story twice as close as I checked anyone else's. And after she made that statement on the tape, I got Dave Thatcher to use his contacts over there to check out the American stuff. I felt ashamed doing it, but I bloody well did it all the same. It all checked out, right down the line. She's true diamond, Pete, true bloody diamond, and anyone who tries to tell me different had better have an affidavit signed by Jesus Christ himself to back it up.'

Does he know about her little adventures at the Golden Fleece? wondered Pascoe. Would it matter if he did? Should it matter?

These were questions to tease a man out of thought. More importantly they seemed likely to be questions that could tease a man out of life if put in the wrong way, which was to say in the same room or even town, and without an armed guard of marine commandoes.

He said, 'Sorry, sir, didn't mean to be offensive.'

'Me neither, lad. I'm sorry too. It's the smell of them funny buggers as does it. One sniff of them and I get edgy. What the hell interest can they have in this business, eh?'

'I think you touched on that in your – ah – statement, sir. That stuff about Ashur-Proffitt and the Iran-Contra affair.'

'That's old history, done and dusted,' said Dalziel.

'No, sir, stuff like that's never done. On the surface things change – new treaties, yesterday's enemies become today's allies. But whatever the

477

surface rules are, once you dig deep, they don't apply. Down there it's a whole different ball game – sanction breaking, illegal arms deals, out-of-date-drugs dumping – where only two things matter: profit and not getting caught. It's like the domestic black economy where work gets done without troubling the tax man or the VAT office. Except this is on a much huger scale, and a lot of it has covert official approval, and its colour is red because it's paid for in human lives.'

He came to a halt, somewhat surprised at the passion with which he'd been talking.

'You been reading Ellie's e-mails again?' said Dalziel.

'No, sir,' said Pascoe wearily. 'Just the newspapers and between the lines. I'd have thought 9/11 might have changed things a bit. In fact I'm sure it has. But there are always plenty of people who'd be looking to turn a fast buck even if they saw the four horsemen of the apocalypse galloping across the sky. You say you never heard from Linda Steele again?'

'No, not a dicky. Kept on coming across bits and pieces she'd left around the house and it were funny, despite what she'd done, or tried to do, I'd feel I really missed her. But she never showed her face here again, nor back home so far as Dave Thatcher could trace. But, like I say, she were a bright lass, bright enough to know there was little future in going back home to tell her creepy boss she'd screwed up. So I'd guess she did what she'd told me she'd done in the first place: quietly resigned and went off somewhere exotic to start a new career.'

'And you never found out exactly how Kay got the negatives back?'

'Not from her, but I could guess. Who else? Would hardly be Kay, would it? No, she must've told Kafka what Linda was up to and he sorted it out. I didn't ask questions, I were just glad to be off the hook.'

'You never wondered if something unpleasant might have happened to her then?'

'Something . . . ? What are you trying to say, Pete? Something unpleasant like something fatal, you mean? For Godsake this is Mid-Yorkshire not the Middle East. Any road, people don't get killed on my patch without me hearing something. And Kay might turn a blind eye to a bit of illegality but she'd never stand by and let another woman get hurt, that I'm sure of. No, Linda's sitting somewhere as we speak, comfortable and warm, with a smile on her face and a glass in her hand, and if ever I met her, I'd say give us a kiss and let's down a noggin for the sake of auld lang syne.'

If you want blind faith, convert a cynic, thought Pascoe.

He said brusquely, 'OK, sir. Where do we go from here?'

'It's your case,' said Dalziel. 'All I would say is, try and remember just what the case is about.

Did Pal Maciver kill himself, that's what. Nowt else. If he did, all this other crap's irrelevant.'

'Do you still think he did, sir?' asked Pascoe, wondering if this were the time to admit that he too was starting to come round to this way of thinking.

'I've heard nowt so far to suggest different. And I'm beginning to think we won't hear owt either, not unless we try a bit of table tapping and make direct contact with the dead!'

With perfect timing there came a rap at the door.

'Oh hell,' said Dalziel. 'Talk of the devil.'

And Pascoe turned and found himself staring Death in the face.

Happily the face in this instance belonged to Arnold Gentry, Head of the Forensic Lab, of whom it was alleged that once he had fallen asleep in a hospital waiting room and woken on a slab just in time to grasp the pathologist's wrist before he made his first incision. Police wit prefers the path most trodden, and naturally his cadaverous appearance had won him the sobriquet Dr Death.

'Andy,' he said. 'And Peter. So there is life in CID.'

'Oh aye? And how'd you recognize it, Arnold?' said Dalziel.

'By its rudeness mainly. What I am trying to convey is that there seems very little sign out there. But to my business. Some interesting things have come up as a result of our further examination of the Moscow House material and as I was passing on my way to an appointment, I thought I would show how sensitive we were to Peter's plea of urgency by conveying the findings myself.'

'Don't think we're not appreciative,' said Dalziel unpersuasively. 'So what've you got, apart from the verbal runs?'

From his briefcase Gentry produced a plastic file which he laid before the Fat Man.

'I'll read this on the bog later,' said Dalziel impatiently. 'Just give us the gist.'

'If you insist, though all this talking does dry the throat,' said Gentry, his eye fixed on the bottle of Highland Park.

'Jesus,' groaned Dalziel.

He produced another tumbler, poured a generous measure and topped up his own. Pascoe shook his head.

Dalziel raised his glass to his lips.

'I'd say *slainte*, only it seems a bit of a waste in thy case, Arnold,' he said. 'OK, get on with it.'

'Following the DCI's strict instructions, the SOCO team had despatched to us everything they could remove from the room including, I should point out, several hundred rather dusty volumes which I would rather not waste my staff's precious time on.'

'I didn't mean them to remove the books, except to facilitate their search,' apologized Pascoe.

'Then they must have taken your instructions over literally. The portrait of the mountaineering gent, did you want us to look at that also?'

'No. Sorry.'

'Good. We did, however, examine a coil of rope that showed no signs of ever having been used to hang or even whip anyone. There was also an ice axe which, interestingly, beneath the dust and rust did have some faint residual traces of blood. But they had clearly been there far too long to have any connection with the present investigation and are presumably a relict of some occasion on which our intrepid mountaineer hit his thumb instead of a piton.'

'For crying out loud,' exploded Dalziel. 'If you've got owt to say, Arnold, say it, even if it's only goodbye!'

'I see you are impatient for the nitty-gritty, Andrew. Very well. First the lock. We noted that it had been recently and liberally lubricated with a high-grade lubricant with the effect that the turning of a key in it would meet with minimal resistance. Further, we found adhering to the lubricant some traces of ash, as we did on the key itself . . .'

'Not surprising,' interrupted Dalziel, 'seeing the dead man had lit a little bonfire in his waste bin afore he topped himself.'

'Certainly it would have been easy to explain any traces on the key thus,' said Gentry. 'But with the key inserted, the ash therefrom would hardly have penetrated the lock. Analysis reveals that the internal ash traces, and some of the traces on the key also, derive from a source other than the fire in the waste bin.'

'Where's this leading us?' demanded Dalziel.

'It leads us to the gramophone,' said Gentry. 'The only ash traces we found on its exterior were clearly from the waste bin. But when we dismantled the machine we found twisted round the turntable spindle a length of thread. High-quality thread, thin but very strong, the loose end of which shows signs of having been severed by flame.'

'Tell me you're not telling me what you're telling me,' growled Dalziel.

'I tell you nothing,' said Gentry. 'I merely present the facts. Though I should add we are conducting various experiments in the lab and it does seem possible that if a thread had been tied to the turntable spindle then passed out through the power-cable aperture, wrapped round the head of the key, and fed through the keyhole, and if the key were placed in the lock on the inside then turned almost to the point where the bolt was engaged, then when a record was played on the player and the slack taken up by the spindle, sufficient pressure could be exerted to turn the key and lock the door. Of course, the player could be turned on from the outside simply by using the mains switch.'

'Oh-oh, me brain's beginning to hurt,' moaned Dalziel, taking a long analgesic pull at his scotch.

Gentry followed suit, draining his glass.

'Nice scotch,' he said hopefully. But something in the Fat Man's gaze told him he was reaching too far and he went hurriedly on. 'The thread or a substantial part of it having been soaked in some form of accelerant – ordinary lighter fuel would do the trick – all the perpetrator would have to do would be to listen at the door on the landing till they heard the lock click then set a light to the loose end of the thread dangling from the keyhole. The flame would run through the lock, and burn round the key head, at which point the length of thread running to the spindle would be free and the record would resume playing.'

'And you're saying this is what happened?' demanded Dalziel.

'Certainly not. Like I say, we simply present our findings and offer any hypotheses that seem germane. But we leave conclusions to CID. The rest of our findings, analysis of the ash in the waste bin, et cetera, you will find in the file.'

He stood up, then said, 'Oh, and one thing more. The SOCO team faxed through a palm print for us to check against the one found on the door. It looks a good match. This second version they found in the lounge in which I gather an *accouchement* took place the same night as the suicide. What extraordinarily interesting lives you lead in CID! You see what this means. Someone who was in that lounge had also been up on the landing, crouching outside the study door.'

'Could have been one of our lot,' said Dalziel. 'Or just old prints. The house is up for sale, there must have been people shown round.'

Gentry smiled, like a pirate ship breaking out its colours. The bastard's saving the best – or worst – till last, thought Dalziel.

'Not one of your lot,' he corrected. 'DCI Pascoe, meticulous as ever, had made sure we had all their prints for comparison. You will be interested to hear, Peter, that the sheet of paper you left with us a little earlier today held exactly the same palm print. Presumably you know whose that is, so that's one mystery solved.'

Pascoe avoided Dalziel's accusing stare by pretending to lick the last drops from his tumbler with his tongue. He felt he might be going to need them.

Gentry went to the door, opened it, then turned back.

'I nearly forgot. You'll recall there was a partial, not the deceased's, on the study key. Not really significant forensically speaking as there aren't enough points of comparison to put before a court. But, for what it's worth, it also seems to match a print we found on your sheet of paper, Peter. Thank you for the drink, Andy. Now I really must dash to my appointment.'

'Aye, bugger off to Samarra,' snarled Dalziel after him. 'Well, Pete, you who don't have secrets, are you going to tell me what the hell all that was about?'

'It sounded to me as if Gentry was suggesting the possibility that someone went to considerable trouble to fix things to create the illusion that Maciver locked himself in the study then shot himself,' said Pascoe.

'Aye, that much I got. What I'm talking about is these prints.'

'Ah. Those. Yes, they seem to suggest that whoever it was that set up this rather Heath Robinson apparatus to make it appear like suicide inadvertently left a partial on the key. Then, as they knelt outside to light the thread running to the gramophone after they'd heard the lock click shut, they leaned against the door with the palm of their hand.'

'I know that, I've worked all that out too. How to see the fucking obvious is the first lesson they learn you at superintendents' school. It's the name I want, the fucking name.'

Pascoe said, 'I think you've probably worked that out too, sir. We'll need to take her prints properly to get absolute confirmation, but this, plus what Novello found out from the Avenue girls, makes it pretty clear Kay Kafka was in Moscow House at or about the time Maciver died.'

Dalziel nodded.

'Then we'd best talk to her,' he said.

'We?' said Pascoe.

'It's your case, Pete. But it's been my call. If I've got it wrong, do you not think I'm entitled to be around to see for myself?'

Pascoe nodded.

'That sounds fair. Do you want to do it now?'

The Fat Man looked at his watch.

'No. Cap's due back tonight, if she's not been arrested, that is. She's been away on one of her demo's. Don't ask me what, sometimes she tells me, sometimes she doesn't, and it's the times she doesn't that worry me most.'

'I know the feeling,' said Pascoe. 'When then, sir?'

'First thing tomorrow. And it'll give us time to think a bit. There's a lot going off here we need to think about, Peter. That OK by you?'

Pascoe hesitated. His instinct was to head straight out to Cothersley. On the other hand, it was Friday night and he and Ellie were due at a school concert where Rosie would be playing the clarinet in public for the first time. It was his private opinion that his daughter's playing should be an experience reserved for consenting adults in a large empty desert, but while admitting he understood little about the complexities of the female mind, he understood enough not to even hint a hint of this.

Mistaking the cause of the hesitation, Dalziel said, 'She's not going anywhere, lad, not with them new babbies gurgling away in the maternity ward. And if you're worried I'm going to be ringing her, forget it. I'll be too busy discussing American foreign policy or summat with Cap.'

'That what you call it these days?' said Pascoe,

smiling. 'I assume this means that my twenty-four-hour deadline has been expunged?'

'Aye. Wiped out like someone's peed on it from a great height,' said Dalziel. 'Like I'm beginning to feel someone has.'

'Till tomorrow then,' said Pascoe. 'See you here at nine?'

'Suits me,' said Dalziel with an affectation of indifference that didn't quite come off.

Pascoe went in search of Wield and found him at his desk behind a mountain of paper.

'What's this?' he asked.

'Edwin's book-dealing chums have their big thrash tonight. Thought I'd take the chance to get the department records in sight of the millennium.'

'Not invited then?'

'In-house only. You've got to be two hundred years old and leather bound. Something you want, Pete?'

'Maybe. But it could turn out even more boring than paperwork and probably less productive.'

'Try me,' said Wield, pushing his paper mountain aside.

22

walking on water

As the last drinkers began to drift away from the
Dog and Duck, St Cuthbert's clock struck eleven.

It was a rather splendid chime, fit for a cathedral or a town hall, the old Cothersleyans used
to boast. A man a mile or more away, tending a
sick beast in the dead of night or ploughing a
heavy field in heavy mist, need never be uncertain of the right time with Cothersley clock to set
him true. But one man's boast is another man's
burden and a couple of years earlier after petition
from light-sleeping incomers, outvoting the native
opposition by five to one, the quarters had been
silenced between the hours of ten in the evening
and seven in the morning. The objectors would
have been glad to silence the hours too, but David
Upshott (it was the first big test of his ministry)
had offered this compromise, saying that anyone
who could not get to sleep within an hour ought
to consult his doctor or his conscience.

Dolly Upshott, rather to the surprise of the pub

regulars who weren't used to seeing her so late and alone, had come in at ten, ordered a large vodka and tonic and sat in a corner, nursing her drink and her mobile phone. She had replied politely but shortly to attempts at conversation and shown no desire to have company at her table. So the regulars had returned their attention to the less edifying but more entertaining sight of Sue-Lynn Maciver, who was more than happy to share the sorrows of her new widowhood with anyone who cared to buy her a drink.

Dolly was the last to leave the pub.

'You all right, Miss Upshott?' enquired the Captain, who was in a benevolent mood brought on by the realization that, far from being a turn-off, the presence of the grieving widow had actually bumped his takings right up.

'Yes, thank you. Fine,' said Dolly, looking across the green to where the bulk of the church stood black against a gloriously star-spattered sky.

The church getting in the way of the heavens. It was a conceit that pleased her.

But the stars were out of her reach and in times of trouble we turn to whatever comfort is most readily to hand.

When the pub door was closed behind her, she walked over the green and up the path towards the church.

Moscow House too loomed dark against the sky as Kay Kafka walked up the drive. She recalled taking the same walk two nights before. She hadn't been frightened then and she wasn't frightened now. She had surfeited on fear all those years ago when she'd gone running to the crèche with Emily's poem beating through her mind and by the time she stood two days later looking down at the still form of her daughter, so incredibly small it seemed impossible that life had ever informed those tiny limbs, those of her neural circuits that recorded fear had been burnt out.

Only on very few occasions since then had they shown any flicker of life. Once when after her first husband's death it had seemed possible they might find a way to take Helen away from her. A second time when Helen had shyly but at the same time so hopefully confided in her that she was desperately in love with Jason Dunn. And yet again, here at Moscow House when Helen went into labour.

But such conventional terrors as might be expected to accompany a solitary visit to a house which held the memories this one did had no power over her.

This time the front door was shut but she had Helen's key, the key Helen insisted on having when the house went on the market. And this time she did not need to rely on finding a stub of candle and a book of matches. Providently she had a pencil torch in her pocket.

Its thin beam led her up the staircase to the study door. She turned the handle and pushed.

It swung open and without even a second's hesitation she stepped into the room where her husband and her stepson had both died.

Now her mind did register something, but it was surprise not fear, caused by the room's emptiness. She let the torch beam stray hither and thither. Everything had gone. Furniture, picture, even the books. How very thorough. Andy had told her DCI Pascoe was a man for fine detail but she hadn't expected anything like this.

But their thoroughness had not taken them quite all the way. They had not attempted to remove the gun cabinet from the wall.

She went to it and opened it.

The dust that had gathered inside looked undisturbed.

She reached in, took hold of the gun-retaining clip, twisted it anticlockwise and pulled. It swung out easily on well-oiled hinges and she let the torch beam play into the revealed chamber.

At the same time the room's central light came on and a voice said, 'Once saw a movie where there was a safe hidden behind a safe. Should have thought of that.'

For a second she froze but when she turned, her face showed nothing but the pleasure of a welcoming hostess.

'How nice to see you, Sergeant,' she said. 'I'm so glad to have been of assistance.'

'You've certainly been that,' agreed Wield. 'So what brings you here, Mrs Kafka?'

'It was Mr Pascoe, actually. He asked me if I knew anything about another gun. I said no, but later I got to thinking, and I had this recollection of seeing my husband, my first husband that is, closing this cabinet one day. It struck me as odd that it should swing out completely but I never really thought there might be another cabinet behind it, not till Mr Pascoe made me think, that is. And once I got the notion in my head, that was it. I found I couldn't rest until I'd seen for myself.'

'Didn't think of just ringing Mr Pascoe?'

'And send him on a wild-goose chase? No, I thought I'd come down here myself and ask the policeman on duty if I could test out my theory.'

'And when you saw there wasn't a policeman on duty?'

She smiled at him.

'But of course, there is, Sergeant. You. So here you are. One little mystery solved. Now, if you'll excuse me, I must be getting home. My husband's away and he will probably try to ring me from his hotel. Good night to you, Mr Wield.'

She walked towards him.

He watched her approach, his face giving away nothing.

Then he stood aside and said, 'Good night, Mrs Kafka.'

In St Cuthbert's church Dolly Upshott had no idea how long she'd been sitting.

It was cold in here, but not cold enough to mask the unique smell of the place, what her brother called the odour of sanctity. It comprised wood and leather and cloth and stone and dampness and the ghost of incense and hyssop (David was quite 'high'). The stained-glass windows, beautiful with the sun behind them, were too heavily tinted for starlight to penetrate. Only to the south-west where a gibbous moon glanced on a high narrow window did a diffused light pass through, and she'd taken her seat here.

She didn't move, not even when she heard the church door, which she'd left ajar, creak fully open and footsteps come up the aisle.

'I saw the door was open as I drove by,' said Kay Kafka. 'It seemed like an invitation. But if I'm disturbing you . . .'

'No more than life. Have a pew.'

Uncertain if this was an English joke or not, Kay sat down and looked up at the window where the moonlight set the stained glass glowing. The design showed two haloed figures walking towards each other across a stretch of water. This was usually interpreted as Herbert of Derwentwater visiting his chum Cuthbert of Lindisfarne, or maybe vice versa. One of the figures (probably Herbert) looked a lot less certain than the other, as if not quite able to get it out of his mind that the slightest flicker of faith could have him plunging to a weedy grave.

'I know how he feels,' said Kay.

'Sorry?'

'The picture in the window. Walking on water's fine till something comes along to remind you it's water you're walking on.'

'Like a ship, you mean?'

'Or a shark.'

They shared a moment of humour, but soon they moved beyond sharing, each into some private space where they looked for whatever it was that had brought them into this place at this time.

It was the church clock striking midnight that brought them out of their reveries.

Even now neither spoke nor moved till the twelfth note had sounded across the green, rolling out beyond the sleeping cottages and farms, past the near meadows, over the still streams, finally fading to nothingness in the neighbouring valley-glades.

Now they rose and walked down the aisle together.

Outside they stood for a moment looking up at the brilliant stars above the dark unheeding village.

'Looks set fair for tomorrow, doesn't it?' said Kay.

'You think so?' said Dolly. 'Doesn't matter. Even if it rains, water's not the end of the world, is it? We can always swim.'

'So can sharks,' said Kay.

March 23rd, 2002

1

a lady calls

Peter Pascoe awoke on Saturday morning feeling good. Drowsily he tried to give shape to the as yet amorphous causes of this pleasant state. It was the beginning of a free weekend; last night's concert had been close to a triumph, Rosie playing with a brio which visually more than compensated for her somewhat cavalier attitude to musical notation; he and Ellie had put her to bed with love and kisses, and not long after put themselves to bed with even more; and one of the shapes which was contributing largely to his euphoria, or perhaps one should more accurately say two of them, was, or were, pressed invitingly close against his belly at this moment.

Then a thin wail from his mobile phone brought him out of his dream.

He grabbed it from the bedside table, switched off the sound, checked the display. It was Wield. What the hell did he want at ten to eight on a Saturday morning?

LEEDS COLLEGE OF BUILDING
499
LIBRARY

As he staggered out of the room to find out, it occurred to him that his irritation was misdirected. His long lie-in was already spoken for. He had a date with Dalziel to pay a visit to Cothersley Hall. Plus, and even more imperatively, he had an agreement with Rosie to drop her off for her nine a.m. clarinet lesson on the way in to the station. After last night she would have the Royal Festival Hall in her sights, or at least the Wigmore. Indeed, as he settled on the loo seat to answer his phone, he could already hear her running up a scale whose atonality would have left Schoenberg gasping.

'Yes?' he yawned.

'Morning, Pete,' said Wield, sounding disgustingly wide awake. 'Wanted to catch you before you set out.'

Briefly he described the events at Moscow House the previous night.

'You didn't bring her in for questioning then?' said Pascoe.

'No point. Would have meant rousting you and Andy out of bed, and for what? She had her story ready anyway.'

'Which you believed?'

'No way. I reckon she wanted to check what might be in there. Anything she didn't fancy us finding, she'd have removed. Then some time today she'd have "remembered" about the hidden cabinet and passed on the info like a good citizen.'

'Tell me again what you found.'

'A silver whisky flask, initials P.M. A silver cigarette lighter, same initials. A medicine bottle, empty, but the label says it contained Valium capsules prescribed to Mr P. Maciver. A micro-cassette. And a diary, stamped with the year 1992. I've not done anything with them yet other than photo them in situ and bag them. I'm at the lab now. I rang Dr Death and told him I needed some bodies down here a.s.a.p. Soon as they show, I'll get this stuff tested and printed. Of course it may turn out it's all covered with Mrs Kafka's prints, and she was in the study to recover the evidence. But if that's the case, why'd she leave it there in the first place?'

'Good question. I wish you'd got in touch to ask it last night.'

'For what? To spoil your sleep? There was nowt to be done till this morning, at least nowt I could think of,' said the sergeant, sounding slightly aggrieved at the DCI's reproachful tone.

He was quite right, thought Pascoe. Dalziel might have said, read the diary, play the tape, bugger the risk of cross-contamination! But he knew he would have contained his impatience till the lab did its work.

Also there was the memory of what Wield would have disturbed if he had rung . . .

He said, 'Sorry, Wieldy, you were quite right. Listen, there's something else you can do for me now that you're out and about so bright and early. Once you've got those idle sods at the lab work-

501

ing, could you give Tom Lockridge an early call before he makes for the golf course or whatever it is he does on a Saturday morning? Shake him up a bit. Tell him he'll have to be suspended from our medical examiner list for concealing his intimate connection with a key witness in a case he was advising on.'

'OK. Anything special you want me to shake out of him?'

'It's clear Sue-Lynn imagined she was going to benefit substantially when her husband died . . .'

'But the photo gives them an alibi,' interrupted Wield.

'I know. But it's more her reaction now that she knows Pal changed his will . . . and Pal's reasons for changing his will . . . and one or two other things . . .'

'Sounds to me like you're coming round to Andy's point of view, Pete.'

'Yes. Ironic, isn't it? Just when I feel I'm making headway getting him round to mine! Anyway, my point is, while I can still see lots of motives for murder, I can't yet see any for suicide. But Sue-Lynn will clearly be desperate to prove he was going doolally. And I've got a feeling Tom Lockridge is on the case too. So shake away. Keep in touch, will you? I'll be out at Cothersley.'

'And the best of luck,' said Wield. 'I reckon you'll need it.'

Pascoe switched off the phone, turned the shower on and stepped underneath.

As he towelled himself down, he heard the front door bell. Jesus, he thought. Doesn't anyone have a long lie-in on a Saturday morning any more? The clarinet fell silent, which suggested Rosie was taking care of things. He went back to the bedroom where he found that one person at least was set for the long lie-in. She had rolled over, throwing the duvet off her naked body and he groaned with frustrated longing as he pulled his clothes on.

He was buttoning up his shirt when the door opened and Rosie came in.

She said, 'There's a lady to see you.'

'A lady? You mean a woman,' said Pascoe, loyally adding his weight to Ellie's attempts to purge the child of prejudice in all its forms.

Rosie thought, then said, 'Yes, of course she's a woman. But she looks like a lady and she talks like a lady.'

She turned and left with the Parthian shot, 'You know I mustn't be late.'

Behind him there was a sound as Ellie awoke.

'Was that the door bell I heard before?' she yawned.

'Yes. Rosie got it. Seems I've got a visitor.'

'At this time on a Saturday morning? Jesus.' Then with sudden suspicion, 'It's not that fat bastard, is it?'

'Reasonable guess,' he said. 'But no. This one's a woman. Sorry. A lady.'

'Well, if she's here with your love-child, tell

her to go and find some bulrushes,' said Ellie.

'God, you're sexy when you yawn,' he said.

'That sounds like an argument for boring sex,' she said, sinking back on to the pillow.

On another occasion he might have read that as a hint. This morning, with Dalziel, Rosie and a lady weighing in the counterbalance, he turned and went out of the room.

As he descended the stairs he guessed that his daughter, with a sense of precedence which wouldn't have been out of place in a Victorian society hostess, would have put her lady in the lounge rather than the kitchen.

He was right. And Rosie was right too. At least as far as she could see.

Standing by the patio window looking out into the garden was Dolly Upshott.

She looked pale, with dark shadows under her eyes. The short brown hair was even more hectic than usual. Looking at her young form clad in a Fair Isle sweater, sensible tweed skirt and flat brogues, it was still hard to believe what her presence there must surely mean was the truth.

Which with admirable directness, she now confirmed.

'Got your message,' she said. 'I thought of doing a runner, but decided there was no point really. I looked you up in the phone book. I'm really sorry to be bothering you at home like this, but I thought that showing up at the cop-shop would probably remove any chance I had of keeping this thing sub rosa. I mean, I'd be straight into the torture chamber there, wouldn't I? Tape machines, witnesses, red-hot irons, all the apparatus.'

Her attempt at humour was more revealing of her agitated state of mind than hysterical tears would have been.

He said, 'Please sit down, Miss Upshott. I haven't had any breakfast and I need at least one cup of coffee before I can function properly. Can I get you something?'

'Coffee would be nice,' she said.

He went out and ran lightly up the stairs. Ellie opened her eyes as he came into the bedroom.

'What?' she said.

'Sorry, can you take Rosie to her lesson?'

'Jesus. You mean it really is the love-child?'

'Far more serious than that,' he said. 'Could even be serious enough to make me late for Fat Andy.'

'In that case, what does a little inconvenience to me matter. OK.'

'Thanks. I owe you.'

'And you'll pay,' she called after him.

He collected a microcassette recorder from his study, went into the kitchen, made a couple of mugs of instant coffee and took them through to the lounge.

'Right, Miss Upshott,' he said.

'What do you want me to do?' she said. 'I want to get everything out of the way, here, now. I heard what you said in your message about

505

coming round to the vicarage. Please, I couldn't bear that. I'll do anything, but David must never hear any of this, all right?'

Though he never liked doing it, Pascoe had long ago learned the detective art of making non-binding promises, unenforceable agreements.

He smiled sympathetically and said, 'Your best way to ensure that, Miss Upshott, is to tell me everything, as fully and frankly as you can.'

As he spoke he set the microcassette between them on the table.

She didn't seem to notice it but continued to examine his face closely till he felt the sympathetic smile must resemble a cynical leer.

Finally she closed her eyes as if to compare what she saw with some inner picture.

When she opened them again after nearly a minute she said in a small childlike voice, 'All right, then. I will.'

2

Dolly

Gosh, where on earth shall I begin? I mean, you'd think that something that's ended up where this has ended up would have a pretty definite starting point, wouldn't you? On your mark – get set – bang! But that's not the way life works, is it? I suppose it really began when Mother died. Or perhaps when Mother got ill. I was still living at home, you see. That was in Chester, do you know it? Sorry. Not relevant. I had a job then, in a bank, nothing exciting. After a while even all that money becomes boring, though I sometimes used to dream . . . but I shouldn't be telling you that! Then Mother got ill and needed more and more looking after. The bank was very good, and arranged for me to work full-time part-time, if you see what I mean. But eventually even that was too much. I was needed at home all the time for the last six months till Mother passed on.

After that, back to the boring old bank, I thought. But David said why not come and stay with him for a while, I deserved a rest, and having his sister about the vicarage might help fend off all the lady parishioners who were determined to marry him off.

So I came to Cothersley. That was three years ago. My rest didn't last long, I'm a busy bee by nature and very soon I was helping out with things – parish finances, timetables, fêtes, that sort of thing – till eventually I found I was doing what felt like a full-time job, except of course I got nothing for it, except my keep.

I kept telling myself I had to break away, get out and find a real job again, but I can't say the thought of going back to the bank really turned me on. David said, 'Hang on, don't rush into anything, something is sure to turn up.' And it did!

I'd got to know Pal as a neighbour and also as one of my brother's parishioners, though really I didn't see much of him except when I was doing the rounds with my collecting box when he was always very generous. Then one day I was in town, shopping for a birthday present for David, and I saw this little musical box in an antique shop window, and I went inside, not really registering the shop's name, and Pal said, 'Well, hello, this is nice,' like we were old friends. The box was a lovely thing, early nineteenth century, silver with beryls and topazes, and it played a sweet little tune which Pal said was by Haydn, but its price was far more than I could afford even when he offered me a discount. Well we chatted about antiques for a while – Mother had been interested so I knew a little bit – then suddenly he asked if I'd be interested in a job. He was looking for someone to help him in the shop, someone he could rely on to take over while he was away on buying trips.

Sue-Lynn, his wife, helped sometimes but he said she wasn't really interested and if I could see my way . . .

I didn't hesitate. The thought of being at least partially independent again was marvellous. I said, 'Yes please. How much will you pay me?' And he laughed and said if I was going to be an antiques dealer, I'd have to learn a better haggling technique than that.

So I took the job, and it was great. I really enjoyed it and after a while I think I became pretty good at it.

That was just over eighteen months ago. The sex began three or four months later.

It wasn't an affair. It was never an affair, not like in Brief Encounter, which was Mother's favourite movie – in the end I knew the script by heart – no, this was certainly nothing like that. One day in the shop he touched me. Not an accidental brush. No ambiguity. A hand on my . . . you know. Well, I didn't know what to do. So I touched him back. He put the closed sign up.

I suppose that was my on your mark, get set, bang!

I wasn't inexperienced, but for a long time, what with looking after Mother then living in the vicarage, there hadn't been much opportunity. But this was worth waiting for.

Like the job, it was great. I really enjoyed it. And after a while with Pal's help I think I became pretty good at it.

The Dolores thing started casually. We asked each other to do various things and the Dolores get-up was one of the things he asked me to do. It was like children dressing up! Well, a bit more than that, of course, but you know what I mean. Then he asked if he could bring a friend. I got rather frightened at this, but he said I should ask myself if that wasn't Dolly Upshott speaking, and why didn't I check with Dolores, which was who I'd be to this friend, he need never know anything about Dolly. So I did check, and though it was still a bit scary, Dolores found the prospect rather exciting, and the actual encounter more exciting still.

I hope I'm not shocking you, but you said the franker I was, the less chance there was of David ever needing to hear any of this, and I couldn't bear that.

Things developed. Pal said the friend would like to be by himself with me. He took a hotel room. I went to it. When he went, he left an envelope by my clothes. I opened it. There was two hundred pounds in it. I was furious and I went to Pal and had a row with him. I asked him what he thought I was. He told me that all that mattered was what I thought I was. If I wanted, he said, he'd give the money back to his friend, but if he could find a girl who left him a couple of hundred quid every time they had a fuck, he'd jump at it. I threw the money at him and said, 'There you go then.' And he threw it back at me and told me angrily not to be stupid. And I said, 'What's the difference?' And he said he wouldn't object to being paid as a stud but he had no ambitions to be a pimp. And we both started laughing.

After that, well, it became . . . not routine, not even regular, and not for the money either though that was nice . . . but whenever Dolores felt like it. Dolores was part of me, of course, but only a part, and I, me, Dolly Upshott, was completely separate from Dolores.

Pal got me a phone so that his friends – there were two or three of them, no more – could contact me and leave a message, and I could get back to them if I wanted to. And sometimes I did and sometimes I didn't. But with Pal, I always wanted to.

Sorry, I'm boring you a bit, aren't I? It's information you want, not analysis. Trouble is, Dolores doesn't give a toss what you think, but Dolly would like you to understand . . .

Anyway, sometimes Pal took me to Moscow House. He told me how it had been put on the market after all these years and his car turning up there wouldn't draw much attention. It was very eerie going into an old house with a lot of the furniture shrouded in dust sheets, but that only made it more exciting for Dolores. This after all was her kind of territory, though Dolly almost put in an appearance when Pal eventually told me about his father committing suicide there. He went on about it not really being suicide, insisting that his stepmother was somehow responsible. He used to get very angry when he talked about her, but I noticed that he also got very excited too so I often deliberately brought her into the conversation.

Then he asked if I'd mind if he brought someone else along to Moscow House. I did mind. It was our place. But when he explained it wasn't like the others, this wasn't someone who would want to ring me up and fix to meet me in a hotel room and leave an envelope, this was personal, this was family, Dolores got interested and said, 'Why not?'

That's how I met Jason. Jase. You know him? Of

511

course you do. He's Pal's brother-in-law and you must have met all the family while you've been investigating the case. He is gorgeous, isn't he? And the sex! Pal once said, 'For God's sake, Jase, slow down, you make me feel like an old man!' So from that point of view it was great. But I always felt there was something else.

Then one night we were all lying there, shagged out – sorry, sounds awful, doesn't it? But I mean it quite literally. And as well as shagged out, the two chaps were spaced out – they'd got into the habit of doing a line or two of coke, Pal's treat. He offered me some too, but Dolores wasn't interested. The sex was enough for her, and besides when they were like this, they'd get to talking like she wasn't there, and it's a bit of a giggle eavesdropping on you men when you think you're all alone.

This time Pal started talking about Kay, that's his stepmother. Sorry, you know that. Not his usual angry stuff but just sort of dreamily recalling how he reckoned she fancied him when he was in his teens and how there'd been a couple of occasions when they were alone together and he was sure he could have had her, only he was too nervous to try. And Jason said that he'd missed a great chance, on a scale of ten he'd give her ten plus; and Pal said, 'You mean, you have had her?' Jason sort of hesitated – I think he was just enough in touch with the real world to think that maybe this wasn't a road he wanted to go down, not with his wife's brother – but Pal said something like, 'Hey, Jase, it's OK, buddy, you're among friends, what anyone says here, stays here.' And Jason relaxed again and he said, oh yes, he'd certainly had Kay, but it was long before he married Helen – that's Pal's sister; sorry – in fact it was because of Helen he'd met Kay. She used to come to parent–teachers' meetings at Weavers School where he taught. Jase had no reason to talk to her – the girls have a woman PE teacher – but he'd spotted this good-looking bird, as he put it, and he'd caught her eye one night and given her his come-on look, and she'd responded, and not long after the meeting ended, he was having one of the best times he'd ever had.

Pal asked how long this went on and Jase said not long, he never let these things go on long enough to get serious. He tried to sound real casual about it, but somehow I got the impression it was really her who'd done the dumping and she'd made it hurt.

Then Pal asked if it hadn't been awkward when he started going out with Helen. Jase said that in fact there was no way he'd have started with Helen if he'd real-ized who she was, but he'd met her in a club, they had a great time, good enough to make him look out for her the following night. This time they exchanged rather more information, but even when she mentioned she'd just left Weavers a few weeks before and had always fancied him, he didn't make a connection between this Helen Maciver and the Kay Kafka he'd had a fling with, otherwise, he said, he'd have run a mile.

Whatever Kay had done to him, she'd left her mark.

Jase boasted he was used to being fancied by the older girls at school but he made very sure he kept them at arm's length or even further. He really likes his job and he doesn't want to risk losing it for something that's in plentiful supply in the outside world. His words. Once the girls left Weavers, though, they were fair game for a couple of sessions on the training track. His words again.

But after he'd been out with Helen three or four times, he began to think this one might be different. He really liked her. He sounded rather surprised when he said it, as if really liking a woman he'd bedded was a novelty. He listened to her talking about the two of them as an item and found he didn't mind. Still no notion of her connection with Kay. Helen told him later that her stepmother's approval meant so much to her, she kept putting off inviting him home for fear things might go wrong. But she was far too close to Kay to keep it secret for long that she'd met the man she loved and wanted to marry, and one day Jase answered the bell to his apartment and found Kay on the doorstep.

When he realized she was Helen's stepmother, he said he felt the world was coming to an end. What she said made such a deep impression he was still able to quote it verbatim. Me too. I've always had a fantastic memory.

She said, 'Mr Dunn, I know what you are capable of, in every sense. Helen finds you irresistibly attractive and has got it into her head that you are the man she wants to marry. I think this would be a huge mistake. I haven't told her this, nor my reasons for so believing, because of the damage it would do to our relationship. In fact I suggested she should invite you round to tea next time you meet. When she does, I would like you to tell her, no way, you've no desire whatsoever to get

your feet under the table, this thing between you is a
casual fling and if she's got other ideas she'd better
disabuse herself. If you fail to do this, I will have to
intervene, whatever the consequences. And by the way,
one of those consequences would be the loss of your job
as I should make it quite clear to the education author-
ities that this relationship had begun while Helen was
still a pupil at Weavers.'

Jase said he was scared shitless – his words – but
what was even more scary was he heard himself telling
Kay that he didn't give a toss, she must do whatever
she felt she had to do, but even if it meant losing his
job and having to start over, Helen was the only girl for
him and he was going to marry her, come what may.

He said Kay didn't speak for a long time, just sat
there looking at him, so still and intense he began to
think maybe she was going to turn him into a frog.

Then she said, 'OK. In that case when she asks you
to tea, you'd better come.'

Pal let out a great whoop of laughter and said,
'That's my girl! Nothing but the best for her beloved
little Helen. Good stud line, lovely mover, beautifully
schooled, top-class foals guaranteed. Only thing she
didn't reckon on was how frisky you might get if
deprived of your regular oats.'

Then Pal laughed again, only in a more friendly
fashion this time, and said, 'No need to look so worried,
my son. I know this is just a bit of fun while my kid
sister's out of commission, no harm done. And there
won't be any tales out of school. Dolores and I are as
discreet as a pair of dodos, and that's dead discreet.'

So things went on as before, until last time.

We all used to meet up in the sports centre car park, at the dark end near the river. Jase and I would get into Pal's car and he'd drive us off to Moscow House so that his was the only car anyone would see going up the drive. Only this night our usual time went by and there was no sign of Pal. Finally I got into Jase's car so we could decide what to do. I tried to ring Pal on his mobile, but it was switched off. Then I tried the shop, but got no reply. After that Jase used my phone to ring Pal's home number. He spoke to Sue-Lynn, who had no idea where Pal was. After that we drove to the Avenue and went slowly past the entrance to Moscow House in case Pal had gone directly there for some reason. But it was very misty and, even if it hadn't been, you can hardly see the house from the road. We turned and came back and this time as we approached we saw a police car turn into the driveway.

This really bothered Jase and he headed back to the sports centre. He dropped me in the car park. He was going to go into the club and do a bit more phoning around to see if he could track down Pal. He said he was sure everything was all right, but I could tell he was worried. He said I should just go home, wherever that was. I almost told him it was the vicarage at Cothersley, just to see his face, but that would have been very silly. I got into my little Fiat. Usually I change in there and get my make-up off, if the car park's quiet, but tonight I was worried too, so I decided to take another drive down the Avenue.

I got there just in time to see an ambulance with its

siren wailing turning into Moscow House. I could see what looked like a police car's flashing lights up by the house. I parked around the corner and got out and walked back. I knew that a lot of prostitutes hung out along the Avenue, so I thought a woman walking by herself wouldn't attract any attention, but the place seemed deserted and I realized that at the first sign of the police most of the pros must have realized that business was over for the night and headed off elsewhere.

Gosh it was eerie, but I had to find out what was going on. There was a policeman stationed at the gate. He nearly jumped out of his skin when he saw me, and realizing that he was even more scared than I was gave me confidence. I put on my best Dolores voice and pretended I was one of the Avenue girls rather put out at having her evening's trade ruined. What he told me really chilled my blood. He said they'd found a dead man in the house, looked like suicide but they didn't know for certain yet, and the body was still to be identified. I knew it was Pal, I don't know how, but from the start I was sure.

Some other cars came and I hid. Then I made my way back to my own car and drove back to Cothersley as quickly as I could. I was in such a state I almost forgot to get out of my Dolores gear. Gosh, what a shock it would have given David if I'd walked in dressed like that!

As far as I was concerned that was the end of Dolores. I only got the phone out last night to throw it away and if I hadn't checked for messages, I wouldn't be here.

But then I suppose you would have come round to the vicarage and that would have been far worse.

Please, I've told you everything I know. It hasn't been easy, but I didn't want to leave any reason for you to need to question me again ever.

So I've done what you asked, as full and frank as I can make it. You look like a good and honest man, to me, Mr Pascoe. Please, can I have your assurance again that this is the last I'm ever going to hear of this business?

3

middle name

Pascoe paused to get his breath before he passed through the general CID room en route to Dalziel's office. He didn't want his subordinates to think he'd been running up the stairs because he was late, but Novello's welcoming grin gave the impression that she knew anyway.

To his surprise, Hat Bowler too was sitting at his desk, gazing vacantly at the wall. He looked pale and unhappy.

'Hat, what are you doing here?' asked Pascoe, concerned.

'Super said he thought it would be a good idea, sir. Break myself back in gently.'

'But you're still on the sick list.'

'Yes, sir. But I'll be seeing the doc on Monday to get signed off.'

'I think that will be for the doctor to say,' said Pascoe gently.

Now he recalled Dalziel's concern lest the lad was somehow getting mixed up with funny-bugger business by spending time at Lavinia Maciver's cottage. And the fat sod accuses me of flights of fancy! thought Pascoe.

But today did not seem a good time to start countermanding orders from the Godhead.

He said, 'Well, don't overdo it,' a comment which brought a cynical snort quickly modified into a sneeze from Novello. Pascoe shot her an admonitory glance and went to meet his doom.

The Fat Man was replacing his phone as Pascoe entered.

'Sorry I'm late, sir, but . . .'

'Bugger buts. Late's late,' said Dalziel without any real force. 'I've just been talking to Kay and told her we'd be out to see her a bit later.'

'But we didn't have an appointment,' protested Pascoe. 'In fact I'd have preferred to take her by surprise.'

'You'd need to get up a bit earlier to do that, lad,' said Dalziel. 'Any road, I didn't ring her, she rang me.'

'How convenient. What for?'

'Two things,' said Dalziel, ignoring the slight sneer. 'One was to tell me about what went off at Moscow House last night. Seemed surprised I didn't know about it. Not as surprised as me, but.'

He looked questioningly at Pascoe who said, 'Sorry, sir, just heard what happened from Wieldy myself this morning. I was going to put you in the picture.'

'I really appreciate that, Pete. The other thing

she rang about is she's worried about her husband.'

'Like Mrs Dale used to be?'

'No joking matter, this, lad,' said Dalziel heavily. 'Seems he went off to London yesterday so's he could catch a morning flight to America from Heathrow.'

'Yes, I was there when he left,' said Pascoe. 'I think he said he had to go in to Ash-Mac's first.'

'That's right. Well, she expected him to ring her some time last night . . .'

'So why did she go out?' interrupted Pascoe.

'You not heard of mobiles, lad?' demanded Dalziel with a scorn ill becoming in one who had once opined that if he wanted something that whistled in his pocket, he'd fill it with twigs and buy a canary. 'And answer services? There was no call, no message. This morning she rang the airport hotel he usually stays at. He was booked in but he hadn't showed. His flight goes in half an hour and he's not checked in for that yet either. I got on to the railway car park and they went and had a look and they've just confirmed Kafka's car is parked there.'

'So what do you think's going on, sir?'

'Could be in the boot, I suppose, but I doubt it. Have you read your paper this morning?'

'Haven't had time, sir.'

'No? Coming in at this hour, I'd have thought you'd have had time to read *War and* sodding *Peace*. Bit in it about Ashur-Proffitt in the States.

Seems the authorities are taking a long close look at the business like they did with that Enron mob. And it seems one or two of their top execs saw what was coming and have taken to the hills.'

Pascoe said, 'And you think that Kafka . . . ?'

'Why not? You go out scrumping apples and you see the farmer coming, you run like hell.'

'Just like that? Leaving your wife to fend for herself. Or do you think she might know something, sir?'

Two days earlier, even yesterday, he would have expected such a suggestion to trigger a violent rebuttal, but now the Fat Man just glowered at him. He felt no triumph at having been party to sowing seeds of doubt, only a sense of loss.

He said, 'The reason I was late, sir, was Dolly Upshott came to see me. This is her statement.'

He took the microcassette out of his pocket and pressed the 'play' button.

When it finished, Dalziel said, 'And what did you tell her?'

'I told her that if she thought we had an agreement she was mistaken,' said Pascoe, unhappy at the memory.

'Oh aye? I bet that bleeding heart of thine were leaking like a sieve.'

'She was very upset,' said Pascoe.

'Didn't try any of her Dolores stuff on you, I hope?'

'Of course not,' snapped Pascoe. 'I advised her

to go home and get on with her jumble sale and try to put it all out of her mind and, with a bit of luck, she might not hear from me again.'

'God, you're a bigger liar than I am,' complimented the Fat Man. 'This turns into a murder case, how're you going to keep Dolores out of it?'

'Yes, but if it stays as a suicide case, there's no reason to involve her.'

Dalziel did his gobsmacked face.

'Am I hearing right? After running around squawking like a headless chicken these past days, you're saying you think this might be suicide after all?'

'I never said it couldn't be,' protested Pascoe, slightly indignant at the characterization. 'All I know is there's a lot of oddities, and a few pointers to suggest that Mrs Kafka might have been involved in some way. There's a history of bad blood between her and Maciver, and now Miss Upshott's statement suggests she might have had a more immediate motive for wanting rid of him.'

'Which is?'

'Not to put too fine a point on it, Kay Kafka seems to make a hobby out of putting young men through the ringer. I'm sorry, sir, but it seems there's been quite a stream of them.'

He paused to make room for a Dalzielesque explosion, but none came. Why should it? If the Fat Man was interested in you, it was hard to do a lot in Mid-Yorkshire that sooner or later wouldn't come to his notice.

He went on, 'It's not hard to understand her motivation after listening to that tape you gave me . . .'

'Spare me the psycho-crap, lad,' growled Dalziel. 'Just give me the gist of your so-called argument.'

'All right. She'd shagged Jason then given him his marching orders like the rest. Then a couple of years later she discovers Helen is crazy for him. She thinks she can frighten the guy off, but to her surprise he stands up to her. Now she has a real problem. If she pulls the whole shebang down around their ears it could end with them taking off together anyway, leaving her without what seems to be the most important person in her life. So she takes a long hard look at the alternative. And she gets to thinking, is this really such a bad thing anyway? Helen's going to marry some day anyway, and here we have a handsome lad, a really hot lover, good breeding stock, in a good secure profession, not too bright, but bright enough not to want to risk his job by amatory adventures. Plus, and I'm certain this was of the essence, she believed he was really deeply in love with the girl. So she gives the thumbs up, but only after making sure Jason is fully apprised of the rules.'

'Pity the stupid bastard didn't stick to them,' grunted Dalziel.

'As I've often heard you say, sir, a man can't turn aside from his cock. And he had Pal Maciver on his case. If Kay wanted the Dunn household to be a little paradise, Pal was the serpent, only this time he went for the fellow.'

'And why'd he do that?'

'Malice. Long-standing hate of his stepmother. At first he probably just thought it amusing to know that any time he wanted he could distress Kay by sowing a little discord in his sister's marriage. But infidelities are forgivable. Chances were that Jason would be taken back into the fold and wicked old Pal hurled into the outer darkness forever. But once Jason let slip that he'd screwed Kay, Pal had a weapon of mass destruction. This wouldn't just rock the marital boat. This could destroy Kay's relationship with Helen forever.'

Dalziel shook his great head, whether to express disenchantment with his fellow man or disagreement with Pascoe's theory wasn't apparent.

'So why'd he not just blow the gaff?'

'And miss out on the fun? No, he'd let Kay know that he knew. He probably set it up as a blackmail operation, which would explain those payments into his account. But that was never the real object. That was just a way of keeping Kay dangling. He could jerk the cord from time to time, by asking for more money, say. Or by pretending a crisis of conscience and suggesting to her it might be best to let it all come out in the open. Making Kay pay, that was the name of the game.'

'Pay for what?'

'For whatever he believed she'd done to him and his family. We may never know the truth of that.'

Dalziel said with a force no less strong because his voice was unusually quiet, 'I know the truth, lad, never doubt that. Get on with your fairy tale.'

'Kay is a clever lady. She knows what Pal's playing at. She knows her own little bit of heaven on earth is at serious risk. She guesses that Pal may think the perfect time to strike is shortly after the birth of the twins when her paradise will seem complete. So she decides to get in first. She arranges to meet him at Moscow House. Perhaps she hints that sex might be on offer rather than money. What more fitting rendezvous in view of all that had happened or almost happened there? She gets there in advance to get things ready. When he comes, they have a drink together. When he starts feeling woozy, she says she'd like to look in the study. He sits down in his father's chair. She puts the shotgun under his chin and blows his head off. She's shown us she knew where the second gun was hidden.'

Dalziel said, 'Do you really believe any of this, Peter?'

'I believe it's possible, sir. And I believe we've got to proceed on the lines of that possibility.'

'Then let's proceed,' said the Fat Man, standing up. 'But remember, Pete. She's worried about Kafka. OK, I know you think mebbe she knows what he's up to, but you can't be sure. So I don't want you going in there clogs flying.'

'No, sir. I'll just get Novello, shall I?'

'Ivor? What do you want her for?'

Because I want an independent witness to this interview, thought Pascoe.

He said, 'If Mrs Kafka is really upset, sir, it's good procedure to have a woman officer in attendance. Is that all right, sir?'

'You know me, lad. Good procedure's my middle name,' said Dalziel.

No it's not, it's Hamish, thought Pascoe.

But this was one piece of arcane knowledge he thought it wise to keep to himself.

4

a bucket of cold water

Edgar Wield's fist was beginning to hurt from hammering at the door.

A man passing by said, 'Surgery's shut on a Saturday. Hurt your face, have you, mate? You'd best head down to Casualty.'

Wield carried on knocking. Finally after several minutes more the door opened.

'What?' snarled Tom Lockridge.

Haggard, unshaven, with the reek of whisky on his breath, he looked like an illustration for a Graham Greene novel.

'Your wife said I'd likely find you here,' said Wield.

What Mary Lockridge had actually said was, 'I'd try that whore's gin-palace at Cothersley. Failing that he could be dossing down at his surgery. And failing that, I don't give a damn.'

The surgery being closer than Cothersley, Wield had come here first and his persistence was due to the presence of Lockridge's Audi badly parked in the street.

'Oh yes. Any message?' said the doctor with heavy sarcasm.

'No. Can I come in?'

'You got an appointment? Yes, why not. Better than performing out here.'

They went inside. Lockridge sat down in the waiting room and said, 'So what brings you into town on a fine Saturday morning, Sergeant, when you could be tiptoeing through the tulips with your mate out at Enscombe?'

It was an undisguised gibe, and it brought home to Wield just how unprivate a man's private life could be. Also, up to now uncertain whether to go in hard or soft, it provoked him into a choice.

'I'm here to ask why, once you had identified the corpse of Pal Maciver, you subsequently failed to disclose your connection with his wife,' he said harshly.

'I told your boss she was my patient,' protested Lockridge.

'You didn't tell us you were shagging her,' said Wield, who when he opted for hard could come close to the Fat Man's high standards.

'I didn't see what my personal relationship with Mrs Maciver had to do with anything,' the doctor blustered.

'Come off it, Doc! You don't need me to spell it out, do you? If it was suicide, keeping quiet was bad enough. But if it wasn't . . .'

Suddenly the bleary eyes were alert.

'Not suicide? Why? What's happened?'

'Nothing,' said Wield, backing off. 'I'm just saying that when you examined the body you didn't know anything for certain about the circumstances of death except that it had been violent.'

'And certainly not an accident! So if it wasn't suicide . . .'

'That would leave murder, in which case you and Mrs Maciver might look like pretty good suspects. Except you seem to have an alibi.'

'Eh?'

Wield showed him the date-inscribed photograph.

'Did she give you that? The cow. Well, at least it gets me off that hook.'

'Mebbe. Puts you on another with the Medical Council.'

'You reckon? I doubt it. She knows if she makes a fuss there, I could get struck off, and she's probably already calculated what that would do to the alimony.'

'You could be right about your wife's reaction,' said Wield. 'But she's not the only one who knows, and I'm not sure I can see any incentive for us to keep our mouths shut.'

'Oh shit. You wouldn't? Why? I've always got on well with you lot, haven't I?'

He looked appealingly at Wield, who returned his gaze impassively. Dalziel might have the edge on him when it came to hard but in the field of impassive he yielded the palm to no man.

Then, when he saw the man was looking into the pit and seeing nothing but darkness, he relaxed, and said in a milder tone, 'Best tell me all about it, Doc, and we'll see if we can find a way through this crap, eh?'

The soft approach did the trick.

Lockridge launched into an account of his affair, self-justifying and defensive, but falling on Wield's finely attuned ear as pretty comprehensive and accurate.

'I often wondered if Pal knew and just didn't care,' said Lockridge. 'He dropped me as his doctor, you know. No reason. Just felt like a change. That made me wonder, but he went on being as friendly as ever. But since he killed himself, I've been wondering if there mightn't have been another reason . . .'

'Such as?' encouraged Wield.

'Well, I do a bit of work down at the hospital. To be honest, I'd like to get out of general practice and specialize. Anyway, to cut a story short, a couple of months ago, I spotted Pal coming out of Vic Chakravarty's consulting room. Thought nothing of it, I knew they sometimes played squash together, but when Sue-Lynn rang the other night and told me about the will, I got to thinking . . .'

'Sorry, Tom, you're losing me,' said Wield.

'You know the bastard changed his will, cut her off with hardly a penny? It all goes to his sister, the older one, and some dotty aunt. I told

Sue-Lynn it would never stand up in court. I mean, the very fact that he made such changes then topped himself is sufficient to suggest he wasn't in his right mind, isn't it?'

'Some folk might think that cutting your adulterous wife out of your will was a pretty rational thing to do,' said Wield. 'What's this got to do with Chakravarty?'

'He's the neurological consultant. If it wasn't a social call but a medical one, then this could be the evidence we need that Pal was mentally unstable . . .'

'We? You said "we"?'

'Did I? Yes, I did. And I meant it. I'm in it too, aren't I? I mean, things are definitely over between me and Mary, our marriage had been on the rocks for a long time and this has just pushed it off the reef so that it can slide gently into the sea. I love Sue-Lynn and she loves me, but love's not enough, is it? You need bread as well as roses. To be quite honest, by the time Mary is finished with me, I expect I'll be a bit strapped. Sue-Lynn should have been sitting pretty, and as long as she's got enough for herself, she's the soul of generosity with those around her. Neither of us is really mercenary, you understand, but I can't see any future for us unless we can get the will overturned. Which is why I need to get Chakravarty to come clean. I'm sure there's something there. I thought I was getting somewhere with him, I laid all my cards on the table, then suddenly he went all coy on me, said he hadn't got anything to tell me and, even if he had, patient confidentiality would be his watchword. That was the giveaway, I thought. Why say that unless there really was something?'

'So what you're saying is that you think this Chakravarty guy might know something about Pal Maciver's health which could support the widow's assertion that he was off his head when he changed the will?'

'You've got it! Look, could you lean on Chakravarty? Don't mention you've been talking to me, though. That bastard wields a lot of power, he could scupper my chances of getting established in the hospital if he set his mind to it. Could you do that for me?'

'I'm not sure I could,' said Wield. 'And I'm not sure I should. I mean, what would my reason be?'

'Because you want to know why he topped himself, don't you? What if he had an inoperable brain tumour? That's the beauty of it, you see. You get your motive for suicide. Sue-Lynn gets her case for contesting the will. It's perfect!'

'We're talking about a dead man here,' said Wield coldly. 'Not only that but I've seen the post-mortem report. No mention of a tumour.'

'There wouldn't be. No one would be looking for it and, if they did, where would they look? Did you see the state of the poor bastard's head? I did, close up. It was fragmented. There was more brain on the desk and floor than there was left in his skull, and I can't see you lot sweeping it all up and putting it back in a plastic bag like chicken giblets.'

Wield had heard enough. He stood up.

'Dr Lockridge,' he said, 'I have been asked to tell you that until such time as your behaviour and involvement, direct and indirect, in this case has been carefully considered, you are suspended from the official police list of attending physicians. You may be formally interviewed at a later date. In any event you will certainly be hearing from the Police Authority at some time in the future. Thank you for your co-operation.'

It was like dumping a bucket of cold water over the man.

And as he drove away, Wield admitted to himself with some surprise that the only thing he'd have enjoyed more was actually dumping a bucket of cold water over him.

5

a lovely cup of tea

No one spoke in the car on the journey to
Cothersley Hall, but Shirley Novello's head was
abuzz with excitement. She knew it was only her
gender that had placed her here, but for once it
didn't matter. When the brass invite a WDC to
join them in talking to a woman, it means that
things are getting serious, and even if her main
function turned out to be escorting Mrs Kafka to
the bog or standing over her as she changed her
clothes, Novello knew that involvement in the
serious was the way to the stars.

She also knew that there was something more
personal at issue here between Dalziel and Pascoe
and felt a natural curiosity to find out the truth
of it.

In response to Dalziel's warning that he was
coming, the gates of Cothersley Hall stood open.
Novello drank it all in, the imposing entrance, the
tree-lined drive, the extensive grounds whose
dewy grass was still chiffoned with mist as the

spring sun's weak warmth got to work, and finally the house itself, the kind of place she only knew through the kind of heritage movie she hated. Moscow House had been bad enough, but at least there were other buildings within screaming distance and five minutes' brisk walk would bring you in sight of some shops. What kind of woman would choose to live out here by herself, or even with a fellow, which, bed apart, Novello regarded as being to all other intents and purposes, alone?

The door of the house opened as they got out of the car and Kay appeared at the top of the steps in a bathrobe. Her hair was just a touch dishevelled. The distraught wife, thought Pascoe. But not overplayed.

She came down the steps to greet them.

'Andy, thank you for coming. And you, Mr Pascoe.'

She expressed no curiosity about nor interest in Novello.

Dalziel put his arm around Kay's shoulders and urged her back up the steps into the house. Pascoe and Novello read the legend on the back of the robe, then exchanged glances, like Sweden and Switzerland, each vying for the greater neutrality.

Novello thought, *Is he going to suggest a tour of the grounds while that pair cosy up to each other inside?*

Pascoe thought, *Two seconds here and she's got him performing like a dancing bear!*

He said, 'Let's get inside.'

They caught up with the odd couple in the spacious room he'd sat in the previous day.

Kay Kafka was apologizing for her dishabille, occasioned, she explained, by the fact that since waking this morning she'd been attempting with increasing concern to contact her husband. It occurred to Pascoe that she might have thought Dalziel would turn up alone, in which case the loosely tied bathrobe could have been intended as a useful distraction. The impression he got of there being nothing beneath it certainly distracted him. Then he dismissed the suspicion. Anyone as bright as Kay Kafka would long since have sussed out that she had more chance of diverting a charging rhino with an amusing anecdote than taking the Fat Man's eye off the ball with a glimpse of groin.

'I'm sorry to have troubled you with this, Andy,' she concluded. 'I didn't know who else to turn to.'

'You did right, luv. Look, there's probably nowt to worry about, simple explanation. I've set the wheels in motion. Why don't you go and get yourself dressed while I check if there's any news. Young Ivor here can make us all a nice cup of tea.'

Fuck that! thought Novello angrily. But when Kay Kafka made for the door she found herself meekly following and saying, 'Where's the kitchen, Mrs Kafka?'

By the time the two women dead-heated back

into the room – Kay Kafka immaculate and composed in slacks and sweater; Novello bearing a tray laden with mugs and teapot, plus a jug of cranberry juice and a plateful of buttered scones – the last two items her own choice; if she was going to be a skivvy, she might as well be a well-fed skivvy – Dalziel had checked that there was nothing new.

'Right,' he said. 'It's still early days. Let's have a cuppa and I don't doubt we'll hear summat in the next half-hour or so. Shall I be mum?'

'No, I think I can manage that, Andy,' said Kay. 'Excuse me, my dear, I think you've forgotten the sugar and, as I'm sure you know, the super likes his tea hot and sweet.'

Oh, but you're living dangerously there, thought Pascoe. In a duel of words, you can probably slash our Shirley to pieces without breaking sweat, but if ever it comes to the real thing, I reckon she'd snap you like a twig.

But Novello showed neither resentment nor antagonism as she rose and went out of the room in search of the sugar basin.

Kay poured the tea and passed it over, then said, 'While we're waiting, it occurs to me that perhaps Mr Pascoe's presence here might have more to do with my encounter with Sergeant Wield last night than with my concern about Tony.'

She fixed him with an encouraging smile. At the same time, Dalziel gave him a look which would have frozen a basilisk, but the DCI was not going to let this chance pass. If they turned up some bad news about her husband she was going to move right out of his reach for some time, but at the moment all that the situation meant was that her usual super-efficient guard might have dropped a little. Such opportunities, he had been taught by someone not a million miles away, were not to be missed.

He said, 'Actually, I wanted to see you again even before the sergeant mentioned your encounter. Yesterday I got called away before our really interesting discussion had reached its conclusion. You'll recall we'd been discussing the possible reasons your husband had for using one of Emily Dickinson's poems as a farewell note, so to speak, and you offered a very moving explanation of what you thought he was trying to say. But what, I wonder, do you imagine his son was trying to say by leaving the same poem open on the desk?'

The power of Dalziel's gaze was now so intense that Pascoe thought, if I duck, birds in a direct line will be falling out of the sky for several miles.

'I've really no idea, Mr Pascoe,' said Kay. 'Only Pal could tell us that, and I suspect the poor boy was so confused at the end, even he might not have been certain of his own motives.'

'No? Possibly you're right. It's just that I thought he might have given you some indication of how he was thinking when you saw him at Moscow House that same evening.'

She was excellent. Not by a flicker of the eyes, a tremor of any visible muscle, did she let him see if he'd registered a blow or not. He got more sense of reaction from his two colleagues whom he wasn't looking at, Dalziel still and menacing as an unexploded mine left on a resort beach by the ebbing tide, Novello – who'd slipped back in at some point with the sugar bowl – just as still but completely rapt, mouth open, scone poised a couple of inches in front of it, like a freeze-frame in a telly ad.

'I didn't see him at Moscow House that evening,' said Kay Kafka gravely.

'But you did go to Moscow House,' said Pascoe. 'Before you turned up with your stepdaughter, I mean.'

'Yes, I did,' she replied, as if surprised there should ever have been any question about her earlier visit. 'But I didn't see Pal.'

The ease of the admission surprised him for a second but no more. She must guess he had strong evidence to put the accusation, so why deny it?

Perhaps she'd even been forewarned.

He put that thought from his mind and said, 'You never mentioned this visit earlier?'

'If anybody had asked me to account for my movements, then of course I would have mentioned it. But if you didn't think my movements were of interest, why should I?'

'That's just a touch disingenuous, don't you think, Mrs Kafka?' he said with a slight smile.

'But, putting that question aside, let's address some larger ones. Why did you go to Moscow House, and what happened when you were there?'

She relaxed slightly as if they'd passed some dangerous point and now she was on safer ground.

She said, 'I went because Pal invited me to go. I arrived. The door was open. I went inside. I could find no sign of life. I came away.'

'I think a little more detail might be helpful, Mrs Kafka.'

'I'm afraid I can't really recall any more detail at the moment, Mr Pascoe. But be sure, if and when it returns to me, I shall be assiduous in relaying it to you.'

She spoke with a calm courtesy. He admired the way that not once did her gaze move from him towards Dalziel, whom he estimated it would take very little to bring blundering in.

He said, 'Nothing I've heard in the past couple of days suggests to me you were on very good terms with your stepson. So what was it, I wonder, that he said to make you agree to meet him in a deserted house on such a dark and dreary night?'

She laughed and said, 'Really, Mr Pascoe, you make it sound like I had a rendezvous at Wuthering Heights at midnight. It wasn't long after six o'clock in the evening and the house in question is one where I'd lived for several years.

As for the weather, OK that was pretty gothic, but not desperately so, and in any case it could just as easily have been a bright moonlit night.'

'Even so, I can't believe your stepson said, or wrote – how did he contact you, by the way?'

'He rang.'

'I see. Said, "Hi, Stepmomma, why don't we meet at Moscow tonight and have a little chat about the good old days?"'

She said, 'No, he didn't say that.'

'So what did he say?'

'He said he wanted to talk about his father's, my husband's, death. He said he had things to tell me which I ought to know.'

Pascoe did dubiety well, head cocked lightly to the left, teeth pressed tight, lips stretched wide, nostrils flared to draw in an audible breath. He gave it the full Henry Irving now and said, 'And that was enough to make you agree to meet him in a deserted house where I gather your previous one-to-one encounters had been, to say the least, distressing?'

Now she did look at Dalziel.

'You gave him the tape, Andy?'

The Fat Man nodded as if not trusting himself to speak, and she turned her attention back to Pascoe and said, 'If you've listened to it, Mr Pascoe, you'll understand pretty well all there is to know.'

'Yes, I've listened to it, as I've listened to almost everybody else who could throw any light on the life and times of the family Maciver. If not exactly dysfunctional, certainly not the most functional of families, wouldn't you agree?'

He leaned forward and tried to stare her out. It wasn't the cleverest move. Like the Fat Man said, never start a fight you're not pretty sure of winning. And this was like taking on La Gioconda.

When she didn't respond, he sat back and said, 'OK. So what precisely happened when you went to Moscow House?'

'The front door was open. I went inside and called. There was no reply. I tried the light switch but the electricity was switched off. I noticed a stub of candle and a book of matches on the sill by the door. I lit the candle and called Pal's name. There was no reply but I got a sense of . . .'

For the first time her fluency deserted her.

'Of what, Mrs Kafka?'

'Of a presence. I'm not sure. The mind can play tricks. And I thought I heard . . . something.'

'Something? Some particular thing?' pressed Pascoe.

'A piece of music . . . rather the ghost of a piece of music, so faint and distant it might have been from another world . . .'

'What kind of music.'

'Piano. Just a few notes. But I recognized them. It was "Of Foreign Lands and People" from Schumann's *Childhood Scenes*. The first classical piece that Helen learned to play . . .'

'The piece on the record in the study, right?

And the same piece Pal played to lure you into the music room ten years ago . . .'

'That's right. And that's where I went the other night. The music room.'

'Despite the fact that last time you were in there according to you Pal attacked you?' said Pascoe with the sceptical raise of his left eyebrow that he'd perfected in front of the bathroom mirror.

'Got something in your eye, Chief Inspector?' said Dalziel.

Kay smiled at him and said, 'I'm sorry if I'm disappointing your expectations, Mr Pascoe, but I am not a gothic heroine. All I felt was curiosity. But the music-room door was locked and the key wouldn't turn. So I went upstairs. I tried the study door. It was locked too. I stopped to look through the keyhole, but I couldn't see anything.'

'Because it was dark inside or because the key was in the lock?' said Dalziel.

He might have known the old sod couldn't keep quiet.

'I don't know. All I know is I felt this weird joke had gone far enough. I went downstairs, put the candle back where I'd found it and left.'

'Anyone see you?'

'I saw a couple of women. Hookers, I think. One of them said something. I think she was asking if I were looking for sex. I walked back to where I'd left the car and drove round to my stepdaughter's house. I always go there on a

Wednesday evening when Jason is playing squash. Sorry, Andy. I should have told you all this before, but it didn't seem relevant and, to be quite honest, the thought of getting close up to another Maciver suicide was more than I could bear.'

The change of focus to Dalziel was something Pascoe had been looking for, even before the Fat Man opened his mouth. She'd need to know if she still had him on board or not. He sat back and waited to see if Dalziel was going to take the next step or leave it to him.

His phone rang.

Shit!

He took it out and checked the display.

It was Wield.

He stood up, caught Novello's eye, mouthed *Stay!*, and left the room.

In the hallway he said, 'Wieldy, it's me.'

'Sorry to butt in, Pete, but you did say to keep you posted.'

'It's OK. Shoot.'

Wield gave him a succinct account of his visit to Tom Lockridge's surgery, then went on, 'After I left him, I dropped in at the hospital to see if I could have a word with this Chakravarty guy. His secretary was blocking like Boycott, but when I told her to mention the name Maciver, I got shown straight in. At first I got the impression he was ready to cooperate, but when I explained what I wanted, for some reason he seemed to change his mind and all he would say was that he was unable to confirm at this time whether Pal Maciver had been his patient or not. You any idea what's going on, Pete?'

Pascoe thought for a moment then said, 'I do believe I have. You leave him to me, Wieldy. Now what about that stuff from Moscow House.'

'I've just rung the lab. I hope you've not arrested Mrs Kafka, Maciver's prints were all over everything. No sign of hers. There was a bit of piano music on the tape in the microcassette. Dr Death thought it was Schubert maybe.'

'Schumann,' said Pascoe.

'Whatever. But the diary might be interesting. No forensic except for Maciver's prints and someone else's, a lot older, most likely Pal Senior's. It's his diary for 1992, and it finishes a few days before he topped himself. Death's done with it now and I'm on my way there to have a read.'

'Great,' said Pascoe. 'I'm heading back to the station myself shortly so I'll see you there.'

He switched off the phone and turned to see Novello coming out of the sitting room.

'Mr Dalziel wants his document case from the car, sir,' she said apologetically. 'I played deaf the first two times he said it, but I think if I'd stayed any longer, he'd have thrown me out of the window.'

'That's OK. We're done here. Why don't you go and start the car?'

'But the super's document case . . .'

Pascoe said, 'The super wouldn't recognize a document case if he found one in a document case shop with "document case" stamped all over it.'

Then he winked and said, 'You make a very nice cup of tea, Shirley. I hope your getaway technique's up to the same high standard.'

This has got to be that post-operative irony you hear those plonkers with the verbal squits talk about on the telly when you're too pissed to switch it off, thought Novello as she went outside. It means he wants me to know he really appreciates me. At least that had better be what he means!

In the sitting room Dalziel and Kay Kafka hadn't moved but somehow it felt as if they were closer together.

Pascoe said briskly, 'Sir, that was Sergeant Wield. I need to get back to talk to him. No need for you to come, though. I thought you might want to hang on a bit with Mrs Kafka to see if any new information comes through about Mr Kafka.'

'You're finished with me, Mr Pascoe?' said the woman.

'Yes, ma'am. Thank you. I'm sure you'll get some good news soon.'

He took in the Fat Man's faintly puzzled expression without catching his menacingly demanding eye as he turned on his heel and moved across the hall almost at a trot.

The car was at the bottom of the steps with the engine running.

He slipped into the passenger seat and said what he'd never expected to hear himself saying to Novello, 'Fast as you like, Shirley.'

She gunned the engine and they were already thirty yards down the drive and accelerating before the rear-view mirror showed him Dalziel erupting out of the front door of the Hall.

'I think the super's trying to attract your attention, sir,' said Novello.

'Really? No, I think he's just waving goodbye.'

In fact what the Fat Man was now doing was running back inside. Then they were into a gravel-spraying skid on the bend which took them out of sight of the house and heading down the straight towards the gateway.

'Sir,' said Novello. 'I think the gates are closing.'

Pascoe looked ahead. She was right. The fat bastard must have found the switch and thrown it.

'I heard you were a fast driver,' he said sceptically.

Novello heard and accepted the challenge. They got through the gates with only a lightly affectionate clip to the passenger mirror.

Pascoe wound down his window and adjusted it.

'I think we can drop within hailing distance of the legal limit now, Shirley,' he suggested.

'Yes, sir,' said Novello, maintaining her speed.

'That would be so you can tell me what's going on, would it, sir?'

And Pascoe, recognizing an offer it would be foolish to refuse, said, 'I was going to anyway.'

6

an Irish joke

Shirley Novello listened with an intensity matched, to Pascoe's relief, by a proportionate deceleration as he described Wield's encounter with Kay Kafka the previous evening and the subsequent forensic results.

'So instead of making Mrs Kafka look more guilty, her showing up at the house last night and opening the cabinet puts her in the clear?' she said.

'You sound doubtful, Shirley. Or is it disappointed?'

'Doesn't worry me one way or the other,' she said. 'So now what you're thinking is that Maciver deliberately set up his suicide so it would look like Mrs Kafka murdered him?'

'That's how it's looking.'

'But that's stupid!' she protested.

He said, 'Yes, I suppose it is, though I'd like to hear your reasons for saying so, Shirley.'

She said, 'Well, it's like the Irish joke about the

guy who found his wife in bed with his best friend and he drew out his gun and put it to his own head and said, "Right, this'll show you." The wife fell about laughing and he said, "I don't know what you're laughing at – you're next!" I mean, what's the point of Maciver killing himself to put one over on his stepmother? She's still going to be alive and he's going to be dead.'

'You put it well,' he said. 'And I like the analogous anecdote. But ask yourself, can you think of any circumstance which might render the concept less like an Irish joke?'

Novello, whose classical education didn't go much further than the acquaintance with church Latin inculcated by a Catholic upbringing, would have been baffled by reference to the Socratic elenchus, but after an initial resentment at being as she saw it patronized by the DCI and his little questions, she had come to recognize their serious intent was not just to show her the path, but make her take it herself. In other words he wasn't trying to put her down by showing her what a clever clogs he was, he was teaching her to be a clever clogs too.

She said slowly, 'Fitting up Kay had to be an afterthought. He had to have another reason for killing himself, a real reason, not an Irish joke one.'

'And, remembering he wasn't a good Catholic, what might a real reason be?'

She said, 'That he was going to die anyway, but slower and with more pain.'

'Excellent,' he said. 'Let's find out, shall we?'

He took out his phone and dialled the number of the Central Hospital and asked to be put through to Mr Chakravarty. After the usual obstacles which are put in the way of non-paying applicants who wish to talk directly to consultants, he got the great man's secretary who was back in full Boycott mode.

'Mr Chakravarty has already spoken to an officer this morning about Mr Maciver,' she said reprovingly. 'And in any case he is a very busy man and I don't know when he'll be available.'

'That's fine,' said Pascoe. 'I'd hate to interrupt his hospital work. Tell him I'll be happy to interview him at his home, if he prefers. Oh, and by the way, tell him it's not Mr Palinurus Maciver I want to talk about, but Miss Cressida Maciver.'

He removed the phone from his ear and smiled at Novello. They were passing through Cothersley village now. There was something happening outside the Dog and Duck but the car was still moving too fast for him to make out what.

'Sir,' said Novello. 'I think someone's trying to talk to you.'

A small tinny voice was rising from his lap.

'Really? Ever been to hospital, Shirley?'

'Yes, sir.'

'Then you'll know how much time you spend there sitting around, waiting for some godlike consultant to arrive. Sometimes the whirligig of time does indeed bring round his revenges.'

Slowly he raised the phone and said, 'Mr Chakravarty, how kind of you to spare me a moment.'

The conversation lasted less than a minute.

When it finished, Novello, marvelling that anyone could be so threatening while remaining so polite, said, 'Wow.'

'You got that, did you?' said Pascoe.

'The poor bastard had an inoperable brain tumour. And Chakrawhatsit had been banging his sister. But I don't see why this stopped him coming forward when he heard about the suicide.'

'He might well have done so eventually, even though doctors are naturally reluctant to share their patients' secrets. But he received a strong disincentive when Tom Lockridge approached him. You see, Lockridge must have explained to him that anything he could say about Maciver's possibly diseased brain might be very useful in helping the widow overthrow his will. His mistake was to mention that, in the new will, Pal's sister, Cressida, was one of the main beneficiaries. And the prospect of standing up in court and giving evidence for the plaintiff in a will dispute case involving Cress was not very attractive to our Mr Chakravarty.'

'Because . . . ?'

'Because,' said Pascoe, 'while one can see why the playwright said that hell hath no fury like a woman scorned, I think that a woman scorned and then done out of a large sum of money by the same guy would be several times more furious.'

Novello digested this.

'So he'd dumped her and she wasn't pleased?'

'So my informant tells me.'

That would be Mrs Pascoe, she guessed, but this time she was wise enough not to display her cleverness. A police car passed them heading towards Cothersley. It was moving at a fairly stately pace which, she felt, matched its inmates, whom she recognized as Jennison and Maycock.

She said, 'I reckon the wife will win the case.'

'Why so?'

'Because even though it makes a bit more sense, he must still have been off his trolley to try and set things up the way he did. He didn't have a cat in hell's chance of getting away with it, did he? I mean, OK, you want revenge on somebody and you know you're dying yourself, so why not just go round to their house and blow them away? You've got no worry about the consequences, have you?'

'And that, you feel, would have better indicated that Maciver was of sound mind than doing it the way he chose?'

Novello thought for a moment then said, 'All right, probably not. But I still say it was a bloody stupid way of going about things.'

'That depends,' said Pascoe, 'on what he thought he was going about.'

She thought this might be a prelude to

another elenctic bout but instead he lapsed into a brooding silence allowing Novello to concentrate on trying to break whatever speed records existed for the journey from Cothersley to the station.

Here Pascoe made straight for his office, leaving instructions that Wield was to be ushered straight in the moment he showed his face.

While he waited, he went online and accessed the Ashur-Proffitt website to see if news of the Commission investigation had touched it yet.

It hadn't. There it was, as solid and impressive as Ozymandias's statue must once have seemed, with its network of partners and subsidiaries stretching across the world. Junius, he recalled, had described it as a rat warren. The beasts could emerge anywhere and you'd have no idea where they went in.

He checked to see if the Junius hyperlink was still in place. It was, or it had been renewed. He read through the newsletter again. Against the displayed might of the corporation it seemed like a puffball blown against behemoth. But there was a final paragraph that brought it right up to date. Junius rejoiced at news of the investigation. He drew a parallel with the Capone empire of extortion and racketeering back in the twenties, and forecast that the accountants might be able to do what the forces of law seemed powerless to do and bring the monster to book.

Pascoe sat back, closed his eyes and brooded

on the links, as yet intuited rather than educed, between this and Pal Maciver's death.

When he opened his eyes, Wield was standing before him.

'Make my day, punk,' said Pascoe.

The sergeant dropped a leather-bound diary stamped 1992 on to his desk.

Pascoe looked at the volume but didn't touch it. Later he might browse it at his leisure but when you had before you a man famed for his speed-reading and almost eidetic memory, it was silly not to take the short cut.

'Sit down and give me the gist, Wieldy,' he said.

'Jake Gallipot. Pal Senior hired him to help check out what was going on at Ash-Mac's. He wanted an out-of-town PI for extra security, but he didn't pick Jake with a pin. He knew him from a Masons' meeting, knew he'd been a cop and that he was crooked enough to need to resign but clever enough not to get caught. He wanted someone who'd be willing to bend the law if necessary. He fixed it for Jake to get taken on in the Ash-Mac Security section. Ex-cop, he had all the qualifications. And that gave him the chance to go poking around at night when everyone else was asleep. What old Pal suspected was that Ash-Mac's was being used, either directly or sometimes as a staging post, for the export of material and machinery with military applications to countries on the sanctions list. At first Jake came up with some good stuff, memos, bills of lading – all circumstantial, but old Pal clearly felt he was close to discovering a smoking gun. But it was a long time coming and Pal got impatient. He'd sounded off to Tony Kafka a couple of times, trying to bluff an admission out of him by claiming he knew more than he did. All he got in reply was a polite warning that modern business was a much harder game than it had been in his day and he ought to be careful what he said. In the end, he decided he and Jake were getting nowhere alone and that was when he contacted the papers. His last entry was on the eve of his trip down to London. He was full of hope.'

'Now let's see,' said Pascoe, unearthing the old Maciver file. 'He went down on the fifteenth of March, 1992, came back two days later. Kay and Helen flew to the States first thing next day. Pal Senior topped himself the day after that, the twentieth. Now, I assume he kept this diary hidden in his concealed cabinet in the study, which would explain why there were no entries for days he was in London. But you'd think when he came back he'd have wanted to scribble something about what happened down there.'

'Perhaps he was just so disappointed at the reception he got that he didn't feel up to it. Remember, he didn't even feel able to write a proper suicide note.'

'No, he didn't. Anything about Kay and the children in the diary?'

'No. He was obsessed by the firm, it seems. But I did notice something, could be owt or nowt. He mentioned a couple of meetings with a VAT investigator. Seems it was the business, not him personally, being investigated. And he seemed to have hopes that this might be a way to get at the new management if all else failed.'

'The Al Capone technique,' mused Pascoe. 'This VAT man, any name?'

'No. But some initials: L.W. I had a word with Bowler. That guy Waverley he mentioned, friend of the bird lady, retired VAT inspector, his first name's Laurence.'

'Whom Lavinia Maciver met for the first time at Moscow House ten years ago when she showed him the green woodpeckers.'

'No law against that,' said Wield.

'Perhaps not. But it's interesting, particularly as the bird lady says that the only times she's visited her old home in the past decade have been connected with violent death.'

Pascoe glanced at his watch and stood up. Abandoning Dalziel at the Hall had seemed an amusing idea at the time, but it was a joke to be enjoyed from a safe distance.

'Bowler still out there?' he asked.

'Yes. Why?'

'I think I'll take a little trip out to see Miss Mac and, from the sound of it, I may need a guide!'

7

a load of bullshit

After his attempt to close the gates on his exiting
car had failed, Andy Dalziel went back into the
big living room. Kay Kafka hadn't moved.

'Looks like it's just thee and me, luv,' said
Dalziel.

'I've got no complaints,' she said, regarding him
affectionately. 'Your Mr Pascoe is a very pleasant
man but there's something . . . do you know
Lamia?'

'Would that be Lamia Shufflebottom, kept a
disorderly house in Neep Street?'

She smiled.

'Keats's poem. There's a philosopher in it,
Apollonius. He sees to the heart of things and by
fixing his severe eye upon Lamia turns her from
the beautiful woman who has seduced his star
pupil back into the serpent she was. I think Mr
Pascoe fancies himself as Apollonius.'

'Waste of time, then, as you're not a serpent.
Are you?'

'What do you think, Andy?'

He shrugged.

'All yon magic stuff's way beyond a simple soul like me. Give me a decomposing head in a plant pot any day. I'll just do a bit of ringing round, see if they've got a line on your man yet.'

He took out his mobile and started making calls. She sat and watched, wondering, as often before, what to make of him. If you listened carefully to what he said, you started noticing juxtapositions which could be significant, or might simply be the product of your own over-subtlety. She liked the way he didn't go out of the room to make his calls. If there were bad news, he was strong enough to give it to her upfront, and he believed she was strong enough so to take it.

Or perhaps he wanted to observe her reaction to his reaction as he talked.

'Nowt,' he said finally. 'Which is good. But only 'cos it's not bad. Could be he's sitting on a plane somewhere over the Atlantic. Does he ever travel under another name?'

'Why should he do that?'

'Don't know. Mebbe Kafka's not his real name, just one he uses professionally, and his passport's in his real name.'

'What a curious idea.'

'Why? He's not Czech, is he? I mean, I know he's Yank now, but he's never struck me as very Middle Europe. Funny cheekbones, but they're not Czech cheekbones.'

'You're very observant, Andy.'

'You've noticed?' he said complacently. 'Aye, well, I learned the hard way. When I were a young DC, I described someone as looking foreign and my boss tore a strip off me. "What the fuck use is that?" he said. "It's like saying you saw a vehicle and it looked like a car. You'd better start thinking in 3-D, lad, or you're no fucking use to me."'

'Sure you weren't talking to yourself, Andy?'

'Eh? Oh, I see what you mean. Yes, I picked up a few tips from old Wally. Any road, you've not answered my question.'

She said, 'No. Kafka is the name on his passport. It was the name he got from his father.'

'But mebbe not from his granddad?'

'I don't think he went back beyond one generation,' she said. 'But that didn't bother him. He was a good man, Andy. A good American. That was important to him.'

'You said *was*. Twice.'

'I know. The first time was a slip. The second time it felt true. Andy, I've got a bad feeling about this.'

'I thought you did,' he said. 'Any particular reason?'

'No. What reason could there be?'

'Threatening phone calls. Nasty letters. Sinister strangers hanging around the garden. Or mebbe he's just been acting odd lately.'

'None of those. Just a feeling in my stomach. Do you know what I mean?'

'Not unless it's hunger,' he said. 'Which reminds me, I've eaten nowt since breakfast and you look like you could do with something to keep your strength up. How about we raid your larder? Or I could take you down yon pub. I've only been in there once since they tarted it up.'

'And it's kind of you to offer to grit your teeth and brave the horrors again on my account,' she said, smiling. 'But no thanks, Andy. Don't worry about me. I'm not going to sit around here all day. I've promised Helen I'll call in at the hospital.'

'Means a lot to you, that lass, doesn't she?'

'Children are a gift from heaven, Andy. A very precious and fragile gift. I got mine twice. And now twice more.'

'Perfect is she, then?'

She laughed and said, 'Don't be silly. Love can be perfect but not people. In fact I'm beginning to get just a little worried about Helen. She seems to have difficulty contemplating any version of the future that doesn't involve lying in a nice comfortable bed with nurses at her beck and call and people dropping by to tell her how wonderful she looks.'

'Understandable. Twins is a pretty big stone to have dropped in your nice calm pool,' said Dalziel. 'That husband of hers, he going to be a help or a hindrance?'

'Sorry?'

'You know, these PE guys, all brawn, not much brain,' he said. 'I just wondered if he were going to give her the kind of support she'll likely need.'

'Don't worry about Jase,' she said firmly. 'He'll pull his weight. Now, if you'll excuse me, I'll just fix my face to meet the world.'

She stood up.

'Looks good enough to me,' he said. 'You'll need to drop me off somewhere. Them buggers have hijacked my car.'

'My pleasure, Andy.'

Twenty minutes later they were driving through Cothersley.

'Hello,' said Dalziel. 'What's going off here?'

On the green right in front of the pub reared what looked like a model of Great Gable, as if some gigantic mole had been at work under the earth. A police car was parked nearby and Constables Jennison and Maycock were standing there talking to what looked like a very unhappy man.

Kay's attention was focused on the other side of the green where several women were spectating from the entrance to the church hall.

'Oh dear, the jumble sale,' she said. 'I promised I'd look in. Do you mind, Andy?'

She brought the car to a halt.

Dalziel said, 'Never mind about me, luv. I'll get a lift with these lads. Bloody hell!'

As he opened the door of the car the nature of the strange mountain was made manifest. It was potently ripe manure.

Kay got out, her attention focused on the Church Hall rather than the steaming hillock. She started walking across the green. Dolly Upshott detached herself from the knot of watching women and came to meet her.

'You OK?' she said.

'Not sure. You?'

'The same.'

They regarded each other uncertainly for a moment then Kay said, 'What's happening over there?'

'Someone ordered that pile of manure to be dumped in front of the pub,' said Dolly. 'It's the third odd thing that's happened this week. Blue beer, then a bunch of pensioners turned up for a cut-price lunch. I know it's incredible, but I've got a feeling that Pal might be behind it. He hated the Captain and he loved a joke.'

'Yes, I do believe he did,' said Kay, sniffing the air. 'Can't be helping your sale much though.'

'They don't seem to mind. Are you coming in?'

Kay said, 'I don't think I will. But I wouldn't mind a talk.'

'Me too. Tell you what, let's slip into the church.'

'But your sale . . . ?'

'They can manage without me for a few minutes. For a few years even!'

'OK,' said Kay.

Dalziel watched the two women go up the path

to the church, then strolled towards the two constables who had their backs towards him.

'Hello, hello, what's going off here then?' he cried as he approached.

Jennison glanced round, did a comic double-take, and muttered out of the side of his mouth to Maycock, 'Bloody hell, is there a CID holiday camp round here?'

Then to the Fat Man he said, 'How do, sir? Seems that some joker thought it would be funny to deliver the Captain here a load of bullshit.'

'Now why on earth should anyone want to do that?' said Dalziel.

8

birdland

When Pascoe told Hat Bowler that they were going to see Lavinia Maciver, the young man was bewildered. No fool, he'd picked up the message over the past twenty-four hours that the brass, for reasons best known to themselves, were bent on keeping him away from Blacklow Cottage, and this morning he'd thought mutinously of ignoring Dalziel's suggestion that he might like to spend Saturday at his desk, easing himself back in to work. He was after all still officially sick, and the sweet medicine of fresh-baked bread shared with Miss Mac's family of birds was surely the better therapy.

But a suggestion from Dalziel was like an offer from a Mafia godfather – you rejected it at your peril.

In the car he sat in silence, his bewilderment changing visibly to distress.

Pascoe tried light conversation but in the end he pulled over to the verge and said, 'Right, Hat.

My idea in bringing you along was, first, to make sure I didn't get lost. And, second, to reassure your friend, Miss Mac, that she had nothing to fear from my visit. But with you sulking and brooding in the background, she's going to think at the very least I've come to put her birds in an aviary. So what's bugging you?'

'It's just that I don't know what's going on, sir,' he said.

'Join the club. But it's part of a DC's job description that much of the time he won't have the faintest idea what's going on, so there has to be more. Either spit it out, or I'll get on the radio and rustle up a car to take you back to the station.'

The thought of Pascoe going on alone did the trick.

Hat said at a rush, 'It's just that there's something you might notice when you're there, and I didn't mention it because I didn't think it was any of our business, not in the circumstances, and what with the new guidelines and everything . . .'

'Whoah!' said Pascoe. 'Take it slowly, Hat. Like you were giving evidence in court. Then maybe I'll have some faint idea what you're talking about.'

Hat took a deep breath and started again.

'The first time I was there, I noticed there was a bit of a smell but what with bread baking, and the windows open so that the birds can get in and out, it didn't really register. Then yesterday I started working in the garden, and though the stalks were all dried up I thought, hello. Then I checked in the lean-to greenhouse and there were these trays of shoots and, though I'm not an expert, I thought I recognized what they were.'

He halted as though he'd reached a conclusion.

'Radishes?' suggested Pascoe. 'Spring onions? Jerusalem artichokes? Come on, Hat. Spit it out.'

'Cannabis,' blurted the youngster wretchedly.

'At last. So let's get this straight,' said Pascoe. 'You're saying Miss Maciver smokes cannabis? And grows it in her garden?'

'Yes, sir, but it's medicinal, it's for her MS and, like I say, I thought with the new guidelines coming in . . .'

'We apply the law. We don't interpret it, nor do we anticipate it,' said Pascoe sternly. 'Have you talked to her about this?'

'No, sir.'

'That at least is a relief.' Pascoe looked at the unhappy young man for a moment then went on, 'Are you going to lighten up or would you rather stand by the roadside looking miserable till the car comes to pick you up?'

Hat said, 'I'll be fine, sir. Really.'

He wanted to ask what Pascoe was going to do about the dope but, though young, he was wise enough to know that some answers were like plastic filler – they only hardened up when exposed to air.

He didn't know whether to be pleased or not

when, on approaching the cottage, he saw the wine-coloured Jaguar parked outside.

'Mr Waverley's here,' he said to Pascoe.

'So I see.'

On setting out, if asked, Pascoe would have declared a preference for finding Miss Maciver alone. But now, instead of disappointment, he began to see a way of short-circuiting matters.

The front door was open so Hat led the way straight in with the confidence of an habitué. He found there was no need to affect relaxation and pleasure; the smell of new-baked bread, the welcoming smile on Miss Mac's face, the excited flutter of wings, all these combined to flood his heart with content.

Even Mr Waverley, seated at the kitchen table, seemed pleased to see him, though his gaze grew speculative as it passed to Pascoe whose nose so far had picked up nothing but the mouth-watering smell of baking.

'Hello, Miss Mac,' said Hat. 'How're you doing? You've met Mr Pascoe, I think. He said he was coming out this way, so I got a lift.'

Pascoe noticed the not too subtle effort at disso-ciation and smiled.

'Good morning, Miss Maciver,' he said. 'And Mr Waverley, too. How are you, sir?'

'I'm feeling particularly well at the moment,' said Waverley. 'The year's at the spring and day's at the morn: God's in his heaven, all's right with the world.'

'I'm glad to hear it, said Pascoe. 'Though you might get an argument in Whitehall or Washington.'

Miss Mac had pulled out a chair for Hat and when he sat down she pushed the loaf on the table invitingly towards him and a couple of tits fluttered down from the roof beam to settle on his shoulders.

'And Mr Pascoe, won't you sit and have a bite or a cup of tea at least?' she said.

'Yes, Mr Pascoe, why don't you take my chair?' said Waverley, rising. 'I have to be on my way, I'm afraid.'

'You keep busy for a retired man then?' said Pascoe.

'Oh yes. When you've spent a lifetime in my kind of work, even in retirement you're always in demand,' said Waverley, meeting his eye and smiling. 'Tax problems never go away, do they?'

'Indeed not. In fact, you might be able to help me there, if you wouldn't object to my picking your brain,' said Pascoe.

'By all means. Why don't you walk out to the car with me?' said Waverley.

He said goodbye to Miss Mac and Hat. Pascoe noticed that though the birds were unfazed by Waverley's proximity, they didn't seem to treat him with the same easy familiarity they displayed to Hat, but that might only have been down to the youngster's energetic way with a loaf of bread.

As they walked down the garden path together,

Waverley said, 'So, how can I help you, Mr Pascoe?'

'By telling me the truth,' said Pascoe.

Waverley made no effort to look puzzled. He walked on in silence as if considering his reply, then shook his head.

'No, Mr Pascoe, you've got it wrong. That is not how I can help you. In fact that would be quite the reverse of helping you.'

Pascoe said, 'I think I should be the judge of that.'

A rather sad little smile touched Waverley's lips.

'Mr Pascoe, all the portents are good for you, all the smart money is saying you will go far. According to your confidential file, which of course doesn't exist, you have most of the right qualities. You are clever, perceptive, sensitive, discreet, articulate; you have a natural authority but you are not a bully; you are willing to listen to the opinions of others but you are not afraid to make hard decisions. And you do not make the same mistake twice. But there are some mistakes it is fatal to make even once. If you examine the credentials of all those who have climbed the slippery pole before you, you will find one thing they have on top of all the qualities I have just listed. They are able to recognize there are things they should not be the judge of. This is one of them. It is unnecessary for you and it would be unhelpful for you to be told the truth. I have a telephone number you can ring to receive confirmation of this, but in the greater scheme of things it would be marked down as a mistake for you to have found it necessary to make such a call. So let us part friends, me to resume the even tenor of my retirement, you to continue along the busy highway of crime investigation. I'm sure there is work enough there to occupy all the livelong day.'

They had reached the Jaguar. He opened the door and slipped in behind the wheel, put his key into the ignition, looked up at Pascoe, and smiled.

Good exit, thought Pascoe. Silence. I watch him go. The Jag disappears down the lane. I shake my head as if bringing myself back to the real world then turn back to the cottage. The curtain falls. Tumultuous applause.

He leaned down to the open window and said, 'You're quite right. I have a huge backlog of work and new things drop on my desk every day. I have to make decisions about them, which I'm not afraid to do, though, as you say, I'm always happy to listen to the opinions of others before I do so. What, for example, would be your opinion about a case like this one that's just come to my notice? It involves a woman of about sixty who suffers from multiple sclerosis. Happily at the moment she seems to be enjoying a period of remission, but when her symptoms become too troublesome, she attempts to alleviate them by smoking marijuana. Now I am of course aware that the law relating to the use of marijuana has been relaxed slightly, and attitudes have relaxed even more. But according to my information, this woman grows the stuff herself, and possibly in quantities in excess of what might be needed for personal use.'

He paused and raised an enquiring eyebrow at Waverley, who was sitting very still with his fingers still gripping the ignition key.

'So what is the nature of your problem, Chief Inspector?' he asked.

'How do I proceed? Do I summon a team to search this woman's house and dig up her garden? Do I have her brought in for questioning? Do I charge her with possession, cultivation, and possibly distribution? She lives in what some people might regard as rather eccentric conditions involving wild birds, some of which may be protected species. Do I involve the social services? Do I, when her case comes up, have a quiet word with the magistrate and suggest that an official psychological examination and report might be useful? Will the RSPCA or the RSPB wish to investigate? And what steps should I take to protect the woman's property from the intrusive interest of the popular press? I'd be interested in your opinion, Mr Waverley.'

Now the man's eyes were filled with coldness which in a real VAT investigator would have had Pascoe burning all his financial records.

'You could find it in you to do all this to a woman whose only crimes are that she is ill and she values her privacy?'

'It would be a hard decision to make, but from what you just told me, not making it could be seen as a sign of weakness which might affect my long-term prospects.'

Waverley said, 'I don't believe you could do that, Mr Pascoe.'

'In that case, goodbye, Mr Waverley.'

'But it's not a risk I am willing to take. Would you care to join me?'

He opened the passenger door. Pascoe got in. There was an opulent smell of leather. They must have a good pension scheme, these funny buggers, thought Pascoe. Perhaps when they offed anyone, they inherited their benefits.

Waverley said in a businesslike tone, 'I shall speak to you as briefly as I can. I will not be interrupted and I shall not answer questions. There will be no further interviews after this, and of course no record.'

Pascoe switched on the mini cassette recorder in his pocket and said, 'Agreed. In your own time, Mr Waverley.'

9

Mr Waverley

The world is a botched palimpsest, Mr Pascoe. From time to time attempts are made to obliterate what has been written before and inscribe something completely new. But the ur-writing always shows through and there we may read two inerasable though apparently contradictory truths. One is the economic imperative; the other is the holiness of the heart's affections.

The latter we may see evidenced by the apparently aberrant behaviour of myself in regard to Miss Lavinia Maciver, or of your Mr Dalziel in regard to Mrs Kay Maciver, later Kafka.

The former at all levels drove the takeover of Maciver's by Ashur-Proffitt.

To the world it seemed simply another step in the process of commercial globalization, or in the Thatcherite sell-off and sell-out of British industry, depending how one regarded such things. In fact it was, as I believe you understand now, merely a small movement in the constantly changing pattern of that global black economy which unifies the world despite all the temporal surface shifts of elections, revolutions, and all other forms of political change.

This gap between appearance and reality becomes more evident if I point out that, at a time when the thaumaturgic word in the corridors of Westminster was privatization, *this takeover was in fact a sort of covert nationalization. What I mean is, the activities and the security of what was now known familiarly as Ash-Mac's became, albeit sub rosa, the responsibility of certain people in Whitehall and Westminster with a watching brief accorded to some others in Washington DC.*

I am sure you have worked this out. It won't have been difficult. Rumours always abound. But the government – any government – has any amount of machinery dedicated to spreading other rumours, counter rumours, more interesting rumours.

What became a matter of concern was the subsequent behaviour of Palinurus Maciver Senior, the former owner of the firm, now, as they thought, safely side-lined into a meaningless advisory directorship. When a man of his standing begins to make accusations of sanction busting and other forms of illegal trading, eventually people will start taking notice. And if he could produce hard evidence to back up his claims, then we would have a scandal on our hands.

And there are always plenty of people in the agencies of government, both public and covert, who will be delighted to advance themselves and their causes on the back of a scandal.

The American management at Ash-Mac's assured us

the matter was under control. Nevertheless my masters, who have a view of good old American know-how only matched in its scepticism by the American view of British savoir-faire, despatched me to Yorkshire to get an unbiased view of the state of play.

The cover I used was a favourite one of mine, that of a Value Added Tax Investigator. It goes deep. You will find a detailed CV of Laurence Waverley in the Customs and Excise personnel records. And it is a job which attracts such natural suspicion that no one imagines I might be something worse. In this case, as I was ostensibly looking into possible VAT irregularities at Ash-Mac's, it meant I could present myself to Maciver in a very favourable light under the pretext of wanting to compare the record-keeping systems presently in operation with those used before the takeover. Once he got the message that I wasn't happy with the new regime, he was putty in my hands, as they say. Soon he was sharing with me his own concerns about the firm, and it was from his own mouth that I discovered he was employing the services of Jake Gallipot in his efforts to get hold of the hard evidence he desired.

My investigation of Gallipot revealed a ruthless, ingenious and not untalented man with a deep vein of venality and a very dodgy past. A combination of threat and bribery soon had him on our side, but Maciver remained a nuisance. Not a great one. He had obviously been completely isolated from legitimate access to all sensitive areas in Ash-Mac's, which was why he needed to employ Gallipot. So it seemed the best he could now do was kick up a fuss with no supporting evidence and it would be fairly easy to have him publicly ridiculed as just another bad loser who couldn't come to terms with his loss of power. My recommendation was to take all necessary steps to undermine his credibility and let things take their course.

It was his relationship with his wife that altered things, radically. His growing suspicions about the firm had caused a coldness between himself and Kay. From the start he warned Gallipot that she must be kept in the dark. She was still an employee of Ash-Mac's, and her relationship with Tony Kafka was close. I suspect that in those dark moods which will always overtake an older man with a young wife, Maciver had sometimes asked himself to what extent their romance and marriage had been aimed at facilitating the takeover. In addition, Gallipot during the course of his investigations had visited the Golden Fleece Hotel where Ash-Mac's had a suite on permanent reserve for distinguished visitors. His aim was to get a look at the registration book to discover who these VIP's were. He was successful in this, but the chambermaid whom he suborned also let drop the information that Mrs Maciver had on at least two occasions to her knowledge used the suite for sexual assignations. She had no names but they were in her words, as Gallipot recorded them, 'young fellows, you know the type, think they're the bee's knees, but by the time she'd done with them, they'd lost their sting, know what I mean? Chewed 'em up and spat 'em out, she did!'

But the sexual predilections of Mrs Maciver seemed to me irrelevant to my work. Indeed, if as Gallipot

578

believed, Maciver too had his suspicions about her, then that just gave him something else to distract his mind. A cuckold who couldn't come to terms with being a nobody, the more noise he made, the more absurd he would look.

So one day in March I started packing my bags, thinking my task here was done. Then the phone rang in my hotel bedroom.

It was Gallipot asking me to call round at Moscow House. His form of words was studiedly casual, but I read the urgency underneath.

I was there in five minutes.

I found Gallipot in the lounge with Kay. She was in a semi-catatonic state, sitting bolt upright, pale as death. Looking utterly beautiful. Yes, that struck me very forcibly. Tragedy often destroys female beauty. Not in her case. Quite the opposite, she seemed made for grief.

Upstairs in the study I found Maciver. He was dead with a deep wound on the top of his head. On the floor close by was a bloodstained ice axe, the one which you will recall seeing mounted on the wall alongside the portrait of Mr Maciver in outdoor mode.

There was a letter on the desk. I read it.

It was from his son and it accused Kay of attempting to seduce him during a recent visit home, an attempt which was the culmination of a whole series of incidents of sexual harassment ever since his stepmother had come into the house.

The sequence of events seems to have been that Maciver was returning from London where he had been attempting to interest a newspaper in his campaign.

Their response had been cautious. They get this kind of thing all the time and they aren't interested in committing time, money or personnel unless there's some real evidence there's something in it for them.

But Maciver, ready to take any interest as encouragement, was much enthused, and he'd rung Gallipot on his way back to fill him in and demand a progress report. Gallipot, wanting to get a fuller picture of just what the paper had promised, arranged to call at Moscow House for a consultation. In the meantime – we pieced this together later – Maciver got home, read the letter, and confronted his wife with its contents. She denied it, blaming the son. Maciver, his mind already dark with suspicion, did not know what to believe. In any case, there was no comfort to be found in any version of the truth. But one thing he was certain of. He wasn't going to let Kay out of the country with his daughter. They were due to fly out from Manchester the following morning. Maciver told her the trip was off. Kay protested. Maciver got angry, and I do not doubt his anger made him talk as if absolutely persuaded that his wife was totally to blame for the situation. He told her that she should go to America herself, that he didn't care if she never came back, and that in any event he didn't want her anywhere near his family, and in particular Helen, ever again.

For this and for what happened next we have only Kay's account. She said that when she reacted strongly to this threat – she seems to have been genuinely, indeed almost obsessively, attached to the girl – he became physical and tried to manhandle her out of the room, perhaps intending to throw her right out of the house.

They struggled and crashed against the wall with such force the ice axe became dislodged from its mounting and came tumbling down, unhappily landing point first on her husband's balding skull.

Now though it is certainly possible that a violent collision with the wall could have disturbed the display mounted there, whether an axe falling a matter of a few feet could attain a momentum sufficient to cause this damage I cannot say. A proper forensic examination would doubtless have established this one way or the other.

But it did not seem to me that this was either necessary or desirable. I deal in facts and practicalities. The way I looked at it was that, no matter how sceptical their initial response, any newspaper which had just been offered the kind of story Maciver was touting around was going to sit up and take notice when they heard that, a few hours after he left their offices, he'd died in very suspicious circumstances.

My first concern was Kay Maciver. It was no use doing anything if she proved hellbent on ringing the police and telling them all. But as she came out of her initial shock, I realized that here was a woman of extraordinary mettle. She didn't know who the devil I was, of course, but I'd rung Tony Kafka and explained the situation and he came straight round to talk to her.

Mr Kafka is a man of rapid thought and ingenious device and finding he shared my appraisal of the situation we rapidly worked out what had to be done to protect the interests of all involved.

We were completely open with Mrs Maciver. There

was no other way. I told her that we had to devise an explanation of her husband's death which did not involve her. She said again that it was an accident and I said it didn't matter. His death in unusual circumstances so soon after his attempt to persuade the newspapers that something fishy was going on at Ash-Mac's was bound to arouse their suspicions. She appreciated the undesirability of this, being, of course, privy to all the firm's officially unofficial dealings, but I think it was her awareness of how the truth could affect her relationship with Helen that made her co-operate so fully with our proposals for a cover-up.

Suicide was the obvious solution. Jumping from a high place might account for the damage to the head, but that involved getting him out of the house and taking him to the high place. Also it made it more difficult to make the tragedy unexceptionable even to the most sceptical tabloid eye. No, it had to be in situ, behind a locked door. The shotgun cabinet in the study provided the obvious weapon, and careful channelling of the shot would provide a means of obliterating the earlier head damage.

We didn't go into this detail with Kay, of course, but she did appreciate the need to authenticate the death in all ways possible and rather than run the risk of a forged suicide note, it was she who, at Kafka's prompting, suggested the use of the Dickinson poem.

She had her cases already packed and her stepdaughter's. I now instructed her to take them with her when she went to pick up Helen from school but instead of bringing her home as planned, tell her that a severe frost was forecast for that night which would make the cross-Pennine roads very dicey early in the morning, so they were going straightaway and would spend the night in an airport hotel.

Once in the States, we told her to hire a car and get lost. The longer it took to find her with the sad news, the more time she'd have to get herself together.

Kafka had no doubts from the start about her ability to cope and the more I saw of her, the more impressed I was. Once motivated, she moved with speed and determination and soon she was on her way to pick up Helen. Kafka and I agreed it would be best to put as much space as possible between Kay's departure and Maciver's death to dilute any suspicion of cause and effect. We fixed on March the twentieth. Kafka undertook to provide evidence of Maciver making increasingly agitated attempts to contact him during this period, while I set about applying my specialist skills to stage-managing the fake suicide.

The mechanics of how I set it all up you have of course already worked out, including no doubt the burning of paper in the waste bin to help cover any traces of ash left by the burnt threads. What I actually burnt was his son's letter – I didn't want that lying about – plus several more sheets of writing paper, to give the impression he'd tried to compose a farewell note but found it beyond him, and opted for the poem.

It was all rather Agatha Christie, I fear, but I had to extemporize. Given a little more time and with the aid of a fully equipped technical team, I would have done things very differently, but it is only in the never

never world of the movies and television that such expertise can be conjured up at the drop of a hat. In any case the English suburbs have a thousand eyes and the less activity there was around the house, the better. As it was there was a close scrape. With everything done, I let myself out of the house after of course checking there was no sign of activity outside. I had just closed the door when I heard a noise and I turned to see a woman coming through the shrubbery. It was, I found out later, Miss Lavinia Maciver. Her greeting was, I felt then, eccentric, though as I came to know her better, I realized it was in fact typical.

'Hello,' she said. 'I'm so glad to see the green woodpeckers are still here.'

'Are they?' I said.

'Oh yes. Come and see.'

And I found myself led across the garden to peer into a hole in a semi-decayed beech tree and invited to admire the allegedly clear signs of new nesting activity.

I expressed interest and admiration and eventually managed to establish who she was. Myself I introduced in my role as VAT inspector. I said I'd been ringing the bell for some time but had got no reply. We returned to the house and tried again. Finally, and without anything more than a natural exasperation at a wasted journey, she bade me good day and set off down the drive. Her MS had barely got a hold back then and she could still stride out, but it was just beginning to drizzle and when I overtook her in my car, I halted to ask if she needed a lift. She replied no, she'd come by taxi from the bus station and would walk to the nearest phone box and call up another to take her back. I of course insisted that she got in and when I discovered that her journey home involved catching a bus which didn't depart for another ninety minutes, and then, after a roundabout journey of over an hour, being dropped in a small village from which it was forty minutes' walk to her house, I ignored her protests and drove her there myself.

My motives were mixed, I admit. She was a possible loose end which I wanted to be sure was tied up. But also I found myself intrigued by her. She seemed, I don't know, to have a kind of independence of spirit, to be free of any agenda, or at least any I recognized. I don't meet many people like that.

My first reaction when I saw her cottage, with doors unlocked, windows open, and birds flying in and out at will, was disappointment. Perhaps after all she was simply mad! But there was nothing mad about the way she invited me to sit down and then provided tea and the most delicious scones.

Curious that. A man in my line of business not infrequently has his loyalty tested by the offer of bribes. But the only time I ever bent the rules, it was done for little more than a buttered scone. Could Mr Dalziel's fall be occasioned by something so slight, I wonder?

I am not unadept at oblique questioning and once Miss Mac got used to my presence she treated me rather like one of the birds with whom she shares all her thoughts and feelings.

It appeared that her brother had called to see her the previous week in a somewhat agitated frame of mind which seemed to have something to do with Kay and Helen's imminent trip to the States. He didn't seem altogether happy about it and was particularly concerned that urgent business in London meant he would have to go away for a couple of days and wouldn't get back till the day before their planned departure. He seemed to be asking if it would be possible, should the need arise, for Lavinia to come and look after his household for a while, as she had done when his first wife died. But when she attempted to get details out of him, he backed off, changed direction, and spent the rest of his visit talking about their childhood at Moscow House, when the family firm was flourishing and the future lay before them like a sunlit beach. Her words. Or perhaps his words.

It was this harking back to the days when they had been most at ease with each other, before his growing irritation at her growing dottiness, as he saw it, came between them, that bothered her in the following days and she was concerned sufficiently to make the effort of this rare visit to Moscow House to see for herself how things stood there.

I reassured her as best I could, surprising in myself a certain discomfiture amounting almost to guilt at the thought that her brother's body was growing cold in his study as we talked. But not too cold. To confuse the issue of time of death, I'd programmed the central heating to stay on at full blast for the next couple of days until the twenty-second, the day before his son in his letter had said that he'd be coming home. Later I visited Tony Kafka at Ash-Mac's to give him an update, and also to check the measures he'd taken re Maciver's alleged contacts. I needn't have worried. He was so thorough he'd thought of details I wouldn't have bothered with myself. But he didn't fall into the trap of being over-fussy. He could have been one of the great illusionists, I think. The only thing that bothered me slightly was that his main concern seemed to be for Kay Maciver. His attitude to her was protective to a degree almost paternal, with Ash-Mac's interests a poor second. He it was who drew my attention to Kay's special relationship with your Mr Dalziel and suggested this might come in useful in smoothing out any snags in the investigation, as indeed proved to be the case.

Did I have any guilt feelings about letting the son find the body? Not really. I had no way of assessing the truth of the letter he'd written to his father, but from what Gallipot had told me of Kay's proclivities, it seemed at least possible that it wasn't righteous indignation at an attempted seduction which motivated him but injured pride in being, as the chambermaid put it, chewed up and spat out.

Human motivation remains a mystery to me, Mr Pascoe. Including my own.

I called again on Miss Maciver the following day on the pretext, to her, of checking whether I'd left my gloves there, and to myself of keeping an eye on a possible loose end.

The true reason was I wanted to go back. She fascinated me. You may find this odd in a man of my professional background, but consider again the spell Kay Maciver has clearly cast over your own Mr

Dalziel. Is my deep affection for Miss Mac any odder than that?

I should of course have kept well away. The more she saw of me, the more likely she was to mention our encounter at the house to one of your colleagues. No harm in that, of course, as it was soon established that Mr Maciver had been alive and well for at least another twenty-four hours. But mention of a Customs and Excise investigator might arouse the interest of a coroner concerned with establishing the deceased's state of mind, and my masters do not like their officers to tread the public stage, no matter how good their cover.

But I ignored best practice. Worse still, after the discovery of the body, I waited till mention of it had been made on the local news, then went out myself to Blacklow Cottage so that she would hear about it from my lips rather than from, saving your presence, some tongue-tied bobby.

As it turned out, I was never mentioned so I never put myself in the way of a reprimand. The inquest went exactly as planned. The only possible fly in the ointment was young Mr Maciver. His changing of the locks at Moscow House so that his stepmother couldn't get back in took me by surprise but gave me warning that he could cause some real trouble. Not that it would have affected our preferred scenario, of course. Indeed it might have helped it, distracting attention from his father's relations with Ash-Mac's and focusing it on family problems. My masters were of a mind to encourage him in his revelations and accusations. But the thought of the effect of such a scandal on Kay, on the daughter

Helen, and above all on Miss Maciver disturbed me considerably and I was already examining contingency plans for keeping him quiet when it turned out that Kay had made her own arrangements.

It was now that the real value of Kay's friendship with Mr Dalziel became apparent. It was I believe a spin off from an earlier operation undertaken by my department in relation to Ash-Mac's security, though I am not sure precisely how Kay used it to get Mr Dalziel so deeply in her debt. I do know, however, that having him in charge of the enquiry made everything so much easier, and it was something of a relief to be able to stand back and see the unpleasant young Maciver silenced without having to dirty my own hands.

I have talked long enough. You will have to be content with a mere digest of the next ten years.

I left Mid-Yorkshire, not without regrets, and returned to my daily toil. Very soon afterwards I was involved in an altercation which left me with a gunshot wound to my leg. On the road to recovery, I chose to return here for a convalescent holiday and of course to renew my acquaintance with Miss Mac, which was absolutely against the rules. I found her condition had begun to deteriorate noticeably but, as is her nature, she was struggling gamely and uncomplainingly on. I was able to help in various ways, one of which that pleasant young man, Mr Bowler, has clearly brought to your notice. My reward has been to see her enter the long period of remission which she is still enjoying. Incidentally, she never let her family know the serious-

ness of her condition, and they are all too self-absorbed to have noticed anything more than could be put down to the debilities of age.

My own condition, it became clear, was going to leave me with impaired movement in my leg, which I may have exaggerated slightly, so that I was informed I would not be returning to field work. On hearing this, I looked suitably disappointed, refused the offer of a routine desk job, and opted instead for what we call sleep mode. No one ever really retires from our business, Mr Pascoe. And resignation is the agency's euphemism for death!

Normally an operative in sleep mode is able to pass the rest of his life in what seems to the outside world a normal state of retirement from whatever job he may claim to have had. But in times of need, you are always likely to be reactivated.

When I heard of young Maciver's death, I went straight round to Blacklow Cottage, bearing the sad news purely as a friend. But I was duty bound to report the odd circumstances of the death to my masters, since when I admit I have been acting as their ears here in Mid-Yorkshire. My conclusion about the affair is I am sure the same as yours, Mr Pascoe. Young Pal came across something which made him think again about the circumstances of his father's death. Perhaps it was simply a record of his dealings with Gallipot. Pal followed his father's road pretty exactly here too, hiring the man ostensibly for one purpose then gradually bringing him round to the other. How he did it I'm not sure – bribery, alcohol, drugs, perhaps a combination –

but eventually he got Gallipot to reveal all, or at least as much as he knew or suspected, of the true circumstances of his father's death. You would of course have a much fuller picture if it were not for the tragic accident which deprived you of a chance to question Gallipot. Strange are the workings of fate.

This information must have been shocking to young Pal, but I cannot believe it overthrew his reason to the point where he decided to take his own life. That decision must surely have had some other much closer occasion – I see from your face, Mr Pascoe, that I am right – but once taken, his mind was quite clearly so deranged that he opted to repeat the circumstances of the paternal death as closely as possible, using whatever garbled version Gallipot had fed him as a template.

My reactivation period has been most interesting and I am glad to have been of service to my country again. But I will not disguise the fact that now that everything is satisfactorily settled, I am looking forward to going back to sleep.

All's well that's ends well, a sentiment I am sure Mr Dalziel will agree with. He I would gauge has most to lose by any public airing of these affairs, and I should hate to see a noble career end on such a sour note.

But if I am any judge of character, I doubt whether you, Mr Pascoe, will let it come to this.

The world is a stranger place than you or I can begin to imagine. We must each cultivate our own garden, Mr Pascoe. Except for young Mr Hat, who I would guess will benefit greatly from being allowed to cultivate Miss Mac's.

Good luck in your career, Mr Pascoe. I shall follow it with interest.

And now I bid you good day.

10

and having done all, to stand

Pascoe switched off the tape.

He looked at Edgar Wield, who looked away.

The third person in the room, Andy Dalziel, shifted in his chair, adjusted one buttock as if contemplating breaking wind, changed his mind, and settled instead for a long exhalation of breath midway between a sigh and a whistle which had a quality of infinite distance in it.

Perhaps he's calling something up, thought Pascoe.

He had thought long and hard about what to do with the recording.

After a while he realized he was simply looking for reasons not to play it to the Fat Man.

Upon which he'd headed straight for Dalziel's room, pausing only to pick up the sergeant on the way, as a witness, or simply as a supportive friend, he wasn't sure which. He suspected Wield wasn't grateful.

The whistling sound faded away.

'Did he know you were taping him?' said Dalziel.

'I didn't tell him. But I don't think he cared. He took precautions.'

'Precautions?'

'He refers to your relationship with Kay at least five times. So who apart from ourselves are we going to play it to?'

'You could have burnt it, said nowt.'

'No, I couldn't.'

'Why not?'

'Because I was concerned some future situation might arise in which I wished I had played it to you.'

Dalziel whistled again, this time the breath going in not out, then said, 'You any idea what he's talking about, Wieldy?'

The sergeant thought for a moment.

'Yes,' he said.

'Bloody hell. If this were a sodding democracy, I'd be outvoted. All right, let's play the democratic game. We've all heard it. What next?'

'Now we burn it,' said Pascoe.

'Why?'

'Because, like I said, we can't use it. And because we don't know how much of it is true.'

'Which bit in particular?'

'Any of it. For instance, we don't know what really happened between Kay and her husband. Did he lay hands on her? Was there an accident? Or did she take the ice axe and hit him in self-defence? Or was she so angry and fearful when he threatened to keep her and Helen permanently apart that she deliberately and with premeditation drove the axe into his head?'

'Or mebbe he wasn't dead at all,' said Wield.

'Eh?' said Dalziel.

'Waverley's right about an axe falling on you from a wall. Could knock you out, leave a lot of blood, but chances of it killing you are pretty small. Even a single blow by a woman isn't all that likely to do the trick. Top of the head's one of the hardest parts of the body. When Waverley realizes Maciver's just unconscious, he's got a problem. Call ambulance and police? Suddenly him and Gallipot have got to explain themselves. It's going to be a headline case, this business about the wife trying to shag the son, all that. Very messy once the papers get their big yellow teeth into it. But if Maciver's dead, and he can fake it as suicide, all the problems go away. And Kay thinking she did it means her cooperation is guaranteed for ever.'

'So it's not a corpse he fakes the suicide on,' said Pascoe. 'That would be a lot easier than fooling a pathologist about the cause and time of death. Which means all that stuff about the central heating was just a smoke screen for my benefit.'

'Yes. He'd be willing to admit a lot to get you off his back, but likely he reckoned that murder would be an admission too far. Which is what it was if he just tied Pal Senior up and came back to finish the job a day or two later.'

'Jesus Christ!' exclaimed Dalziel. 'You two have got more stories than yon Arabian bint who didn't want to get topped. How about it's all a lie, and Maciver really did kill himself, and Waverley just thinks he can make me run scared, thinking I've got myself involved in a cover-up?'

'Possible,' said Pascoe. 'Possibly also Waverley really is just a VAT inspector with a very active fantasy life and an obsession with Miss Maciver. We don't know. In fact we've got a whole bunch of statements from just about everyone involved in this business, and I'll tell you what, there's not a one of them I'm one hundred per cent certain of. And that includes even those I think believe they're telling the truth.'

'So what are we going to do?' said Wield.

Pascoe liked the *we*. A lesser man would have said *you*.

He looked at Dalziel and said, 'Sir?'

He said, 'There's nowt we can do about any of the big stuff, sanction busting, politics, all that shit. And despite your fancy theories about murder, I reckon this guy Waverley's untouchable. The best we could do by hassling him is get his boss, Mr sodding Gedye, nervous enough to have Waverley permanently retired. But we're all happy that Pal Junior actually did kill himself, right? For which in my book he deserves a vote of thanks. Always had him marked for a right nasty bastard.'

'The blue beer and the bullshit were quite amusing,' ventured Pascoe.

'I give you that. Yon so-called captain had it coming,' agreed Dalziel. 'But it don't make up for trying to destroy his kid sister's marriage, does it?'

'I didn't say that. His mental condition was, to say the least, suspect. But in fairness to him, I don't believe he ever thought there was a real chance of getting Kay sent down for murdering him. Embarrass her, piss her off, yes. But in the end he knew we were bound to work it out. His real aim was to make us think seriously about the circumstances of his father's death.'

'So why not come to us with his suspicions? Or leave a letter detailing them?' asked Wield.

'Perhaps because he thought that with Kay having such good friends in high places, any suggestion that Ash-Mac's management might have been involved would be kicked into touch without a second thought. In any case, accusations contained in suicide notes are always treated with a pinch of salt and he had no real evidence to offer. So he set out to show us how it could be done. By imitating the exact circumstances, he ensured that any investigation of his own death would be an investigation of his father's also. He dropped the letter addressed to the Officer i/c the Maciver Murder Enquiry in the post after the last pick-up on Wednesday evening so that it wouldn't reach us till Friday. He left Gallipot's card in his wallet so that we'd be straight on to him. And he'd given Gallipot a key to Casa Alba and instructed him to e-mail any incriminating photo he got to Mrs Lockridge, to give us another possible link to the man.'

'Some link, with the bugger dead,' growled Dalziel. 'You saying that was down to Waverley?'

'That would be my guess,' said Pascoe. 'The funny buggers, certainly. Pal knew that when they caught on what was happening, Gallipot would be at risk, but he thought we'd get to him before they did, and that Jake would reckon the best way to defuse a potentially deadly secret was to share it.'

'So everyone's been jerking us about,' said Wield. 'And we don't know the half of it. I don't much care for being kept in the dark.'

'Aye, where do we go from here, Pete?' said Dalziel. 'You started with one suspicious death and now you seem to be saying there could be at least two more, Gallipot and Pal Senior.'

'And what about Tony Kafka? Is he on the run, or what?' said Wield.

Tony Kafka who wanted to be a good American . . .

In his mind's eye Pascoe was seeing Kay Kafka run out of Cothersley Hall to embrace her husband as he left the previous afternoon. There had been something very final in that embrace. She had clung to him as if she meant to keep him with her by main force. He had turned away from the intensity of the scene, feeling like a voyeur.

When she came back into the room she'd said, 'Tony is a good man. He wants to be a good American,' as if this were an aim fraught with difficulty and peril.

He pushed the scene out of his mind like a slide and replaced it with another.

After talking with Waverley, he had watched the Jag drive away and then returned to the cottage.

'Time to be off, Hat,' he'd said.

'So soon, Mr Pascoe?' said Miss Mac. 'Wasn't there something you wanted to ask me about?'

'No need. Just a small matter that Mr Waverley was able to clear up. Ready, Hat?'

Bowler clearly wasn't. He began to rise with all the reluctance of a small boy told it was time to abandon his computer game and go to bed.

Miss Mac said, 'I must say I don't reckon much to the youth of today, Mr Pascoe. In my time, if I'd offered to help a poor old pensioner with her garden, I'd have been too ashamed to leave the job half-done. What do you say?'

Pascoe said, 'I think it would be most reprehensible behaviour. What on earth are you thinking of, Bowler? But I've got to go so you won't have a lift.'

'Got my mobile, I can easily ring a taxi,' said Hat.

'You'll stay for supper then we'll see about that,' said Miss Mac firmly.

'Goodbye then,' said Pascoe. 'I'll see myself out.'

At the front door he'd paused and glanced back. Hat was sitting at the table again. He had picked up his wedge of bread and was laughing at something Miss Mac had said. There was a flutter of birds about his head.

Pascoe smiled at the memory then realized his two colleagues were watching him very seriously. It occurred to him that *a propos* the Maciver affair they were looking to him for words that would give them, to use the modern cant term, closure.

Why should it be down to me? he asked himself angrily. How come I get elected moral arbiter of this odd little trinity?

He'd once said something similar to Ellie, demanding rhetorically, *Why do they treat me like I'm CID's moral conscience?* To which she'd replied, *How else should they treat you?* and would not stay for an answer.

Right, he thought. If that's what they want . . .

He put on a parsonical voice and declaimed, 'For we wrestle not against flesh and blood, but against principalities, against powers, against the rulers of the darkness of this world, against spiritual wickedness in high places. Wherefore take unto you the whole armour of God, that ye may be able to withstand in the evil day, and having done all, to stand.'

He smiled at the baffled expressions before him and said, 'That's one way of looking at things. How does it grab you?'

Dalziel said, 'Me, I'm a dedicated flesh and blood man.'

'Me too,' said Wield.

'Then we have a majority. Pal Maciver found he had an inoperable brain tumour and he took his own life. That will be the inquest verdict. Whether it will mark the end of the affair I don't know, but it will certainly mark the end of our part in it. We have done all we can, I think. Whether we've done enough, we won't find out till the evil day, whenever that is.'

He rose to his feet.

'End of sermon. Andy, the tape's all yours. Try to be a bit more careful with this one. I'm going home and I shan't be in till Monday. Not unless someone starts a war, that is.'

'I'd sleep light then,' said Andy Dalziel. 'The world's full of mad buggers. It may not come tomorrow, it may not come this year, but it'll come, sure as eggs. I'd sleep bloody light.'

11

midnight

Three times the phone rang in Cothersley Hall that night and three times Kay Kafka snatched it up almost before it had started ringing.

The first voice was American.

'Mrs Kafka?'

'Yes.'

'Good evening, Mrs Kafka. I'm hoping you may be able to help me. I was expecting to meet your husband Mr Tony Kafka off a flight from London, UK, earlier today, and he hasn't showed. I wonder if there's been some change of plan he hasn't told anyone about.'

'Not that I know,' said Kay. 'You work for Joe Proffitt, do you, Mr . . . I didn't get your name?'

'Hackenburg. In a way, yes, I'm working with Mr Proffitt at the moment. So Mr Kafka isn't there with you at the current time? If he were, I'd really appreciate it if he could come to the phone.'

'No, he's not. What do you mean you're

working with Joe at the moment? Just who are you, Mr Hackenburg?'

'To be honest with you, Mrs Kafka, I work for the Securities and Exchange Commission. We're looking into one or two apparent anomalies in the Ashur-Proffitt accounts at this present moment, and Mr Kafka's name has been mentioned as someone who might be able to help us with our enquiries. So when we learned that he was expected to land here in the States today . . .'

'Mr Hackenburg, I've no idea where my husband is. I wish I did know. I'm putting the phone down now as I'm hoping to get a call either from Tony himself or the authorities, giving me information as to his whereabouts. Good night.'

She replaced the receiver.

Next time it rang, it was Andy Dalziel.

'Andy, you've heard something?'

'Sorry, luv, nowt. I'm just checking how you are.'

'I'm fine. Worried sick, but fine.'

'I know the feeling. Listen, Kay, it doesn't look like Tony had an accident or anything, so we need to ask . . . well, was there any other reason he might just have decided to take off? Trouble at work, summat like that?'

'You mean has he headed for the hills because of this investigation into A-P that's just hit the headlines? The answer's no. I'm sure he knows nothing about what's been going on back there. He's been away from the centre of things so long . . . he's been here, with me, because of me . . . that's been the trouble.'

Dalziel said, 'You OK, lass? You sound a bit upset. Shall I come round?'

A moment of silence, then Kay spoke again, her voice at its normal controlled pitch.

'Andy, if your lads heard you being so *galant*, I think you'd have to resign. Thank you, but it's truly not necessary. I'm fine. And I'm sure Tony is too. The next time the phone rings, it will probably be him.'

'Well, let me know if it is,' growled Dalziel. 'And I'll give him a big wet kiss when I see him, but only after I've kicked the bugger up the arse first for causing you so much grief.'

'That I would like to see,' said Kay. 'Good night, Andy.'

She put the phone down and looked at her watch.

Time for bed. Routine is the best way through darkness. It doesn't matter that you can't see if you know your foot is going to hit solid familiar ground with every automatic step.

She stood up. The phone rang again. She snatched it up and sank back into her seat.

'Yes?'

'Mrs Kafka?' said a dry-edged voice.

'Yes. Who is this?'

'I'm a friend of your husband's, Mrs Kafka.'

The voice was like dead leaves drifted across a pavement by a chilly wind.

'Where is he?'

'Don't you know, Mrs Kafka? Let's assume you don't. He needs to be out of things for a little while. No doubt he'll contact you when he can. But meanwhile he feels the best thing for you to do is nothing that might draw attention. Yes, that would be best.'

'Best for who? For Tony? For me? For you?'

'For all of those, Mrs Kafka. And for your step-daughter and her family too, I daresay. They all depend so much on you, Mrs Kafka. Don't let them down. Goodbye now.'

'Wait! I want to . . .'

But the phone was dead.

She dialled 1471. To her surprise she got a number. She pressed 3 to ring it back. After three rings a very English voice came on the line.

'Good evening. This is the Mastaba Club. I regret there is no one in attendance to take care of your call at this time. If you wish to leave a message for one of our members, speak after the tone and we will endeavour to pass it on at the earliest convenient opportunity. Thank you. Good evening.'

All kind of rudenesses came into her mind but she put the phone down before they found utterance. You do not make faces at wolves.

She stood up once more. There would be no more calls.

As she crossed the entrance hall towards the stairs, the American long-case clock began to strike midnight.

She went to it and opened the pendulum cupboard.

As the eleventh note sounded, she reached in and stopped the pendulum.

Then she went upstairs to bed.

April 2003

1

by the waters of Babylon

The war had been over three weeks.

A young marine called Tod Lessing sat on a pile of rubble and lit a cigarette to mask the faint smell of decay which hung over all such ruins. He was attached to a unit searching for weapons of mass destruction in which he personally had little interest. This had been his first spell of active service and he'd rapidly learned to focus his attention on weapons of personal destruction, to wit those likely to be an immediate danger to himself and his comrades.

So now while the men in white suits went about their so far unprofitable work in a relatively undamaged building a couple of hundred yards away, Tod grasped the chance for a spot of R and R.

But he still remained vigilant and when he heard a noise behind him, he twisted round, bringing his weapon to bear with the unthinking instinct of a hunting dog scenting danger.

It was a kid who called to him and beckoned.

Tod rose and went towards him, but he didn't relax. Weapons of personal destruction came in all shapes and sizes.

The boy spoke excitedly and pointed downwards. Tod let his gaze follow the pointing finger.

The high sun slid a ray of light deep between shattered concrete slabs till it bounced back off white bone. The rats and flies had pretty well finished their work here but the after-smell of decay was strong. Tod drew deep on his cigarette and looked enquiringly at the boy. In this country where the smart bombs had done their smart work, corpses were sadly too commonplace to be remarkable.

The boy pointed again impatiently. Tod peered down once more and this time saw that there was something round the corpse's neck. A chain with some kind of amulet. The kid was jabbering away, clearly irritated at Tod's lack of understanding. Then suddenly he seized the marine's arm and held it up and shook it fiercely.

It took a moment for Tod to confirm he wasn't being attacked and another to get the message.

The kid's arm was too short to reach.

Motioning the boy to one side where he could keep an eye on him, Tod inserted his arm into the crack. He had to lie flat on the rubble before his groping fingers found the chain. He pulled. It resisted. He jerked hard. It snapped.

Slowly he withdrew his arm. A graze so close to a decomposing body could be nasty.

The boy came close, impatient to see what they'd found.

He looked puzzled when he saw what it was but Tod recognized it instantly. The bust of Washington bedded on purple and framed in gold.

A Purple Heart.

He turned it over and read the name. *Amal Kafala.*

Sounded Arab. Weird but not very. Any American phone book was full of weird names. Maybe this was some poor bastard taken prisoner by the gooks who ended up getting popped by his own side. Could be he was a left-over from the first Gulf War. Smelt a bit fresh for that. Or maybe the guy down there had plundered the Heart from some dead soldier.

Whatever, it wasn't his business. First chance he got, he'd pass the medal on to the unit's i-officer with details of where he'd found it and let the machine take it from there. Knowing the way it worked, they wouldn't rest till they were knocking on someone's door with the sad news. Unknown soldiers were OK for foreign monuments, but the US Army prided itself on keeping a close check on its own up to the grave and, where necessary, beyond. It was a thought at once comforting and disturbing.

He scrambled off the heap of rubble.

The kid was looking at him expectantly.

He dug into his pack and produced a choc bar and a can of cola.

'There you go, son,' he said.

The boy took them, snapped a flamboyant salute, said stumblingly, 'Have a nice day!' and ran off.

'I'll surely do my best,' called Tod after him.

Then, grinning, he made his way back towards the white suits who looked like they'd decided they were wasting their time here.

As the small convoy of vehicles drove away, they passed a shattered statue of the country's late leader. The head was dented, the nose knocked off, but the features were still recognizable. And those eyes, which had once gazed down upon his people with such menacing benevolence, now stared sightlessly from ground level across the ruins into the desert where, boundless and bare, the lone and level sands stretched far away.